What Matters Most

a novel

by Bette L. Crosby

BENT
PINE
PUBLISHING

Cover Design:
Michael G. Visconte
Creative Director
FCEdge - Stuart, Florida

© Copyright 2013 by Bette Lee Crosby

This is a work of fiction. While, as in all fiction, the literary perceptions and insights are based on life experiences and conclusions drawn from research, all names, characters, places and specific instances are products of the author's imagination and used fictitiously. No actual reference to any real person, living or dead, is intended or inferred.

ISBN # 978-0-9891289-0-2

BENT PINE PUBLISHING

Port Saint Lucie, FL

Also by Bette Lee Crosby

SPARE CHANGE
2010 Royal Palm Literary Award
2011 Reviewer's Choice Award
2012 FPA President's Book Award Silver Medal

THE TWELFTH CHILD
National League of American Pen Women
Women's Fiction Award

CRACKS IN THE SIDEWALK
2011 FPA President's Book Award Gold Medal
2009 Royal Palm Literary Award

CUPID'S CHRISTMAS
A holiday romance

To read more about this author, visit:
www.betteleecrosby.com

For Geri,
My Sister and Best Friend

Clay Palmer

Uncle Charlie died a month ago today. He was nine years older than Pop, but he lived twenty years longer. Pop was a nose-to-the-grindstone man; Uncle Charlie wasn't. I suppose that's the difference.

It's funny how something like this suddenly gets you thinking about your own life. I look back and I don't like what I see. I see me too busy to come for a visit, too busy to take time for frivolous things like fishing. I'm Pop all over again. I'm even starting to look like him.

I try to recall the last time I was truly happy. Happy enough to let go of a belly-shaking laugh like Uncle Charlie's. I can't remember a single one. I'm not unhappy I tell myself, but I'm beginning to wonder if not-unhappy is the same as happy. I don't think so.

I wasn't always like this. When I started working at the bank, I was young and full of great ideas. I figured I'd stay a year, maybe two, get some experience under my belt, and move on. It never happened. Thirty years I've been there. Day in, day out, the same routine, the same complaints, the same weary faces.

Summer before last Herb Kramer retired and I thought for sure I'd get the district manager spot, but I didn't. A kid thirty years younger than me got it. The president's nephew.

So why do I stay? That's what I've been asking myself. Unfortunately, I've got no answer. Something has to change, but I'll be damned if I know what that something is.

The Inheritance

Early on Louise Palmer came to the conclusion that life was somewhat like a jigsaw puzzle. First you envisioned the picture. Then you assembled the pieces. Louise began when she was eleven. She started with a brown shoebox, then added snippets from magazines—a square of blue sky, smoke rising from a chimney, lace curtains, a red door, a wedding gown, a gold ring, photographs with obscured faces—images of what she saw as a picture-perfect life. Night after night she pulled the shoebox from its hiding place and spread the contents across the floor, arranging and rearranging the dog-eared pieces until everything was as she imagined it should be. By the time she was sixteen, Louise knew exactly what her life would look like.

Through the years she painstakingly slid those pieces into place—a loving husband, a house with black shutters, an oak tree in the yard, a baby boy, and then a girl. Once the youngsters had grown into a son and daughter she could be proud of, the picture was perfect. Louise could now sit back and enjoy the completeness of a well-planned life. In her mind she simply had no reason to scramble the pieces and start over again. Her husband, Clay, didn't see it in quite the same way.

The long gray envelope from Horace P. Fredericks, Attorney at Law, arrived on the second Saturday in January, smack in the middle of an icy New Jersey winter. Had it been July or August, Clay might have approached things differently. But as fate would have it, that Saturday was the coldest day of the year. Icicles hung from the trees, six inches of frozen snow covered the yard, and a gusty wind that had howled throughout the night rattled a metal garbage can down the middle of the street.

When they first read the letter, it seemed a stroke of good fortune. Not the part about Uncle Charlie dying, but the fact that Clay would inherit the entire estate—a house in Florida, all the furnishings, a bank account, and a car to boot. It was unexpected, to say the least, for Clay hadn't seen his uncle in fifteen years, maybe more. He called the old man on Christmas and wrote a note every so often, but one would hardly consider Clay a devoted nephew.

Louise craned her neck and peered over Clay's shoulder as he read the letter aloud for a second time.

"In accordance with the Last Will and Testament of the late Charles Palmer, you have been designated sole beneficiary and heir to his estate." Clay paused for a moment and let out a long, low whistle, a bit out of character for the stoic man seldom given to any display of emotion.

"Estate," Louise repeated. "Good gracious."

"This estate consists of the single-family residence located at Seventeen Blossom Tree Trail, all furnishings, a Buick Century, and a First National Bank savings account in the amount of two thousand three hundred six dollars and thirty-nine cents." Clay rambled past several other details then read the last line again, what Louise had been waiting to hear.

"Please advise if you plan to take physical possession of the property or would prefer that I make the necessary arrangements for liquidation to cash."

For what seemed a rather long time, Clay stood there staring at the piece of paper and fingering his chin. Finally he dropped the letter onto the table and turned to refill his coffee cup.

Several minutes passed, and when Louise could no longer stand the silence she said, "Well?"

"Well what?" Clay replied.

"Aren't you going to say something?"

"I'm thinking about it."

"Thinking about it?"

"Yes," he answered and said nothing more.

Louise, a woman who openly shared the thoughts inside her head, had little patience for such secretive thinking. At times Clay could be downright miserly with his thoughts, hoarding them as if they were something too precious to part with. He claimed he simply wanted to save her from needless worry, but she suspected otherwise.

Years ago at the Somerset County Fair they each paid two dollars to have their fortune told by a gypsy. The woman looked into a crystal ball and saw Louise's future clear as day, right down to predicting how one day there would be a blue-eyed granddaughter. But when it came Clay's turn, the gypsy had to give back his money. She'd looked into her crystal ball and found it as blank as the expression on his face. Not even the gypsy could zero in on Clay's thoughts, past, future, or present.

After she'd waited a few minutes longer, Louise gave an exasperated sigh. "With news like this it seems you'd be excited."

"I am," Clay answered.

"Oh, really?"

Clay ignored the whisper of sarcasm and shook his head sadly as a washboard of ridges settled on his brow. "I'm pleased about the inheritance," he finally said, "but I feel bad about losing Uncle Charlie."

"Well, of course you do," Louise replied sympathetically. She hesitated a moment then gave a sigh, sloping the corners of her mouth and shaking her head in synchronization with Clay. Even though one could hardly expect her to bemoan the fate of a man she had never laid eyes on, she felt certain her performance appeared adequately mournful.

"At least Uncle Charlie had sense enough to enjoy the last twenty years of his life," Clay said. "He knew how to live. He didn't keep working until the day he died like Pop did."

Clay's father, like Clay, had been a quiet person, a banker who kept his thoughts private as he carted himself off to work each day and trudged home again in the evening. That was until the day he keeled over dead at his desk. A robust sort of man, barely fifty-six years old, swooshed off the face of the earth by a heart attack that came without a whisker of warning.

Louise waited for Clay to continue, waited for him to get back to their discussion of the estate he'd inherited. Instead, he began reminiscing about the time Uncle Charlie won a truckload of watermelons in a radio contest. For several minutes she tried to look interested, but when Clay segued into the story of a monster catfish Uncle Charlie once caught, Louise found it impossible to keep looking interested. When he paused between words she jumped in.

"This house of your uncle's," she said. "How much do you think it's worth?"

"No idea." Clay cradled his chin in the valley between his thumb and forefinger as if deep in thought.

Louise naturally assumed he was working up an estimate. All that property had to be worth something—maybe enough for a European vacation, a new car or a backyard pool. *Maybe even...* As she pictured a new bedroom set and burgundy-colored carpeting Clay announced, "The value of the house doesn't matter, because I'm not going to sell it."

"Not going to sell?" she echoed. "But why?"

"Well, I'm almost fifty-four years old and before long we'll want a place..." His voice trailed off.

"Want a place? Why? What would we do with a house in Florida when we've already got—" Suddenly the reality of what he was thinking smacked Louise in the face and left her so faint she had to steady herself against the table.

"You can't possibly mean what I think you mean—?" she gasped. "It's impossible!" Not waiting for—or perhaps not wanting—his answer, she peeled off a paper towel and began mopping a droplet of coffee that had spilled on the table. *How*, she wondered, *could he even think of living in some other house?* This was where they belonged, where they'd raised their children. Why, she'd planned to live the rest of her life in this house. She'd even imagined herself dying in the upstairs bedroom.

She finished wiping the table, then continued across the counter over an already-spotless chrome faucet and along the edge of the sink. Wadding the paper towel into a tight little ball, she dropped it into the garbage can and turned back to Clay. "In my opinion," she said, "it would be downright foolish not to sell the house and take the money like the lawyer recommended."

"Mister Fredericks didn't recommend anything," Clay replied. "He simply indicated what our options are."

"Well, it's obvious. Taking the money *is* the best option," Louise reiterated. "We have a lovely home right here. We don't need a house way down in Florida."

"Actually, Florida's the perfect place for people like us," Clay said. "I've been thinking of retiring, and I'd like to do it now while I'm still young and healthy enough to enjoy life."

"Retire?" Louise's face fell. "Why, you're barely fifty-four years old!"

"Fifty-five, end of next month."

"So what?" she argued. "Fifty-five is still too young to retire."

"Not really," Clay said. "Since the merger the bank has cut back on personnel. Now we've got fewer people but the same amount of work. There are days when I can barely see over the pile of papers on my desk." He picked up his cup and turned toward the living room. "This job is a thankless thing. It feels like I'm banging my head against a cement wall, day after day after day. Why should I settle for a life like this?"

Louise followed a step behind. "Why? Because it's your job. It's how we pay the mortgage, gas and electricity, buy food, clothing—"

Clay stopped her mid-sentence. "Hold on a minute. All I'm saying is if we moved to Florida and lived in that nice little house of Uncle Charlie's, I wouldn't have to keep working. We wouldn't have a mortgage. We wouldn't have all these bills and expenses. I could take it easy and start enjoying life."

"Instead of moving, why don't we just cut back on spending?"

"It's never going to happen. Our expenses are what they are. What would we cut back on? Going to the movies? An occasional dinner out?"

"I'm sure there's more than—"

"Louise, it's not just the expenses. It's this job. It's killing me. If I continue working the way I have been, one of these days they're gonna find me slumped over my desk just like Pop."

12

"Oh," she gasped, taken aback by the thought. "You've never mentioned anything—"

"I'm not saying it'll happen, but I am saying it's a possibility." Clay wove a thread of weariness through his words. "With all the pressure I'm under..." He left the remainder of that thought hanging in the air like an ominous threat.

"I had no idea you felt this way," Louise replied, her voice sad.

"I didn't want to worry you."

"How can it not worry me? I love you, Clay. Nothing is more important than your health. If you feel that job is too much, I don't want you to stay. I'll understand and support whatever decision you make." A sly smile tugged at the corners of Clay's mouth. "Okay," he answered. "Then it's settled."

"Settled?" Louise noticed his expression of weariness had departed as suddenly as it had come. "What do you mean settled?"

"Well, since you're willing to support my decision, I'll write this Fredericks fellow and let him know we're gonna keep Uncle Charlie's place."

Louise felt her stomach lurch the way it did on those carnival rides that turn everything upside down. "That's not what I meant." Suddenly she had the terrible feeling that this would turn into one of those occasions when her words carried her off to a place she had no intention of going. She should have said flat out that the idea of moving to Florida was crazy, that it wasn't something she would expect from a reasonably sane person. Irresponsible wanderers like her father might yank up his family and cart them off to some place they didn't want to go, but not a banker. And certainly not Clay! She wanted to say his settled-down way was the very thing she loved. But it somehow seemed as if she had already said too much. So Louise stood there with her mouth hanging open and all the things she should have said drifting into nothingness.

They stood an arm's length apart, but a canyon of silence separated them. Louise knew that a stalemate such as this could be the forerunner of everything in years to come. To speak first was to surrender, but to be trapped in silence could be infinitely more painful. She was wondering what to do when her thoughts were interrupted by the sound of Yoo's tail thumping against the chair.

The large black dog, always hungry and bumping into things, provided a welcome intrusion. It gave Louise a few moments to reorganize herself, to get back the thoughts that she'd allowed to slip away. "Go lie down," she said waggling her finger toward the kitchen.

The memories always nudged her off track, the fleeting recollections of other times and places. Long after she should have forgotten, they still stayed. Memories that belonged to the past. Memories with no relevance to the here and now. *Not this time*, she told herself. She squared her shoulders and turned back to the conversation.

"Clay," she said trying to give crispness to the sound of his name. "I'm okay with the decision to quit your job, but I'm not okay with the thought of moving. We have some money saved, and we can cut back on expenses. But I want to stay here. We're comfortable in this house. Our children and all our friends are here. There's nothing for us in Florida." A whoosh of air rattled from her chest as she repeated, "Nothing."

Without turning to look at her, Clay answered. "Not right now maybe, but we'll start over again, the way Uncle Charlie did. Think about it," he said. "A new life, new outlook, new friends, and adventures."

Louise did think about it and answered with a sigh. It seemed that Clay, of all people, should understand. Given her nature, moving from one side of the street to the other would have been traumatic. Yet here he was, asking her to uproot her entire life. Asking her to leave everything she knew and loved to live in a place thousands of miles away, an obscure finger of land poking out into the ocean. As it was she had no love for the South. Not that she'd ever been to Florida, specifically, but she only had bad memories from Alabama, Georgia, and South Carolina. She thought back on the run-down rooming houses, the dusty back roads, and the daddy who didn't care a twit about his daughter. The memories churned inside of her with the sourness of curdled milk.

"Think about it," Clay repeated, oblivious to the way Louise's lower lip had begun to quiver. "An opportunity such as this coming along precisely when I'm burnt out and worn to the nub. Our moving to Florida was meant to be. It's destiny."

Louise tried to focus on what he said, but she'd already slipped away to remembering how it felt to sit in the back of her daddy's shiny black Packard and watch the only home she'd ever known get smaller and smaller until it disappeared from the rearview mirror. She could still feel the sting of salty tears rolling down her cheeks.

"What about Amanda?" she finally asked. "What's a five-year-old supposed to think when her grandparents pick up and move thousands of miles away?"

"It's only twelve hundred miles," Clay said. "A two hour plane ride. The kids will come to visit."

"Visit?" Louise replied flatly. "Visit like out-of-town strangers? Our son? Our only granddaughter?" The thought of it caused her heart to pound hard against her chest. He'd obviously not given one ounce of consideration to her volunteer work at the library or her quilting club, the women who'd been her friends since the children were babies. Louise knew she had to change his mind. She started to explain how picture perfect their life already was, but when she opened her mouth a flurry of angry words jumped out. "I'm not moving!" she said. "Not to Florida, not anywhere!"

She'd expected him to argue, to come right back at her, but instead he just stood there staring out the window with a bluish-gray glare of snow reflected in his glasses. Louise reeled in her anger and softened her tone. "I don't care if you quit your job," she said. "That's fine. Take an early retirement if you want to. I know it's less money, but we'll manage. At least we'll spend the rest of our years here in our own house."

"Ah, Louise," he sighed. "That might be fine for you, but what kind of a life would it be for me? Squirreled away in the house all winter long, the weather too cold to do much of anything except maybe shovel snow. Why, that's worse than working."

Louise felt herself losing ground. "You don't even know if you'd like living in Florida," she argued. "You might get down there and hate it. What if the heat's unbearable and the place is loaded with mosquitoes? Okay, Uncle Charlie left you a house, but you don't know what kind of house. For all you know it could be a fishing shack or a roadside shanty."

"It's not a fishing shack, it's a house. Not as nice as this, but nice enough."

"How can you be so sure? You haven't been there for over fifteen years. By now it's probably a run-down mess with a dozen broken windows and weeds as tall as a tree."

Clay smiled. "I'm certain it's nothing like that."

"Oh really? Well, I'm not so certain, and I'm the one who has a sixth sense about things like this."

Maybe Clay didn't remember the gas company meter reader— the fellow everyone else thought was harmless. She'd said the man acted suspicious and the whole family had a good chuckle at her expense. "Shifty-eyed," she'd said, and they laughed even harder. But sure enough, a year later the police arrested that meter reader for burglary. Louise knew she had a born-in instinct for seeing things in their true light, not simply an over-active imagination as Clay claimed. When the story appeared in the newspaper, she clipped the article and stuck in on the refrigerator. Beneath the man's picture she wrote, "I told you so!"

"Houses don't change that much," Clay said. "A house is a house. Trust me, you'd like it down there. It's a friendly neighborhood, and the weather is nowhere near as hot as you think. You could have a year-round flower garden, and I could fish, maybe learn to play golf or tennis."

"Tennis?" Louise groused. "A man your age? If you're worried about having a heart attack, how can you think of playing tennis in the hot sun?" She waited for Clay's reaction, but none came. He just stood there staring at the snow that had started to fall again. There was a faraway look in his eyes and when he finally spoke his voice seemed brittle, weighted with a seriousness she was unaccustomed to hearing.

"Almost thirty years I've been at that bank," he said. "Week after week watching people come and go. Some people use their money to take cruises or go on vacations. They buy things, boats and such. Then when those things are gone, they move on to other things. Most everybody, that is, except me. I'm like wallpaper that's grown colorless and ragged around the edge but still stuck to the wall. I catch sight of myself in the mirror and see I've begun to look like some of the old customers—the weary ones who complain about the service, complain about the weather, complain about any little thing they can think of. Those people have no joy. Week after week they hold out a few extra pennies to make a pitiful deposit. Then what happens?"

Clay turned back to the window, his voice noticeably more fragile as he answered his own question. "One day they die, and all that's left is some scrabbly little account for their relatives to argue over." He shook his head sadly. "There's got to be more to life than that."

"But up until now…" Louise stammered. Clay was not a man to pour his heart out and unnecessarily alarm a person. He was generally an easygoing sort, set in his ways perhaps, but then what man wasn't? To look at him anyone else might see a rather undistinguished face, a middle-aged man with worry ridges rolling across his forehead, and a mop of unruly brown hair woven through with strands of silver. She saw past those things. She saw the truth of who he was in his eyes, eyes that were dark brown with flecks of copper. Eyes that reminded her of a cavern with a wealth of untold secrets.

"I've had this on my mind for quite some time," Clay said solemnly. His voice did not sound angry, but flat and definitive. "I've given it a lot of thought," he said, "and now I intend to do it."

His words landed with a thud like a boulder that had dropped into place and could no longer be moved. Louise waited, hoping he'd take stock of what he'd said and rethink it. But he didn't. He simply stood there waiting for her response. When it became evident he would not budge, she spoke.

"We have family, a home and a life here. Those aren't things you toss away just because you're tired of working."

"I'm not asking you to toss them away," he answered, "just change them."

"Change them?" she shot back. "Sensible people change their underwear, not their house. Once a house becomes your home, you stay there forever."

"It doesn't have to be that way," Clay answered. "We could move on to an easier life. We could leave here and get rid of all these responsibilities. Instead of shoveling a pathway to get the mail, we could spend our days in a place where the sun warms our bones."

Louise listened to his words tumble one on top of another and she knew it would be impossible to change his mind, to move him back to where he'd been before he opened that dreadful letter. He wouldn't just reverse course; she needed to offer an alternative. As Clay continued to speak, she searched her mind for an idea. When it finally came, she strolled across the room and began to massage his shoulders.

"I understand how you feel," she said sympathetically, "but I think there might be another solution."

"Another solution?"

"Yes. You remember Billie Butterman's cousin, Mildred?" she said. "Lives in that big blue house over on Lakeside Drive? Married Walter Krumm? You must remember. His family is the one who owns that sanitation trucking company?"

"Walter?"

"Yes. Tall, dark hair, a thin mustache, he looks like the actor in that Claudette Colbert movie where she's dying from this horrible disease, and her sister—"

"Louise! I know who Walter Krumm is. I was just asking if it was his family or her family who owned the trucking company."

"Oh, his. His stepfather, actually. Well, when he retired—Walter, not his stepfather—they bought a cute little place in Florida. It's one of those inexpensive condo-things, you know, where they cut the grass for you. Mildred says Walter doesn't have to do a lick of work at that place. Everything is taken care of by the same folks who cut the grass. Anyway, every winter they go down there and spend two months, sometimes even three. Then they come back and spend the rest of the year right here in Westfield, in the same house they've been living in since the day they got married. See? They have two places. Walter gets away from the snow and cold weather without Mildred having to give up her home. Great idea, huh?"

"It would be a fine idea," Clay said, "if we could afford it."

"You mean we've got no—"

"We've got money, so don't worry. There's no mortgage on Uncle Charlie's house, and we'll have my pension to live on."

"Well, then—"

"Unfortunately, my pension payment will be a lot less than I'm making now. There's no way we could possibly afford two places, unless I work for another ten years."

"Oh."

Louise noticed how the mention of another ten years wrapped itself around Clay like a weighted overcoat. It made him seem older, more like his father. She pictured him trudging through the snow with his hands jammed into his pockets and shoulders hunched forward, just as Father Palmer had done on that last day of his life. It was strange that she'd not seen it before but with him standing there as he was, she could almost see the weariness chipping away at him.

Louise knew Clay's words held an element of truth. Many a man worked himself into the ground only to have his wife discover that once he was dead and buried, she spent the rest of her days alone. Of course that wasn't true of everyone. People like Claudia Marquardt remarried time and time again. She'd already buried five husbands, and there was no telling how many more there might be. Just months after poor Harold was in the ground, she sent out the invitations to her next wedding. Most people didn't even realize Harold was gone until the mailman dropped off that wedding invitation. Oh, the neighbors talked, but Claudia didn't care. She hauled out her white wedding gown, had it dry cleaned, and marched down the aisle with a happy-looking smile on her face.

Such behavior was fine for Claudia Marquardt, but Louise knew she couldn't do that. Despite any differences they had, she loved Clay Palmer. She'd loved him since the day they first met. They'd built a life together, bought a home, had children. Clay planted the oak tree in the front yard, planted it when it was no more than a sapling. Now after all those years…

The image of Clay lying stone-faced in a coffin flickered across Louise's mind and before she knew what happened, a single word came tumbling out.

"Okay," she said, but even before the sound of her voice cleared the air, she began to think she'd made a terrible mistake.

Louise Palmer

Ask me why I fell in love with Clay Palmer and I'll tell you. It was because he was the exact opposite of my father. The first time I saw him, I noticed the serious expression tacked onto his face. Right away I suspected he was a settled-down man, a man who'd be content to spend the whole of his life in one place. When he proposed and said we'd buy a house nine short blocks from where he'd lived as a boy, that was proof positive.

After living with the man almost thirty years I know his heart as well as I know my own, and I can assure you, Clay doesn't want to move. He's just feeling the dreariness of this winter weather. The truth is he's as happy in this house as I am. Why would anyone leave a place where they've got everything a person could wish for?

It's that job. I'm glad he's going to retire. Once he's out of the bank he'll have a new outlook on life. He imagines he'll be bored, but he won't. Lord knows there are plenty of things that need fixing around here, and he's already got that nice little workshop in the basement.

So, we'll have less spending money. That's okay. I can stretch a dollar. When we were first married he was only making half of what he makes now and even with raising two kids, we got along just fine. We did it then and we can do it again. As far as I'm concerned, hamburger's the same as steak. It's just ground-up.

The Sorry Truth

Louise breathed a sigh of relief on Monday morning when she heard the plow truck rumble down the street a few hours before dawn. If not for that letter from Horace P. Fredericks, she might have welcomed the idea of Clay taking an unexpected day off. But given this sudden obsession with moving to Florida, being snowbound for another day was the last thing she wanted.

All day Sunday she'd tucked herself away in the little sewing room piecing together patches for Aunt Rose's Tree of Life quilt. For the most part Clay had busied himself with cleaning the basement and sifting through a stack of cartons stored behind the furnace. Twice he'd tromped upstairs to ask her something. The first time he wanted to know if they needed to keep the oscillating fan, seeing as how it no longer revolved. The second time he came asking for his green bathing suit.

"Why, I threw that old thing out ages ago," Louise answered without looking up from the speckled patch she was working on.

"The green one?"

"Yes."

"The one with a black stripe down the side?"

"Exactly."

"Well, if that doesn't beat all," he grumbled, then disappeared back downstairs.

That was it. For the rest of the afternoon Louise didn't hear another word from him. He clattered around the basement, whistling, and banged in and out of the back door. When Louise finally ventured downstairs to start dinner, she noticed a sizable mound of trash piled up alongside the driveway. For ages she'd asked Clay to get rid of some the clutter that had accumulated in the basement but now, in addition to the broken lawn chair and dried-up cans of paint, he'd thrown out a perfectly good pair of skis and a sled that needed nothing more than a new rope.

Louise was setting dinner on the table when Clay came huffing and puffing through the back door, his nose and ears nearly scarlet.

"Well, at least that's done!" he said, flicking bits of snow from his hair. "Working outside in this weather can give a man a heart attack."

"Nonsense," Louise answered, then plunked a huge pile of green beans onto his plate.

"Hey, hold up on those," Clay said. "Give me some mashed potatoes instead."

"If you're worried about your health, you should watch your weight."

"Yeah, well, I see *you've* got potatoes." He slid himself into a chair and grabbed a Parker House roll. "I don't suppose there's any reason to hang onto that leaf-blower," he mumbled, slathering the roll with an oversize ball of butter.

Other than that, there was no mention of moving. Not during dinner, not during the evening news, and not even when Phillip called to ask if his father needed help clearing the driveway.

Phillip was good about lending a hand anytime they needed help. He was the first-born and would have been named Prescott, if Louise had her say. But Clay wouldn't hear of it. "A sissy-pants name," he'd complained. So they settled on Phillip. Both of the Palmer children had names starting with the letter "P." That was something Louise *had* insisted upon. She knew nothing was luckier than two-of-a-kind initials, which is why she'd stood firm on matching initials for the children. Phillip and Patricia Lynn. The Lynn, a name given to humor Clay's mother, had been a mistake, because now that Patty was a grown woman she used it with "P. Lynn Palmer" printed on her business cards and stationery.

Louise knew believing in lucky double initials had more to do with real life than people realized. It had proven itself true over and over again. Millie Moskowitz won seventeen hundred dollars in the lottery. Claire Comstead weighed one hundred and ten pounds and could eat a whole chocolate cake without ever gaining an ounce. Anne Ainsley got a three-karat diamond ring for her engagement. Granted, Anne did get a divorce two years later, but it was understandable because she married a man named Harbinger and that took away her two-of-a-kind initials.

The list went on and on. But Louise's best friend, Billie—a once-cute teenager who had grown into a glamorously slender woman with polished red fingernails and dark hair clipped close about her face—topped them all. She married Bradley Butterman, a man with two-of-a-kind initials. She had a double set of matching initials in her household, so naturally Billie never had to worry about making meatloaf to stretch the food budget. Why would she? She had married Bradley Butterman, and everything he touched turned to gold.

Monday morning Clay left for work at the usual time. Although the temperature had eased its way back up to forty degrees and the thin crust of snow was not quite ankle deep, he tugged on black galoshes and wrapped a much-too-heavy wool muffler around his neck. In doing so, he emphasized every step of the process, moaning and groaning at times, twisting the corner of his mouth half-open as if he was about to say something, then heaving a pitiful sigh and slouching over to button the next button or pull on a glove. Louise noticed it but kept to herself, cleared away the breakfast dishes, and refrained from asking what might be wrong.

"Drive carefully," she said as he started out the door. "Remember, the road is still slick in spots." Thankful he didn't bring up the subject of moving, she chose to believe he'd realized the foolishness of such a notion and moved on.

Men could go off on tangents at times, react to a bad day at the office or some other thing, but sensible men got hold of themselves before doing anything drastic—and Clay was indeed a sensible man. *Best to forget the whole thing*, Louise thought.

Once Clay's car disappeared down the block, she set about getting her day in order. It was Monday, her day to clean the house top to bottom and then spend the afternoon with Aunt Rose. Pushing any thought of moving from the forefront of her mind, she swung into action. After she had changed the sheets, plumped the pillows, and smoothed the comforter into place, she sat down at the dressing table.

The face in the mirror looked round as a dinner plate and almost as flat, the eyes a worn-away color, not blue, not green, not gray, but a changeable blend her driver's license listed as hazel. Louise smacked a dollop of cream on her forehead, then spread it along her cheekbones and across her chin. Except for the tiny lines gathered in the corners of her eyes she looked younger than her fifty-three years, but she didn't see herself that way. She envisioned her face a plain beige canvas, crisscrossed with more cares than she could remember. The uncontrollable corkscrew curls that had once been the rich golden color of butterscotch pudding were now threaded with silver and dulled to a lifeless blonde nearly the color of her skin.

Louise eyed herself critically, squinting to soften the ridge settling between her brows. Even with blurred edges she had an uncomplicated face, completely without the mystique that makes a person interesting. Little wonder people still called her Squeezie, a ridiculous nickname left over from high school, a name originally intended to be a fun-loving version of Louise but now more reminiscent of toilet paper. The name certainly didn't befit a grandmother. Such a foolish tag would never have stuck to a double-initial person like Billie Butterman. Louise dabbed on a spot of Pinker than Pink lipstick and told the pie-faced reflection, "I should have changed my name to Pamela when I married Clay Palmer." She bent over and scooped up the dirty sheets. "Then things would have been different."

Louise kept a crate of "should have's" locked inside her head, and once the box opened she pored through them one by one. She should have known...should have said...should have insisted...A storehouse of little regrets. Not all things she'd change, just things she'd mishandled.

In fact, there were some things she wouldn't change for anything in the world. Amanda, for example. Sure, she'd crayoned the bedroom wall and swallowed Louise's wedding ring, but those things Louise blamed on herself. She should have kept a closer eye on her granddaughter. Other than a few such mishaps, Amanda was an angel, a blue-eyed angel who looked more like Grandma than she did her parents. Phillip had his father's olive coloring and dark hair. Rachel, with those big brown eyes—well, if she wasn't Phillip's wife she might have passed for his sister.

When the phone rang, Clay spoke before she could say hello. "We're going to need a realtor," he announced in a rather business-like tone. "I'm caught up with paperwork. Could you call a few people?"

"Huh?" Almost certain Clay had forgotten his thoughts of moving, the request stunned Louise. "Realtor?" she repeated.

"Yeah. Find out what they'd suggest as an asking price."

"Asking price…"

"For our house. Ask what they think it's worth." He hesitated for less than a half-second, then added, "Better yet, call three, get comparisons."

"Three!" she gasped.

"Okay, do more if you want."

"Clay—"

"Sorry. I'd take care of it, but I've got a meeting in five minutes. Don't worry about making a decision, just get the estimates. We'll talk tonight." With that he hung up. No goodbye. No listening to what she had to say. No anything. He just hung up.

For a moment Louise stood there looking at the receiver. Then she hauled off and kicked a footstool clear across the room, kicked it so hard that a sharp pain shimmied up her shin bone. "Damn you, Clay Palmer!" she cried and dropped onto the chair. If he thought she'd help him destroy what they'd worked so hard to build, he was sadly mistaken. "Call a realtor?" she grumbled. "Fat chance!"

Cleaning now seemed of little consequence. If Clay wanted to sell the house, then he could sell it dust and all. Louise tossed the furniture polish back into the bin under the sink and went upstairs to dress for lunch. Hopefully Aunt Rose would not be in one of her moods.

The lunch was a once-a-week obligation, not necessarily something to be enjoyed. Through the years Rose had forgotten how to laugh, and although she could be pleasant enough when things went her way she was often crotchety and given to fits of contrariness. Still, forty-two years ago, when Louise was dumped on the Elkins' doorstep, Rose took her in without a word of resentment. An occasional lunch was certainly not overpayment for such a kindness.

Louise heard the telephone ring moments after she stepped from the shower. She hurried across the bedroom, leaving a trail of wet spots on the carpet.

"You won't believe who's having a sale," Billie Butterman announced. "Thirty-five percent off of everything. Even the new pre-season stuff."

"Not Steinman's?"

"Yes!" Billie answered triumphantly. "And I've got a preferred customer coupon for an extra ten percent."

Billie, it seemed, always got Steinman's coupons. Louise got coupons for things like Betty Crocker Scalloped Potatoes or some off-brand pancake mix. Never Steinman's.

"How soon can you be ready?" Billie asked.

"I don't think I can go," Louise answered wistfully. "It's my day for Aunt Rose."

"You can't possibly pass up a sale like this."

"I don't want to, but Aunt Rose—"

"Reschedule. You can see Aunt Rose anytime, but a sale at Steinman's—"

"Maybe…"

Billie had been sure of herself since the day she was born. She never hemmed and hawed over things as Louise did. But then, she'd been born a Balsas with two-of-a-kind initials right from the start. Louise suspected a gold American Express card and a Steinman's coupon were tucked into Billie's first diaper. People like that were gifted with a special brand of magic, and if you were lucky enough to stand close to them a tiny bit sometimes spilled over onto you.

"Forget maybe," Billie said. "You're coming. Meet me at noon and we'll have lunch at Jumping Jack's."

"Okay," Louise agreed. She hung up, then called Aunt Rose and concocted a story about a chipped tooth and a last-minute appointment at the dentist.

"Oh, dear," Rose Elkins said with a dramatic sigh. "I was so counting on our little lunch today. I have a taste for something grilled. A steak, or lamb chops maybe."

"Well, why don't we just switch our lunch date to Wednesday?"

"I suppose that would be okay. I could make do with a can of spaghetti for today. Maybe heat up one of those frozen things that have no nutrition whatsoever."

"Now, Aunt Rose, you have plenty of things in the freezer. Why, just a few days ago I brought over some homemade chicken stew and a tray of stuffed peppers."

"Those tasteless old things?"

Rose Elkins, at seventy-eight, had perfected the art of manipulating people into doing exactly what she wanted. And when necessary, she'd resort to something that generated either guilt or pity.

"Now don't you worry about me," she said with an air of melancholy. "I can manage with a bit of soup and some saltine crackers."

In truth Rose Elkins didn't have to manage. The cupboards were full of food, food she herself had selected from the supermarket shelf. Going to lunch on Wednesday was a fair substitution, but nonetheless the feeling of guilt took hold, and before Louise knew it she blurted out, "You'll do no such thing. You'll have dinner at our house tonight."

Louise didn't actually *want* Aunt Rose to come for dinner, but it seemed a small enough price to pay for easing her conscience. Once that was done, the day took on a new perspective. Louise eyed the gray turtleneck and plaid slacks lying on the bed. Too drab. Far too drab for an outing with Billie. She returned them to the closet and chose instead the green wool dress, the one that gave color to her eyes and made her appear pounds thinner than she actually was. "Much better," she told her reflection.

Twenty minutes later, with a package of chicken defrosting in the sink and the dog sleeping in the sun of the dining room window, she backed the car out of the garage and turned toward the center of town.

Westfield was one of the few places that still had a bustling town center. Little stores lined Broad Street, and shopkeepers smiled when people came through the door. Scoops, with its giant balls of ice cream, Crane's Book Nook, Doc's Drugs, The Shoe-in, Martha's—these stores weren't part of a mammoth mall, they were friends, people Louise had known for as long as she could remember.

Steinman's was in the center of town, Jumping Jack's further south, close to the railroad station. When Louise stepped from the glare of day into the dimly-lit restaurant, the lack of daylight blinded her. She waited until the blackness shaped itself into shadows and the shadows gave way to faces, then eased her way through the room and slid into a booth across the table from Billie.

Two glasses of wine already sat on the table, one half-empty. Before Louise settled in her seat, Billie downed another gulp.

"Problem?" Louise asked jokingly.

"Same as always," Billie answered. "Miserable old Missus Butterman."

"Aunt Rose was a bit testy today also. They get crotchety at that age."

"No, Squeezie, Rose Elkins is a piece of cake compared to Bradley's mother. That woman is driving me to drink." Billie gave a throaty chuckle.

"How so?" Louise took a sip of her wine.

"Does everything she can think of to get Bradley's attention. She expects one of us to come running over there every time she loses a key or stubs a toe."

"Hmm."

"Her latest trick is firing the housekeepers, one right after the other. Then she wants me to find a replacement on the very same day. This morning she fired Clarissa. 'Now, what was wrong with Clarissa?' I asked her."

Louise waited.

"She tells me, 'The girl is a thief. Pilfered my Sam's gold coin collection and took every last piece.' Why, I know for certain Missus Butterman sold that coin collection. It was right after Bradley's daddy died. She sold those coins and bought herself a brand new Lincoln Town Car. I remind her of this and she says, 'Not me, I'd never do such a thing. It must've been Clarissa.'"

"I know what that miserable old biddy is angling for." Billie downed the last few drops of wine. "She wants Bradley to suggest she come and live with us. She sees those upstairs bedrooms sitting empty and figures she'll move in and aggravate me for the rest of my days." Billie rolled her eyes. "That is *not* going to happen."

The thought of hanging onto a place called home struck a chord, and Louise said sadly, "I don't blame her for wanting to move in with you. I wish I could."

She had not intended to tell anyone. She had planned to discuss the move with Clay and somehow convince him to forget such foolishness, or at the very least find a middle ground for compromise. But after his telephone call, there seemed little chance of either.

Before Louise could stop herself, she spilled the entire story. She began with the letter from Horace P. Fredericks and went straight through to the part where Clay had asked her to call a realtor. Who better to tell? she reasoned. Billie was her best friend.

"Squeezie, why do you insist on acting as if you're a doormat?" Billie said. "You've got to tell Clay flat out, 'I am not selling this house, and I am not moving to Florida!'"

"That's what I did. I said we've got a wonderful life here and I'm not moving anywhere. But—"

"But what?"

"Clay started talking about how his father had a heart attack and died when he was only fifty-six. He said if he keeps working the way he is, he'll end up exactly like his father."

Billie gave a groan of disbelief. "Oh, give me a break! Didn't Clay just have a physical?"

"Yes," Louise nodded. "But that was three months ago."

"See? He was healthy enough three months ago, and he's fine now. You've got to realize, this is his way of manipulating you into doing what he wants."

"Maybe, maybe not. There's no way to know for certain. I said quitting his job doesn't mean we have to move, but he's convinced it does. He told me he couldn't stand being cooped up in the house all winter with nothing to do. After that I stopped arguing. If something actually happened to Clay, I'd feel as though I'd murdered him."

Just then the waitress appeared with the salads they'd ordered. "Another glass of wine?" she asked.

Both women answered, "Yes."

Louise found it hard to focus on the food, but Billie made quick work of two black olives and the artichoke heart. Then she bunched up a forkful of chunky greens and shoved it into her mouth.

"Of course I don't want to go," Louise said, absently poking at a piece of red lettuce. "It means leaving the kids, little Amanda, the girls in the quilting club, you." She thrust an angry jab at the lettuce, and it jettisoned off the plate.

"Well, that's exactly what you have to tell Clay," Billie garbled as she crunched down on an oversized crouton.

"Okay, but what if I take a stand," –without straying from her thoughts, she scooped the lettuce from the edge of the table and put it back on the plate— "and Clay keels over with a heart attack? I couldn't live with that. Clay has his faults, but I love him. Just because he's set on having things his way doesn't mean—"

"Get real, Squeezie. What you've got here is a slight difference of opinion. It's not a life-or-death thing. If you're concerned that the job is affecting Clay's health, tell him to retire and tinker around the house like Francine's husband does."

"I'd be fine with that, but now that he's got his uncle's place in Florida he wants to live there. He'll argue me blue if I refuse to move."

"Then don't flat out refuse, use a more tactful approach."

"Like what?"

"Hmm. I've gotta think about it." Billie shoveled a wedge of cucumber into her mouth and started chewing.

Louise watched her friend's jaw move up and down as she waited for words of wisdom to come floating across the table. The only thing she heard was the din of the room, sounds of people laughing, drinking, and having fun.

"I've got it!" Billie finally said. "You haven't called a real estate agent yet, have you?"

"No, of course not."

"Get Henry Hornock." Billie nodded with an air of authority.

"Gloria's husband?"

"Yeah. He's working for Bliss Realty."

"But he's such a klutz."

"Exactly! He's lazy as a log, never succeeds at anything. You give him the listing, then sit back and wait while nothing happens. Let Clay go ahead and retire, settle into some hobby, and start puttering around the house. Eventually he'll come to his senses and give up this obsession with moving."

"You think?"

"I know." Billie turned back to her salad.

Leaving her food almost untouched, Louise leaned back and thought about the suggestion. Billie had a point: Henry Hornock, a walking disaster, defied the double initial rule. Why, he'd had more than twenty different jobs in the last year alone. A streak of bad luck, he called it. A streak of bad luck that started the month after Gloria married him and never stopped. That's why the poor woman had to keep her job at Belinda's House of Beauty. Year after year while other mothers sat in the park with their children, Gloria stood inside the plate glass window of Belinda's teasing silver blonde hair into bouffant dos. Here she married a man who by all rights should have been lucky, and look what happened. The only thing that could account for such bad luck was the fact that he'd switched to using the nickname Lurch when he played football in high school.

Billie swabbed her plate with a chunk of bread and then pushed the plate aside. "So?"

"Hmm. I don't know…"

"How can you possibly have a problem with this?"

"Well, it is kind of deceitful."

"Of course it is. That's the idea. You fight fire with fire. He's trying to manipulate you into moving, so you have to devise a better plan and manipulate him into staying. Trust me, it's better than living in some steamy swamp."

"Swamp?"

"All right, it might be a bit deceitful," Billie said with a laugh. "But for all we know, this might be the one thing Henry Hornock is really good at."

"That's true." Louise grew fonder of the idea after hearing Billie's rationalization. "Anyway, Gloria's a friend of mine. I owe it to her to give Henry a chance. Could be his bad luck has ended. Maybe this is just the break he needs."

After lunch the two women window-shopped their way down Broad Street. They stopped at Pauline's Perfumery and the Book Nook. Louise thumbed through the latest issue of "House and Garden" then carried it to the register before she remembered that unless their plan worked, she wouldn't be doing any decorating.

Inside Steinman's they drifted off in different directions. Billie, who could drape a shower curtain over her shoulders and still look glamorous, headed for designer sportswear. Louise strolled aimlessly toward the petite department where some little kid played underneath a rack of blouses. "William!" the boy's mother screamed. "You come out of there! William! I'm warning you!"

Louise thumbed through a row of skirts and slacks, but even the red dot price tags couldn't generate any enthusiasm. It seemed foolish to consider buying a winter outfit with her life up in the air like this. Moths could eat a wool sweater before she'd have a chance to wear it. And summer things—well, if she didn't succeed in making Clay forget the move to Florida, clothes would hardly matter. In the pictures she'd seen, Floridians wore only skimpy bathing suits, skin tight tee shirts, and shorts above the level of decency.

Her thoughts were interrupted when William tumbled a whole display of brassieres to the floor. "William!" the mother screamed again. After that Louise decided to leave. She wasn't in the mood to shop for clothes, not even at 35% off.

"Don't forget tomorrow's meeting," Billie called out as Louise waved goodbye.

Forget? How could Louise possibly forget? She was more likely to forget breathing. She loved the wonderfully predictable routines of her life. The weekly meeting of the quilting club; Aunt Rose on Monday; Wednesday at the library. The pieces fit together perfectly. Some might consider her life ordinary but it fit Louise as comfortably as a soft pair of slippers, never pinching or causing a blister to rise up unexpectedly. She loved the day-in, day-out simplicity of her life. When the kids were small it was one catastrophe after another—a lost skate, a dead hamster, a broken arm, chicken pox, always something. Now it was such a pleasure to wake up in the morning and know exactly what the day would bring. No surprises.

Well, at least not before this business about Florida got started.

By the time Louise arrived at Aunt Rose's it was almost five o'clock. The old lady stood in front of her apartment building, impatiently tapping her toe and glowering at the walkway. She was dressed head-to-toe in navy blue—hat, dress, shoes, and gloves, but there in the middle of all that navy blue her snow white face looked knotted up like a lace doily.

"Sorry," Louise apologized. "I'm running late."

"Have you not learned that tardiness can be avoided with proper planning?"

If nothing else Rose Elkins was certainly proper. She had an Emily Post book that she revered only slightly less than the family Bible. "Just look at you," she groaned, lowering herself into the car, "no hat, no gloves."

"Nowadays women don't bother with those things," Louise replied.

"So you've said." Rose gave a worrisome shake of her head as she squared her navy blue purse in the middle of her lap. "I suppose it's what the world has come to—war, pestilence, and a lackadaisical attitude toward dressing." She gave a deep sigh, then asked, "Exactly what are we having for dinner, dear?"

"Chicken."

"Chicken? Didn't I mention I had a taste for lamb chops or maybe a steak? Don't you have either of those?"

"Sorry, but chicken was all I had in the freezer."

"With all your hatless running around, it would seem you might have stopped in the butcher shop. But since you failed to make time for such a thing, chicken will have to do. Just be mindful of how you prepare it. My stomach can't take those rich spices you use."

"It's just salt and pepper."

"So you say."

As soon as they arrived at the house, Aunt Rose walked into the family room and snapped on the television. "Your tardiness has caused me to miss most of the evening news," she grumbled as she swatted Yoo off the recliner and plopped down.

Louise had just finished snapping the tails off the string beans when she heard the front door close and knew Clay was home. She could hear him talking to Aunt Rose, but for the most part their conversation was muffled, drawn under by the grumble of the television. Then in one of those moments when there was a break in the newscaster's chatter, she heard Clay's voice loud and clear. "Has Louise told you the news about our moving to Florida?" he asked.

A crash and the sound of breaking glass stopped Rose before she could respond.

"Louise?" Clay called out.

When no answer came, he hurried to the kitchen. "Louise?"

She was not in the kitchen but the back door stood open. Pieces of raw chicken and the splintered remnants of a Pyrex baking dish had scattered across the floor. "Louise?" he called again. Then he spotted her marching across the yard with red checked oven mitts on both hands.

"Louise?"

Louise

I never believe what I don't want to be true. I fool myself into thinking something will change. The truth could walk up and smack me in the face, and I still wouldn't recognize it. I pushed the possibility of moving aside and told myself Clay would never do something like that. But that was before I heard the determination in his voice. Now I know he's set on doing it. He's so preoccupied with looking across the horizon that he's lost sight of what's right here in front of him.

For Clay, Florida is the pot of gold at the end of the rainbow. But the reality is a rainbow has no end. It's just a patch of promise in the sky. At times it looks close enough that you think you can chase it down. But if you try that rainbow disappears as quickly as it came, and you're left with nothing. I know, because my daddy spent his life chasing rainbows, and when he died all he left behind was an angry wife and an orphaned daughter.

After all our years of being together, I thought Clay would have a better feeling for what's inside my heart. I never want to leave here. It's the only place I've ever truly belonged. It's not the biggest house or the fanciest house, but it's our *house. I love having the kids close enough to hug, having a granddaughter whose eyes light up when she sees me. I love having my friends close by and being part of their lives, just as they're part of mine.*

Yes, I love Clay too. But why should loving him mean that I have to give up all the other things in my life?

Maybe Billie is right. Maybe it's time for me to face up to the truth.

Priscilla's Plan

Louise heard Clay's voice trailing after her, but she didn't stop. She tromped across the frozen lawn and disappeared into the shadows. As she vanished into the darkness beyond the glow of the house, she neither slowed her step nor looked back across her shoulder. A twisted hump of root hidden beneath the snow bordered the walkway where it ended, a root that likely would have tripped anyone else. But after almost thirty years she knew exactly where it was, so she eased her foot over it and kept going. She didn't feel the chill of snow clumped around her ankles until she had passed the big elm.

When she left Louise was bristling with the heat of anger—a pot of resentment boiling over—but now her feet felt like chunks of ice, and the cold night air pinched her skin. She shivered and rubbed the oven mitts along her arms, hoping to generate some warmth. It was so like her to do something stupid. Billie Butterman would never have stomped off into the cold. Billie would have gotten her down-filled jacket from the hall closet and taken time to pull on her weatherproof boots. *Then* she would have stomped off. More likely, she'd have *driven* off in that big Cadillac of hers.

Louise crossed to the far side of the yard and squeezed through the side door of the metal storage shed. She was the one who kept the shed straightened, putting things where they belonged, and she knew precisely where everything sat. But with almost no light to see by, it seemed things were moved about. She barely stepped inside the door when she banged her shin against a broken lawn mower, a lawn mower definitely in a place where it didn't belong. A welt came up, and when she bent to rub it she went headlong into an unfamiliar pile-up of folding chairs, rakes, and shovels that tumbled down onto her back.

A glimmer of light came through the tiny window at the far end of the shed, a speck of moonlight, nothing more. Not enough to see what she wanted. She inched deeper into the clutter. Once past the jumble of stuff left in the wrong place she could grab a rain slicker or camping blanket, something to keep her warm. Hopefully she wouldn't be here all that long. Surely Clay would realize how his words had angered her and he'd come to apologize. He wasn't the type to let her stay outside in this freezing cold weather. He'd worry that she'd catch a chill or, worse yet, pneumonia. At least she hoped he would.

Louise felt her way past the baby carriage she'd used for Phillip and Patty, then reached for the row of hooks where she thought she'd find a sweater or jacket. Maybe even that worn quilt they took to the beach. Running her hand along the wall, she felt the first hook, a large S-shaped piece of metal with a residue of rust and nothing more. The second hook was also empty. The third and fourth held only a straw hat and dirt-clumped gardening apron. She gave a groan of disappointment; then, recalling that most body heat is lost through the head, plopped the hat atop her frizzed curls. Hat or no hat, she grew colder by the second and began to shiver. When her teeth began to chatter, she shook a splatter of dirt from the plastic apron and shrugged it around her shoulders. It was cold and stiff but hopefully would lock in what little body heat she had left.

Louise peered out the shed window and wondered how long it would take for Clay to come looking for her. If he were the man she gave him credit for being, he'd be pleading for forgiveness and insist that she come back inside the warm house. Of course she would, but only after he promised to forget this nonsense about moving to Florida. She sat on the splintery picnic bench and watched the amber square of light coming from the back door. Any second that door would swing open, and Clay would step outside calling her name. She waited. The minutes stretched into what felt like hours, and the longer she sat the more she thought things weren't working out the way she'd anticipated.

A sense of aloneness settled over Louise, and she drifted back to thinking of the yellow house and the night she'd hidden Molly in the barn. It wasn't supposed to end the way it did, but things happened and as usual she had no say in her life. She was tossed into the back seat of her daddy's Packard and hauled away without a word of discussion. When her mama found out about Molly, she simply said they were not going back to the house and that was that.

"It's just a doll," she'd said. "You can't expect your daddy to drive eighty miles back for some raggedy old doll."

They never understood. Molly wasn't *just* a doll. She was Louise's best friend. Her only friend. Molly was the one who was there when she needed somebody to love. On the nights when her daddy didn't come home and her mama whimpered like a hungry dog, Molly was the only one she could hold on to.

Looking back, Louise knew she should never have expected anything different. Her mother was a woman who had fallen victim to life, buckled at the knees and caved-in, her hope flattened out like a threadbare doormat. She turned cold and uncaring, resolved to keeping a store of bitterness in her heart forever. "I'd once planned on being an actress," she'd say. But the truth was she wasn't much of anything, just an irresponsible frump of a woman who trailed along behind her husband mumbling, "Yes, Walter. No, Walter. You decide, Walter."

Louise worried that heredity might cause such traits to be passed along from mother to daughter. Sometimes she'd do something, then find herself thinking, *This is just what Mother would do,* and it was like a sharp smack in the head.

Suddenly Louise could almost hear her mama saying, "Yes, Walter, I'll be glad to drag myself off to Florida." She jumped to her feet so quickly that a planter toppled from the shelf and fell to the floor. Instantly she shot out the door and headed back up the walkway, the plastic apron tied around her shoulders billowing like Wonder Woman's cape.

As she neared the house, she heard the whine of Aunt Rose's voice and slowed her steps. Louise wanted to meet this issue head on, but maybe that wasn't the best approach. She recalled Billie's words, and by the time she reached the porch she knew exactly what she would do. Removing the apron, she calmly stepped inside.

Clay crouched close to the floor, gathering bits of broken glass and raw chicken. With a wide-eyed expression he glanced up and asked, "What happened?"

"An accident," Louise replied calmly. "I was getting ready to put the chicken in the oven, and the bake dish slid out of my hands."

"That's it?" Clay's expression didn't change. "You dropped a dish—that's it?"

"Yes."

"Then why'd you take off like you did?"

"I needed a breath of air to calm myself."

Not one to hold her tongue, Aunt Rose piped up. "Well, I'm not eating *that* chicken! You'd better scurry down to the market for a steak or maybe some lamb chops."

Louise had already decided she wasn't her mother, and she wasn't going to scurry anywhere. "That's not necessary," she said. "Just relax and watch your show. Dinner will be ready shortly." She opened the cupboard and shuffled around boxes of cereal and potato flakes, hoping to find a package of macaroni and cheese.

Rose Elkins wrinkled her face into a frown. "Well, hurry it up," she said. "My system gets out of kilter when I eat too late." With that she turned back to the family room. "Wheel of Fortune" had already started, and it was a show she never missed.

Clay still looked bewildered. "That's all that happened?" he asked again.

"Yes," Louise answered, emptying the box of macaroni into a pot.

As she listened to Clay's footsteps fading off down the hall, Louise heard Aunt Rose shout, "R, dimwit! You need an R!"

Louise had settled herself into a sense of resolve. She was now determined to handle this situation not as her mother might, but as Billie Butterman would. It was never too late for a woman to change and if she could change her ways, why not also change her name? *Penelope. Maybe Priscilla.*

She was thinking through the specifics of her plan when they sat down to dinner.

"Macaroni is what we're having?" Clay said. "No meat?"

"No meat," she answered and handed him the bowl of string beans.

"No meat?" Rose repeated. "No steak? No lamb chops?"

"Sorry," Louise said.

"Sorry?" Rose Elkins scowled. "*Sorry?* I can't eat sorry! Didn't I mention I had a taste for steak or lamb chops?"

They shared very little conversation during dinner, but when Louise set a plate of fudge brownies on the table the mood changed. Rose smiled, and Clay put aside the newspaper he'd been reading. It seemed now they had something to talk about.

Rose spoke first. "So, what's this about Florida?"

Louise, not yet ready, said, "We can talk about that later."

Unfortunately, there was no stopping Clay. He swung into the full explanation of how he'd inherited a house in Florida. He segued from that into how he would quit the rat race before it killed him. When he got to the part about fishing and golf, he interrupted himself and asked, "Louise, did you call any real estate agents?"

"Well, actually…" For a second she felt a trace of hesitation, a moment when the burgeoning Penelope or Priscilla might be pushed aside by that thing handed down from her mother.

But it didn't happen. Louise took a deep breath and said, "After looking into it, I've decided we should ask Gloria Hornock's husband, Henry, to handle it. He works with Bliss Realty."

"Henry Hornock?"

"Uh-huh. I've heard he's quite good."

"Henry Hornock? The same Henry Hornock who worked at Patioland last summer and Shoe City the year before?"

"Yes."

"But…that guy is a—"

"Don't be so opinionated," Louise said before Clay had the chance to finish his thought. "Henry's had a bit of bad luck, but is that all you can focus on? He also has plenty of good qualities, the sort of qualities we need in a real estate agent. Why, just today Billie said she thought he'd be perfect for us."

"Henry Hornock?"

"Yes, Henry Hornock. You know Gloria is almost one of my dearest friends, and I couldn't possibly say we're not willing to work with her husband."

"I didn't think you and Gloria—"

Louise rolled her eyes. "Only since high school," she said.

"Okay, okay," Clay conceded. "But I still want you to get three appraisals. Henry Hornock can be one of them."

"Three? Why bother with—"

"Three. And we go with the agent who thinks they can get the highest price."

Rose, who had not been a part of the conversation, purposely rattled her coffee cup against the saucer and grumbled. "Am I to assume the two of you are planning to move to Florida without a bit of concern for me?"

"You?" Clay asked.

"Yes," she answered, doubling the wrinkles in her face and pinching them into a quarrelsome frown. "Me!"

"Well, I don't see what—"

"You don't? With Louise gone, how am I supposed to get back and forth to the hairdresser? The doctor? The grocery store? Were you planning to sign me up for some charity wagon to deliver a lukewarm bowl of soup and bologna sandwich?" Rose Elkins angrily pushed her pointy little nose into Clay's face, daring him to answer in the wrong tone of voice.

He didn't. He just sputtered something about how that was never his intention.

"Maybe not," Rose snapped back, "but that's exactly what will happen!"

Clay tried to switch the conversation to another topic, but Rose went on to tell of all the disasters that could befall an elderly woman alone in the world. When she got to the part about axe murderers, Clay picked up his newspaper and turned to the sports section.

Louise considered taking Aunt Rose aside and telling her of the plan, but Rose never was one to keep a secret. The best Louise could do was reassure her. "We'd never leave you here alone," she said. "You're part of our family and that will never change, no matter what happens."

"Bear in mind," Rose replied grumpily, "I'm none too fond of hot weather."

Without saying a word, Clay lowered his newspaper and gave Louise a look.

Later that night as Louise patted cream around her eyes, she noticed something in the mirror. Her face looked different—younger, less lined, more confident. Already she had started to look like a Priscilla or maybe a Pamela. A smile slid across her face. *Whoever you are, I think I like you.*

The next morning Louise kissed Clay goodbye ever so sweetly, but before his car had left the driveway she'd reached into the closet and hauled out the Yellow Pages directory. Within half-an-hour she had a list of twelve real estate agents. Carefully selected agents. The ones with obscure names and single-line listings. She also had Henry Hornock's number at Bliss Realty.

All twelve agents agreed to come over and look at the house. She scheduled the appointments thirty minutes apart, hoping no one would be either late or early. With a dozen different realtors, she could be relatively certain at least two would come back with an estimate lower than whatever Henry Hornock might submit.

The first agent came from Homes-4-U. He arrived promptly at ten. Louise walked him through the house, room by room. "The storm windows don't fit snug as they should," she told him. "Feel that draft on your feet? And these bathroom tiles are loose." She pushed in on the one tile that did jiggle a bit. "See? Hanging on by a thread. Plumber thinks water got in behind the faucet and rotted part of the wallboard."

"How about the water heater?" Homes-4-U asked.

"Oh, it works just fine if only one person takes a shower. More than one, you'll have to wait an hour in between."

"And the neighborhood?" Homes-4-U asked. "Quiet?"

"It was. Not that I want to be the one to carry tales, but word is the family next door's planning to take in nine foster children, all with drug problems. Imagine," she said with an air of sadness, "nine uncontrollable teenagers living right next to you!"

Truth be known, Dilbert and Olivia Graham lived next door, an elderly couple with little use for their own grandchildren and less use for anyone else's. But Louise thought the addition of wayward teenagers added an element of color.

"Yes, yes, I understand." When they finished going from room to room, Mister Homes-4-U took out a packet of papers and handed them to Louise. "These are comparison forms," he said. "They'll give you an idea of what other houses in this area are selling for."

Louise wondered if she'd been discouraging enough. "Ah, yes," she sighed, shuffling through the stack. "It's obvious some houses are selling for considerably more than we'd expect. We know there are problems with this house, and we're not looking for top dollar. The last thing in the world we'd do would be try and take advantage of some poor unsuspecting buyer. Why, that would be absolutely unforgivable."

"Absolutely," Mister Homes-4-U commiserated as he scribbled notes on his pad. Then he took out a form and started filling in the blank spaces, all the while humming like there was a nest of bees in his head. Finally, he handed Louise the paper. "Under the circumstances," he said apologetically, "this is probably the best I can come up with. Your house looks real good, but with all these repairs it needs, well…"

Louise shrugged as if she understood the problem but was saddened by it.

"You know, Missus Palmer, you did right telling me these things. There's a law that says you've got to tell the prospective buyer when there's stuff wrong with the house. So, it's good you did. Most people, they try to hide stuff like this, but it always comes out in the end. You—well, you're one of the honest ones."

His last comment made Louise swallow hard, and for a brief moment she wondered if she'd gone too far with the drug-addicted teenagers.

The second agent, Sarah Waterman-Jones, came from Lovely Lifestyles. Her delicate hands and soft-spoken nature made Louise felt even guiltier about the tall tale she had spun, so she eliminated the part about nine foster children. Instead, she added in a tidbit about a rumored reassessment of property taxes.

As the agents paraded in and out of the house Louise fine-tuned and polished her story, removing the nine foster children altogether and adding in a faulty furnace, leaky pipes, and a dishwasher constantly on the fritz.

Following Sarah Waterman-Jones, an elderly gentleman from Crestridge Realty said he could do without seeing the upstairs bedrooms as the arthritis in his knee was acting up. After him came a gum-snapping bimbo from Homes-a-Million. "Kristi, with an i," the bimbo said, and she handed Louise a business card with a smiley face drawn in where the dot should have been. Kristi wore leather boots that came up to the middle of her thigh, but her skirt ended considerably above that point.

"Aren't you cold?" Louise asked.

"Nah." Kristi bent to pet the dog, and her skirt rode up even further. "Cute dog. What's his name?" With that she lifted Yoo's front paws and checked his underbelly. "You are a *him* aren't you, sweetie?"

"Yoo. His name's Yoo."

"Well, now," she said and rolled the dog over so that she could rub his belly. "Who gave you such a funny name?"

"Nobody gave it to him. It just sort of happened."

"Oh?"

"He was a stray, not a puppy we'd planned to keep. Got into everything imaginable. It was always, 'Hey, you, get outta that! Hey, you, leave that sock alone!' Hey, you, this. Hey, you, that. Eventually, his name just became Yoo."

"Cute," she said and unfolded herself from the floor. "Well, I'll think this house thing over and get back to you. Right now, I gotta scram. Got a lunch date. This guy I met yesterday. My boyfriend would have a hemorrhage if he knew."

"You don't have comparison sheets to show me?"

"Afraid not. I was gonna bring some, but when this guy called we kind of got talking and I ran out of time. Me, I never like to be late for appointments."

"Well, do you want to go through the upstairs? Ask questions?"

"Nah. I already got the picture. I got a good eye for sizing up houses without making a big thing over it."

"Oh."

"I'll get back to you. Gimme a few days, a week maybe."

Kristi waved goodbye and trotted her bare little thighs down the walkway without ever knowing about the tax reassessment, the faulty furnace, or the leaky pipes.

The parade continued all afternoon, and Louise continually got more creative with her descriptions of what was wrong with the house. "Poor insulation," she'd say. "Might need a new roof. Heard a highway is coming through next year." Once she'd slipped into the role she was playing, she even began trying on a double initial name for size and feel. She began by introducing herself as Priscilla Palmer to the agent from Rossman's Realty and then as Pamela to the next one.

The last agent of the day arrived at four-thirty; it was Henry Hornock. He wore a crumpled plaid jacket and looked just as frumpy and down-at-the-heels as ever.

"Ah, the same old Henry," Louise said and breathed a sigh of relief.

"Well, well, now. Aren't you a sight for sore eyes? Pretty little Lulu Fogal, all grown up and fancy."

"It's Palmer now."

"Palmer? Oh, right. You married that skinny guy from the bank. Pleasant sort. Clifford, wasn't it?"

"Clayton."

"Nice house," Henry said, showing himself through the hallway into the living room. He stopped beside the coffee table, picked up a porcelain vase, and turned it over. "You get this at Walmart?"

"No, it belonged to Clay's grandmother."

"My sister got almost the same thing. Hers came from Walmart." He eyeballed the rest of the room. "How come you wanna sell a nice place like this?"

"Clay's uncle died and left him a house down in Florida, so we're thinking of possibly moving. But," she quickly added, "we're only thinking. We may actually decide not to sell this house."

"Depends on what?" Henry asked, lifting the sofa skirt and looking beneath it for no obvious reason.

"We'd be asking a fairly high price," Louise said, working to paint a different picture. "The house is in excellent condition, and it's in a wonderful neighborhood."

Henry worked his way through the dining room into the kitchen. Unlike his predecessors he didn't bother with notes or offer critique as he went. He simply bobbed his head up and down saying, "Nice, real nice."

"All hardwood floors," Louise noted. "And the storm windows, why, they keep the place warm and cozy as can be."

Uninvited, Henry tromped up the staircase and wandered through the bedrooms one by one. He flipped the light switches on and off but did not ask a single question. Louise followed along, offering her unsolicited comments. "New wallpaper, lots of closets, view of the pond, plenty of hot water." She wanted to talk about the house, but he wanted to talk about their high school days.

"Gloria and me, we saw Pete Schneider at the County Fair last year. Almost didn't recognize him, fat and bald as the rump of a newborn baby. Pete, he was always a ladies' man, fancy red car, a roll of bills in his pocket. Who'd of thought he'd end up packing it around like an overstuffed sausage?"

"Well, now, about the house—"

"Nice. Now, Kenny Millburn, he still looks like that Redford guy. Got a place over in Warren that would knock your socks off. Big stone house, white pillars, the whole nine yards. That place is worth at least a dime or two."

"What about our house?"

"It's a fine place. Likely fetch a pretty penny."

"Oh?"

Henry scratched his head like he might be thinking about the price. "Funny," he finally said, "in school Kenny Millburn was a real drippy guy. Nobody ever figured him for making the big bucks."

After what seemed an eternity of reminiscent chitchat, Henry finally reached into his breast pocket, pulled out a gray estimating sheet, and started to write. Louise fidgeted nervously as she waited. The other agents had shown her all kinds of comparison sheets, discussed the matter thoroughly before they set pen to paper, but not Henry.

"Don't you think we ought to talk about the price?" she asked hesitantly.

"Nah, I'm good," he answered and kept on writing. "I can see you got a real nice house here." He handed her a piece of paper that was crumpled and smudged with fingerprints. "I'm gonna do okay for you, Lulu. You stick with old Henry Hornock, and you'll get a sweet deal."

A wide smile stretched across her face when Louise read the proposal form. This was even better than she'd hoped for. Clay couldn't argue with her choice. Henry had quoted the highest price by far.

When she showed him to the door, Henry took Louise's hand and pumped it up and down vigorously. "Good to see you, Lulu. Real good. We gotta get together, you and Clifford, me and Gloria, talk about the old times. Maybe have a few beers down at Bullwhacker's. Yeah," he said wistfully, "those were the days."

"Clayton," Louise said again.

Henry turned to go as if he expected nothing more, but as he lumbered down the walkway she shouted, "I'll give you a call, tomorrow probably."

He glanced over his shoulder, grinned, and said, "Yeah, call me." As he walked off, he mumbled again, "Yes, sir, those were the days." Louise watched the once-dapper football star wearily climb into a beat-up old Chevy and understood why he wanted to relive the past.

Before Clay came home from work, Louise carefully gathered all the estimate sheets and tucked most of them safely away in her lingerie drawer. She left out only the three she would use—the lowest one from Valu-Rite Realty, the mid-estimate from Sarah Waterman-Jones, and the highest, which came from Henry Hornock. On the way out of the bedroom she stopped at the dressing table, applied a fresh coat of Rosy-Posy Pink lipstick, and fluffed her hair. Now that she had the situation under control, a younger, more confident reflection in the mirror suggested the possibility of a nickname. *Pinkie? Pansy? Prissy?*

"Definitely not Prissy," she said and turned away.

Louise hurriedly squished together a meatloaf and tucked it into the oven along with two small potatoes. When the garage door clamored up, she poured Clay a glass of wine and shoved it into his hand the moment he entered the house. "Dinner's ready," she said sweetly.

"I don't have time to change my clothes?"

"No. Meatloaf's nice and hot. You know how much you hate cold—"

"I don't mind it cold." He looked at the glass in his hand. "Wine with meatloaf?"

"It's good for your digestion. Help you relax while we go over things."

"Go over things?"

"Yes, of course, unless you want me to choose the realtor by myself."

"I don't think—" Clay loosened his tie as he settled into the chair. "Were you able to get all three estimates?"

"Isn't that what you wanted?" She followed Billie's instructions and answered each question with another question so she couldn't be tricked into revealing the plan.

"Well, yes," Clay stammered. "But are we in some kind of a rush here?"

"Rush? Me? Aren't you the one who wants to move?"

"I suppose I am. Today I filled out the retirement forms. Come April first, I'm gone from the bank." He gave a wide grin, the kind she hadn't seen on his face for quite some time. "It's time for us to start making our plans."

Louise tried not to notice how happy he looked when she shoved the three estimate sheets under his nose. "Check these out."

"Hmm."

Louise's eyes would have jumped directly to the bottom line but Clay seemed to read every word on the page, absorbing each and every detail.

"What's this notation mean? 'Needs repairs'?"

"Well, that's to be expected. There's not a house in the world that doesn't have something or another that needs attending to."

"Hmm."

He read on. Every word. Even the fine print. "I'd have thought the house worth more," he finally said, then turned to the next page.

It was a true test of patience for Louise to wait and say nothing, but she held fast.

When he finished reading the second page, Clay muttered, "Well, this price is better, but still pretty disappointing." He then turned to the estimate form submitted by Henry. Scowling as he smoothed the grimy sheet of paper, he began to read, starting with the very first word at the top of the page. Halfway down, he stopped and asked, "Is this here a thumbprint or an eight?"

Louise leaned over Clay's shoulder. "Why, that's an eight," she said. "Actually, two eights, sitting side by side."

"Hmm. More like what I thought the price should be."

Louise set the plate in front of Clay. Meatloaf with a freckled brown potato and a handful of peas that had rolled to one side. Afraid of giving herself away, she said nothing.

Clay pushed his glasses low on his nose and peered over them. "Henry Hornock did this?" he asked suspiciously.

"He's the one who signed it, isn't he?"

"Yes, but something—"

"But nothing. You said the highest estimate."

"So I did, but—Henry Hornock?"

"What's wrong with Henry?"

"Well, he's not exactly—"

"I think he's *exactly* the type of agent we need."

"Hmm." Clay stuffed a bite of meatloaf in his mouth and began chewing.

Meatloaf wasn't like a steak—it wasn't something a person needed to chew—yet it seemed to Louise he'd chomped on that same bite for far longer than necessary. Finally she said, "Well?"

"Is this the same meatloaf you always make? It seems tougher."

"It's the same," she answered, even though it wasn't. What with all those realtors coming and going, she'd rushed and used a packet of mix that had sat in the back of the cupboard for ages. "So what about Henry?"

"Ah, yes, Henry. I've got a number of misgivings. The man always seemed like such a goofball. Why, back in school—"

"Clay!"

"Okay, okay. He has the highest estimate, so go with him."

While Clay still sat at the kitchen table chewing on the meatloaf, Louise phoned Henry. The telephone rang four times before Gloria answered. "Hi, Gloria," Louise said in her cheeriest voice. "I was wondering if Henry could pop over this evening so Clay can sign the listing agreement."

"Who's this?" Gloria asked.

"Louise Palmer."

"Who?" Gloria repeated.

"Louise Palmer," she whispered. "Used to be Fogal. Remember? Westfield High? We were both in Mister Cooperman's history—"

"Well, I'll be! How long has it been? Forty years, I'll bet. Thirty if it's a day."

"I suppose so," Louise said with a put-upon sigh, trying to hide the gist of the conversation from Clay. "That Henry, he's something. Just this afternoon he was over here, and we're convinced he's the right agent to sell our house. If Henry has time—"

"Henry's got nothing but time," Gloria answered. "He's eating right now, but I suppose he could be there in an hour or so."

When the doorbell rang Louise was finishing up the dishes so Clay set aside his newspaper, pulled himself from the recliner, and opened the door.

"Hey, Cliff. How you doing?"

"Clay," Louise said, coming up behind her husband. "Henry, you remember Clay, don't you?"

"Sure, sure. Me and Clay go back a long time." Henry didn't bother with formalities such as wiping his feet, so he tromped right in. "You used to go by the handle of Cliff, right?"

"No," Clay said. "Never."

"Oh. Funny, I could've sworn…" Now familiar with the house, Henry headed for the kitchen. "Got any coffee? I could sure use a cup." He pulled off his jacket, hung it over the back of the chair, and flopped down in Clay's spot. "Anything sweet, that'd be great too."

"Cookies?" Louise offered.

The three of them gathered around the table with the paperwork. "Now, you see here, what this means…" Henry began, and then he went through the entire contract word by word.

When he pulled out a magnifying glass to read the disclaimer, Louise began to grow nervous. "I think we can skip that part," she said, but Clay insisted on hearing every last word. Louise could have cared less about the disclaimer or how many days before the contract would expire; she simply wanted to get the listing agreement signed and shoo Henry out the door before something went wrong.

Unfortunately, Henry was still caught up with the good old days. "Albertina Morrison, tight sweaters, remember her?" he'd ask, and Louise could see a serious look of doubt crawling across Clay's face. "What about Freddie Hopmeyer, the guy who used to barf in biology?"

At ten o'clock that night, when she watched Henry whistle his way down the walk with the signed contract, Louise breathed a sigh of relief.

Clay

Okay, I know Louise doesn't want to move. She hates the thought, I'm well aware of that. I just hope she's not trying to pull a fast one by hiring Hornock to sell the house, because I'm giving this guy three months at most. After that, I'm getting somebody who can actually do the job. If Louise had her way, we'd stay here until we died of dry rot. But I don't plan to let it happen. I've seen how Uncle Charlie enjoyed life, and I intend to do the exact same thing. Louise will just have to get used to the idea. In time she will. I'm sure of it. If working with Hornock makes this easier for her, then I'll go along with it—but, as I said, for three months. That's it!

Personally, I think Hornock is a brainless twerp. But I'm guessing he'll put the house on multiple listings and some savvy real estate agent will snap up the sale. The sooner the better, as far as I'm concerned.

The more I think about living in that nice little house of Uncle Charlie's, the more I know I'm doing the right thing. Louise should be able to see how good this is gonna be, but she's not always the best judge of circumstances. She's too emotionally involved. She's worried about leaving the kids and her friends. What she doesn't realize is that those ladies in her club aren't the last people on earth. She'll make new friends. After she does, everything will be fine.

I know once we get to Florida, my life will be a whole lot better and hers will too. She just doesn't know it. Once we get settled in the house, she can fix things the way she wants. Within a month or two she'll be as attached to that house as she is to this one.

As for me, I don't need any convincing. I'm already picturing myself fishing, maybe playing a little golf. I'm gonna be enjoying a life of ease from here on in.

Yesterday I had a customer complain about the two dollar charge he'd been billed for a stop payment order. For almost fifteen minutes he stood there complaining, even after I'd already credited his account for the two bucks. All the while I'm listening, I'm thinking, "Two months. That's it." And I'm laughing on the inside of my face.

A Miracle of Misfortune

After he marched off with the agreement to sell their house tucked into his jacket pocket, the Palmers did not see hide nor hair of Henry. "I'll be in touch," he'd said, then waved goodbye and climbed back into that rusted Chevy of his. The thirty-year-old engine choked and sputtered like it didn't have another mile left in it, but after a dozen or so tries he got it started and chugged off down the street. Louise kept her fingers crossed until she saw the Chevy's tail-lights disappear around the corner. Then she smiled at Clay who was standing in the doorway and looking as dazed as a man who'd staggered off of a roller coaster.

"Well, now, that's done," she said.

"I don't know," Clay replied, shaking his head. "I just don't have a good feeling about this."

"Nonsense. Henry will do the right thing for us. You'll see."

Louise figured it wasn't an out-and-out lie. It *was* the best thing for them. Although Clay might have thought retirement meant they had to move to Florida, he'd realize the truth once he settled into a routine of having his second cup of coffee on the front porch and puttering about the yard all afternoon. She felt certain of it.

A twinge of doubt nipped at the edge of her thoughts, but Louise brushed it back. It was way too early to start worrying, she told herself. Clay wouldn't retire until April, and by then the weather would start warming up. There'd be green buds popping out all over the big oak tree and spring flowers that needed planting. The storm windows would have to be taken down and the screens put up, the back porch painted—why, there was any number of things to keep him busy. They could spend an afternoon on one of those ferryboat excursions along the Hudson River, take a picnic lunch to Central Park, and maybe even ride the carousel.

That was something they hadn't done since before the kids were born. It would be no time at all before Clay forgot about moving. "Leave here?" he'd ask. "How could you expect that I'd ever leave here?"

Louise planned on answering with nothing more than a sly smile; then she'd hand him another list of things that needed his attention. Confident she was doing exactly what needed to be done, she let go of her last smidgeon of doubt.

Then this morning, two weeks to the day they signed the contract with Henry Hornock, Louise woke up with a troublesome tick in her head. *What if?* she began thinking. When she'd exhausted one scenario, she'd move on to another and find something new to worry about. Half a dozen snowflakes had fallen during the night, no more than a dusting across the lawn, but it pushed her into thinking about the day Clay's father died. It happened on an icy cold February day, the coldest anyone could remember. The night before it had snowed seven or eight inches, and poor old Mister Palmer climbed out of his bed that morning to shovel the drive before he went off to work. He came back in the house—his face red as an apple, to hear Missus Palmer tell it—kissed her goodbye, and went off to the bank.

"You'll catch your death of cold going out when you're so perspired," she told him. But she was wrong; he didn't catch a cold. He didn't have time enough.

That year no one hung laundry on the outside line because shirts, sheets, even the socks, would turn to ice before a clothespin could be clipped on. That's why Missus Palmer was in the basement that afternoon. Clay's daddy had tacked up a clothesline behind the furnace, and she was hanging the sheets when the phone started ringing. At first she ignored the call, thinking it couldn't be of much importance. But when the phone kept ringing and ringing, she knew it had to be important or the caller would have hung up long ago. She let go of the sheet she was in the midst of hanging and went scurrying up those narrow wooden stairs—which is how she fell and broke her hip. For three hours she lay there listening to that phone ring and just knowing it had to be something really important. It was almost suppertime when Clay finally got there and told her that the guard down at the bank had found her husband at his desk, dead. "He was slumped over like a man taking a nap," the guard said, "his head atop a stack of loan requests that had yet to be processed."

"It was the shoveling snow that killed him!" Missus Palmer cried over and over again. From that point on her heart was broken and with nothing more to live for she followed Clay's daddy to the grave less than a year later.

Thinking back on how poor Mister Palmer had spent his last hours on earth shoveling snow, Louise decided she would insist Clay get a snow blower. A measure of sadness settled into her heart as she rolled another loaf of pinwheel sandwiches. If only Missus Palmer had insisted that her husband get a snow blower; then Clay wouldn't be worrying that he'd die like his daddy.

Louise sliced the loaf and arranged the tiny sandwiches on a platter. Today the Material Girls Quilting Club would meet at her house. As she tucked a sprig of parsley beneath the last pinwheel, she drifted on to thinking about the time Margo's Volkswagen got stuck in the snow, a much more pleasant memory. It happened years ago, but her mind's eye could still see it. They'd left the store with shopping bags full of presents and discovered the car almost buried in a pile of snow pushed aside by the plow. Lucky for them a group of Phillip's friends happened by, five gangly boys who laughed uproariously at the sight. After they'd had their fun at Margo's expense, they heaved that little VW bug over the mound of snow and set it ready to go in the middle of Broad Street.

Pulling a second platter from the cupboard, Louise arranged bite-sized chunks of cheddar cheese in a circle and skewered each of them with a bright red cherry tomato or olive. Not randomly—it was tomato, black olive, green olive. Tomato, black olive, green olive. Some of the girls went all out with fancy spreads; others ordered a six-foot sub from Wattinger's Deli. But whether they used crystal glasses or plastic picnic ware, the Material Girls stayed the same year after year. There was a schedule, a schedule everyone kept. They met at Claire's house, then Ida's, then Barbara's, then Eloise's—each person took a turn. And at every meeting you could count on Billie to complain about grumpy old Missus Butterman, Maggie to swear Joe was drinking again, and Ida to announce that she had either lost or gained another pound.

As she set out the china dishes and linen napkins, Louise wondered why anyone would want to leave such a delightfully predictable life.

"You deaf or something?" Eloise poked her head into the kitchen.

"Oh!" Lost in thought, Louise came up startled. With a swaddling of scarves around her head, Eloise was barely recognizable.

"We rang the bell twice," Eloise said, sounding a bit put out. "I'm prone to the sniffles, and it's too cold to stand there waiting forever."

"Sorry. Didn't hear a thing," Louise said. "I was thinking back on the day when Margo's car got stuck in the snow—"

"That was twenty years ago!"

"Yes, but—"

"Nobody wants to hear *that* story. You've told it forty times already!"

"Have I?" Louise asked absently as she moved off to greet the others.

One by one the women bustled in, stomping bits of snow from their feet and untangling themselves from layer after layer of wooly clothes and zipped-up, flapped-over, buckled-down parkas.

"Donna Swift can't make it today," Ida said. "Her dog had six puppies. Happened just before she went to bed, and she couldn't sleep a wink with those pups squealing."

"Well," Claire said as she twisted her arm loose from an extra heavy sweater squeezed under her coat. "Not that I don't feel sorry for Donna, but I didn't close my eyes last night either. Ken has taken to snoring. All night long, I poke him and say 'Turn over.' He does, but ten seconds later he's right back to chugging away like a locomotive and, believe me, he makes a lot more noise than six newborn puppies."

"You could use more hangers in this closet," Susan said as she hung her plaid jacket over someone else's coat.

That's how every meeting of the quilting club was; one thought didn't lead into the next, but the conversations were pieced together in a patchwork pattern of friendship.

Unable to top Claire's snoring story, Ida jumped from puppies to quilting. "I've designed a new applique pattern that's the easiest ever," she said. But before she got to the details of how she'd worked the pattern through, everyone had turned to listen to Maxine.

"The Klinefelds are getting a divorce."

"Wilma Klinefeld?" Claire gasped. "The Wilma Klinefeld who lives in that brown house across from Ida?"

"Yes." Maxine nodded. "I thought it was still a secret, but yesterday when I was at the bakery Margaret Bloomer said half the people in town already knew."

The other voices stilled, everyone pausing to listen.

"Poor Wilma," Maxine said, stretching the words for added emphasis. "She'd been having problems with George for a while, but all along she figured it was her fault. Claimed it was because she was fat and colorless. So she went out, bought herself one of those Stairmasters, and loaded her hair up with henna until she looked like Lucille Ball. Then come to find out it wasn't one bit her fault. George had a mistress!"

"Disgraceful," Ida exclaimed.

"Worse than disgraceful! Poor Wilma was jumping around on that Stairmaster all day long, then slaving over a hot stove to make George his favorite meals. And all the while he was running around with some chubby blonde half his age."

"Outrageous!" the women told one another. Wilma wasn't the friendliest person around, but she certainly didn't deserve that type of treatment. Worrying aloud, they went to great lengths to assure each other that *their* husbands would never do such a thing.

"Not Ken," Claire said. "Snores maybe, but cheat? Never!"

"What did Wilma do?" Louise asked.

"Do?" Maxine repeated. "She did what any one of us would do. First she washed all that henna out of her hair. Then she threw the Stairmaster *and* George out of the house!"

"Good for her," the group mumbled as they sat down to lunch. The conversation then moved on to patterns and binding techniques, as Louise poured everyone a glass of punch and carted dishes of pickled mushrooms and pinwheel sandwiches to the table.

Mildred Libowitz was in the middle of her explanation of the stack-and-whack method when the doorbell chimed several times—ding-dong, ding-dong, ding-dong—with no pause in-between. "Oh dear," Louise said, eyeing the empty sandwich platter. "I thought everyone was already here."

When she opened the door Henry Hornock grinned and edged an unfamiliar young couple forward. "Hey, Lulu," he said. "The Spotswoods here would like to see your house."

Louise's face fell.

"Are we interrupting your day?" the dark-haired woman asked apologetically. "If so we can come back another time."

Louise was going to answer "Yes, please do" but Henry led the couple right past her and into the center hall. "Interrupting?" he said. "Why, we ain't interrupting Lulu. She's always got time for friends. Right, Lou?"

"Um, well, I do have company. The girls from my quilting club—"

"Quilting club?" the woman asked. "Part of the New Jersey Guild?"

"Yes. But it's not an open club, just friends getting together."

"Well, if this isn't a small world. My mom is Virginia Gluck. Her quilted vistas won first place at the Pieces and Patches Show." She extended her hand toward Louise. "I'm Nancy. This is my husband, Steven."

"Louise. Louise Palmer." She returned the handshake and smiled pleasantly enough, but an uneasy feeling had churned up inside her stomach. The kind of queasiness she got when trouble was on its way.

It wouldn't have taken a lot of effort for Louise to instantly dislike the couple. She just needed one thing, one little thing that would enable her to scoff at the way they did this or that. Steven Spotswood had two-of-a-kind initials, which didn't make it any easier. His face, friendly enough, looked studious and round as a ball. He also had round eyes, round glasses, and a rounded over shirt collar. In short he looked like a walking bowl of Cheerios with sandy blond hair. Not much to like or dislike.

Nancy stood the same height as Steven, but where he was round she was angular—high cheekbones, dark eyes with lashes that fluttered as she spoke, and a twist of satin smooth hair clipped into a tortoiseshell barrette. She had the look of someone who would never dream of fussing with her hairdo, a person who stepped out of the shower ready to go without a lick of mascara or a splat of rouge. Although she was tall she didn't seem tall, because she had narrow hipbones as obvious as question marks. All in all, she looked like a skinny long-legged model from the pages of *Miss Perfect* magazine. It was impossible to find fault with the woman, which was something that unnerved Louise.

Nancy glanced into the living room. "Your home is beautiful," she said. "With the children, our place just seems to sprout clutter."

Louise saw beyond the words and she knew underneath that nauseatingly pleasant exterior Nancy Spotswood was already thinking of how she'd arrange her furniture in the room. All morning Louise had cleaned and polished until everything fairly sparkled, but now she regretted doing so. It would have been far better if the Spotswoods had come on one of those days when Clay's newspapers and shoes were strewn about, and the dog was slobbering all over the sofa.

Henry grabbed Nancy's arm and led her toward the staircase. "You gotta see the upstairs first." He clunked his way up the steps, crusty boots dripping bits of snow. "Four bedrooms, just what you wanted."

Louise tagged along behind feeling like a caboose. "One is *very* small," she said. "Teeny. Not much bigger than a closet."

"Good schools," Henry came back with.

"Yes, but they're at least seven, maybe eight blocks away."

"Nice," Nancy said. "Some kids don't get enough exercise. We like ours to do a bit of walking." She stuck her head in the first bedroom. "Lovely, just lovely."

"Park nearby. Wonderful neighbors. Good size yard." Henry commented on one thing after another as he led the couple through the house. Nancy had something flowery to say about almost everything, but Steven just slouched along with his eyebrows squeezed together and his index finger constantly pushing his glasses up on his nose. He didn't seem to have an opinion one way or the other. Not until they started down the stairs; then he put his arm around Nancy, smiled, and said, "You like it?"

The Material Girls, busy with their quilting and gossip, had taken no notice of what was going on until Henry steered the couple through the dining room. As she tiptoed past the chair, Nancy glanced over Ida's shoulder and asked, "Is that the Star of Bethlehem?" All conversation stopped; all eyes looked up.

"And who are you?" Billie Butterman challenged the newcomer.

"Sorry." The young woman moved back a step. "Nancy. Nancy and Steven Spotswood," she said. "I apologize for interrupting. I just can't pass a beautiful quilt without looking at it. My work's not nearly as nice as this."

"You quilt?"

"Oh, yes, for years and years. Our whole family does. My mom won first place at the Pieces and Patches Show last year."

"Virginia Gluck?" Ida gasped.

"Why, yes. You know her?"

"Everyone's heard of Virginia Gluck," Millie interjected. "Her quilts have won a dozen or more prizes in the New Jersey Guild alone. Lord knows how many elsewhere."

The Material Girls were a closed group of friends, not some hobby club that allowed people to wander in off the street. Yet Ida turned all the way around to face Nancy. "Pull up a chair and join us," she said.

"Oh, thank you. I can't right now. Perhaps another time?"

Unimpressed, Billie still glowered across the table, but Millie said, "Yes, yes. We meet on Tuesday. Do come. You must tell us Virginia's secret of success."

Nancy laughed in a way that seemed overly ingratiating. "I'm not sure I know any real secrets, but I'd love to come." She reached for Ida's hand. "Thank you."

Henry, apparently anxious to move along, nudged her toward the kitchen.

It seemed pointless for Louise to continue mentioning things that could discourage Nancy's interest in the house. No matter what she said, Henry put a positive spin on it. The backyard wasn't small, but manageable. The family room wasn't stuffy, just nice and cozy. The kitchen wasn't cramped, it was conveniently accessible. If the dog had pooped in the middle of the living room, Henry would have said it just showed how well the carpet could resist stains. When he steered the Spotswoods toward the basement, Louise gave up and returned to her friends.

"What an absolutely charming woman," Ida gushed. "Since she was so impressed with my Star of Bethlehem, I may enter it into this year's competition."

"When Nancy comes to the meeting, ask what she thinks," Susan suggested.

With a lopsided grin on her face, Claire said, "Imagine, Virginia Gluck's daughter at our meeting. Why, I never dreamed!"

A dour sort of woman who usually found little to like about anyone, Eloise asked, "Do you think she'll really come to a meeting?"

"She said she was going to."

Billie looked at Louise. "What are those people doing here?"

"I do believe Henry's found a buyer for our house," Louise said sorrowfully.

"Your house?" a number of women asked in unison.

"Did you expect...?" Billie didn't finish the question but waved her finger in the general direction of the door the Spotswoods had gone through.

"Of course not," Louise answered. "Henry Hornock has been unreliable for as long as I've known him. Why would I think he'd change now?"

"Excuse me," Eloise grumbled. "But would somebody mind explaining?"

After the Spotswoods had gone, Louise hauled out the letter from Horace P. Fredericks, Attorney at Law, and read it aloud, her voice quivering at each mention of Florida. "That's it," she said tearfully. "Now Clay wants to sell this house and go live there."

"Oh my," Millie murmured. "What a wonderful opportunity."

"Wonderful? Why, it's awful!"

"Awful?"

"Yes. It means leaving everything behind—friends, family, this house."

With her usual grim expression Eloise mumbled, "Seems to me you're a lot better off than poor Wilma."

"Ah, yes. Poor Wilma," Maxine added.

"Well, I for one don't believe it!" Billie set aside the quilt she'd been stitching. "I don't think Henry Hornock will ever close this sale. Remember the paving company?"

Louise did remember. It was in the newspaper for three days running. Gloria told friends she was planning to quit her job at Belinda's, but once the scandal broke, Henry's hopes of making a million were gone along with the owner of the fraudulent company.

But this wasn't the paving company, and the Spotswoods looked more than reputable. Louise gave a weary shrug and said, "I hope not."

It was nearing suppertime when the women wriggled back into their coats and left for home. As Louise cleared the table and straightened the chairs, thoughts of the yellow house came to mind. She could still remember how the place seemed so big, standing high on a hill as it did. It had the look of a storybook castle. In the late afternoon the sun would drop behind the peak of the roof and make it look as though there was a rainbow inside the attic window.

"Daddy," Louise recalled saying, "why'd we have to move away from that nice big yellow house?"

"Why, that wasn't so big," he'd answer. Hardly worth thinking about."

Although it happened a lifetime ago, it was the start of her troubles.

Louise dimmed the light and turned toward the kitchen. She stopped, glanced back at the darkened dining room, and saw Nancy Spotswood sitting in the chair, showing the Material Girls exactly how Virginia Gluck won those awards. A familiar dread settled in Louise's heart, and she knew it was going to be the yellow house all over again.

That weekend Louise hovered around the telephone shouting, "I've got it!" the moment the first jangle sounded. She skipped taking a shower and held off going to the bathroom for as long as possible. Regardless of what sacrifices had to be made, she had to keep Henry Hornock from getting through to Clay. When they left for the movies on Saturday night, she discreetly slipped the plug from the answering machine. No machine, no messages.

On Monday morning Louise breathed a sigh of relief. It looked like the Spotswoods had not been so taken with the place after all. Henry Hornock's streak of bad luck was apparently still intact. By the end of the week she felt certain the crisis had passed, so she agreed to go shopping with Billie on Friday afternoon. They met at the mall, then went to the Drift-on-Inn for lunch and lingered over a full carafe of wine.

"Here's to Hard-Luck-Henry," Billie said, and they toasted one another.

"Yes, indeed," Louise answered. She knew some things were a given. Life scheduled people for so many strokes of bad luck and so many strokes of good luck. A person could change the ratio sometimes by having matching initials or a four-leaf clover that actually came from Ireland, but nobody escaped a certain amount of bad luck. After first losing Molly, then her daddy and mama, Louise thought she had pretty well fulfilled her bad luck quota, but a week ago Tuesday it seemed ready to start up again. Now it was turned back around. Today she even found a heads-up penny.

That's why she was so unprepared for what happened when she got home.

Clay was sitting in the recliner, a can of beer in his right hand and a smile that looked like a monkey's grin stretched across his face.

"What are you doing home so early?" she asked.

"They finished up the audit." He chuckled playfully and waggled his finger at her. "You sly little fox."

"Huh?"

"You never said a word."

"About what?"

"All the while I thought Henry was a jerk, but you knew better."

"I did?"

"You sure as blazes did."

Louise started to sense something had gone wrong.

"When you're right, you're right."

"About?"

"Henry selling the house."

Now she knew something had gone wrong.

"That offer shocked the living daylights out of me."

"Offer?" She leaned into the word, the muscles in her face falling slack.

"Yeah." Clay smiled. "Henry called fifteen minutes ago, told me they'd agreed to our asking price and said they'd add another thousand if we'd leave the appliances."

"Oh no," Louise said with a moan. "It's not possible."

"What do you mean, not possible? They love this house, and they're willing to pay top dollar." Clay leaned over and rumpled his hand across Yoo's belly. "We're gonna like living in Florida, huh, fella?"

"Oh, Clay, how could you?"

"How could I what? Take the dog?"

"No. How could you take me away from here? Ask me to leave my friends, go off to some strange place where I don't know a single solitary soul? Don't you understand? This is exactly the kind of thing my father would do!"

"Why, your father was an irresponsible philanderer! A man who never once held a steady job. I'm no such thing."

"Then it seems you'd realize a woman needs *some* stability."

"Louise, we've lived in the same house for almost thirty years. That's not stability?"

"No," she answered tearfully. "Living in a place until the day you die—that's stability."

Louise

What's done is done. I suppose God has a reason for wanting me to give up this life that's made me so happy, but for the love of me I can't figure out what it is. Didn't I go through enough with Mama and Daddy, I ask Him—but so far I've gotten no answer.

It broke my heart when Henry Hornock actually found a buyer for the house. The truth is I never expected he would. I figured Clay would retire and after we started doing some of the fun things we used to do, he'd be perfectly content to stay here where we belong. Obviously, that's not what happened.

As much as I hate the thought of moving, of leaving all the people and places I've grown to love, I'm resigned to it. Resigned doesn't mean I'm happy with the idea; it just means that I know it's going to happen regardless of how I feel. When my spirit gets so low that I have to reach down and scrape it off the floor, I tell myself this is God's plan. He knows things I don't. Maybe this move is the difference between Clay living and dying. If I thought that was the case, I'd be a lot more accepting of it. But sometimes when I watch the way Clay walks, the way he runs, the way he can do almost any chore without being winded, I can say truthfully he sure doesn't have the look of a weary man.

I told Billie that God most likely had a hand in Henry selling the house and she said, "Hogwash!" She claims it was nothing but a stroke of dumb luck. Me, I'm not so sure.

The Countdown

"That's it for January," Louise said as she drew an X through the last open square of the month. She lifted the calendar pages and counted the days until the first of April—sixty, including today. Sixty-one, if she also counted April first. Hardly enough time to sneeze, let alone pack away her entire life. Time, it seemed, thumped along like a square wheel when she was eager for something—a baby to arrive, a package to be delivered, a cup of tea to finish brewing—but if she had cause to dread the coming of a thing, well, that was another story.

Once, right before Phillip went off to college, she'd gone a whole month without crossing the days off the calendar. She'd hoped it would slow time, stretch days into weeks, weeks into months. But it didn't change a thing; he left anyway. Then all she had was an empty bedroom and a blank August. It seemed a cruel irony that she, such a settled-down person, should end up in such a transient world.

Louise started to create a store of memories she could call upon when the house was gone from her life. She studied every little detail, counted the number of steps leading to the bedrooms, snipped off bits of fabric from curtains, and tugged strands of carpet from each room. Those things had to be left behind, but she could take the memory of them with her.

In February she tried to take a photo of the front yard, but through the lens of the camera the ground appeared brown and the shrubs a tangle of stringy branches knotted together, not at all the way she wanted to remember it. So she crayoned her own version—a cream-colored house framed with cloudless blue sky, a gray squirrel scampering down the trunk of the big oak, thick green forsythia hedges, and flowers. Lots of flowers, like brightly colored impatiens. She forgot to sketch the broken garage window, the patch of paint peeled loose from the front door, or the dark shadow falling across the walkway.

At first, only the singular vision of Nancy Spotswood sitting in the dining room alongside the Material Girls tormented Louise. But as the days wore on the image moved into the kitchen and eventually into the rest of the house. She began to imagine clusters of toys sprouting in the family room, bicycles cluttering the back porch, and Nancy's skinny little jeans tumbling around in *her* washer and dryer. When those images prickled her heart Louise grew angry with Clay, but the picture of him lying in a brown metal casket always returned to mind and resolutely she'd move on.

On a Tuesday morning, with forty-six days to go, Louise decided there was no reason to hold onto clothes they wouldn't be using anymore. She gathered a stack of shopping bags and tromped upstairs to clear the closets, starting with Clay's. Hot as it was going to be in Florida he certainly didn't need sweaters, so she packed all of them into shopping bags. Every last one. Even the gray cashmere he claimed was his favorite. After that she tackled the sweatshirts, which he also wouldn't need. Then it was a row of suits, some dress shoes, and an entire drawer of socks. Even the underwear—he had far too much of that. She almost ran out of shopping bags before she got to her own things, which, as it turned out, did not require anywhere near the same number of shopping bags.

As soon as she opened her closet door she noticed the red reindeer sweater. Christmas just wouldn't be Christmas if she didn't wear that sweater, so she left it on the hanger. She passed right by the black sequined dress, thinking a person never knew when they might need something for a dressy occasion. If she kept the dress, it would certainly stand to reason that she should keep the matching shoes and bag. And the navy blue wool suit—well, it would be almost impossible to find anything to fit the way that did. The tweed slacks were her favorite. The leather boots had cost ninety-five dollars. When Louise finished up with her closet she had parted with a skirt that had a broken zipper and a ski sweater which was too small for her anyway.

"At least that's done," she said, lowering herself onto the side of the bed. Then she picked up the telephone and dialed the number for Goodwill. "Good morning," she said. "I'd like to schedule a pick-up."

The next day Louise planned to pack the good china, then the silver, and the fancy glasses. That would be the hardest part, packing away things she'd held on to for almost thirty years. A few things she'd had even longer, things such as the yellow and pink vinegar pitcher that according to Aunt Rose had once belonged to Harry Truman's grandmother. For such fragile treasures, she'd need good sturdy cartons.

She set the shopping bags aside, went downstairs, pulled on her boots, and drove to the Food Rite Market. A pile of empty boxes usually sat alongside the last check-out counter; not the flimsy chipboard type, but strong corrugated cartons, sturdy enough to carry a load of canned goods. Breezing through the door she glanced down the line of check-out stations, but there in the spot where the boxes ought to have been a pimple-faced kid was building a pyramid of canned green beans.

"Excuse me," she said. "Where are the boxes?"

"I dunno," he answered and stacked two more cans on top of the others.

"Empty cartons? The ones you're finished with?"

"Oh, those. They're already in the trash."

"Would anyone mind if I took a few?"

"Nope. But they're squashed."

"Squashed flat?"

"Yeah."

"Oh. Don't you have any not-squashed boxes?"

He shook his head, stepped up on a stool, and kept stacking green beans, which made no sense to Louise because the tower of cans already stood a foot taller than the top of his head. A customer couldn't possibly dislodge a single can of beans without toppling the entire pile. She was about to point this out when a silver-haired woman tapped her on the shoulder.

"Dearie," the woman said, "I'm not usually one to butt in, but I'd try the moving company if I were you."

"Moving company?"

The woman nodded. "The movers have nice clean cartons," she said. Then she leaned over and whispered, "The market boxes have bits of lettuce and broccoli stuck inside. Sometimes even a nest of fruit flies. You bring fruit flies home, and you'll never get rid of them."

"Well, I certainly don't want that," Louise said.

"Besides," the woman smiled, "moving company cartons have a place on top to write your name and address so nothing gets lost."

Clay had selected Fatso's, a moving company on the far side of town a good ten miles away. With no other choice, Louise climbed back into her car and pressed down on the gas pedal. She drove in the left-hand lane the entire way, took a shortcut through the elementary school parking lot, and whizzed right through three amber traffic signals. It was five-twenty when she arrived, ten minutes before closing time. When she burst through the door the old man behind the counter looked up and frowned. Skinny and rippled as a sheet of corrugated cardboard, he wore a shirt embroidered with the name Fatso.

"Thank heaven you're still open," she said. "I need boxes."

"What size?" he asked.

"Size?"

"Yeah. We got wardrobe, large, medium, and small. Barrels too."

"Wooden barrels?"

"Yeah. They're twenty-five. Wardrobes are fifteen. Boxes are ten, eight, and six."

"I have to *pay* for boxes?"

"We pay. You pay."

To pay for moving boxes when she didn't want to move seemed somehow injurious. Louise rolled her eyes and grimaced.

"You want them or not?" The skinny Fatso looked over at the clock. "I'm outta here in five minutes," he warned.

Feeling the pressure of Skinny Fatso's quitting time, Louise said, "Okay. Give me ten large, four medium, and...um, maybe two of the small ones."

The man disappeared into the back of the store and returned with a stack of flattened corrugated. "Here you are," he said.

"Those boxes are squashed!"

"They're not squashed, they're flat. They come flat."

To Louise flat looked a lot like squashed, but she had become a woman with very few options. "Okay," she sighed. "I'll take them."

Louise spent the days that followed packing the contents of the house in her paid-for boxes. She carefully wrapped every piece of china in newspaper—not single sheets, but layer after layer. For a single teapot she used the entire Sunday Review section, and a chipped candlestick took nine pages of stock market news. She crumpled the *Parade* section page by page and used it as extra padding along the sides, top, and bottom of each layer.

Nothing was left behind: not the cups with broken handles, not the single saltshaker that years earlier lost its pepper mill, not even a half-empty box of laundry detergent. When she ran out of newspaper, she gathered the bath towels and wound them around platters and soup tureens. Once the towels were gone, she turned to sheets and pillowcases. After that she used the remainder of Clay's tee shirts to wrap a photo album filled with long-forgotten faces. Before she was finished the stack of cartons had begun to smell of dampness, because of the tears dropped in alongside her belongings.

On the Wednesday before they were to leave, Louise stopped packing at one o'clock and drove to the Lloyd P. Hopkins Elementary School. She parked in the lot and watched as groups of children ran to find mommies or aunties or grandmas—hundreds of tiny little hands clenched around drawings that would one day be yellowed and still hanging on the refrigerator. They were so young, so very trusting. For them the future was this afternoon, and there was nothing to worry about. In years to come they might fret over relationships and jobs, maybe even the troubles of where they would live when their lives wound down. But right now they had no worries. Even a dead hamster could be forgotten by the next morning.

Louise's thoughts were drifting back to the time when her own children were this age when she spotted Mandy's yellow curls bouncing toward the car.

"Where's Mommy?" Mandy asked.

"Mommy said I could pick you up today. We're going shopping." Louise pulled out of the parking lot and headed toward Broad Street.

"Are we going to the toy store?"

"Yes."

"Can we go to Scoops too?"

"Scoops too? Well now, that's asking a lot, but I suppose..."

"Grandma, you're my very best friend." Mandy scooted across the seat and pushed closer to Louise, so close Louise barely had enough room to maneuver the gearshift.

Before they left the toy store, Mandy had pulled the doll from the box and was lovingly clutching it in her hand. "This is my most favorite doll ever," she said. "Thank you, Grandma."

Louise smiled, but behind her smile was a trace of sadness. She knew that within days or, at most, weeks this doll would look like the others in the toy box. The fancy hairdo would be undone and the blue satin gown missing. Being the most favorite was a momentary thing. It was only for the short span of now. Not even a Barbie could count on a lifetime of stability.

The day the sale of the house was to be finalized, the Spotswoods arrived at the attorney's office with both of their children in tow. The younger one, a petite-nosed little girl, had her mother's dark hair. The redheaded boy bore no resemblance to either parent and looked as if he might have been picked from someone else's family tree.

"Elizabeth, Tommy, come meet Mister and Missus Palmer," Nancy said.

"Hello." Elizabeth smiled shyly and scooted into the chair beside her mother.

Tommy grunted, "Hi," the word sounding as if it were squeezed from him.

With that they all gathered around the mahogany conference table, everyone smiling except Louise. Her face was longer than the stretch of turnpike going to Florida.

Winston Boomer, a white-haired blimp of a man, was the attorney handling the transaction. His red cheeks puffed out and his stomach heaved with every breath. "This contract states the sale of the specified residence will be finalized today, but the Palmers will lease the house for the next twenty-four hours and will vacate the premises by noon tomorrow," he said. "Are these terms acceptable to all parties?"

Everyone nodded except Louise. She sat there looking as if she'd turned to stone.

Winston Boomer took no notice of her and rumbled on. "Well then, since you're all in agreement sign the first page, initial the second, review the financial statements at the top of four, blah, blah, blah." A sheath of papers passed from person to person. When all of the forms were signed, countersigned, and initialed, Steven Spotswood handed Winston Boomer a check, and in turn Boomer handed one to Clay. In less than an hour it was done. Most everyone was smiling but unable to get past the fact that for the next twenty-four hours they would be *renting* their own house, Louise was felt downright dour-faced.

Steven stretched his Cheerio-shaped mouth into a smile, then leaned over and kissed his wife on the cheek. "Well, Sweetie, you've got the house you wanted."

Ah, yes. Sweetie. Sweetie Spotswood—that explains it all!

Her house was gone. It now belonged to Sweetie Spotswood. How could she have allowed such a thing to happen?

Louise tried to remember exactly when she lost control of her life. There were instances where she had no say in a situation; for those she couldn't blame herself. But there were other times, times when she did some innocuous little thing, and it led her down a pathway she hadn't intended to travel.

As a girl she'd dreamt of becoming a schoolteacher, someone who stayed in the same place year after year, decade after decade. She'd looked forward to a life where young people spent a few semesters under her tutelage then moved on, recalling her wit and intelligence long after they were married and had children of their own. But that didn't happen. Instead of lounging in the sun the summer after graduation, she took a temporary job at the bank. That was where she got to know Clay Palmer, a handsome young man with unruly hair and eyes that brought to mind a Hershey's chocolate.

He was a shy settled-down sort—the type who by all rights should have been content to stay in one spot forever. Seven or eight times a day he'd saunter past her desk on his way to the water cooler. For the longest time he'd do nothing more than give a nod. Then he began saying "Morning," or "Afternoon." Finally he stopped to chat. They started dating right after the company picnic and were married the following spring.

Getting married and having babies was something that should have been as permanent as being a schoolteacher, but look what happened. What on earth, she wondered, had gone wrong?

As they crossed Winston Boomer's parking lot on the way back to their car, Louise looked at Clay. His dark hair was now peppered with strands of gray, his body no longer lean and lanky. But as he strolled along, absently whistling "We're in the Money," he held his back straight as a tree trunk and his step seemed more confident than ever. He had the look of a happy man, carefree almost. Definitely not a person concerned about his health.

Clay was still whistling when he pulled open the car door for Louise. He segued into "You Are My Sunshine," then circled around and slid in on the driver's side.

As soon as he was settled, Louise said, "Aunt Rose is coming with us."

"Coming where?"

"To Florida."

"To Florida..." he stammered. "Aunt Rose?"

"Yes. You can't expect me to leave her here alone. She's getting on in years, and we're practically her only family."

"What about—"

"She hasn't spoken to Minnie for ages. They just don't seem to get along."

"Yeah, well."

"She's coming with us, Clay, I've already told her." Louise angrily turned her face toward the window, thereby ending the discussion.

After riding in silence for several minutes, Clay said, "Having Rose for dinner every so often is one thing, but you surely can't expect me to live with—"

With a quick twist of her head, Louise turned and glared at him. "Don't worry," she said sarcastically. "Aunt Rose doesn't want to live with you anymore than you want to live with her!"

"Oh?"

"She's planning to stay with Floyd, Uncle Elroy's brother."

Elroy Elkins was married to Rose for thirty-three years, but despite his two-of-a-kind initials, he died young and left her to spend his money.

"Floyd?" Clay repeated. "Floyd's a bachelor. Does he know she's coming to live with him?"

"He invited her. She's not planning to live there, she's just visiting." Louise said nothing about how Aunt Rose would eventually get home.

"Okay then." Clay gave a grunt of resignation. "But I'd venture to say it's going to be a long twelve hundred miles."

"Eleven hundred. She's only going as far as New Smyrna Beach."

"Well," Clay muttered. "That's a relief."

The sun had not yet crossed the horizon when Fatso's Moving van arrived the following morning. Three men, each one big-bellied and round as a barrel, climbed from the truck. Two of the men hauled out a loading ramp as the third pounded on the front door. Clay was still asleep, but Louise was up and fully dressed. In truth, she had not gone to bed. There was no way she could spend her last hours in the house curled up under a comforter, sleeping as though it were any another night. As she swung open the door, the burliest of the three was reaching to knock again, his fist jutted out, and narrowly missed clipping her nose.

"Sorry," he said, glancing down at the snip of paper in his hand. "You Palmer?"

"Unfortunately," she answered.

"Huh?"

"Yes, we're Palmer." As he lumbered by, Louise called out, "Don't get dirt on my carpet." Then she remembered it wasn't her carpet anymore.

Fatso ignored the warning and swung into action. "Fred, you and Jack get the sofa," he said as he toted out a tiny lamp.

"Then get the recliner," Fatso ordered as he bent to pick up an itty bitty footstool. "Step it along now, we've got a few more loads going out today."

Louise said nothing but stood aside as bureaus, chairs, large boxes, and small boxes were swallowed up by the moving van. Jack and Fred heaved, sweated, and groaned, while Fatso delegated one task after another. When Louise could no longer watch them carry off her things, she left to pick up Aunt Rose.

At eight-thirty in the morning, traffic was at its very worst. People were heading off to work, the school bus stopped on every corner, and there was a line of cars a block long trying to get in and out of Dunkin Donuts. The drive across town was so slow that it made Louise edgy. At Ogden Avenue she scooted forward in her seat and leaned into the steering wheel, trying to push the Toyota in front of her to move a bit faster, but it didn't work and in the end she arrived at Senior City a nervous wreck.

Louise couldn't recall even one of Aunt Rose's friends who owned a car, yet the Senior City parking area was jammed full. The closest space she could find was at the far end of the lot. She slid the car into an angled slot, hurried into the building, and pushed the intercom button for Elkins.

"About time," a voice crackled. The entrance lock clicked one short buzz, not nearly long enough to allow her to make it from the keypad to the door handle.

Louise rang the intercom again. "Aunt Rose, hold the button down."

"Okay, okay."

When the click sounded a second time she jerked the glass door open and dashed across the lobby into the elevator. As she pushed the button for seventeen, Louise could still hear the buzz-buzz-buzz of the lock release.

Rose Elkins stood in the apartment doorway outfitted from head to toe in pumpkin orange, a symphony of matching color. Every piece, from her squat-heeled little pumps to her brimmed hat, was the exact same shade of pumpkin.

"Louise, dear, could you arrange for someone to take my bags down?"

"There's only me."

"Well, then," she said, nodding at the row of baggage lined along the wall.

"Aunt Rose, all this luggage won't fit into the car."

"Certainly it will, dear. You just need to shuffle things around a bit."

"Even if I got it all in the trunk, where would we put our suitcases?"

"On top of the car, I suppose."

"Oh, you mean in a luggage rack? But we don't have—"

"Well, then, you need to buy one."

Louise gave a sigh of resignation and hoisted the first suitcase. "I can't imagine why you need all these clothes if you're only going for a visit."

Rose raised a disapproving eyebrow. "Would you rather I look shabby? Uncoordinated?"

On the way home, or what was once home and had now become a twenty-four-hour rental, Louise stopped at Buddy's Auto World and had a luggage rack installed.

It was almost eleven-thirty when they arrived back at the house, and Fatso's van was gone. Louise parked in the driveway and entered through the front door. The place was empty, picked bare as a rib bone, nothing left behind but a lone dust ball and a wisp of cobweb clinging to the corner. Yoo sat in the foyer alongside his blue bowl, three suitcases, and a large cooler. Like everyone else, he was ready to leave.

"Okay, let's hit the road," Clay called out as he came through the hallway with a camera swinging from his neck.

Rose eyed his jeans and sweatshirt. "You're going like *that*?"

"We'll be sitting in the car for a long time. I'm dressed for traveling."

"More like a vagrant, I'd say."

"There's nothing wrong with jeans."

"Not if you don't care a fig about what people think."

"What people?" Clay said as he reached for the first suitcase. "We won't see a soul we know between here and Florida."

"You never know," Rose came back at him. "Those rest stops are crowded with people. There's no telling who you'll meet. And then there's Floyd—"

"Floyd?"

"Yes, Floyd. I certainly hope you don't plan to embarrass the lot of us by walking into his place dressed like a rag-picker."

"I have shorts in my bag. When we get further south, I'll change into shorts."

"Shorts?" she gasped. "With your hairy legs?"

"Just get in the car, Rose."

"Louise," Rose complained. "Will you listen to what this man is planning to do?"

"Don't worry about it, Aunt Rose. You look so lovely no one will notice him."

"That's probably true, but it hardly excuses his lack of appropriate dress." Rose eased herself into the back seat, pushed Yoo to the far side, and placed the pumpkin purse squarely between the two of them.

"I don't remember us having this luggage rack," Clay mumbled as he swung the suitcases to the top of the car.

For a long moment Louise stood in the driveway, looking at the house, studying it, trying to memorize every detail, right down to and including a spot of paint that had attached itself to the lower edge of the windowpane. Then all alone she went inside to say one last goodbye. With a heavy heart she walked through the rooms, one by one. Even though the house was stripped clean, completely devoid of any trace of her ever having lived there, she envisioned it differently. Without closing her eyes, she could see all the furniture still in place, smell a roast sizzling in the oven, hear the banter of chatter that came from the Material Girls as they gathered around the dining room table. Sweetie Spotswood was nowhere in sight, and that was exactly how Louise planned to remember it.

She bent over, picked up Yoo's blue bowl, and tucked it under her arm. Then she reached for her purse. As she did so, the bowl came loose and crashed to the floor. It splintered into pieces, sending shards of glass flying across the kitchen floor and into the dining room. If the bowl had simply broken into two or three pieces, she would have scooped them up and taken them along to be glued together at some later date, but shattered as it was Louise turned and walked out the door, leaving the splintered pieces behind, the same way she had years ago left Molly.

The garage door rumbled down with a clanging that had the sound of something in need of repair. This was the last time Louise would hear it, and she knew even that she would miss. As the door closed, Clay reached back and placed the remote control on a shelf inside the garage.

Louise did not turn around as they pulled away, nor did she allow her eyes to linger on the houses they passed as they moved along the block—houses that belonged to the Blaine family, Missus Marquardt with her rheumatism and newest husband, the Kramers, friends they would most likely never see again.

Their house had seemed bigger than life as they backed out of the driveway, but when Louise caught sight of it in the side mirror it was little more than a speck.

The words along the bottom of the mirror read, "Warning: Objects are closer than they may appear," and Louise realized that it was heartbreakingly true.

Clay

When the garage door came down, I said that's it. No more snow. No more raking leaves. No more hauling my butt out of bed before dawn. From here on in, I'm a man of zero responsibilities. A few days from now I'm gonna be stretched out in a hammock, snoozing the afternoon away. Of course until then I've got Rose Elkins to contend with.

I'm hoping I can tolerate the woman for two whole days. Rose is a pimple on the tailbone of progress. If she had her way, men would be walking around in spats and bowler hats. Proper dress, she calls it. I call it being an old fart who's out of touch with reality. Thank God she's only going to be with us two days. I doubt I could take much more. I may not like it, but I'm going to try not to say one cross word to Rose. I owe Louise that much.

I know at first Louise wasn't too crazy about making this move to Florida, but she's come around. I think she's okay with the idea now. Why else would she have hired Henry Hornock as our real estate agent? Obviously, she saw something in him that I didn't. The truth is I wouldn't have picked Henry if he was the only realtor in the state of New Jersey. I've never known him to be anything but a goofball. I guess people change.

Well, most people change, but Rose Elkins? Not likely.

As I said, thank God it's only for two days.

The Journey Begins

The cozy houses with clean-swept walkways disappeared when Clay turned onto Route 22, a highway lined with strip malls, gas stations, and fast food restaurants. They'd driven this route any number of times to shop at Home Depot, the Sherwin Williams Paint store, or Fabric Mart, and despite Louise's objections Clay generally insisted on stopping at Fat Fred's for a burger, a burger that inevitably dripped ketchup on his shirt. Today he sped right by the roadside stand as if it had vanished from sight.

"I could sure go for one of those burgers," Louise suggested, but by then Clay was a half mile down the highway and focused on humming "The Battle Hymn of the Republic."

The incident with Yoo's bowl made Louise think back to a different time, a different place, a different car, and a different driver behind the wheel. A sinking feeling settled into her chest, the same as it had when her mama started packing to leave the yellow house in Oak Ridge.

"I won't go!" Louise shouted. "You can't make me!" But the truth was they could make her. Could and did. Anger and tears didn't change things. They did nothing more than cause her to be chastised. "Stand in the corner," her father, a gruff-tongued man, commanded. "Stand there and face the wall until you're ready to apologize." She stood there until bedtime but did not apologize.

After everyone else was asleep, she slipped from the house and took Molly to their hideaway far back in the barn. Louise went past the empty horse stall, past the rakes and shovels hanging along the wall, all the way back to the corner where a split in the weathered boards splattered specks of moonlight across the floor. She and Molly had come here so many times to play and share secrets. But that night Louise sat on the matted straw and cried as if her heart would break. That's when she came up with the plan to leave Molly behind. Mama and Daddy would have to come back for Molly and once they saw a reminder of the wonderful place they'd be leaving, they'd be sure to change their minds.

Lots of times Louise's daddy had intended to do one thing or another, but as soon as he caught sight of something more to his liking everything changed. She expected him to do it again, but he didn't. When she said she'd left Molly behind, he grew red-faced and claimed she'd done it out of pure spite.

"Well, we're not going back," he snapped. "Let this be a lesson to you."

"Yes," her mother echoed. "You ought to have considered the consequences before you did such a spiteful thing."

"Please, Mama!" Louise cried. "Molly's my friend, my only friend."

"Nonsense. It's just a raggedy old doll. We're not going back, and that's that. Now keep it up, missy, and you'll never get another doll."

They didn't go back, and Louise sobbed all the way across West Virginia. "I'll never ask for anything else," she promised. "Never ever."

After a long while her daddy said he'd buy her a new doll when they got to the next town, but by then Louise had decided she didn't want another doll. It was too painful to love something that could so easily be lost.

Strange; after all these years the hurt felt as fresh as yesterday. Molly was supposedly a doll, but Louise could still remember the warmth of her muslin body. It was the kind of warmth that came from sleeping alongside a sister. Of course, Louise never had a real sister. All she ever had was Molly. You didn't get to have sisters when you yourself were considered an accident.

After South Carolina they moved on to a run-down rooming house in Georgia, then a roadside motel in Alabama, and from there on to dozens and dozens of other places too awful to remember. Those places were just a blur of sad memories and forgotten faces.

As she brushed back a tear, Louise saw the sign: Turnpike south, bear right.

Clay moved the car into the approach lane and stretched his neck to the right as he eased in front of a bus bound for Philadelphia. "Rose," he grumbled, "take your hat off. I can't see out the back window."

"You expect me to travel hatless?" Rose answered haughtily. "A person of breeding would never—"

"I need to see what's behind me!"

"Don't be gawking at what's behind you. The proper way to drive is to face forward and keep your eyes on the road. A good driver—"

"Take that blasted hat—"

Louise cut into his words with an angry glare. "Did you not hear Aunt Rose say she wants to keep her hat on?"

"And risk having an accident?"

"Oh, Clay." She gave a disheartened sigh. "That is so typical of you. When someone doesn't do what you want them to, you threaten them with disaster."

"What are you talking about?"

"You know what I'm talking about," Louise replied. "First you say you'll die of a heart attack if we don't move to Florida. Now you're trying to scare Aunt Rose into believing we'll be killed if she doesn't take off her hat." Her words held the churn of emotions turning resignation into resentment. "Shame on you," she said. "Shame on you."

"I never said—" Clay decided to leave it at that because Louise turned her face to the window, and Rose had already removed the hat.

Minutes later he pulled up to the turnpike booth and collected a ticket. "Have a nice day," he said as he settled into his seat and drove off.

Before long Clay began humming an off-key version of "Blue Skies."

Louise had a lot more she wanted to say but knew it would fall on deaf ears. Clay whistled and hummed like a man happy with life. Apparently his worries of dying like his daddy had disappeared the day they sold the house. He didn't mind yanking up the roots of a lifetime and moving off. It didn't bother him at all. He'd lived in Westfield his entire life, grown up with the same group of friends, lived in a real house, had his own bicycle. He couldn't possibly understand what it was like to always sleep on a pullout sofa and never belong anywhere.

Louise knew he'd feel differently if he'd had years of straggling from one ugly town to another. The longest her mama and daddy ever stayed in one place was the year they lived in Oak Ridge. That was a real house, the kind of a place a kid could think of as a home. The others were mostly one-room apartments, over a Laundromat with machines rattling from dawn till dusk or back behind some noisy bar where fights broke out all the time. Instead of thinking back on a bright red bicycle, she remembered worn-thin blankets, chipped dishes, and no furniture to call their own. Louise gave a weary sigh and closed her eyes. She was lost in thought when Aunt Rose called her for the third time.

"Louise!" Rose shouted. "Have you lost your hearing?"

"Oh. Sorry. I suppose I was daydreaming."

"Well, even a daydreaming person ought to be able to hear me asking if you've taken notice of the time."

Louise glanced at her wristwatch. "It's twelve-fifteen," she said, thinking how three days from now, at precisely this time, the Material Girls would be getting together. The meeting would be at Ida's house, and she'd no doubt serve those cherry cobblers everyone loved. And wine. Ida always served wine, which was why everyone talked more and quilted less at Ida's house. Louise wondered what the girls would talk about this time. More than likely it would be her.

"I know it's twelve-fifteen," Rose said pointedly. "Haven't you heard my stomach rumbling?"

"Poor Louise." That's what the Material Girls would say to one another. "Poor Louise. Her husband forced her to move to Florida where she has no friends or family. You'd think she would have stuck up for herself instead of allowing this to happen! Such a tragedy…"

"Louise, are you listening?

"Um, sorry. I was thinking of something else."

"Well, pay attention. It's past time for my lunch."

"Okay, Aunt Rose. Clay will stop at the next restaurant."

"The next plaza's eighteen miles," Clay said. "Twenty minutes or so."

Rose gave an agitated huff. "My sensitive stomach's not going to like that."

"Sorry," Louise repeated half-heartedly. She'd moved on to imagining Sweetie Spotswood sitting in the midst of the Material Girls.

"Sorry? Sorry will be of no use when I pass away from lack of nourishment."

Clay glanced at her in the rearview mirror and said, "Gimme a break. Nobody dies of hunger in twenty minutes."

"Maybe not," Louise said sorrowfully, "but sadness can kill a soul instantly."

"I'm not the least bit sad," Rose Elkins grumbled, "just hungry."

When they finally arrived at the rest stop, Aunt Rose was first from the car. She set the pumpkin hat back on her head, smoothed her skirt, then marched across the parking lot toward the restaurant.

"You go ahead," Louise told Clay. "I'm going to walk Yoo."

"You want me to order a sandwich for you?" Clay asked as he walked away.

Louise shook her head. Out of the corner of her eye she saw a silver Trailways bus parked on the far end of the lot. From where she stood she could see the large black letters: NEWARK. Newark was a stone's throw from Westfield, close enough to take a taxi cab or call a friend to come and pick you up. Newark was almost home.

Louise had never before considered doing anything so rash, but the bus standing there and calling out to her seemed like a sign. A sign that she had to return home instantly. Without hesitating to think about it or consider the consequences, Louise grabbed her purse and took off in the direction of the Trailways bus. The driver was nowhere in sight, but the door stood open. Another sign. She boosted Yoo up the steps and then climbed in behind him.

Most of the seats were empty but marked with a magazine or a hat or a sweater, something that warned other passengers "Don't sit here!" Several times Yoo tried to stop and poke his nose under a seat or sniff a bag of food sitting beside a newspaper, but Louise hurried him along until they found two seats midway down the aisle.

"Are these seats taken?" she asked the woman sitting directly across.

"Unh-unh," the woman answered. "But you can't bring no dog on here."

"He's very well behaved," Louise said. "Never barks. Once he's in the seat, I doubt that anyone will even notice he's a dog."

"Not notice? Look at the size of his head!" The woman turned back to her magazine. "Besides," she said. "Even a no-good man don't smell like that."

Louise nudged Yoo up into the seat, then rummaged through her purse, pulled out a tiny spray bottle, and spritzed him with Estee Lauder's Beautiful.

The woman across the aisle chuckled. "Now, he smell like a French whore *and* he still got big ears sticking up."

Louise got up, eased her way toward the front of the bus as if she might be looking for someone, then turned and started back down the aisle. As she passed the third row, she snatched a checkered cap from the seat and kept moving. When she spotted the uniformed driver returning to the bus, she pulled the cap over Yoo's ears and tried to appear nonchalant.

One by one, people trudged back onto the bus—a young girl with a hamburger dripping ketchup, a woman with a container of hot coffee, two kids with candy bars, and a red-eyed man with a bottle of beer wrapped in a brown paper sack. Yoo sniffed and snuffed a bit, but Louise kept a tight hold on him.

The driver climbed aboard last and the doors whooshed shut behind him. So far, so good. No one had noticed the dog, and it looked as though she was in the clear. Just as the engine of the bus roared to life Louise looked across the parking lot and saw Clay standing outside the restaurant, looking first to the left and then the right. For a moment she was tempted to open the window and call out to him, but something stopped her. Perhaps she suddenly realized how foolish her actions were, or maybe she feared he'd do nothing more than wave goodbye. The moment passed. Then

Louise, like all the other passengers, eased back into her seat and closed her eyes.

As the bus moved toward the exit ramp, the driver spoke into the intercom, "Settle back, folks," he said. "We'll be arriving in Newark, Delaware in one hour."

"Delaware!" Louise screamed and jumped up from her seat, which started Yoo barking furiously.

"There's a dog on this bus!" the man behind her shouted. "I'm allergic to dogs!"

A fat woman stood up shaking her fist in the air. "What kind of bus line allows dogs? I didn't pay to ride with no dogs!"

All the while Louise was shouting, "Stop! Stop! I'm on the wrong bus!"

The driver slammed his foot down on the brake and a number of passengers flew forward in their seats. The man drinking beer from a brown paper sack tumbled out into the aisle, and Yoo leaped on top of him. "Stop!" Louise shouted again as she tugged at Yoo's collar. "There's been a mistake!"

"I'll say there's been a mistake!" the fat lady yelled. "And, sister, you're the one who made it! I say we toss that dog out onto the highway!"

The driver stepped from behind the wheel and shot an angry glance at Louise. "Lady, where'd you come from, and how'd you get a dog on this bus?"

"The door was open," she stammered. "I had every intention of buying a ticket, but there wasn't anybody to buy it from. Before I knew it the bus started moving."

By now every head on the bus was turned toward Louise, but it was the man in the third row who jumped up and shouted, "That lousy fleabag's wearing my cap!"

"I'm sorry," Louise mumbled as she tugged Yoo up the aisle. "I wasn't really stealing the cap. Maybe I should have asked before borrowing it, but, honestly, Yoo doesn't have a single flea on him. And your cap's not one bit harmed." She stretched out her arm and tried to return the hat to its rightful owner, but the man grabbed hold of it and threw it back into her face.

"I'm gonna file a complaint!" the man growled. "I'll sue for damages! You can't steal my property and get away with it."

"Let's all simmer down," the bus driver said. "No harm's been done. We get started on complaints about who did what to who, and we're not gonna get to Delaware until midnight. Now, we don't want that, do we?"

"I got somebody picking me up at two-thirty," the fat lady called out. "We damn sight better be there by then, else I've got no way to get where I'm going."

"Me too," echoed several other passengers.

"Okay then. How about if I escort this woman and the dog off the bus, and we continue on our way?" the driver asked.

"What about my hat?" the man in the third row argued.

"Forget about it!" one passenger called out. Then another shouted, "Shut up and let's get going!" and a third yelled something about the hat being so ugly only a dog would wear it anyway.

"Quiet!" the bus driver shouted, then he turned to the hat man and asked what the cap had cost. Sixteen dollars was the answer. "How about this lady gives you twenty bucks, and the dog keeps the cap?" While the hat man thought the deal over, the driver asked Louise if she had twenty dollars.

"Of course," she answered. "I'm not a vagrant. I simply got on this bus by mistake." She started digging through her purse. "It was an honest mistake, one anybody could have made. I thought it was Newark, New Jersey. If this bus is going to Delaware, it should say Delaware!" She handed the driver a twenty dollar bill and he in turn handed it to the hat man. The doors whooshed open, and as Louise stepped off the bus the other passengers applauded loudly. The only exception was the woman who had been sitting across from her; that woman just shook her head and mumbled something about having done said dogs ain't allowed on buses.

The Trailways bus roared off and left Louise standing in the parking lot. *I should have known*, she told herself, *I should have known that going home wasn't going to be so easy.* Good things never came easy to her. They came easy to people like Billie Butterman, people with double initials, but never to her. Just as she was about to start recalling specific instances, she heard Clay's voice.

90

"Where in the world have you been?" he shouted as he hustled across the lot.

"Me?"

"Yes, you. We've been waiting for almost twenty minutes."

"Twenty minutes?"

"Yes!" Clay answered impatiently. "And what's that?" He pointed to the checkered hat Louise was holding.

"A cap. It belongs to Yoo."

"Since when does Yoo wear a cap?"

"He just started," Louise said. She squatted down and pulled the checkered cap over Yoo's ears. "Looks good, huh?"

Clay gave her an exasperated sigh and shook his head. "Hurry up," he said, "we've got to eat and get back on the road."

After lunch they climbed back into the car and resumed their journey. Louise said nothing but stared absently out the window and pictured herself on the right bus, a bus headed for New Jersey. She could envision the northbound scenery rewinding itself back to where the thread of her life broke off.

Of course, there would still be the problem of where to live once she got to Westfield, because old Missus Butterman had finally moved into Billie's guest room and apparently didn't plan to leave anytime soon. She could probably camp out on the Buttermans' sofa, or perhaps Wilma Klinefeld would want a roommate now that she and George were getting a divorce. The Klinefeld house was on the corner of Baker Street and Lakeside, close to Billie, but a mile-and-a-half from Mandy. For the briefest moment Louise even considered going to live with Phillip so she could see Mandy all day, every day. But after recalling Rachel's rules for this, that, and the other thing, she thought better of the idea.

They'd been rolling along for almost an hour before Clay said, "You're awfully quiet, Squeezie," he reached across and patted her thigh. "Whatcha thinking about?"

There was nothing he could have called Louise that would have angered her more. She had tolerated a thousand things— being taken from the place she loved, getting thrown off a Trailways bus, and left standing alongside the road, but to be

91

forever tagged with a name that sounded like toilet paper was more than she could stand. She turned to face him, her eyes narrow with anger.

"Stop calling me that," she said icily.

"Huh?"

"I hate that name!"

"But I've always called you—"

"Yes, and I've told you a thousand times, I hate it."

"Okay, I'll stick with Louise."

"Don't call me that either."

"What am I supposed to—"

"Find a name that starts with P—Precious, Princess, Penelope."

A look of confusion stretched across Clay's face. "But—"

"Persnickety," Rose snapped. "That's what you ought to call her, persnickety!"

"Rose, this doesn't concern you," Clay replied, his voice firm.

"Persnickety," Rose mumbled again, then said nothing more.

Louise turned back to the window. It wasn't just the name, it was life. A life that twisted and turned down the pathways she tried to avoid. A Trailways bus headed to the wrong destination, twenty dollars for a horrible old cap, people applauding when she was set out on the parking lot, Sweetie Spotswood taking her place in the Material Girls.

Never having had double initials was just the teeniest part of it. She was losing the things she valued most, just as she had lost Molly. She wanted to open the car door, take a giant step out onto the New Jersey Turnpike, and start walking back to where she was once happy. But even that would have been fruitless.

Happiness was a fickle visitor. It came, stayed for a while, and then disappeared in the blink of an eye. Even if you remained in the same spot forever, it would up and leave. There was no holding onto happiness. If you went in search of it, it stayed behind and thumbed its nose at you as you drove off.

Clay gave up humming one song after another and allowed a look of worry to settle on his face. From time to time he'd glance over at Louise and see her still turned to the window. "You all right?" he'd ask, but she gave no response. So they rode in silence for mile after mile.

Shortly after they crossed the Delaware Memorial Bridge, he said, "How about Penny?"

"Penny?" Louise repeated cautiously and turned to face him.

"Uh-huh. Lucky Penny." Clay took his eyes from the road just long enough to sweep a glance her way. "Having you is like having a lucky penny."

It wasn't the same as being born with double initials, but it was better than nothing. Louise curled the corners of her mouth ever so slightly. "Lucky Penny," she repeated slowly. "Okay, Penny sounds good."

"Foolishness," Rose mumbled. "Utter and complete foolishness."

Although it came at his suggestion, Clay stumbled over Louise's new name as if it were a speck of phlegm caught in his throat. "*Penny*," he said, "would you like the radio on?"

Louise shook her head.

"How about a stick of gum, *Penny*?" He glanced her way with a smile that seemed to sit sideways on his face.

Louise started to wonder why, after almost thirty years of marriage, did he suddenly discover she was his lucky penny? The name was nothing more than his way of putting a Band-Aid on her broken heart. It didn't change anything. The look on Clay's face told the truth of the matter. There was no turnaround on the road to Florida.

He looked over and smiled again. That's when Louise saw it. A glimmer. A certain slyness she'd not noticed before. It was the same look Phillip had when she caught him with a package of cigarettes, and he swore they belonged to a friend. She knew. A lie might slide from Clay's lips without warning, but the truth was hidden in the folds of his smile.

Now that they'd sold the house, he'd shed his weariness the way a snake sheds its skin. He was now full of happiness and good health—rosy cheeked, smiling, whistling one happy song after another.

Louise turned back to the window.

Louise

You'd think after years of living with my father I'd be wise to every trick in the book. I'm not. I'm as gullible as the day is long. Just like Mama believed Daddy would one day give up gambling and settle down, I believed Clay would give up this idea of moving. Right up until the last minute, I thought something would happen. Something would change his mind. The sad truth is I thought his love for me would be big enough to outshine the luster of Florida.

Now I know for certain that's not the case. So the next move is up to me. I can be my mama and follow along with no regard for what my heart wants, or I can be Penny Palmer. For the first time in my life, I'm choosing Penny Palmer.

I say that with a mouthful of bravado, but the truth is I'm afraid. Afraid of being like my mama, but just as afraid of losing Clay. It seems impossible that after all these years we can't find some middle ground, some way for both of us to have a little piece of what we want.

I believe Clay loves me, but he can't understand that a broken heart hurts every bit as bad as a broken body. If tomorrow I was to become a cripple, I know Clay would lift me into his arms and carry me wherever I needed to go. But the hurt is inside. He can't see it, so he believes it's not real.

Right now I am in bad need of a friend. A friend who'll listen or maybe tell me everything is gonna work out okay. It's an awful thing to be alone inside of yourself. I know. I've been there before, and I sure don't want to go back again.

A Friend in Need

Early in the afternoon Louise placed her first call to Billie Butterman. Ever since that disastrous incident on the bus she'd been mulling an idea over, but when they left Delaware and moved into Maryland she knew it was time to swing into action. "Aunt Rose needs to use the restroom," she told Clay. "We'll have to get off at the next exit."

"I've no such need," Rose Elkins said. "You're the one. You drank that great big Pepsi-Cola, and now you've got to pee. Just say so and be done with it."

Louise turned toward the back seat and winked her right eye. "Now, Aunt Rose, I can tell you need a break, too, right?"

"Well, I suppose..."

"And Yoo, he needs to be walked again," Louise continued. "Otherwise he's liable to have an accident right here in the car."

"There'll be the devil to pay if this dog pees on me!" Rose said and began shoving Yoo to the far side of the seat.

Once Rose got started, there was no stopping her. Reluctantly Clay left the highway and pulled into a Super Speed Gas Station. "Think I'll just gas up while we're here," he suggested. "Then we won't have to stop again for a good long while."

"Don't start hurrying me," Louise replied. "There's a Stuckey's right down the road, and since we've already stopped I believe I'd enjoy a piece of their fudge."

"Is that absolutely necessary?" Clay made a point of looking at his watch. "We're already behind schedule because of all the time we wasted at that last rest stop."

"What's the rush?"

"There's no real rush," he said. "But I figure if we make it partway through North Carolina by nightfall, we'll be in New Smyrna Beach tomorrow evening. That would save us a full day."

"We've don't need to save a day," Louise said icily. "You're retired, so we've got plenty of time." She turned on her heel, trotted off to the fast food counter, handed the clerk a five-dollar bill, and asked for twenty quarters. Since Clay had their cell phone in his pocket and she didn't want him to hear what she was saying, she had to resort to a pay phone.

Billie Butterman answered on the first ring and the moment she heard Louise's voice, she asked, "Where are you?"

"Some town called Aberdeen," Louise answered. "I would have been in Newark by now, but the bus was going to Delaware."

"Bus?"

"It's a long story."

Louise told of how she'd smuggled the dog aboard the wrong bus, only to get thrown off and be forced to pay twenty dollars for the ugliest cap she'd ever seen. "On top of it all," she said with a sigh, "I left my very best sweater on that bus. Do you think if I call the bus company they might—"

"Oh, hell," Billie moaned, "Missus Butterman is ringing that damn bell of hers again. She sits upstairs and rings that thing every five minutes. If it isn't another cup of tea or a drink of water she wants, it's some lost magazine. I told Bradley his mama ought to be in a nursing home instead of here jingling for me to come and wait on her. Now, what were you saying?"

"I called because I need your help. The thing with Henry Hornock didn't work out, but that doesn't mean I've got to give up. I thought maybe you could come up with another plan to convince Clay to come back to New Jersey."

"What kind of a plan?"

"If I knew, I wouldn't need your help."

Louise waited for a moment thinking that Billie would jump right in as she usually did, but when there was nothing but the far away tinkling of a bell she finally asked, "Got any ideas?"

"Maybe I could get Bradley to offer him a job at the store."

"Work? Why, Clay would never come back for work!"

"What about pretending Phillip needs his help with something or another?"

"Clay would say that know-it-all doesn't need my help with anything. He loves Phillip, but they squabble about everything. Last year when Phillip was putting a new rail on their porch Clay went over to help, and they ended up not speaking for three weeks. Personally, I think it's Rachel. She instigates—"

"I've got it!" Billie interrupted. "Tell him you absolutely *must* go home because Patty has discovered she's pregnant."

"Bite your tongue."

"Hmm. I've gotta think. Call me back in an hour, and try to slow Clay down."

"Slow him down? How?"

"Do whatever you can, but keep him from driving farther away. Say you're too sick to travel, hide out in the restroom, let the air of the tires if you have to. Just remember, the closer he is to Florida, the less likely he'll come back."

Louise knew such a thing was easier said than done. Clay had already made it perfectly clear he intended to drive straight through to Rocky Mount on the first day. The idea of hiding out in a restroom wouldn't work, because he'd just send Aunt Rose in after her, and she couldn't let the air out of his tires because she didn't have the foggiest notion of how to do such a thing. Instead, she went about it in her own way.

"I'm dying for a cold drink," she said and insisted Clay stop at a roadside stand. Fifteen miles later she told him she had an urgent need to stop at a restroom. Then Yoo needed to do his business. A few miles down the road she started to crave a doughnut and then it was a bag of pretzels. After that she was thirsty again. Then there was another stop at a restroom.

"I'm trying to make Rocky Mount before nightfall," Clay said impatiently. "This is the last stop we're making for at least two hours."

"But, what if we've some sort of emergency?" Louise protested.

"What kind of emergency?" Clay replied, a dubious overtone in his voice.

Caught without a plausible emergency, she shrugged.

Although a number of times Louise indicated she might like to visit the restroom, Clay kept his foot on the accelerator and refused to stop for a full two hours. Only after Yoo began to whine did he exit the highway and pull into a rest stop plaza.

"It's about time," Rose grumbled. "I'm stiff from sitting."

In an obvious display of impatience, Clay huffed loudly and scrunched his mouth to one side. "Try to hurry it up," he said. "It's almost four-thirty!" He then took out his roadmap and began calculating how far behind schedule they were.

Louise headed for the pay phone and dialed Billie's number. "Got anything?" she asked.

"Not yet," Billie answered. "I thought someone else might have an idea so I called an emergency meeting of the Material Girls, but they didn't come up with much either. Lucille said she has a brother who lives in Florida, and if you need a ride home maybe he'd be willing to drive you."

"That's it?" Louise sighed.

"Well, Norma volunteered to take the issue up with her pastor, but I said she'd better wait until after I'd discussed it with you."

Of course Louise vetoed that idea, because Reverend Brice and Clay had gone to school together; they were boyhood friends. "See what else you can come up with," she told Billie. "Clay's determined to make Rocky Mount today and I'm not having a whole lot of success in slowing him down, but I'll keep trying. Call you later."

Seconds later Clay tromped in, looking for her. "It's after five," he grumbled. "We're never going to make Rocky Mount by nightfall."

"What's the rush?" Louise said. "Now that we're on the road, we ought to take it easy, maybe stop and do a little sight-seeing like you said. Aunt Rose would love to visit some of the outlet stores, and I wouldn't mind getting more of that delicious fudge from Stuckey's."

"Take it easy?" Clay gasped. "A person could walk to Florida faster than we're going. We've stopped a dozen or more times!"

"That's an exaggeration. Anyway, what's wrong with me wanting a little bit of candy?"

"You've already been to Stuckey's," Clay said. "Three times!"

"Yes, but that fudge is all gone," Louise replied. She shoved the still-full bag of candy to the bottom of her purse.

"Okay," Clay said with his jaw clenched. "Stuckey's. But that's the last stop we're making until we get to Rocky Mount." When he pulled back onto the highway, Clay began whizzing along at a steady seventy miles an hour.

Louise pressed her nose to the window and watched the landscape fly by. As daylight dwindled, a purple shadow of dusk drifted across the sky and a scattering of lights began to appear in the distance. Louise imagined the women living in those houses, women without friends or neighbors living next door, women with nothing but long stretches of farmland between them and the rest of the world.

Oblivious to her thoughts, Clay continued the trek southward.

On the dot of six o'clock, Rose Elkins complained her stomach was grumbling. "It's way past my dinnertime," she said, but Clay kept his foot pressed down on the accelerator. "Did you not hear me?" she said loudly. He upped the speed to seventy-eight miles an hour and leaned into the wheel.

"Slow down before you get a speeding ticket," Louise said.

"I've got to make up for lost time," Clay answered, pressing down on the accelerator. The needle of the speedometer wiggled past eighty.

After that there was very little conversation. Rose flipped through her magazine. Clay sat hunched over the wheel, eyes fixed on the road and a grim look of determination on his face. Louise was lost in thoughts of what to do now.

When the darkness finally closed in on them, Clay begrudgingly agreed to stop for the night. "But I plan to start early tomorrow to make up for lost time," he warned.

He pulled off the highway at Smokey Falls, a town with not much to choose from in the way of motels or restaurants—no Best Western or Holiday Inn. Those were further down the road in Rocky Mount. At the end of the exit ramp, Clay made a left and traveled east for close to three miles before spotting a neon sign on the opposite side of the highway: "Stay n' Snooze, low rates, free breakfast." The oo's in snooze were eyes with neon eyelids that fluttered up and down. But unfortunately something had thrown off the timing, so instead of looking sleepy they blinked like a person with a nervous twitch.

"Okay, here's a place we can stay." Clay made a U-turn and pulled into the motel parking lot.

Louise looked at the grimy front window. "I don't know," she said apprehensively. "It seems kind of seedy."

"It's fine," Clay snapped. Before she could argue the point he was out of the car and on his way into the registration office.

"I don't know," she repeated as if he were still listening. "It looks like—" Suddenly she realized what the Stay n' Snooze reminded her of: a thousand other places, places her daddy had checked in and out of, places with thin towels and stained sheets. "Wait, Clay!" she shouted and darted into the office after him.

Behind the counter a man so gaunt he seemed barely more than a shadow sat with his eyes fixed on the flickering images of a tiny black-and-white television. He could have been thirty years old or perhaps as much as sixty; there was no way of telling because the crinkles in his weathered face were deeper than those of Rose Elkins. He pushed a slick of long blond hair back from his face and said, "You want a room?"

Louise tugged on her husband's sleeve. It was a gesture meant to stop the tide of things—a gesture much like a kick under the table or a too-loud cough—but Clay didn't seem to catch the meaning and answered, "Two."

"Two people or two rooms?"

"Two rooms."

"I just got one. Two double beds."

"Oh, well," Louise chimed brightly. "There's three of us, so I suppose we'll have to look for another place.

The clerk shrugged. "You won't find it. Leastways, not tonight. Specially not if you're headed south."

"Why not?" she asked.

"Ain't nothing but truck stops for 'least a hundred miles. They fill up early."

"What about west of here?" Clay asked.

The clerk shook his head. "Unh-unh."

"Oh, dear," Louise sighed. "How far do we have to go to get a decent room?"

"More 'n likely, Rocky Mount."

"Rocky Mount!" Clay shouted, and the veins in his neck popped out a bit further.

"Don't get upset," Louise said. "We'll turn around and go back to Richmond, I'm sure there we'll be able to get a—"

Clay's head spun around so rapidly she heard the tendons in his neck snap. "I'm not going back!" he said angrily. "We take this room, or we go on to Rocky Mount!"

"Well, I suppose we could do with one room. It is just for the night."

"Twenty-nine dollars with breakfast. Want it or not?" the clerk asked.

Still grumbling about how they'd not made Rocky Mount, Clay pulled out his credit card and said, "We'll take it."

While Clay waited for the clerk to finish the necessary paperwork, Louise returned to the car. "Aunt Rose," she warned, "this motel only has one vacancy, so I guess you'll be sleeping with us."

"In the same room? With him snoring and you playing the TV?"

"I know it's less than ideal, but they don't have another room."

"Indeed it is less than ideal!" Rose replied, her wrinkled face twitching angrily.

"If we don't take this room we'll have to drive another two or three hours," Louise explained, "and I know how tired you are."

"Well, I guess it will have to do," Rose grumbled. "But right after dinner I take my shower and get into bed, so mind you keep quiet! No television or radio. I get real crotchety when I don't get a good night's sleep."

Clay was still mumbling about how they should have been in Rocky Mount when he climbed back into the car and circled the building in search of their room.

"There it is, number forty-seven." Louise pointed to a darkened room at the far end of the building.

"It's next to a parking lot full of trucks!" Rose exclaimed. "I'm a light sleeper, and that noise will keep me up all night long."

"Those long-haul trucks are parked for the night," Clay said. "You won't hear a thing from them until tomorrow morning, and we'll be long gone by then." He parked the car, carried in the overnight bag and four suitcases, then suggested they get some dinner in the coffee shop.

Clay and Rose trotted off while Louise, who claimed not to be hungry, stayed behind to walk the dog.

"Okay," Clay said. "But don't disappear like you did at that rest stop."

Louise, in fact, wasn't hungry. She was stuffed full of fudge, pretzels, doughnuts, and colas, but more importantly, she wanted to stay behind and call Billie. She slipped off her shoes, sat on the side of the bed, and placed a collect call. Were she not quite so preoccupied with what her next move might be, she probably would have noticed that Clay left the door open.

The phone rang nine times before Billie answered, and when she finally did the snuffling in her voice was obvious.

"What's wrong?" Louise asked, momentarily forgetting her own problems.

"Bradley and I had a huge fight," Billie said, her voice thick and heavy.

"You mean a disagreement, right?"

"No, a fight. A down and dirty, say-the-meanest-thing-you-can-think-of fight." Billie sucked in a gasp of air. "She knew it would come to this. It's what she's wanted all along."

"Who wanted what?"

"Missus Butterman. She hates me. Why, on our wedding day, she told Bradley he should have married Sheila Moskowitz. 'Now, Sheila, she's a girl who's worthy of you,' that's what Missus Butterman told Bradley!"

"Oh, I doubt—"

"Those are her exact words. The woman would be wild with ecstasy if Bradley and I got a divorce. Wild with ecstasy, I tell you!"

"Divorce?"

"I swear it could come to that. Especially after what happened today."

"What happened?"

"Missus Butterman told Bradley that I wouldn't give her a drink of water when she was dying of thirst. Then he jumped all over me and claimed I was spiteful. Spiteful! Can you believe it?"

"I most certainly cannot! The way you run and fetch things when his mama rings her ridiculous little bell, I suppose he doesn't see that!" From the corner of her eye Louise could see Yoo pacing back and forth across the room. Staying with the conversation, she asked, "What did you say when he said that?"

"I told him to go straight to hell, along with his precious mama and her bell!"

"You said that? Exactly that?"

"Yes, I did. What else could I do? Him sticking up for her the way he did."

"Oh, Billie." Louise said. "I ought to be there with you."

"You've got troubles of your own. Speaking of which, I haven't come up with a single new idea. I've been so distracted with this fighting that my creativity is totally stymied. Maybe you ought to go with the Patty Lynn being pregnant thing."

Louise nixed that idea for the second time, then they talked for another twenty minutes. She made Billie promise she'd keep trying to come up with a new plan.

"And if you need someone to set Bradley straight about the way Missus Butterman acts, I will," she said. After that they hung up. That's when she first noticed Yoo was no longer in the room.

"Here, boy," she called and poked her head into the bathroom. "Come on, Yoo, time for a walk," she rattled his leash in the air. Nothing. She checked under both beds—just a gathering of dust.

"Oh, no," Louise groaned when she caught sight of the open door. "Don't tell me he's wandered out there. Yoo? Yoo?" She looked off to the side of the building and back where they had parked the car. Nothing.

Louise then ventured over to the bushes where she saw some movement, but it turned out to be a deer that darted off. Finally she caught sight of the dog halfway across the parking lot. She called out several times but Yoo kept going. He trotted past a long line of cars and then disappeared behind a navy blue Chevrolet. That's when Louise lost sight of him again and took off running across the asphalt in her stocking feet. "Come back here, Yoo, come back!" she called over and over.

The paving ended halfway across the lot and a spread of pebbles replaced it, sharp-edged little rocks that ripped through Louise's stockings and dug into the soles of her feet as she hobbled along calling out for the dog. Finally she spotted a black head bobbing up and down in the back of an open-roofed red convertible. She silently crept up on it and grabbed hold. "Now I've got you!" Louise shouted.

A bare-breasted woman shrieked and jumped up, flapping her arms like a wild bird. Louise immediately released her hold on the woman's head.

"I'm sorry," she said. "I'm looking for my dog and I thought—" By then the woman began screaming for the police, so Louise turned and ran. Before she could make her getaway, a naked man popped up from beneath the woman and screamed, "Pervert!" He jumped from the car, scooped up a handful of gravel rocks, and pummeled Louise as she ran off.

Once she was clear of them, Louise squatted down behind a green pickup truck and remained hidden until she saw the convertible zoom out of the lot. Then she began calling for Yoo again.

The next time she caught sight of him, he was trotting behind a large yellow dog. "Yoo!" she shouted, but when the yellow dog darted beneath a Mobil Tanker Truck Yoo followed. Her stockings were already ripped to shreds and one toe was bleeding, but she continued across the gravel lot to the far side where trucks were parked. The dogs were no longer under the tanker, so she checked beneath a lumber flatbed and three box vans. The Liberty Lettuce truck was the only one left in the lot, parked in an area set off from the others—an area with no overhead lighting and tall bushes on both sides.

Louise inched her way across the lot, then bent down and peered beneath the truck. She could make out the yellow dog and see four eyes glistening in the dark.

"Yoo?" she called softly, but nothing moved. "Yoo!" she said, making it sound like a command. Still nothing. "Come on, Yoo, come on out," she urged, and although the dog rustled around a bit, he stayed put. For a brief while she continued coaxing, suggesting if he'd come she had a treat. But with the ripped stockings and bleeding toe, she lost patience quickly. Finally she slammed her hand against the side of the truck and shouted, "Yoo, get your black ass out of there!"

The cab door popped open and a black man big as a mountain stepped out of the truck. "You talkin' to me?" he thundered angrily and took several long strides toward her.

When Louise saw the man coming at her she gasped, "Oh, dear," but this time she did not back away. "Actually," she said "I was not addressing you." She hesitated a moment then added, "Sir."

"Well, I'm the only one here," he growled.

"I was speaking to him." She pointed toward the darkness beneath the truck.

The man bent over and looked. "That yella dog?" he said. "You got no call to be fussing with her, she belongs to me."

"Not her," Louise said. "Him."

He bent over and looked again. "Him who?" The Palmer dog, black as a shadow, was nearly impossible to see.

"I was calling for Yoo."

"Me?"

"Not you, and not her," Louise explained again. "I was trying to get my dog. He's up under your truck."

The man bent over and looked twice before he saw what she was referring to. "Well, I'll be danged," he said. "There is another one under there. What's the name?"

"Yoo."

"Mine's Jeremiah Buster. Jumbo, they call me."

"I wasn't asking what your name was. That's his name."

"Well now, ain't that something! A dog named Jeremiah!"

"Actually, his name is…um," Louise stammered, ready to start the explanation over again, then thought better of the idea. "It doesn't matter what his name is." she said, "I just need to get him out from under there."

"Well, why didn't you say so?" Jeremiah rooted his arm under the truck. "Come on, doggy." He nabbed hold of Yoo's collar and hauled him out. "This here's a heavy one," he said as he lifted the dog and held him out to Louise.

"Yoo!" she scolded. "You're a disgrace!"

"Don't go picking no fight with me, lady. I fetched the dog for you!"

"Oh, no, not you. Yoo, that's my dog's name. Y-O-O. Get it?"

"Well, I be…A dog named Jeremiah Yoo!"

Louise was soaking her feet in the tub when Aunt Rose and Clay returned. "Have you taken the dog out?" he asked.

"Yes, he's been out," Louise answered wearily.

The Turnaround

Louise had a fretful night. Both Aunt Rose and Clay dozed off quickly and were snoring loudly, but she found it impossible to sleep. Her side of the bed had a lump in the mattress. Not a little pea-sized knot but one that felt like a baseball. And it was in the exact same spot as her hipbone. When she moved, the lump moved. She tried sliding to the far edge of the mattress, but then a row of green lights from the parking lot blinked through a torn spot in the drapery and smacked her in the eye. After two hours of sleeplessly eyeing a brown water stain on the ceiling and thinking about the problems facing both her and Billie, Louise finally reached over and shook Clay's shoulder. "I can't sleep," she whispered. "Maybe we ought to change places."

"Hush up over there!" Rose Elkins shouted. "Or I'll never get to sleep!"

"But Aunt Rose," Louise said apologetically, "you *were* asleep." She half expected an argument, but before she'd finished the sentence Rose had resumed her rhythmic huff-wheezing.

Louise looked back at the ceiling. If she squinted she could imagine the stain as a car, a car that could carry her back to where she wanted to be. Trying not to wake Rose again, Louise inched closer to Clay and whispered in his ear, "This is a terrible mistake. We've got to go back home."

Clay, who had been harummp-whooshing even louder than Rose's huff-wheezing, suddenly slapped at his ear as if he'd felt a bug crawling inside of it. "What the hell?!" he shouted.

"Shhhhh," Louise said. "You'll wake Aunt Rose."

"Wake me?" Rose bolted upright and snapped on the light. "Why, I haven't slept a wink with all this commotion going on!"

"I'm sorry," Louise mumbled. "I didn't think—"

"That's right, you didn't think!" Rose switched off the light. "Now let me get some sleep. And for heaven's sake, keep quiet!"

Clay rolled onto his side and began snoring again. Louise winced, thinking for sure his harummp-whooshing would keep Aunt Rose awake, but apparently it didn't because a minute later they were harmonizing. Once they were both sound asleep, Louise breathed a sigh of relief and went back to staring at the ceiling. But the lump still jabbed into her hip and the car-shaped stain had begun to move. It started over by the bathroom, inched its way across the room, down the wall, and out the door. No doubt, she told herself, it was headed back to wherever it originally came from. That, she supposed, was the way it had to be done. Wait until people are sleeping, then make a run for it. Suddenly the plan she'd been searching for popped into her head.

"You look tired," Louise told Clay when they sat down to breakfast. "Did you get enough sleep last night?"

"I certainly didn't!" Rose said. "All night long it was one disturbance after another."

"I know," Louise replied sympathetically. "Let me get you a nice tall glass of orange juice. That will make you feel better." She popped up from her seat, marched over to the juice bar, and asked for two glasses of orange juice. "The pulpy kind," she said, "with bits of orange in it."

Before starting back to the table she reached into her pocket and pulled out two little white Ambien sleeping pills. She dropped one into each glass, swirled the juice around a bit, and then returned to the table. "Here you are!" she said cheerfully and set the glasses in front of Aunt Rose and Clay. "As for me," she chirped, "I believe I'll have some pancakes, an order of bacon, and a dish of strawberries."

When the food arrived at the table, Louise cut the pancakes into the tiniest slivers imaginable and then chewed each one twenty-seven times.

"Can't you speed it up?" Clay said. "We're already behind schedule!"

"If I rush, I'll get indigestion," Louise replied and started to shave the bacon into even smaller pieces. Twenty minutes; that's how much time she needed. The Ambien would kick in by then, and she'd have no problem.

"Rushing is one thing, but this is ridiculous!" Clay said. Then he yawned.

Rose's eyelids started to droop. "That orange juice didn't help a bit," she told Louise. "Not that I expected it to. A person needs eight hours of sleep!" Rose yawned. "After the night I've had, it's a wonder I've energy enough to eat breakfast."

"I can see that," Louise said, shaking her head sympathetically. "And, Clay, why, you look as if you could doze right off."

"That's how I feel," he said, looking a bit puzzled. "Funny, I could have sworn I slept soundly."

"With all that commotion she was making, how could anybody sleep?" Rose snapped, then covered her mouth and stifled another yawn.

"You're both right," Louise said. "It's my fault. I'll make it up to you. Both of you can lean back and nap. I'll drive for a while."

"That's probably a good idea." Clay yawned again, and Louise noticed that his eyelids had started to droop.

"I don't think I care to finish these pancakes," she said. "Let's get going."

Aunt Rose stretched out in the back seat and fell sound asleep before Louise even pulled onto the highway. Clay sat in the front and tipped his seat back as far as it would go. "We need to get back on schedule," he said. "Try to keep it at a steady seventy." When they passed the sign that read "Rocky Mount – 97 Miles," he was snoring. Louise turned off the highway at the next exit.

She wished she'd had a chance to call Billie and let her know what was happening, but there hadn't been enough time. If she could keep her speed at seventy five or eighty miles an hour she'd be there by tonight; then she'd call Billie. At the end of the exit ramp Louise turned left, circled around under the overpass, and pulled back onto the northbound side of the highway.

With Clay and Aunt Rose both sound asleep, Louise sailed back past Richmond. Then she began feeling so good about her progress she took to humming "King of the Road," but as the words danced through her head she substituted "queen" for "king." She jacked the speed up to eighty and fairly flew past Fredericksburg. At this rate, she reasoned, they might get to New Jersey in time to have dinner at Billie's house. She was closing in on Fairfax when she took the speed up to eight-five, and shortly after that she heard a siren coming up behind her. "Oh, darn," Louise grumbled and eased onto the shoulder of the road. Clay stirred a bit, but when he heard the policeman ask to see Louise's license and registration his eyes popped open.

"What's going on?" Clay said, rubbing the sleep from his eyes.

"Nothing, dear," Louise answered. "I was probably going a tad over the speed limit. I'll straighten it out, you just go back to sleep."

"A tad?" the policeman repeated. "In Virginia, the speed limit is sixty-five. You were doing *eighty-seven*!"

"Virginia!" Clay bolted up and banged his head on the front windshield. "Louise, what are you doing in Virginia?"

"Eighty-seven," the policeman repeated. "I clocked her for ten miles."

"Virginia?" Clay rubbed the knot rising up on his forehead. "How in the name of heaven did we get back in Virginia?"

"It's possible I made a wrong turn."

"Wrong turn? On a straight highway?"

"Have either of you been drinking?" the policeman asked.

Clay took over the conversation at that point. Once he'd explained how Louise had driven almost two hundred miles in the wrong direction, the policeman let her off with just a warning. "However, I'd suggest you take over the driving," the officer told Clay, "because someone else might not be so lenient."

Rose slept through the entire episode and didn't wake until Clay had traveled back past Richmond and was well on his way to Florida. "Are we there yet?" she asked, but no one answered.

Louise sat with sorrow tugging at the corners of her mouth, and Clay had locked onto the steering wheel with the veins in his neck popped out like strings of spaghetti. The look on his face left no doubt that he'd arrive in Rocky Mount before nightfall.

After the Virginia incident Clay stopped only twice. The first time was at a Gas N' Go station where Louise used a key to get into the restroom, only to find out there was no toilet paper and no pay phone. The second stop was at the Snack Shanty where they bought bologna sandwiches in plastic wrap, and she got a chance to squeeze in a call to Billie Butterman. The phone rang twenty-seven times, but no one answered. "Good heavens," Louise murmured, then listened to six more rings before finally hanging up the receiver.

In Rocky Mount they stayed at a Best Western Motel where there was no stain on the ceiling and Aunt Rose had her own room, but Louise still had trouble sleeping. Three times she had tried to call Billie and there was no answer. "Something must be wrong," she told Clay, but he shrugged it off.

"Could be they went to the movies," he said. "Try tomorrow."

"Movies? What about Missus Butterman?"

"Maybe she went too."

Louise wanted to explain how Billie wasn't likely to go anywhere with Missus Butterman, but before she could get her thoughts together she heard Clay snoring.

The third day wasn't any better than the second. Clay hunched over the steering wheel like a driver at the Daytona Five-hundred. "If we keep going, we can make Savannah," he'd say every time Louise mentioned something about stopping.

"Yes, but I'm getting hungry."

"Eat some of those sandwiches."

"They're stale, left over from yesterday!"

"Look at that, we're already in South Carolina. Only twenty-six miles to Florence."

"I ought to call Billie again."

"Did that sign say Savannah was two-hundred-seventy-two miles or was it two-hundred-twelve miles?"

The long stretches of highway made Louise think about other car trips and brought back memories better off forgotten. She could still recall how the fights began with a back and forth bantering of words. Mama would tell Daddy he wasn't listening to a word she said, and then he'd tell her she never said anything worth listening to anyway. It usually started with some minor disagreement, then escalated into a hard-fought battle with bitter accusations and angry voices that drilled into Louise's ears even after she'd buried her head beneath the blanket. "I hate you!" Mama would yell. "You're a good-for-nothing drunkard!"

Daddy would claim Mama was fat and ugly, a hillbilly he should've never bothered with in the first place. Then after a while he'd usually haul off and take a swing at something. More often than not, it was Mama.

It wasn't always that way. Louise could still remember the year they lived in Oak Ridge. She could picture the big square kitchen with its speckled linoleum floor and a window looking out toward the creek. Back then, Daddy didn't drink anything except maybe beer, and Mama made a sit-down dinner every night. Sometimes they'd start hugging or he'd tickle Mama around the waist until she laughed so hard tears rolled down her cheeks, and then they'd go off to the bedroom by themselves.

Louise knew her mama didn't want to leave that house, but she did. She did it because Daddy said she had to. That's when the two of them began hating each other. Mama hated him for his wandering ways, and he hated her because she kept reminding him of what a useless human being he'd become. Eventually they started to hate everything and everybody around them. "We're leaving! Get the kid in the car!" Daddy would scream, and Mama would yell back, "She's your kid, you get her!"

Louise had to straggle along behind two parents who didn't even belong together. Time and again she convinced herself that things would change. They didn't. Well, at least they didn't until her daddy got killed and her mama, who by that time seemed devoid of any feeling, dumped Louise out on the Elkins' doorstep. One suitcase, that's all. An eleven-year-old girl with nothing but a little cardboard suitcase and a mama who claimed to need her own space—a mama so desperate to get away, she drove off before Aunt Rose answered the doorbell. The note said she'd be back as soon as she straightened herself out, which she probably never did, because she never came back. For a long time Louise believed her mama would show up sooner or later, but there was never so much as a phone call.

Despite all that Rose Elkins insisted on impeccable manners and ladylike behavior—no dungarees, no foul language. She was not irresponsible like Louise's mama or mean and bitter like her daddy, but Rose Elkins took proper to a fault. Sloppiness or inappropriate dress was considered practically a cardinal sin.

Uncle Elroy was different. He had a face that never stopped smiling and treated Louise way better than anyone else ever had. Louise knew having Uncle Elroy was better than having a daddy. He wasn't a blood relative, but he was the kindest soul imaginable. He'd smuggle in chocolate bars and slip her movie money every chance he got. When Louise married Clay, Preacher John asked, "Who gives this woman in marriage?" Uncle Elroy was the one who answered, "I do." And he did.

Early in the afternoon of the fourth day, Clay spotted a sign for New Smyrna Beach. At the next exit they left the interstate and headed east along a desolate road marked "Evacuation Route." The arrows pointed back toward the direction they'd come from. Mile after mile they saw nothing but dense thatches of scrub pine and palmettos strangled by snarls of vine. Louise feared that in time she would grow to be like those palmettos, a living thing struggling to break free. She gave a mournful sigh. "Oh, Clay, this is even worse than I'd imagined."

"This?" he laughed. "Why, this is just the access road." Moments later he turned onto a wide thoroughfare with a center island of red flowers and tall palms. Gesturing with a wide sweep of his right arm, he said, "See, this is what Florida is really like! Look!" He pointed toward a barely-visible speck of blue sandwiched between two high rise buildings. "There's the ocean!"

Before Louise could turn her head, the speck of blue disappeared and she only saw a long row of high-rise condominiums—glass-faced buildings that reflected the sun and made it feel even hotter than the actual temperature. On the other side of the car a string of strip malls slid by, one after another, with no break other than a few narrow slits where a side street emptied onto the boulevard. Palm Plaza, Oceanside Shops, Beachfront Boutique—an endless ribbon of pale buildings weighted down with tropical flowers and greenery. Fin and Feather had a live parrot chained to a pole in front of the store. Louise knew that like her, the bird would have flown off were it not tied down.

The further south they traveled, the heavier the traffic became. Youthful drivers were replaced by small white-haired people scrunched down behind the wheel of a big Lincoln or a Cadillac with shark-like fins. Everything moved slower, and cars set their directional signals to blinking blocks and blocks before anyone actually made a turn. The high-rise buildings started crowding closer together, and their names became more obvious—Tropicana Towers, Surfside Arms, Serenity by the Sea. Less than one hundred yards past Coconut Charlie's Bar and Grill, Rose tugged at Clay's shoulder and waggled her finger.

"There it is!"

Dense gardens surrounded Oceanside Palms, a building the color of bleached sand with an entranceway protected by a large, very pink, shell-shaped canopy. Hundreds of tiny terraces crowded with plastic furniture and brightly-colored beach towels flipped across the railing gave the building the look of a resort rather than a place where people would actually live. Clay turned up the drive, edged his way across the lot, and pulled into an empty space alongside the entrance.

With a disapproving glance toward Clay's kneecaps, Rose said, "In the interest of decency, I suggest you tug those shorts down a bit."

Clay let the comment slide without answering.

"What's Uncle Floyd's apartment number?" Louise asked as she opened the door and stepped out of the car.

"As well as I remember," Rose said, "it's seven or seventeen. Or maybe seventy. F, it's definitely F, the same as in Floyd. But,

Louise, dear," she called across the walkway, "don't you want to arrange your hair before you go in?"

Louise checked the directory, then punched in 1-7-0-5.

"Hello," a voice said. "Anybody there?"

"Uncle Floyd, it's Louise."

"Hello?"

She moved her mouth closer to the speaker and shouted, "Louise. It's Louise."

There were several clicks. "Anybody there?" he repeated, then hung up.

Louise pushed the buzzer again. "Uncle Floyd—"

"Hello?"

"He can't hear you," somebody called out.

Louise turned. The voice came from a woman flip-flopping along the walkway in green rubber sandals and a bathing suit dripping water. "Can't nobody hear," she said. "Those speaker things don't work." The old woman, so weathered by the sun her skin had the look of a worn moccasin, came to an abrupt stop and gave the speaker a whack with her cane.

"Oh," Louise gasped, uncertain of where to go from there.

"Who you here to see?" the woman asked, eyeing Louise cautiously.

"Floyd Elkins."

"What business you got with Floyd?"

"I'm his niece."

"Well, it's about time you got here! He's been waiting since early this morning." The old lady stretched her lips back in a broad grin. "I'm seventeen D," she said. "Nellie Sadowski." She reached her free hand past Louise and pushed 1-7-0-5, five times in a row, one sequence of numbers right after the other.

"That you, Nellie?" the voice asked.

By this time Rose had stepped from the car, dusted herself free of dog hairs, and slipped into a sweeter than normal manner of speaking. "Good afternoon."

"Rose?" Nellie asked quizzically.

A smile brightened Rose's face. "Yes, I am," she answered.

"I knew it! Floyd said you might be dressed that way."

The smile flattened itself into a furrowed brow of disapproval. "By 'that way,' I'm assuming you mean proper," Rose replied haughtily.

"I suppose." Nellie chuckled as she led the way to Floyd's apartment, which happened to be 17E as in Elroy, not F as in Floyd. Traveling through the building Nellie whacked several apartment doors with her cane and hollered that there was a get together at Floyd's. "His niece is here," she said. "Come on up."

In a matter of minutes Nellie had several people following along. There was a couple with a half-empty bottle of wine, a woman with a bag of pretzels tucked under her arm, and a man in his bathrobe. "Perhaps Uncle Floyd isn't prepared for all this company," Louise said nervously.

"Company?" Nellie laughed. "You're the only company. We're neighbors."

"Well, I hope…" The last time Louise saw her uncle-by-marriage was ten years ago at Elroy's funeral. Back then Floyd was still married to Helga, a woman twice his size, with a tongue snappy as a leather whip. Helga didn't care for chitchat or socializing, and when she told Floyd to be quiet he'd not speak another word—not even if someone asked him a question. That's why it came as such a surprise when they got divorced. One day Floyd just up and left town. He moved to Florida. Even Aunt Rose was left speechless. Under those circumstances, and with ten years gone by, Louise expected her uncle to look older, weary perhaps, maybe even a bit stooped. Nothing had prepared her for the person who opened the apartment door—a man with dyed brown hair and a youthful twinkle in his blue eyes, a happier-looking man than she ever remembered.

"Rosie, my love!" he shouted and whirled Rose Elkins around so vigorously that her hat slid off. Floyd then hugged Louise just as affectionately, clamped Clay on the back, and patted the dog's head, asking both of them, "How's it going, fella?" With several other people already coming down the hallway, he pushed back the apartment door and propped it open with a little rubber wedge. "Have you met my niece? Rose? Clay?" Floyd asked as the people marched in right behind Nellie.

"What was that? Peace? Nose? Hey?" A white-haired man asked, and then he twisted a finger in his ear and said, "Pass that by me again, if you wouldn't mind."

Within a half-hour neighbors filled the living room. Most came dressed as they were, in shorts or cover-ups. Rose Elkins was the only one wearing a suit. Any number of people brought something to share—a bottle of wine, a bag of chips, a crock of spinach dip. Mary Townsend, a cherub-faced woman from the fourteenth floor, had made cheese puffs earlier in the day but claimed her husband got to snacking on them, so only three were left on the plate when she got to Floyd's. "I do hope you'll try one," she told Louise, "they're really quite good."

The only one who didn't seem to know the others was a young man who drifted in from the hallway, wearing a bathing suit that looked damp in certain spots. He said nothing, just poured himself a glass of wine, circled the room once or twice, ate the three cheese puffs, and meandered out the door. As his hand reached for the last of the cheese puffs, Mary let out a whoosh of disappointment and told Louise, "I *really* wish you could have had one of those."

A tall blonde who lived two apartments past the elevator arrived after everyone else. She came sashaying through the door in a white wrap-around bathrobe and a pair of gold high-heel sandals. "Not a drop of alcohol for me," she warned, then right away started explaining how she seemed to be coming down with a touch of something. "Some sort of flu, no doubt. Why, I could hardly *drag* myself from the bed," she sighed traumatically. She then pulled a pair of rhinestone earrings from her bathrobe pocket and fastened them on.

The party coming together on the spur of moment as it had reminded Louise of the days when she and Clay were first married. Back then everyone had struggled to afford a house, so in the summertime they'd get together and cook hot dogs or hamburgers on a backyard grill. Laura Kidderman always brought that potato salad of hers, and Helen made a pot of chili or, when the weather was too hot, some cold baked beans. Billie Butterman never had to worry about a budget, so she generally brought a keg of beer or some store-bought cake.

In the wintertime the women would visit back and forth, trade casserole recipes, and teach each other how to quilt. That was the first time Louise ever felt she belonged—really, truly belonged. She knew it was the life she was meant to live, and she settled into it so solidly it felt as if roots grew from the soles of her feet and anchored her to the ground beneath their house.

Louise looked around the room—people talking and laughing, passing platters of food from one to the other. An invisible chain of friendship linked them together. This was how the Material Girls would be in another twenty or thirty years. She could picture Billie Butterman with snow white hair and Ida round as a butterball after having given up on her various diets. Every now and again someone might ask, "Whatever happened to that Louise Palmer?" but the likelihood was, they wouldn't remember her face. A tear overflowed Louise's eye, and she brushed it from her cheek.

Without a word to anyone, she turned and walked out the door.

Louise

Seeing the friendship and love circling around that room has made me realize I just can't do this. I can't be where I don't belong. I'm going to call Billie and ask if I can stay with her. She's like a sister to me. Sisters make room for one another, no matter what. Given this problem she's having with Bradley, she needs me as much as I need her. Maybe I can step in and help with Missus Butterman. I don't mind toting a glass of water up the stairs every so often. It's a small enough price to pay for having a place to live.

Anyway, it will only be temporary. Weeks maybe. Once Clay discovers I'm gone he'll have time to think things over. He'll realize that we both belong in New Jersey. Everything we care about is there, just as everything Floyd cares about is here. When a person is where they belong, happiness is written all over their face. Do you know what's written on my face right now? Misery, that's what. I can feel it. Little bits and pieces of my heart have been breaking away and scattering themselves along the highway. The only way I can be whole again is to go back and pick up those lost pieces.

I know Clay loves me, and once he gets a taste of being alone he'll follow me back. I'm certain of it. You can't live with a person for almost thirty years and not miss them.

At least I don't think you can.

Dear God, I hope I'm right.

Missing Person

In the lobby of the Oceanside Palms, Louise found a pay phone and placed a collect person-to-person call to Billie Butterman. The phone rang fourteen times.

"Sorry, no answer," the operator finally said. "Please try your call again later."

Louise reluctantly replaced the receiver. She leaned back and stared at the telephone. A troublesome tick bounced around inside her head just as it had with the suspicious meter man. Something was wrong, she felt certain of it.

She dialed Billie's number again; still no answer. Her tote bag was upstairs in Floyd's apartment and her address book was in the tote bag, so she dialed the operator and asked for New Jersey Information. Louise called Ida first, because Ida knew everything about everybody. But Ida's line was busy. Louise tried another five times; then she gave up and called Claire.

"I've been calling Billie for two days," Louise said with worry in her voice, "and there's no answer. Something's wrong, terribly wrong, I can feel it!"

"Who is this?"

"Claire! It's me, Louise!" Obviously it didn't take years for people to forget. After just four days she'd become a stranger.

"Oh. Well, then, I suppose you haven't heard," Claire said.

"Heard what?"

"About Missus Butterman. It was awful, truly awful."

"What was?" Louise gasped.

"Poor Missus Butterman is dead."

"Good grief!" Aunt Rose was the exact same age as Missus Butterman, and the thought of such a thing happening sent a shiver along Louise's spine. "Heart attack?" she asked solemnly.

Claire's voice was thick with an air of tragedy, but then she was a woman who could make an overdone roast sound mournful. "Worse," she whispered, "much, much worse."

"Stroke?"

"Broken neck! And, as I hear tell, the police think it was murder!"

"Murder! Who?"

"Well, yesterday the police questioned Billie for nearly three hours. Everyone knew she hated the old lady, but Billie said she had nothing to do with it. She claims that when she got home from the beauty parlor Missus Butterman was already dead, lying at the foot of the stairs with her neck broken."

"Missus Butterman fell down the stairs?"

"Fell? Pushed? No one knows for sure."

"Billie would never do such a thing!"

"I wouldn't have thought so either, but we all know how she felt about—"

"Claire, how can you?!"

"Me? I'm not saying she did, I'm just telling you what other folks are saying."

"Gossip," Louise said. "Malicious gossip, that's all it is."

"You can't know for sure, you're in Florida."

"That's true, but I know what kind of person Billie is! Why, she made a thousand trips a day up and down the stairs just because Missus Butterman felt like jingling that bell of hers."

"Not according to Bradley."

"Bradley?"

"Yes, Bradley."

"When did you talk to Bradley?"

"At Missus Butterman's wake. It was certainly a pitiful sight, him standing there all alone, crying his eyes out and Billie too busy to even send a bouquet of flowers."

"Billie wasn't at the funeral parlor?"

"Nope. The last anyone heard was when she called Ida Wednesday night. According to Bradley, he and Billie had a big fight and then she stomped out the door. That's just like Billie. You know how headstrong she can be."

"Maybe so, but still she wouldn't—"

"Well, you've got to admit she's acting pretty suspicious."

Louise didn't have to admit any such thing, so she told Claire she'd be back in touch and hung up the receiver. *Four days.* How could the entire universe change in four days? Louise called Ida and this time she got through, but Ida hadn't heard anything more than Claire. Neither had Eloise, Fran, or Martha. Fran, who lived three houses down from the Buttermans, did say that Billie's Cadillac was gone from the driveway and had been for two days. "Of course," Fran added, "I didn't see actually see her loading suitcases into her car."

By the time Louise returned to the party the crowd had thinned, and Clay, who had been drinking glass after glass of red wine, looked bleary-eyed. "I'd better not drive," he said, and Louise quickly agreed. Although she was anxious to explain the situation—given Billie's predicament Clay simply *couldn't* refuse to turn around and head back to New Jersey—one look at the bright red lines zigzagging across his eyeballs convinced her to wait until morning.

They spent the night on Uncle Floyd's sofa, a pull-out bed that made the lumpy mattress in Smokey Falls seem plush by comparison. All night Louise tossed and turned. She ran the upcoming conversation with Clay through her brain time and time again until she'd decided how to approach it. She had to make it perfectly clear: this was not just a whim. It was an actual emergency. Billie Butterman's life was at stake. Louise had to go back to tell the truth of how Billie had waited on Missus Butterman hand and foot. If no one spoke up on Billie's behalf, she could spend the rest of her days in a penitentiary, or worse, be electrocuted. Louise felt weary to the point of exhaustion, but every time she started to doze she dreamt of Billie and saw her dark hair standing on end as a million volts of electricity coursed through her body.

At eight o'clock the next morning, Louise woke Clay and shoved a cup of coffee into his hand. "Quick, drink this," she said. "I've got to tell you something."

Half-asleep and still feeling the effects of all the wine, he allowed the cup to slide through his fingers and a full mug of hot coffee spilled into his lap. "I'm scalded!" he bellowed, yanking down his boxer shorts and fanning his privates.

"Clay!" Louise gasped. "Aunt Rose will see—"

"See what?" he screamed. "That you've scalded me?"

Louise yanked up the bed sheet and wrapped it around Clay. Things weren't going at all the way she'd rehearsed. "Just forget the coffee and take a cool shower," she said, trying to ease him into a more receptive mood.

Clay had barely stepped from the shower when Uncle Floyd set out a platter of scrambled eggs and sausages along with a pot of freshly-brewed coffee. "Oh, I don't think we can stay—" Louise began, but Floyd cut into her words, insisting they eat.

"How could we refuse a breakfast like this?" Clay said and pulled up a chair.

As soon as they were back in the car and alone, Louise said, "I've got something to tell you."

"What now?"

"We've got to go back to New Jersey."

Clay gave a moan that was so painful Yoo's ears perked up. "We've already been through this," he said. "Several times!"

"Yes, but this time it's different. It's a real emergency."

Clay gave her a sideways glance. "Yeah, I'll bet."

"Billie's in serious trouble. She could be electrocuted!"

Clay suddenly burst into laughter. "You had me going for a minute," he chuckled. "How you come up with such stories is beyond me."

"I'm not fooling! Billie is in serious trouble. She needs help, and I'm her closest friend."

Louise told the story of how Missus Butterman had been found dead at the foot of the stairs, her neck snapped like a twig. "They suspect Billie might have murdered her. It's because of Bradley, he's poisoned their minds—everyone, even Claire and Ida."

Clay was no longer laughing. "Has Billie been arrested?" he asked.

Louise shook her head. "Not exactly."

"Well, then, what?"

"She wasn't at the funeral home. She didn't even send flowers."

"That's it?"

"And she hasn't been home for days. No one has even the remotest idea of where she is or what's happened to her."

"But you know, right?"

"No." The word was hardly out of her mouth when Louise realized it was the wrong answer. "What I mean is, I don't know exactly where—"

"You don't have any idea where she is, do you?"

"Not at this precise moment—"

"You want me to drive all the way back to New Jersey when you don't even know where she is?" Clay took a hard right and pulled onto the southbound side of the road. "For all you know she could be in Alaska!"

"She's not. I'll bet she's trying to get in touch with me right this minute!"

Clay tucked his chin down and leaned into the steering wheel. "Yeah, right. Well, in a few hours we'll be in Tall Pines. Then you can call and leave a message for her."

They drove for two hours and fifty-seven minutes before Clay left the highway and turned onto the narrow roadway that ran westward. "I think this is it," he said, but continued driving as if he were absolutely certain.

"Let's stop and ask directions," Louise suggested. "I'll call Billie again."

"Call her where?" Clay answered, still pressing his foot to the gas pedal.

He didn't stop, didn't even slow down. They sped past a strip mall set back from the roadway and a few houses with toys strewn about the yard and upside down boats pitched on their sides. After that, the road narrowed to a single lane bordered by endless stretches of overgrown brush—pines split by lightning and left to rot, fallen branches, palmettos, and vines twisted together until it was impossible to tell where one stopped and the other started.

Eventually the piney scrub thinned and gave way to a split rail fence with a cluster of thirsty-looking cows huddled under a single shade tree. Florida, as far as Louise could tell, was nothing more than a pitiful wasteland crisscrossed with a latticework of electrical wires. Not that she had expected anything better. Some things never changed. She could still remember how her daddy always promised the next place would be wonderful, but it never was.

By two o'clock the sun was high in the sky and near blinding. Clay squinted to see ahead even though there was nothing to see. "I'm beginning to think we ought to ask directions," he said, making it sound like his idea.

"We could turn back and look for a Seven-Eleven," Louise suggested. Since the cell phone no longer got a signal, she hoped to find a phone to give Billie another try.

But Clay kept heading westward. "We'll stop at the very next place we come to," he promised. A mile past the turnoff for Snake Lake, a faded sign that read "Super Gas and Sundry Supplies" appeared. Clay swung the car around and followed the arrows along a narrow drive. At the end of the driveway they saw a faded building with a nameless gas pump beside the door and a pair of eyes peering through a dirty window pane.

"This is a lucky find," Clay said and pulled up to the pump.

"Lucky find?" Louise echoed, thinking that perhaps this wasn't the best place to make a telephone call. She would have felt more comfortable were it Amoco or Exxon or for that matter a Mobil Station, like that nice one in front of the Seven-Eleven in New Smyrna Beach—anything familiar. This no-name gas might not even be real gasoline. She'd heard of cases where a watered-down mixture was pumped into a tank, and the poor unsuspecting tourist's car sputtered to a stop along some desolate stretch of road. Such a thing had happened in Texas, and the man was lucky to get away with his life. As Clay headed toward the building, she called out, "Be careful."

Her feeling of apprehension increased when a young man wearing heavy jeans and a long-sleeve shirt appeared. He had a suspicious-looking face, long and thin, the kind that sinks into itself when a person's up to no good. Louise tugged Yoo to attention and kept a sharp eye for whatever might happen. Clay could joke about her being a worrier all he wanted to, but she was the one who had seen through the phony meter man.

Louise watched as the man pointed a finger toward the north. Clay leaned to the right, apparently following the finger, and they stood there nodding their heads at one another. After a moment or two the man turned and walked back inside the building. Clay hesitated a moment, then followed behind. Given the narrow set of the man's eyes she could easily imagine her husband being robbed of every cent he had in his pocket, possibly even clunked on the head. She pushed down on the door handle and said, "Come on, Yoo!" Louise climbed out, circled around to the back of the car, and popped open the trunk. She grabbed the tire iron and started for the store, but before she'd gone nine steps Clay reappeared.

"We're almost there," he said, following her back to the car. "It's less than five miles." Spotting the tire iron in her hand, he asked, "What's that for?"

"Oh," Louise answered, "I thought we might be getting a flat tire." She left it at that, figuring the truth would only give him cause to discredit any future warnings she might offer.

Clay circled the car and thumped all four tires. "Nope," he said. "Everything's okay." He slid behind the wheel, started the car, and backed out.

Two miles down the road he saw the landmark he'd been looking for—Hayworth's Feed and Grain Depot. They turned onto County Road Thirteen and almost immediately spotted the wooden billboard. Time and sun had bleached the printing to near white. As they passed by, Louise read the shadowy words, "Tall Pines—3 Miles."

"That's the place," Clay said. "Tall Pines."

"On Route Thirteen," Louise said wearily. "That's a sure sign of bad luck."

"Nobody believes such stuff," Clay chortled.

"Maybe you don't," Louise replied and left it at that.

Clay turned in at the Tall Pines signpost and drove past a long stretch of empty lots and palmetto thickets before they came to the first house. The tiny place squatted alongside the road, a turned-over tricycle and a broken chair on the front lawn.

The next two houses they passed appeared abandoned.

A mile later the road ended, and they had to turn one way or the other. Arrows pointed to the left for the clubhouse and Orange Grove Way. Blossom Tree Trail went to the right. The narrow street, squiggly as a strand of spaghetti, swung first in one direction then twisted around to head the other way. Every house they passed sat squat and low to the ground, a square box dwarfed by the tall pines that like the palmettos were left to grow wild.

"We're on the right street," Clay said as he counted off the house numbers. "One-thirty-nine. Odd numbers on the right side, but it's a way yet. Fifty-seven. Thirty-one."

As the numbers got lower, Louise felt a lump grow in her throat. It swelled to the size of a hard-boiled egg when he got to twenty-three and choked off her breath when he announced, "There it is—seventeen!"

At first glance the house appeared too short for a person to stand inside. It had the look of a decades-old cigar box, tobacco-colored with windows so covered in grime someone just as well might have painted them black. The front door, which at one time had apparently been green, had faded beyond recognition.

Beneath the two front windows sat tin flower boxes, only one of which contained dirt. Louise saw no flowers—not in the boxes, not in the yard, not anywhere. In fact, only a few things looked like they might still be alive, possibly the scrawny bush alongside the step and a solitary palm sitting in the middle of the front yard. "Looks as if no one's been tending the place," Clay commented.

Louise could have said any number of things. She could have told Clay it was the ugliest house she'd ever laid eyes on; she could have told him that he'd lost his mind expecting her to live in a place like this; she could have told him she'd divorce him if he didn't turn the car around and head for home. But as she stood there aghast, all she said was, "I hope the telephone works."

When Clay climbed from the car and started for the front door, Louise followed. He pulled the key from his pocket and slid it into the lock. Rusted and stiff, the lock at first refused to budge. "It's a sure sign," Louise said. "A sure sign that we were meant to leave this place and go home."

"This *is* home," Clay answered and kept jiggling the key until the lock at last clicked. He pushed the door open and stepped inside.

A hazy bit of sunlight drifted through the darkened windows providing just enough light to see, although seeing was not an advantage. Years of dust and neglect covered the windows, walls, and furniture. The air reeked of mildew, fried foods, and stale cigar smoke. The furnishings they'd inherited consisted of a black leatherette recliner with cotton stuffing bulging from a tear in the right arm, a plaid sofa, a coffee table with one end propped up on a cinder block, and a square television sitting on a round three-legged table. On the wall behind the sofa hung Uncle Charlie's prized trophy—a mounted catfish with long whiskers and reflective eyes that followed every movement.

One look at the room convinced Louise that she absolutely had to find a way to get them back to New Jersey. For a brief moment she closed her eyes, blanking out the ugliness and replacing it with the image of their living room in Westfield—down-filled cushions on a brightly-colored chintz sofa, bookshelves lining the walls, porcelain lamps. She gave a despondent sigh and said, "Clay, we've made a terrible mistake leaving our beautiful home for—this!"

"Oh, I realize it needs some fixing up," he answered as he strolled through the dining room in search of a light switch. A moment or so later, a hanging basketball flashed on and filled the room with an orange glow. A few fishing poles were scattered across the floor of the unfurnished dining room like Pick-Up Sticks. Clay kept walking and called back, "The kitchen's in here." Louise followed the sound of his voice.

He opened the refrigerator and a light came on. "Good, it works," Clay said, but once he caught a whiff of the stench from inside, he quickly closed the door. "It's probably better if you don't open this," he told Louise. "Uncle Charlie may have left a fish in there." He moved to the stove. "Now this seems to be in pretty good shape." He swiped his hand across the top, then lifted a burner rack, and that's when a chunk of charcoal fell off. "But it might need cleaning."

"Cleaning?" Louise gasped. "Why, it needs way more than cleaning, it's nothing more than—" She was going to say a piece of junk, but before she got the words from her mouth Clay disappeared around the corner.

"The bedrooms are over on this side," he called back. "There are two."

Once again Louise trailed behind the sound of his voice. In the larger of the two rooms was a double bed with both sides sloping to the center, more a hammock than an innerspring mattress. "This doesn't look at all comfortable," she said. "We'd better think about going to a motel."

"Motel? What for?" Clay marched off to check on the second room. That one didn't have a bed at all, just a student desk, a bookcase, and a recliner in worse condition than the one they'd seen in the living room. He circled back to the utility closet alongside the kitchen and began banging on something. "I'm pretty sure this is supposed to be in working order," he said. After several minutes of clanking and clattering, the air conditioner came on. It rattled and groaned, then finally belched a cool whoosh of air across the room.

Louise kept her eye open for a telephone and finally spotted it on the far side of the sagging bed. She lifted the receiver to dial Billie's number—no dial tone. "Clay!" she screamed. "This phone doesn't work!"

"Don't worry, Sweetie, I'll get it hooked up tomorrow."

Louise didn't like the name Sweetie any better than Squeezie. It was a reminder of Sweetie Spotswood, the woman living in her house, taking her place with the Material Girls. She turned back to the living room and dropped wearily into the recliner. "I really wanted to call Billie tonight," she moaned, and the ugly catfish with a perpetual grin defiantly winked a glass eye.

After Clay carried the suitcases in and stacked them alongside the bed, he suggested going back to Super Gas to pick up a few things for breakfast.

"Did they have a pay phone?" Louise asked.

"No pay phone. Milk and eggs, bacon maybe, and big cans of coffee."

When Clay left, the door slammed shut behind him. It was not because of the wind, since there wasn't any. The air was as motionless as a dead man. Louise listened for something else, but she only heard the scuffle of steps as Clay crossed the driveway and climbed into the car. Once the rumble of the engine drifted into the distance, the only sound she heard was the soft moan of the ancient air conditioner and the call of a night bird—a lone bird that sounded strangely like Billie crying, "Who, Who, Who…who will help me now that you're not here?"

Clay was gone for well over an hour, and in that time darkness drifted across Seventeen Blossom Tree Trail. The solitary palm became a black silhouette against a purple sky. When the last trace of daylight faded, Louise pushed herself forward in the recliner and snapped on the lamp beside the chair. Moments later the bulb popped. A brief flash of light lit up the room, and then nothing but the darkness surrounding her.

A sound as sorrowful as that of the night bird could then be heard echoing through the tall pines. It was the sound of sobbing that came from the dingy little tobacco-colored house.

Louise

When we walked into this house my first thought was, I've been here before. *Not in this house, not in this room, but in hundreds just like it. Even in the pitch dark you know exactly what it looks like, because places like this come with a smell. It's the smell of people passing through. Nobody stays in places like this. They come, camp out until they can find a place that's more livable, and then move on.*

We were staying in just such a place the night Daddy was killed. Mama was always fearful of closing her eyes on nights when Daddy was gone, so she sat up until dawn waiting for him to come home. When we heard the first roosters crowing, she went looking for him and left me alone in that awful room. The daylight came and went before Mama returned, and the whole time she was gone I could feel the dampness of the tears shed in that room. The sadness of a place like that seeps into your skin, and no amount of washing can rid you of it.

Some people may not understand why I was so locked into staying in New Jersey and holding onto the home we had, but this I can assure you: those people have never lived in places like this. It's a terrible thing to have to decide between making yourself happy and making the person you love happy. I wonder if Clay looked that decision square in the eye before he brought me here, before we gave up our home for this.

I love Clay as much as a wife can possibly love her husband, but he's a man who listens to the words I say and ignores the fear thundering through my heart. I need someone to listen, to hold my hand and walk me through this. I need to know he actually cares about the pain in my heart, but that's not what I'm feeling from him.

Worthmore

When Clay returned from the store, only the porch light and the kitchen overhead were burning. He stumbled through the living room calling for Louise but got no answer. He finally found her lying face down across the bed, a box of Kleenex at her side and a pile of crumpled tissues on the floor.

"Louise?"

She pretended to be asleep, but the sniffing of tears indicated she wasn't.

"Louise, are you okay?"

No answer.

"Louise, honey, is something wrong?"

She lifted her head long enough to give a slit-eyed glare across her shoulder, her eyes swollen and her nose red from crying. "Wrong?" she said. "You don't know?" She dropped her face back onto the pillow and began sobbing again.

"Is it the house?"

"It's more than the house. It's this whole place. Can't you smell the sadness?"

"Sadness?" Clay echoed. "I think what you're smelling is the fish that was in the refrigerator, but I've thrown that out."

"It's not just the fish, it's—"

"Give it a chance. I know the place looks bad tonight but it'll grow on you, you'll see. This is the sort of place that once you get to know—"

"It's already grown on me! It's been growing inside my heart since I was old enough to understand what ugliness was."

"Things look different in the daylight—"

"I don't want to talk about it."

Louise hadn't lied. She didn't want to talk about it. But inside the deepest part of heart, she wanted Clay to talk about it. She wanted to hear him say he could understand the sadness she felt and that he'd make it right. Instead he said, "Okay," and turned back to the kitchen with his bag of groceries.

"I got bacon and eggs for tomorrow morning," he called back. "After a good breakfast I'm certain you'll see things in a more positive light."

Louise made no effort to stir from the bed as he clattered around the kitchen, opening and closing cupboard doors. With her heart pounding and her stomach churning, she couldn't bear the thought of food. She buried her head in the pillow. Even with her eyes closed she could see the living room and the trophy hanging above the lumpy sofa. As the tears rolled across her temple and into her ear, Louise imagined the glass-eyed fish laughing at her.

"Foolish woman," it said. "You left a good life to come and live in this dreary old place."

Louise closed her eyes to shut out the shaft of light from the kitchen; then she tugged the pillow around her ears to muffle the rattle of spoons and dishes. Only the smell remained, a smell of stale cigar smoke, mildew, and sadness. As she drifted off to sleep she tried to imagine the fragrance of spring flowers blooming in Westfield. She pictured herself walking through the backyard with the yellow roses in full bloom, breathing in their sweetness. Suddenly an ugly stench pushed its way into her dreams.

"Phew," she said. "What's that awful smell?"

"You have a nerve!" the fish answered. "Criticizing *my* house!" There he was, as big as a man, stretched out on the black recliner, smoking a fat cigar and chomping on a can of sardines.

"Well, as far as I'm concerned you can have this house," Louise answered. "I'm going back to New Jersey."

The fish popped another sardine in his mouth. "No, you're not."

"Yes, I am. I'm going back to my own house."

"Ha!" the fish answered. "You don't have a house. Sweetie has that house."

"I'll stay with friends."

"You don't have friends. Billie Butterman's left town."

"I have other friends."

"No, you don't." The fish curled his slimy lips into a smug grin. "They're dead, the lot of them. They grew old and died waiting for you to come home."

"It's only been five days—"

"Guess again." The fish handed Louise a gold mirror, and she looked at herself. Her hair had turned gray as a storm cloud, and ridges and lines crisscrossed her thin face. "This can't be!" she cried.

"Get used to it," the fish said and flicked the ash off of his cigar.

Louise woke with a start. "Feeling better today?" Clay asked. He bent, kissed her cheek, then sat on the side of the bed.

She turned her head toward the window and blinked at the sliver of light sliding through a tear in the shade. The last thing she remembered was Uncle Charlie's catfish wriggling his whiskers and tucking his fat lips back in an ugly grin. Slowly she realized that she had slept through the night. Clay stretched his arm across her body and spoke.

"I really am sorry about this," he said. "I would have kept my job at the bank had I known you'd be this unhappy." His voice sounded sorrowful, his words weighted and slow. "The house is a disappointment for me also. I didn't realize it was this bad. Uncle Charlie was so happy living here at Tall Pines, and I thought we could be too. I figured it would be wonderful to spend time together and do things before we grew too old to enjoy life. I know you wanted to stay in Westfield, but I honestly did believe that once we were here you'd fall in love with the place, as I had. I was so focused on living the good life that I never stopped to consider Uncle Charlie's house might be in serious need of repair."

The stoop of his shoulders, the gray hairs poking out here and there, the downslide of his eyes, these things and a few others Louise couldn't put her finger on, weakened her resolve. Clay was, after all, a man with good intentions.

"I wouldn't have wanted you to stay at the bank," she said. "I love you and want what's best for you."

"It would have been nice, if not for this house—"

"How could you have known the house was in such bad shape?" she sympathized. "I'm certain at one time it was a very nice place, it's just that—"

"You're right," he said cheerfully. "It was a great place, and I can make it great again. Why should we give up our chance at happiness just because the house needs work? I'll get some paint and start today."

"Well, it's not just the paint—"

"You're right again. It needs a lot of repairs. I'm gonna need caulking, a roll of screening, a pallet of sod, a good strong cleanser, brushes, rags—"

"Even with all of that, I doubt that—"

"In all honesty," he said, "I wouldn't expect you to live in the house the way it is now. But don't worry, I'm gonna fix everything. When I get finished, this place will be polished up like Herb Kramer's fifty-seven Chevy." He rambled on and on without once catching sight of the look on Louise's face.

"Clay, I think we ought to talk about—"

"Outdoor furniture," he said. "We'll definitely need new patio furniture. The stuff out there is rusted through."

After that there was no talking to Clay. He was busy explaining what all he planned to do. Listening to him it would seem he had the ability to turn that drab little house into the Taj Mahal, but Louise knew better. Clay had never once started a repair project and finished it. He'd spent his days working with a fountain pen and ledger sheet, and his tool box consisted of nothing more than a hammer and screwdriver. He wouldn't listen to reason right now, but if she waited a few weeks until he tired of all that work it was quite possible that he'd be willing to pack up and go home.

"Ernie says there's a Giant Hardware and a Bigwig Market over in Worthmore Township," he said. "That's only ten miles north of here."

"Ernie?"

"Ernie Tobias, he works part time at Super Gas. Nice kid." Clay was lost in thought as he turned toward the kitchen.

Louise swung her legs out of bed and reached for the same shorts she wore yesterday. "Before you buy a whole lot of—"

"Don't worry, I'm gonna make a list," he called back.

By time Louise got to the kitchen, Clay had disappeared from sight. "Clay?" she called out. The back door stood open, but he didn't appear to be out there either. "Clay?" she called again, poking her head outside. A broken chaise, two chairs, and the rusted table crowded a patio barely the size of a quilting square. A few yards beyond the patio stood a tall hedge thick with yellow hibiscus flowers.

"How lovely," Louise said, surprising herself with the sentiment as she stepped out into the warm sun. Brushing the dirt from a chair, she sat down. It wasn't Westfield, but it offered a pleasant respite. She had not been there for more than two minutes when suddenly something in the bushes moved.

At first thinking it might be the dog, she called his name. "Yoo?"

The dog padded out from the kitchen and snuffed at the air.

The thing in the bush moved again.

Suspecting any number of wild animals, Louise was afraid to move and afraid not to. "Go get it, Yoo," she said waggling her finger at the hedge.

The dog darted across the grass and nosed his way into the thick of the bush.

"Oooohhh!" a voice squealed. "Shoo! Shoo!"

Louise heard a fair amount of rustling, then the branches parted and a woman with hair as red as a firecracker stumbled out. "Shoo, shoo!" she hollered, frantically waving her arms at the dog.

Louise scrambled from the chair and hurriedly grabbed Yoo's collar. "I'm so sorry. I thought you were a wild animal. A skunk or maybe a raccoon."

"Me?"

"Well, not you precisely, but whatever was in the bush."

"That was me," the woman said plucking a tangle of brown leaves from her bosom. "Cherry, Cherry Melinski. Blue house."

Louise slanted her head in the direction of the hedge. "Blue house?"

"Right next door."

Louise tipped her head to the other side. "Really?"

"You can't see it because the bush is in the way."

"Oh."

"To get there you have to go out your front door and around the walkway or else cut through the bush." Cherry picked a leaf from her hair. "Want me to show you?"

"Oh, no," Louise said. "I believe I know the one you mean." She eyed the hedge again. "Matter of fact, I'm certain."

Once Cherry had straightened out the business of the exact location of her house she said, "Too bad about Charlie. You related?"

"My husband is. Well, was."

"Oh yeah, the nephew. Jersey, right?"

"Westfield," Louise answered thoughtfully. She wanted to describe the lovely two-story house and all the friends she had left behind, but before she could say another word Cherry interrupted.

"So, Ernie says you're gonna fix up the place."

"Clay's thinking of it." Louise began to wonder how Cherry would know such a thing. How did this Ernie find out so quickly? Clay had just mentioned it this morning.

"Giant Hardware in Worthmore," Cherry said, "that's the place. Got everything you need. On Tuesdays they give a twenty percent senior discount."

"Senior?" Louise said, her face puckered like she'd bit into a lemon. "Why, we're nowhere near sixty-five yet!"

"That don't matter! Everybody down here gets a senior discount. Except maybe if you're a teenager or something really obvious."

"But to say you're older than you actually are, isn't that lying?"

The woman laughed with a truck-driver guffaw, loud and big like a boom box playing off-key music, an annoying sound even from her. "Yeah, sure," she said. "Like you think somebody's gonna ask?"

Louise had already come to dislike the woman—the short choppy way she spoke, her frizzy red hair, the clatter of bracelets jangling on her arm, the tacky spandex pants—all of those things perhaps, but mostly because she knew about Clay's plan to fix up the house. She loosed her hand from Yoo's collar.

The broad grin narrowed a bit. "He bite?" Cherry asked.

"Bite? No, never. Yoo's gentle as can be."

"Yoo? Funny name."

Cherry isn't? Louise thought.

"I, myself, am not too big on pets," Cherry said. "For some reason, they just don't take to me." She backed away two steps. "I once knew a German Shepherd who took a chunk right out of its owner's leg."

"Really?"

"Yes, indeed. They shipped that dog off to the pound."

"Well, Yoo would never do that. He'd chase after a squirrel or rabbit, maybe. But never a person. He likes people."

"Well, maybe," Cherry said stepping back a bit further. "Anyway, I've got to be going. Can you grab hold of him till I get back through the bush?"

"Of course," Louise replied, again tightening her grip on Yoo's collar.

Cherry Melinski pushed aside a branch and disappeared into the hibiscus again. "Later," she called back, "I'll stop over with the Mister, see how you're doing."

"Oh, that's not necessary," Louise started to say, but the woman had already left.

Worthmore was a little strip of a town, five blocks from start to finish—a scattering of houses on the side streets, a bank, a library, and a motley array of shops along Center Street, the main thoroughfare. Clay drove past the sun-bleached buildings looking for Giant Hardware.

"Have you seen it?" he asked Louise. She shook her head, even though she hadn't been looking. He circled the block and spotted it the second time around. Then he began looking for a parking space. At the far end of town he sandwiched the car in between a delivery truck and a dusty Plymouth plastered with stickers from places such as the Statue of Liberty, Busch Gardens, and Disney World l

"Giant's a few blocks down," Clay said, taking hold of Louise's elbow and steering her along the street.

They crossed in front of the Good Shepherd Church Second-hand Shop, then passed by a Laundromat whose windows were in need of washing. Louise couldn't help but compare the shops of Worthmore with those of Westfield as they passed storefront after storefront. In every window she saw the reflection of a sad-eyed woman looking back at her.

Giant Hardware sat two doors down from the bank. From the outside the narrow building looked more like a book shop. As Cherry had predicted, they had everything imaginable—ladders, dish racks, garbage cans, brooms, mops, even a display of makeup mirrors and lipstick cases. Unfortunately, things were tossed together and piled on top of each other until it was nearly impossible to find whatever you happened to be searching for.

Behind the counter a man with wire rim spectacles was reading a book. As Clay picked his way through a bin of hammers, the man tipped his head and peered over the glasses. "Holler if I can help," he said.

"Paint department?" Clay queried.

"That's in the back," the man said and motioned them to follow him. He was a dark-haired man, tall, younger than most folks they'd seen in town.

"You Charlie Palmer's nephew?" he asked as they trudged single file around a barrel of nails and screws, past a wall of window shades, and into the paint department, which turned out to be nothing more than a small stack of cans leaning against the back wall.

"Why, yes," Clay answered. "How did—"

"Ernie mentioned you'd probably be in. He gets all his stuff here." The man stuck out his hand and introduced himself. "Howard Gessner, owner and operator of the finest hardware store in the county."

"Clay Palmer. This is my wife, Louise." Clay grinned, grabbed hold of Howard's hand, and shook it vigorously. "Glad to make your acquaintance," he said enthusiastically.

Howard pulled his hand free the moment Clay began to slow a bit. "What color paint you looking for?" he asked.

Clay turned. "Louise?"

"Well." She hesitated, trying to consider what color might best cover the years of dirt and neglect. Finally she answered, "Blue, a soft, slightly grayish blue."

"We don't have any blue."

Clay's smile started to disappear, and the corners of his mouth edged down until his lips formed a perfectly straight line. He fingered his chin nervously. "Can you order it or mix it special?" he asked.

Howard shook his head. "No mixing machine. We only carry standard colors."

Clay's mouth tightened a bit more, and a washboard of ridges settled across his forehead. "Do you suppose another store might have it?"

"Another store? Why, this is the finest hardware store in the county!"

"So you say," Clay answered, "but you don't have a paint mixer."

Louise's patience had already stretched to the limit. What difference did the color of the paint make? They'd soon be leaving the place. "Forget blue," she said. "Just make it buff."

"No buff."

"What colors do you have?"

"Yellow, green, white."

"Three colors? That's it?"

"Afraid so."

Yellow was too much like dried mustard and green walls reminded her of hospitals, so Louise shrugged and said, "White."

"Enamel or flat?"

"You have both?" Clay asked.

"No. But I can special order the enamel."

Clay was still poking through a tub of sanders and scrapers when Howard tallied up their five cans of flat white, two brushes, a bundle of cheesecloth, and the patio set, which required a bit of assembly but was on sale for only ninety-nine dollars. Before the adding machine spit out a grand total, Louise said, "Do you give a senior discount?"

"Twenty percent." Howard click-clacked another number into the machine and said, "That'll be one-hundred forty-eight twenty-seven, with your discount."

Clay said, "Discount?" as he handed two fifties and five ten-dollar bills across the counter.

"Senior discount," Louise whispered in his ear. It seemed an adequate enough explanation to her, but she noticed a puzzled look on Clay's face as he held out his hand for the one dollar and seventy-three cents change.

Howard stacked the cans of paint on the front counter, and two by two Clay carted them to the car. While she waited Louise eyed the windows of the Bluebird, a ladies clothing shop right next door. *It doesn't hurt to browse,* she told herself. It was more like killing time than having a real an interest in buying. Buying such summery clothes would mean she planned on staying, and she had no intention of that. Still, the blue pullover in the upper right hand corner of the display caught her eye. It brought a sense of longing for the blue paint she was denied. *If only it weren't sleeveless.* Louise turned away from the window and shook her head. A person simply didn't need clothes for a place they'd soon leave behind.

Bigwig Market was the largest store along Center Street. Its plate glass windows ran on for the better part of a block and were practically covered over with signs for such things as Florida corn and home grown tomatoes. Despite Louise's reluctance in doing so, she had to admit the store appeared every bit as modern as the PathMark in Westfield. Inside, the produce section was stacked high with several different varieties of lettuce, pale green honeydew melons, fat string beans, and strawberries big and red as an apple. She loaded the basket with zucchini and corn, bright orange carrots, plump tomatoes and half of an already-cut watermelon. Buying groceries was nothing like buying clothes.

Groceries got used up quickly enough and carried no commitment to permanency.

"Get the pulpy orange juice," Clay said. "And one of those fresh chickens." He tossed a steak into the shopping cart, then a package of hamburger and some pork chops, apples, spaghetti, pretzels, potato chips—more food than they were likely to need. By the time they reached the checkout aisle the basket was so full Clay had to carry the two six-packs of Budweiser in his arms. Setting the beer down on the conveyor belt, he commented to the clerk at the register, "Hot day. I could go for one of these right now."

"You're not allowed to drink inside the store," the old guy said. "Not 'cause I got any objection. It's the law what don't allow it."

"Oh no," Clay said with a laugh, "I wasn't going to—"

Louise rolled a cantaloupe along the counter.

"Guess you're stocking up," the clerk said as he tied the handles of the plastic bag into a triple knot that would take ages to undo. He handed the bundle to Clay, hesitated a moment, then asked, "Ain't you Charlie Palmer's nephew?"

"Yes, yes, I am. And you're—"

"Bert."

"You knew Uncle Charlie?"

"Yep. We fished together."

"How did you know—" Clay stammered. "Do I look like my uncle?"

"Can't say for sure. With all those whiskers, I reckon nobody'd ever seen the whole of Charlie's face. But Ernie said you'd be likely to come in and load up."

"Ah, yes," Louise said. "Ernie, again."

"Not again, Tobias. Ernie Tobias. He's real good with tools," Bert said as he pushed another knotted-up bag of groceries toward Louise. "If you folks need help fixing up that place, Ernie, he's your guy."

"Ernie?" Clay said. "From Super Gas?"

"Yep. That fella can do most anything, even knows how to mix paint."

Louise moved the last box of cereal onto the counter. "Colors?" she asked.

"Yep. Pink, red, orange. Not blue or green. He don't do those."

Too-Near Neighbors

The sound of Clay's whistling grated on Louise's nerves. He segued from one cheerful tune into the next with no pause in between, and it particularly annoyed her because the whistling indicated the enthusiasm with which he'd tackled the task of fixing up the house. Back in Westfield convincing him to oil a squeaky hinge or change a light bulb was near impossible. Now he unpacked the "assembly required" lawn furniture as if it were a Christmas present, sorting through bits and pieces, lining them up in accordance with the directions—arms, legs, seats, twenty-one screws.

"A week," Louise said quietly to herself. "One week, and he'll be back to his old ways." She pulled the foods needing refrigeration from the bags then pushed them aside. The fridge was already clean. She'd scrubbed it top to bottom, and the fish smell had been soaked up by a box of baking soda. The second shelf was missing, but other than that the refrigerator was usable. Standing a section of watermelon on end and propping it in place with three tomatoes, she could squeeze in all of the produce. The meat, considerably more than they'd need, she stored in the freezer.

Moving on to the next carton, she opened the cupboard and slid in a can of chicken soup along with a jar of spaghetti sauce. The glass jar caught, tipped to one side, teetered for a split second, then fell and splattered. The sticky red mess dripped down the top shelf onto those below it. As she cleaned up the sauce Louise discovered what she thought was a spill of pepper. A closer look showed the pepper had legs and was still moving.

When Louise was seven they'd lived in a rooming house filled with water bugs and roaches so brazen they'd come out of the walls and march across the countertop. Although she couldn't remember the name of the place, she did remember how her daddy didn't come home for a week. For months afterward, Louise dreamt of those bugs. Before the summer had ended, she'd developed a fear of any and every creepy-crawly thing.

Without giving way to the churning in her stomach, Louise filled the sink with hot water and added a full bottle of Lysol. If this were her own house, she would have had rubber gloves and a Chore Boy scrubby pad. But this wasn't her house, so the best she could come up with was a torn-off piece of towel that was a tad cleaner than the cupboard shelves. She plunged her hands into the hot water and tackled the shelves.

Louise had only half-finished cleaning when she heard the screen door snap open.

"Yoo-hoo, anyone here?"

The dog pricked his ears and snuffed the air. His muscles tensed the way they did when he caught the scent of a cat or squirrel. Then lolloping across the kitchen, he bolted for the front door.

"No, Yoo—" Louise climbed from the stool and followed behind.

"Helloooooo!" the voice called.

Cherry Melinski!

By the time Louise made it to the living room Yoo already had Cherry pinned to the floor, his paws pressing against her ample bosom, his tongue lapping at her face. A round-bottomed woman to start with, Cherry had rolled out of her yellow wedges and lay flat on her back, arms and legs wriggling like an upside-down bug as she tried to get free of the dog.

"Down, Yoo, down!" Louise shouted from the doorway. She hurried across the room and swatted the dog away. "He's just trying to be playful. He doesn't realize how big he is."

"Playful? Why, he flat out attacked me!"

"Oh, he would never—"

"Well, he did!" Cherry's eyes were wide, and her lower lip quivered as she pushed a clump of bushy red hair back into place. "I came over to be neighborly, not rob the house."

"Oh, I certainly never thought…" The truth was Louise would have been delighted to have Cherry Melinski cart the entire place off and leave nothing but a gaping hole in the ground.

"If you didn't think I was a crook, why'd you sic that dog on me?"

"Oh, I didn't. Yoo just wanted to play. I think he likes you."

"Likes me?" Cherry sounded extremely doubtful.

Louise nodded, then extended her hand and helped Cherry up from the floor. "You all right?" she asked.

Hesitating as if it were a question worthy of serious consideration, Cherry shifted her weight from one foot to the other. "I might've sprained my ankle," she finally said.

"Oh, dear." Louise bent down and felt around the supposedly injured ankle. "I don't think anything's broken," she said.

"I'm not so sure." Cherry looked down at her foot.

"Why don't you sit and have a cup of tea?" Louise suggested. "Maybe your ankle will feel better if you rest it awhile." She took Cherry by the arm and helped her to the kitchen.

The uninvited guest settled herself at the table and before long was engrossed in talking about the ladies of the Hands Down Card Club. "Now that's a group who knows how to have fun," she said. "Most of them come for the laughs, but some are real serious about playing cards. Which I suppose is okay if card playing is a thing you wanna be serious about." It seemed the more Cherry talked, the better her ankle felt. "You got any cookies?" she asked, dumping a spoonful of sugar into her second cup of tea.

"Lorna Doones?"

"Yeah, okay. Those or maybe a cheese sandwich."

A sandwich meant lunch, and lunch meant a longer visit, so Louise set out a plate of cookies.

"I was hoping the Mister could meet you," Cherry garbled through a mouthful of Lorna Doones, "but he's gone fishing."

"That's okay," Louise answered. "We're still in a mess anyway."

"Wilfred don't care. He's the kind to pitch in and help."

"Oh, I wasn't suggesting—"

"People might think he's old, but it's just the white hair. He's real capable. Spry almost, and he's got a genuine love of life."

"My Uncle Floyd is like that."

"Wilfred's the reason I've got this red hair." She paused just long enough to chomp down on her fourth cookie. "It used to be brown as a mouse fart, but that didn't bother Wilfred none. Even then, he called me his Cherry-berry. Say, if you've got any more of that tea, I'll take another cup."

Louise dropped a tea bag into the cup and poured hot water over it.

"Thanks." Cherry swallowed a gulp of tea then said. "What about you?"

"Me?" Louise replied.

"Yeah." Cherry stuffed the last Lorna Doone in her mouth. "You ain't yet mentioned your name."

After a moment of hesitation, Louise said, "It's not my given name, but I prefer to be called Penny." The image of a woman called Penny was felt far more gratifying than that of a Squeezie swaddled in toilet paper. Penny would wear a copper-colored silk dress, the sort that swished and swayed with every movement.

"So, Penny's your middle name?"

"No, it's just sort of a nickname." Thinking out loud she said, "I have this thing about two-of-a-kind initials being lucky—so, Penny Palmer."

"Lucky for you, maybe," Cherry said, laughing, "but you sure wouldn't want mine. Mabel Melinski, that's what it was. Who in their right mind would give up a name like Cherry to be called Mabel Melinski?"

"Well, I don't know," Louise said, thinking how she would do almost anything to have the good fortune of matching initials. Then she remembered Billie, who despite her double initials was now suspected of murder. And Bradley, born with double initials, yet his mother was dead and his wife missing. Louise wondered if perhaps misfortune did occasionally strike people with double initials. Probably not as often, she thought and reasoned that she'd have stayed with Mabel if she were Cherry Melinski.

It was close to evening before Louise finished wiping down the cupboards, scouring the countertops, and putting the last of the groceries away. It was late spring, a time when days stretched out longer and people forgot it was past dinnertime.

Feeling the rumble of her stomach, Louise pulled a cast iron skillet from the drawer beneath the oven and took out a package of pork chops. The thought of plain fried pork chops didn't appeal to her in the least, but what could she do? There was no can of seasoned breadcrumbs on the shelf, no potted herb garden on the kitchen windowsill. Everything she owned—the dishes, pots and pans, even the oregano—was in the back of Fatso's moving van, somewhere in Alabama or Georgia maybe. She was lucky to have found the skillet. When the chops began to sizzle, she opened the back door and called out, "Almost time for supper."

"Ten minutes," Clay answered, twisting the last leg of the table into place.

Louise stood and watched. The muscles in his face looked relaxed, not the rock hard knots they sometimes were. He seemed a picture of contentment, focused on his work and all the while whistling and humming—not a tune she could name, just a few bars of some obscure song, then a studied look at the table, then a few more bars. He ignored the red sun sliding behind the horizon.

For a long while she remained there, trying to recall when she'd last seen him so satisfied with what he was doing. As best she could remember, it was the day he'd planted the sapling in front of their house in Westfield, twenty—no, thirty years ago, before the sapling became a towering oak. With a sigh of sadness Louise wondered why such peaceful moments had to be stretched so far apart. She turned back to the kitchen, picked two green plates from the cupboard, and set them on the linoleum tabletop.

Moments later Clay called, "Hey, Lou, come look at this!"

She poked her head out the door and there he was, sticky with sweat but beaming with pride as he stood behind the table and all four chairs. "Looks great, huh?"

"Yes, it looks great," Louise answered. She gave him a smile and tried not to let her disappointment show. She'd hoped that assembling the lawn furniture would be enough to dissuade him from the renovations he planned, but it had gone the other way. He seemed more energized than ever.

"See?" he said proudly. "Once I set my mind to a thing, I'm perfectly capable."

"I thought you would be," she said wistfully. "Come wash up. Dinner's ready."

"Now that we've got lawn furniture, why don't we eat out here?"

"With all these bugs?"

Slapping at his arm, Clay replied, "What bugs?"

Too weary to launch a protest, Louise reluctantly carried the plate of pork chops to the newly-assembled table then settled herself in a chair.

"You know," Clay said, scooping a pile of cold potato salad onto his plate, "I think I'm gonna be good at this handyman stuff."

Louise began searching for an answer when Yoo jumped to his feet and went flying into the hedge of hibiscus.

"Shoo, shoo," Cherry Melinski shrilled as she popped through the bush, this time snapping the dog's nose with a spray of leaves. She glanced at Louise and nervously asked, "Are you *sure* he likes me?"

"I believe so, but then one never knows a dog's mind." Louise didn't want to go overboard making their neighbor feel welcome. Not that she believed it would make a difference, since Cherry was obviously the sort to barge in anyway.

Sure enough, clip-clopping her way across the patio, Cherry wrapped her chubby little arms around Clay and squealed, "Ooh, just look at those brown eyes!"

Louise nearly choked on her pork chop.

Once he shook himself free, Clay said, "I don't believe I caught your name."

"Melinski, Cherry Melinski." She pointed a finger at her bright red hair then jabbed an elbow into Clay's rib. "Cherry, get it?" She guffawed, slapped a hand against her thigh, and then plopped down in a chair. "Did I mention how we got this card club that meets on Tuesdays?" she asked Louise.

"Yes, you did. It's called Hands Down, right?"

"You got a good memory." Cherry beamed. "If you wanna win at cards, you gotta have a good memory."

"Well, you mentioned it just this afternoon."

"You can't win a dime if you don't remember what cards are played."

"I wouldn't know about that. I'm really not a gambler."

"Gambler? Why, Hands Down is not a gambler's club. We get together for lunch and a bit of socializing. Cards, well now, that's just a harmless pastime."

"I didn't mean to infer—"

"No harm done. Anyway, I told the girls I'd be bringing my new neighbor, so mark it down on your calendar. Tuesday, eleven o'clock."

"Hmm, Tuesday," Louise searched her mind for a way out. From day one Aunt Rose had insisted she respect the feelings of others and accept invitations graciously. It was stuck in her head like the memory of the yellow house. Good or bad, one didn't easily forget these things. "Well, I'd love to, but I have a considerable amount of cleaning left, and I don't really think—"

"Cleaning?" Cherry spit the word as if it had a bitter taste. "Cleaning's something that can wait. You need to meet your neighbors."

Clay nodded and looked over at Louise. "Cherry's right," he said. "You should go and let her introduce you to some new friends."

Louise didn't want new friends. She had friends, friends who were waiting for her to come back to New Jersey. "I don't think this Tuesday—" she answered icily.

"I ain't taking no for no answer!" Cherry said, slamming her fist down emphatically. "You're coming, and that's that."

The newly-assembled table began to wobble, and Clay steadied it. "I probably need to tighten those screws," he said pensively.

Ignoring him, Cherry continued. "Not that we're gamblers, but you ought to bring money," she told Louise. "Ten dollars at least. And a casserole or salad maybe. Nothing with seeds, 'cause Bernie has a problem with her gall bladder. No garlic either, on account of Elsie." As she spoke Cherry peered over at Clay's plate. "Those chops look awfully plain. They could probably use a bit of parsley."

When Cherry finally left, they went inside. While Louise washed the dishes, Clay began to fidget with the clunky square box television. He adjusted and re-adjusted the rabbit ears until a snowy picture appeared on the screen; then he settled onto the sofa. "Louise," he called, "I've got 'Law and Order' on, you want to come and watch it?"

He got no answer from the kitchen. First a single tear rolled from Louise's eye; then it became a stream that cascaded down her cheeks and kerplunked into the sudsy dishwater. How was it, she wondered, that he could be so totally unobservant about her feelings? He must have noticed the icy glares she'd given him. He had to have felt the under-the-table kick she'd given his shin when he insisted she go to Cherry Melinski's card club. She'd tried to decline the invitation gracefully, but instead of helping her he'd sided with the loud-mouthed redhead. Was he being deliberately thoughtless or simply had no understanding of the situation? Louise was certain it was the latter. Clay wasn't a person to be deliberately mean.

Louise thought back to the time Clay asked about having a fellow from the bank move in with them while his apartment was being remodeled. "I'd prefer you didn't," is what she'd answered. But that very evening the man showed up with eight suitcases and his stereo set. "Thanks for having me," he'd said, then marched himself right up to the guest room and settled in. When she accused Clay of ignoring her request, he claimed she'd never said *not* to invite the fellow, she'd only said she'd *prefer* he didn't.

Obviously, there were times when more than a subtle suggestion was needed.

When she finished the dishes, Louise dried her eyes and joined Clay in the living room. She lowered herself onto the far end of the sofa, leaving a wide space between them. Unfortunately, that cushion had a broken spring, and no matter how she wriggled or moved about the sharp edge of the spring jabbed at her. Eventually she slid over to the center of sofa, which placed her right next to Clay.

"Isn't this cozy?" he said and wrapped his arm around her.

"There's a broken spring in that cushion," she answered.

"Sure there is." Clay chuckled and gave her shoulder a squeeze. "I know you've been upset about not being able to get in touch with Billie, but now that you've found a friend—"

"Friend?"

"Cherry."

"She's not my friend!"

Clay gave a smug grin as if to say he knew better.

"She came over here, uninvited. I knew those pork chops needed parsley, and I don't appreciate some busybody coming over here to tell me so!" Louise huffed.

The CFLX weatherman ran his pointer along the eastern coastline. "It's right here," he said. "A mass of cold air is edging its way down from the Carolinas. And later tonight it's going to push up against the warm front," he moved the pointer to the tip of Florida. "Looks like tomorrow we'll have showers well into afternoon."

"That's okay," Clay said to the television. "Let it rain. I'll be inside painting all day tomorrow."

"And now for the five-day forecast..."

"She's not my friend," Louise repeated. "I don't even like her."

"Okay, have it your way. Don't go to the card game."

"I don't like anything about this place."

"Haven't we already had this discussion?" Clay looked at her quizzically, as if he thought she might have missed a part of their earlier conversation. "Remember? I told you it'll look better after it's painted."

"It won't feel better."

"I'll start with the kitchen. First the walls, then the cabinets. Once the kitchen's painted—"

"It won't smell better."

"Sure it will. Maybe we ought to think about a new stove."

"I miss the kids."

"And we definitely should get a grill. Food always tastes better when it's cooked over charcoal briquettes. Cousin Stanley, he knows how to make a steak—grills it black on the outside, bloody red in the middle."

"I miss my friends, and I'm really worried about Billie."

"Then we've got that yellow paint for the bedroom..."

"I don't want you to paint anything! I don't want to stay here. I want to go back to New Jersey."

"Don't be ridiculous. Our furniture is halfway to Florida."

"We can send it back again."

"I'm not sending anything back! I'm gonna fix up this house, and we're staying here." Then without missing a beat he reminded her they'd also need new hinges for the screen door.

He wasn't listening. Once again, he simply wasn't listening. "I don't want to live in the same house as that horrible glass-eyed fish!" Louise shouted, flinging out an arm to point at the mounted fish that was supposedly Uncle Charlie's triumph.

"All right," Clay answered angrily. Reaching across her shoulder, he yanked the catfish from the wall, opened the front door, and hurled the trophy out into the yard. "Okay now?" he asked and stomped off towards the bedroom.

Louise remained on the sofa, her back rigid and tears returning to her eyes. Moments later another spring popped loose and jabbed her thigh.

Hours passed before Louise clicked off the television and went into the bedroom. At first she thought Clay was asleep, but when she crawled into bed he casually mumbled, "I'm sorry" without ever turning to face her.

She might have found a measure of solace in those words if she believed they came from his heart, but Louise knew better. They were simply loose words tossed out to placate her, his way of ending an argument. He'd done it thousands of times before—said he was sorry when obviously he wasn't. It was little more than a polite gesture, the sort of thing you'd say if you stepped on a stranger's toe. Clay's sorry sounded like a please or thank you, a courtesy to smooth the harshness of reality. Even if he'd made a heartfelt apology, what was it worth if he was determined to make her live the life *he* wanted?

Without answering him Louise turned over, her face to the wall. She wanted to close her eyes and find the oblivion of sleep, a place where there were no thoughts of Clay, or Cherry Melinski, or Uncle Charlie's house. A place where she could walk away from the quicksand of Florida, quicksand that took hold of a person and wouldn't let go. She squeezed her eyes shut and tried to think of things that made her happy, but they were all back in New Jersey.

Louise remembered the unfinished quilt she'd set aside last November. Every patch symbolized somebody or something important in her life, yet she'd stuffed it in a carton with no special wrapping to protect it. That quilt would have one day been a gift for Mandy, a family heirloom to pass along to her own grandchildren. But now…

Louise lay awake in the wee hours of morning when the rat-tat-tat of rain first began drumming against the tin roof. It started as a gentle patter; then the wind came up, roared through the piney scrub brush, and rattled the drainpipe against the house. Soon a crack of thunder boomed, not immediately overhead but somewhere close by. Moments later lightning lit up the sky and a downpour started. Louise climbed from the bed and tiptoed to the window. She wiped off a patch of condensation and peered into the night. Beyond the pane she saw only darkness and a splash of water overflowing the gutter. In the distance she could hear the caw of a bird. Nothing like the gentle sound of the sparrows that nested in their old oak tree but a screech, harsh and grating like this place.

Near dawn she finally drifted off to sleep.

Louise

The summer before I turned nine, Daddy moved us to Georgia and we lived in a cabin bumped up against a long row of other cabins as small and ugly as ours. If you opened the window even a crack, you could smell the swamp. Claudette and her husband lived two doors down. Claudette could handle most anything—a drunk husband, a fired-off shotgun, even the loud-mouthed motel owner who threatened to throw them out when the week's rent hadn't been paid.

The only thing that scared Claudette was snakes, and she was deathly afraid of them. She wouldn't even wear sandals for fear of a water moccasin catching her on the toe. Claudette used to tell us that she had descended from Cleopatra, and she knew one day an asp would get her the same as it got her ancestor.

Right now I'm as fearful of being here as Claudette was of snakes. I see myself slipping right back into the sort of life we had with Daddy. And the truth is, that life isn't a life at all. It's barely an existence. Mama never had one friend. All she had was me and Daddy, and I know she was none too happy about having me. Mama couldn't have friends because we were always on the move, but me—well, Billie Butterman has been my best friend since high school. Now she's in trouble, and I'm not there to help her. I feel like I'm turning a deaf ear to her, just the same as Clay is turning a deaf ear to me. How can he even suggest that a haphazard woman like Cherry Melinski could ever replace Billie? When something is as wrong as this, nobody understands. They just laugh and say your fear is groundless.

That's exactly what they did to Claudette, and yet one August night when she'd downed a glass of whiskey so she could get some shut-eye a Burmese Python slithered through the cabin window and squeezed the life out of her.

The sheriff said it was a freak accident. He said that snake was probably a pet somebody had let loose in the swamp, but that doesn't explain how Claudette always knew it was coming for her.

I say when such a feeling settles inside of you, it's time to listen.

The Found Fish

At one time Louise used to wish Clay would take a greater interest in the house—help out with the chores, put up storm windows, clean gutters, trim hedges—do the things that Claire and Myrtle's husbands did willingly. Instead Clay would settle into the backyard hammock, his nose in a book or newspaper. How she missed that hammock, missed the sight of him sound asleep with his head nodding against his shoulder and the book flopped lopsidedly across his chest.

He had suddenly become a man of purpose. Not production, just purpose. He rose at dawn and filled the room with the smell of paint before she could even gulp down the first cup of coffee.

Ordinarily she could deal with it. As small as the house was, Louise figured he'd finish in a day or two, but nearly a week had gone by and with each passing day the place became more of a disaster.

On the first day, Clay hauled everything out of the kitchen cupboards and piled it in the center of the floor. He then painted two cabinets and said that was probably enough for one day. After he'd spent an hour cleaning the brushes he'd used to paint for the half-hour, he took a nap. The next day he opened a fresh can of paint and left it hanging off the edge of the ladder. Minutes later the ladder toppled and sent paint splattering all over the green linoleum. It took nearly three hours to mop up the mess. By then he'd decided the kitchen could do with a new tile floor anyway, so he spent another hour measuring the room and calculating how many twelve-inch squares he'd need for the job. Once he'd gotten that out of the way, he said he'd worked up quite an appetite and asked Louise to make him a sandwich.

Clay tore into one project after the other but never finished any of them. He'd paint half a wall, then wander away saying the screen door needed a new hinge. Once the door got stuck in a position where it would neither open nor close, he headed off to attend to the drip in the bathroom faucet. "I'm retired," he'd tell the neighbors. "So what's the rush?" Then he'd invite them in to see the work he'd done. Every time another person came by, Clay stopped what he was doing and sat down for a chat. "Why don't we all have a cup of coffee?" he'd suggest to Louise, or else he'd haul a load of food out of the refrigerator and say it was nearing lunchtime anyway.

Cherry Melinski came over every single day. One day she got there so early that Clay was still walking around in his underwear. "Oh, don't mind me," she said. "I've seen plenty of men's underwear." She then marched herself into the kitchen and started the coffee. About nine-thirty each morning Cherry went home to make Wilfred's breakfast but within the hour she came back, standing around watching Clay paint. "You've missed a spot," she'd tell him, and he'd clamber back up the ladder and dab his brush at the wall.

"Better now?" he'd ask.

"Hmmm. Give it one more swab," she'd answer, then point out another obscure little spot halfway across the room. A dozen times she mentioned how Wilfred thought Ernie could get the job done faster.

Eventually, even the neighbors who lived blocks away began to stop by. They came with Jell-O molds, zucchini casseroles, and already-baked Mrs. Smith's pies. One morning Cassandra Willoughby, a slender woman who lived all the way down by the clubhouse, rapped on the front door carrying a box of doughnuts. She plunked them down on the table and slipped into a chair. "Don't let me touch a crumb," she said. "I'm watching myself." For nearly two hours she hungrily eyed the doughnuts but stuck to black coffee. "Don't misunderstand," she repeated time and again, "it's not that I really need to diet. Pool exercise is what keeps me in shape."

"Do tell," Louise answered impatiently as she bit into a crumb bun.

"Pool exercise, huh?" Clay lowered himself into the chair beside Cassandra and listened attentively as she described every foot roll and leg lift of the program. She was still demonstrating the shoulder shrug when Reverend Horchum arrived.

Like most of the area folks, Horace Horchum did not stand on ceremony but trotted through the still-stuck-open screen door and wandered into the living room calling out, "Anybody home?" When he saw Louise, the reverend, a man as wide as he was tall, broke open a toothy smile, and dimples the size of sinkholes dented his cheeks. "A blessing on your home," he said and waddled off to the kitchen.

Louise set out a fourth cup and the reverend quickly scooted into the chair beside Clay, mumbling something about God blessing this food, then helping himself to a cream-filled doughnut. He was not only a man of God but also one of enormous appetite. He polished off a cinnamon bun, two jelly doughnuts, and a powdered cruller before he invited them to Sunday services and stood to leave.

"Lord of the Land Church," he said. "Just follow the road that runs past the old Henderson farm till you come to the stop sign, then turn right. Can't miss it." He smiled. "Ten-thirty, but we don't always start on the dot."

Not long after the reverend, Beulah Mason came with her strawberry swirl cheesecake. Then the Feingold twins, small round women who dressed alike and anticipated each other's thoughts. "Please pass—" Ernestine would say, but before she completed the sentence, Emma would hand her a napkin, a fork, or whatever else she might have intended to mention. They both sat with their right ankle politely crossed over the left, each used one spoonful of sugar and a dash of cream, stirred their coffee in precisely the same manner, chose the same type of doughnut, even smiled in synchronization. Louise eyed the twins, waiting for one to do something without the other, but it didn't happen. Ernestine even said "Bless you" before Emma sneezed. They were two clocks ticking simultaneously, neither missing a beat. When they finally stood to leave, together of course, Louise breathed a sigh of relief and hoped she'd seen the last of the neighbors.

Unfortunately she hadn't.

Close to noon a gangly string bean of a man ambled up the Palmers' walkway. He had a fringe of snow-white hair and a forehead that extended halfway across the crown of his head. A deep-set frown wrinkled his face from ear to ear as he eyed the house disapprovingly, then rapped on the frame beside the stuck-open screen door.

Clay looked up from his paintbrush. "Hi, there."

"You Charlie's nephew?" the man asked, mincing no words.

"Yes, yes I am."

"Monroe Schramm," the old man announced, as if Clay should know him.

"Monroe Schramm?"

"Yes, sir."

Clay motioned the man to come inside. "Something cold to drink?" he asked.

"Can't do that," Monroe answered. "Not with you."

Clay looked at him with a bewildered expression, "I don't think I—"

"Used to be I'd flop down on that sofa and have myself a cold beer, but no more." He shook his head. "Unh-unh, no more."

"Well, then, a soda? Lemonade?"

"Nope. I come here for one reason and one reason only."

"Huh?"

"I wanna know what happened to Charlie's catfish." Monroe pointed across the room to the rectangle of lighter paint, the area sheltered from years of exposure to dust and smoke, the pale patch that marked the spot where the trophy had been removed. "The catfish that's been hanging on that wall for the past seven years. The catfish that was Charlie Palmer's pride and joy."

"Well now, that—" Clay got a moment's reprieve by the fact that Louise, having heard the raised voice, walked into the room. "Louise, dear, this is Monroe Schramm. Monroe, I take it, was a friend of Uncle Charlie."

"Hello," she said, wiping the dirt from her hand and extending it.

Monroe made no move to accept the gesture but instead glared at Louise. "I want to know what happened to Charlie's catfish."

"Well, now—" Clay repeated, shifting his eyes toward Louise in a silent plea for her to come up with an answer.

Louise stood there looking right back at him but not saying a word.

"Oh, now I know what you mean. The prize catfish, the one Uncle Charlie had mounted." Clay's voice had the edginess of a person who was lying.

"That's the one." Monroe nodded.

"Well, we think the world of that catfish, but with all this renovation going on we didn't want to take a chance on getting it damaged, so Louise stored it away, safe from harm."

Louise's mouth flew open. "Me?"

"Okay then." Monroe turned to Louise, reached into the flowered pillowcase he had brought with him, and pulled out the catfish trophy. "Just how do you explain this?"

"Where did you—"

"It was out by the curb. Tossed away like trash. A thing like this would've broke Charlie Palmer's heart. Broke his heart, I say."

"It couldn't possibly be the same—"

"It's Charlie's catfish all right. See them yellow spots? Right there, right beneath the gill? I ain't ever seen but one fish with them markings. I was with Charlie the day he caught this beauty. Proudest moment of his life. Then you go and—"

"Oh no," Clay said. "Not in a million years. Louise loves that catfish as much as I do, why, she would never—"

She nodded in agreement, even though instinct warned her that the fish would end up right back on the wall, winking its glass eye. "This must've been an accident," she said. "Maybe the dog got hold of it and carried it outside." She turned to Yoo and pretended to admonish him as she affectionately scruffed his ear. "That was a naughty, naughty thing to do," she said in a honeysuckle sort of voice. But Yoo just stood there wagging his tail and waiting for a treat.

"That must be what happened!" Clay said, eagerly pouncing on the thought.

"See," Louise said, pointing to an obscure knick, "there's a tooth mark, right here on the edge of the frame."

Monroe bent over and took a closer look. "Might be..."

"That's definitely it," Clay insisted. He turned to Yoo. "Bad dog," he said in an angry tone. The dog tucked his tail between his legs and lowered his head to the floor. Louise gave Clay a glare that made him to decide to leave it at that.

"Hmm. Let's see if I've got this straight," Monroe said. "You're telling me that old yellow-spot is going back on the wall?"

Louise hoped they'd be able to dance around that issue, but before she had the chance to say anything, Clay answered, "Absolutely."

"Well, then," Monroe said with a smile, "reckon I'll have that cold beer after all." He handed Clay the plaque, then settled in the recliner. His beanpole legs stretched out into the room.

Although Louise was none too happy that Monroe had returned the glass-eyed fish, she neither liked nor disliked him any more than the other neighbors. She simply wished he'd leave so Clay would get back to work and finish painting the living room.

Instead, Clay wiped the paint from his hands and settled onto the sofa. "So," he said, "you and Uncle Charlie were friends?"

"Best friends. Most every day we fished over on Snake Lake. That's where—"

Like one of the Feingold twins, Clay completed Monroe's sentence, "Charlie caught old yellow spot."

"Yes, indeed." Monroe rubbed his forehead thoughtfully. "I tell you that story?"

"Sort of."

"Good old Charlie. Now that he's gone, I don't fish much anymore."

"Don't fish?" Clay said his eyes wide with amazement.

"Nope. No more."

"You mean you gave up fishing?"

"No fun alone. Without Charlie, I'd sooner stay home and watch game shows."

"My uncle wouldn't want that. He'd be the first one to say go fishing with somebody else. You've got to do it. If for no other reason, you've got to do it for Uncle Charlie."

"There's nobody else. It was just the two of us, that's it." Monroe's faced saddened. "Now that Charlie's gone…"

"I'll go. I'll go fishing with you." Clay spotted the look on Louise's face and then backed off. "Um, the thing is, at the moment I'm in a bit of a mess, and there's a lot of painting that needs to get done."

"Bit of a mess?" Monroe shook his head disapprovingly. "Why, these windows are covered with splatters."

"This paint splashes a lot."

"There's streaks all over."

"It may need two coats."

"You ain't even half-finished."

"I can see that."

"If I was you, I'd call Ernie Tobias."

Just as Monroe finished up to tell about how Ernie could do it better and faster, Louise excused herself saying she had to dash over to Worthmore to pick up a few things at Bigwig. She backed out of the driveway, a little uncertain about the directions for getting there, but when Cherry Melinski turned up their walk Louise gave a quick wave and stepped on the accelerator.

The first part of the route seemed easy enough to follow, since she had gone this way before. At the blue farmhouse she made a right onto Route 411, but somewhere after that she went wrong. Last time the trip took about twenty minutes, but today Louise drove for nearly an hour and didn't see a single sign of Worthmore. Once she'd reached the point where nothing looked the least bit familiar, she began to worry she'd gotten lost. Even with the air conditioning rattling at full speed, beads of perspiration began to trickle down her back. Before long her shirt was soaking wet and her hands stuck to the steering wheel.

Louise didn't generally have this much trouble finding her way to some new place, but then back in New Jersey a person could use street signs and road maps. Here she saw nothing but a narrow winding road without any indication of where it headed. Three times she could have sworn she spotted a sign up ahead, but each time it turned out to be an advertisement or another bunch of brown and white cows. Eventually she made a U-turn and headed back.

She drove for almost thirty minutes before she spotted it on the opposite side of the road—a billboard reading "MOOre's Dairy Farm, one mile past Worthmore." The grinning white-faced cow pointed its hoof to the right. "Thank heaven," Louise murmured, and suddenly the air conditioner started working a bit more effectively.

When Louise finally made it to Worthmore, she stepped out of the car and realized that she stood all alone in a strange little town. She didn't feel comfortable with it, and it angered her that she felt that way. *Billie would never be such a wimp*, she thought. *Billie would march into town and...* Louise suddenly squared her shoulders and walked toward the Bluebird Ladies Wear Shoppe. No one in this town knew her. She didn't have to be Squeezie. She could be Billie Butterman if she wanted to. Feeling several inches taller than she did minutes earlier, she strolled into the shop and said, "I'm looking for a blue shirt like the one in the window, only with sleeves."

"We have it in yellow."

"Yellow?" Louise wrinkled her nose disdainfully. She was now a woman of confidence who traveled alone and would settle for nothing less than blue. Had she been herself, she might not have purchased the youthful looking shirt, but as Billie she bought the sleeveless blue top and matching shorts that barely reached mid-way down her thigh.

Once she'd slipped into her new persona Louise felt far too good to waste the day just going to Bigwig, so after leaving the Bluebird she strolled in and out of the other shops along the street. The Drug Depot, Pet Pleasures, The Book Emporium, which hardly deserved to be called an emporium since it was little more than an alleyway of shelves with a scattering of paperbacks. In Grandma's Gingham Shop she bought a blue checked potholder and a worn edition of *Cooking with Key Limes* for fifty cents. She stopped at the Snack Shack for an iced tea, then sauntered leisurely past the optometrist. It was almost four o'clock when she remembered needing rubber gloves and cleaning supplies.

Once again Bert stood at the Bigwig checkout counter. "So, I hear you got Ernie working at your place," he said.

"No. No, he's not," Louise answered in her crisp Billie Butterman voice. "This time the grapevine is absolutely wrong."

"Well, I'll be," He snapped open a plastic bag and loaded in two bottles of Lysol. "I could swear Marty said that Ernie—"

"Unh-unh," Louise interrupted. "He's not." They'd lived in Tall Pines for less than five days, and it was downright presumptuous for Bert to think he knew everything about their business. A New Jersey shopkeeper would never have taken such liberties. Louise crooked her mouth with a smug smile of satisfaction. "Oh, and by the way, I would prefer not to have those handles tied." Billie Butterman would have probably left it at that, but she apologetically added, "It makes them too hard to open."

"Okay," Bert said and pushed the first bag across the counter. "Not working there, huh?" he repeated and then absently looped a triple knot into the handle of the second bag. "Funny, I could've sworn..."

Louise grimaced at the knot then juggled the parcel into her free arm and strode off, leaving Bert with a bewildered look hugging his face.

The drive home took less than twenty minutes and went relatively smoothly since Louise now recognized the right road. She pulled into the driveway and beeped the horn, more from force of habit than truly expecting Clay to hurry out to help her with the bundles. The screen door stood slightly ajar but not cocked open as she had seen it earlier. *At last,* she thought, *he's finished something.* Her arms filled with bundles, Louise pried the door open with her foot, then backed in and turned around.

The door being fixed was a surprise, but the living room shocked her so much that Louise at first wondered if she'd stumbled into the wrong house. Every wall had been painted white as snow. There were no streaks, no puddles of paint on the floor. All of the furniture sat back in its proper place.

"My goodness," she gasped as she carried her bundles through to the kitchen. In the kitchen Louise stopped and blinked several times to make certain she was seeing what she thought she saw— the kitchen was also painted. Not just a single cupboard door or one wall, but the entire kitchen. Even the brass hardware had been polished and put back in place. She now felt a bit guilty about dilly-dallying through the shops while Clay stayed at home working.

As she put the groceries away she heard footsteps scuffling across the living room floor. "Clay?" she called out.

"No."

"No?" Leaving the Brillo pads on the counter, she turned toward the sound. "Clay?" she called again and trotted through the hallway just in time to see a lank-legged stranger with a baseball cap pulled low over his eyes crossing the living room with their television in his arms.

Without casting a sideways glance, the man carted the set out the door and down the walkway. For a second Louise felt so stunned she simply stood there with her mouth hanging open. She wanted to scream, but no sound came out. Once the intruder had moved a distance away Louise darted across the room, slammed the door shut, and flipped the deadbolt. Tall Pines wasn't Westfield, but up until now she'd believed it to be a safe enough neighborhood. Of course, that was before she'd come across someone robbing the house in broad daylight!

He'd already made off with the bedroom television, which didn't matter because it was broken anyway, but Louise was determined not to allow him back into the house. She rattled the door and checked the deadbolt. It was solid as a rock. Clay had repaired that also. "Good thing," she said, grumbling, and hurried back to the kitchen.

The kitchen door didn't have a deadbolt, just an open-close button. Louise pushed it to lock and then jammed a chair under the doorknob. She got ready to call the police when she remembered the box of jewelry in the top bureau drawer. She rushed into the bedroom, hopeful that the burglar hadn't discovered it.

Louise yanked open the drawer, but before she could rummage through Clay's underwear a voice called out, "Anybody here?"

She whirled around.

It was the burglar. The skinny stubble-faced man with ragged jeans and a M.A.S.H. tee shirt. "I ain't finished in here," he said.

"Take whatever you want, but don't kill me!"

"Huh?"

"Robbery is one thing, but murder someone and you'll die in the electric chair."

"You talking to me?" the burglar asked. He glanced back across his shoulder as if he expected there might be someone behind him.

"I'm a mother, a grandmother," she said. "What kind of a man would be heartless enough to kill a grandmother?"

"Not me. I wouldn't kill nobody."

"Fine. Take what you want and go."

"I don't want nothing."

"Burglars always want *something*!"

"I ain't no burglar."

"But—the television set?"

"Needs to be fixed. I was gonna bring it back tomorrow." He pointed an accusing finger at Louise. "You thought I was—"

"Well," she said, "if you're not a burglar, who are you?"

"Ernie Tobias."

"Ernie?"

"Tobias," he repeated.

"What are you doing here?"

"I'm supposed to help with the painting and fixing."

"Who said?"

"Monroe."

"Monroe Schramm?"

"Unh-huh."

"How'd you get in?"

"The first time I come through the front door. This time I came through the back window. I would've come through the door, 'cept the wind blowed it shut."

"Where's Clay?"

"He went fishing."

"Fishing?"

"With Monroe. Over to Snake Lake."

"You mean he left you here to do the work?"

"He's paying me," Ernie said indignantly. He turned away and then stopped as if something else had come to mind. "Oh, yeah," he added, "Mister Clay said never mind making dinner, he'd bring home some catfish."

"He needn't worry, I've no intention of making dinner." Louise replied.

Louise returned to the kitchen and dropped down onto the wobbly spindle back chair. She eyed the unopened bag from the Bluebird Shoppe. Whatever made her think she could be Billie Butterman? Billie had the capability to control her life. Billie deserved to wear sleeveless shirts and short shorts. With a sense of weariness of tugging at her, Louise took the unopened bag from the table and stashed it beneath a stack of dish towels.

The Outsider

Clay came home with a string of catfish. He also came home with Monroe and another friend, both of whom apparently had an invitation to stay for dinner. Louise had not met Bob before, a man with a belly that came through the door long before he did and small eyes squished into the pudgy folds of his face. At first glance he had the look of a man who might topple forward. Younger than Monroe, Bob was probably closer to Clay's age.

"Can't wait to sink my choppers into these babies," Bob said.

"Yep, these is sure gonna be good eatin'," Monroe agreed as he tromped through the living room with water sloshing over the sides of his fish pail.

Clay stopped beside the recliner long enough to plant a peck on the side of Louise's cheek. Then he followed the others into the kitchen. "Honey," he called back, "Bob's gonna show me how to clean these fish. Where's the big cutting board?"

There were several big cutting boards in the back of Fatso's truck, but she didn't remember ever seeing one in this house. Before she had a chance to answer Bob said, "The garage, second shelf on the right."

"Figures," Louise mumbled sadly. Apparently in Tall Pines everyone else knew the facts of your life before you did. It was the way they did things here. People wandered into each other's houses and stuck their noses into your business whether you wanted them to or not. Back in Westfield people wouldn't dream of visiting without an invitation. Why, not even her best friends strolled in unannounced. They respected people's privacy. Ida was the lone exception. She acted as a broadcasting system for everything that happened in the neighborhood.

Louise folded her arms across her chest and pushed back in the recliner. "I want no part of this," she said petulantly to herself.

"If Clay wants to feed those men, he can do it." She settled deeper into the recliner.

Moments later Cherry Melinski came through the front door with a wide smile stretched across her face. "I hear the boys caught themselves a mess of catfish," she said. "Nothing my Wilfred loves better than fresh-caught catfish."

"I don't care for it myself," Louise responded unenthusiastically.

"You haven't had it with my seasoned cracker meal." Cherry rolled her eyes and licked at her lips in anticipation. "I'll get some so they can cook it up proper. I'll fetch us a few beers too. Nothing's better than ice cold beer with fried catfish."

"Oh that's not—"

Before Louise could finish her sentence, Cherry whirled on her heels and hurried out the door. Moments later she came back with a plastic bag of cracker meal and a twelve-pack of Budweiser. "Here you go," she said and stretched out her arm.

"This really wasn't necessary," Louise replied and allowed the bag of cracker meal to be placed in her hand, which was something she probably shouldn't have done. Billie Butterman would have accepted the beer, said thank you, and been done with it. But the sad truth was that no matter how hard she tried, Louise wasn't a Billie Butterman and she never would be. She could pretend for a few hours, perhaps even a day, but when day turned to night or dark turned to dawn like Cinderella she would once again return to her sorry self. With a weary smile Louise said, "Why don't you and Wilfred join us?"

Cherry's face lit up brighter than her hair. "Well, okay," she said. "If you're sure we won't be no trouble." Without waiting for an answer, she hurried back to the door and shouted, "It's okay, Will, come on over."

The next thing Louise knew she stood in the kitchen, setting out six of the least-chipped dishes and chopping a head of cabbage while everyone else squeezed around the table talking about the "really big one" that got away. "If it weren't for that line snapping, I'd've had him for sure," Monroe boasted.

The others nodded their agreement.

For a fleeting moment Louise hoped this would be like the evenings in Westfield, evenings when she'd entertained Billie or Claire or Myrtle. But it wasn't. No one offered to pitch in, help set the table, take out the mayonnaise, or arrange the pickles on a plate. No one commented on the colorful bits of carrot she grated into the coleslaw or asked for the recipe. Instead they chattered on about things like night crawlers and weighted lures, ignoring her completely.

"Down past the cove," Monroe said. "That's where the big ones are."

"No, no," Wilfred argued. "It's back by the dock."

Bob agreed with Monroe and went on to tell them that out by the edge of the swamp Ernie once caught a catfish the size of a baby hog.

"Ernie," Louise replied cynically. "He obviously knows something about everything."

All five faces turned and looked at her. "Why Ernie don't know a thing about fishing," Monroe said. "He knows painting and fixing, but he don't know fishing!"

"He got lucky that one time," Bob explained.

"But painting and fixing's something Ernie knows real well," Cherry declared. "You should have seen the mess this place was in before Ernie got here."

Although she felt left out of the conversation, Louise could find no way to become a part of it. While they talked she listened, puttering about the kitchen, swiping at the counter and setting out bowls of chips and pretzels. Once she asked Cherry if she'd like a glass for her beer, but Cherry just shook her head and went on with whatever she'd been talking about. Louise sighed, thinking how Aunt Rose would break out in hives at the very thought of a woman drinking beer straight from a can.

To Louise's way of thinking, they were a strange group—Cherry as rowdy as the men, leaning back in her chair, guffawing at their jokes and sucking down can after can of beer. A woman who after the third beer challenged Bob to arm-wrestle, then plopped a sizeable portion of her breast onto the edge of the table and won two out of three. Flamboyant as she was, Monroe was the opposite. A solemn sort dressed head to toe in a color that was not black, brown, or gray but some faded version of what at one time could have been any of the three. He had a hard-set mouth and eyes that told nothing about what was going on inside his head. Not someone you could warm to easily.

Bob and Wilfred seemed pleasant enough. Then there was Clay. He was perhaps the most puzzling of all. Louise always thought she knew him inside and out, knew what made him tick, what he'd like or dislike. But suddenly he'd become this stranger who did things her Clay would never do. Her Clay was a reserved man who didn't care for small talk, someone who settled down behind the evening newspaper and bothered with few, if any, friends. Yet here he was, back-slapping along with the rest of them.

Louise fried up three skillets of catfish, then set the platter on the table along with the bowl of coleslaw and a whole plate of sliced tomatoes. "Um-um," Cherry said, reaching with her fingers to grab up a chunk of fried fish. Monroe and Wilfred did the same. Bob hand-shoveled a goodly amount from the platter onto his plate, and Clay, who used his fork for the first few bites, eventually switched over to picking up the greasy fish in his fingers like everyone else. Regardless of what anybody else did Louise believed in proper table manners, so with her knife and fork neatly positioned across the top of her plate she politely handed out another round of napkins.

Anxious for the evening to end, Louise stood and began clearing the table before the food was half-gone.

"Hold up there," Cherry said and latched onto another slab of catfish.

"Yeah," Monroe echoed. "Them end pieces is the best part."

Louise set the catfish back on the table and waited while they picked the platter clean. She expected that once the food was gone everyone would head off home, but they didn't. They stayed and drank more beer. The sky turned red, then purple, then darkened altogether, and they simply moved from the kitchen table to the back patio. Occasionally someone jumped up to swat a mosquito or swish a gnat away, but it never changed the pace of conversation. It seemed they didn't mind the mugginess of the night or the swarms of bugs buzzing in their ears. The moon was full when Cherry got up to fetch a citronella candle and another pack of Budweiser.

Hours later, when even the shadow of the pines disappeared into the blackness of night, the group finally left. The Melinskis were the last to go. Waddling across the lawn to her own house, Cherry called back, "Don't forget, next Tuesday's card club."

"I doubt I'll be able to make it," Louise said and closed the door.

Since she'd not been a part of the conversation, Louise had cleaned up the kitchen while the rest of the group sat out back discussing where the big fish could be found and exactly what went into Cherry's seasoned cracker meal. With the dishes already washed and everything put away, she headed for the bedroom as soon as the Melinskis were out of sight.

Clay lay in bed by the time she pulled her gown over her head. "'Night," he said and snapped out the light.

"Wait a minute." Louise clicked the switch back on. "We've got things to talk about."

"Okay, I'm sorry. I should've told you I'd hired Ernie to do the painting."

The way he jumped right to an apology about Ernie threw her off guard and caused her to forget the speech she'd prepared. "That's it?" she said. "That's it? You're sorry you forgot to tell me about Ernie?"

"It was a simple mistake."

"This is not just about Ernie. It's about this place. It's about all these people. They're nothing like our friends back home. They're strange, different."

"I said I'm sorry."

"For once in your life, stop and listen to me! This is about more than you forgetting to tell me you'd hired a handyman. It's about everything that—"

He interrupted her by shouting, "What now?" Perhaps he intended it as a question, but the words flew across the room like a spear of intolerance.

"What now?" she shouted back. "The 'what now' is that I hate this place! I don't belong here, I'm not part of anything, and I don't like these people."

"Well, I'm not giving up my friends just because you're unhappy!" Clay snapped off the light for a second time and slid down into the sheets. "You'll feel happier tomorrow when the furniture gets here."

"I won't," she said.

He didn't answer.

Louise left the light off this time, but she didn't slide down into the bed as Clay had. Instead she sat with her back pushed up against the headboard, staring out the window into the night. Darkness covered everything, even the tall pines, making it seem as if the tiny house was a world unto itself with nothing beyond its borders. After a long while she said, "Clay, I've got to go home." She got no answer.

Long into the night Louise thought about her life. She wondered why she'd allowed herself to become such a weak-willed person, someone without a spine, no opinions, almost no personality. She wasn't always this way. She could remember how the Material Girls used to say "Louise, you *must* give us the recipe for this dip; show us how you did that stitch; please, give us the name of your hairdresser." She belonged. She was part of something, a person who mattered. Now she belonged to nothing. She was simply a cleaning woman, a Cinderella to sweep the floor and scour the pots while others went to the ball. A stream of tears rolled down her face as she pictured her father and how he would snort, "She's your kid."

The memory of such a life stays with a person forever. It reminds you of all the times you had no one to turn to. It whispers in your ear that things aren't all that different now. It makes your heart ache with the wanting of a friend. Dawn had nearly arrived when Louise finally settled on an answer and closed her eyes.

Weighed down by the ache in her heart Louise ignored memories of the twenty-nine years she and Clay spent living in the same house and raising a family. She bypassed the good times and focused on the emptiness of leaving things behind. It was a strange coincidence, but Louise was a lot like her daddy. She sometimes saw things not as they were but how she perceived them to be. Occasionally that was a good thing; more often it was not.

When Louise awoke Clay's side of the bed was empty. She heard the pounding of a hammer and knew he was somewhere in the house, probably working on another project he would never finish, something he'd eventually call Ernie to do. She climbed out of bed and pulled on her baggy down-to-the-knee shorts. Her eyes were puffy and her shorts wrinkled, but that didn't matter anymore.

She pulled the travel tote from the back of the closet and loaded it with three sets of underwear, two pair of khaki shorts, some tops, a nightshirt, her makeup bag, and the red leash. She would have included the can of hairspray, but she didn't have enough room. She paused for a moment, then plucked a locket and her wedding ring from the jewelry box and slipped them into the side pocket. She zipped the bag closed, set it back in the closet, and went into the kitchen.

Louise fed the dog, then poured herself a cup of coffee and toasted an English muffin. It would be reasonable to think that after making such a monumental decision she'd have little or no appetite, but last night she'd hardly touched the fish and now her stomach grumbled. Apparently only thin people lost their appetite when they were upset; people who could stand to lose a few pounds never did.

She filled the coffee cup for a second time and settled back at the table. That's where she sat when Clay tromped in wearing his paint-splattered work clothes. "You seen the Phillips head screwdriver?" he asked. Without ever looking into her face he began to rummage through a bin of odd-sized nails and rusted tools. Had he looked up, had he focused on her, he might have seen her decision; he would have seen a stone-faced expression of indifference.

Louise didn't answer.

"You know which one I mean? A crisscross at the tip?"

"I know what it is," she said, her voice thin as tissue paper.

"Well, have you seen it?"

"No."

"I suppose Ernie's put it somewhere," Clay complained, then he shuffled out the door with a table knife in his hand. Moments later Louise loaded the tote bag and the dog into the car and backed out of the driveway. Clay never noticed her leaving.

She slammed her foot against the gas pedal and roared down the street, past the blue house, past the thatches of raggedy brush, past the "Welcome to Tall Pines" banner, and out onto the county road. When she whizzed past the red stop sign without even slowing, streams of tears began to trickle down her face. She glanced at the rearview mirror, telling herself she wanted to make certain no flashing red light followed close behind, but in truth she hoped to see Clay running after the car, waving his arms wildly and screaming, "Don't go, Louise! I love you! I'll do anything to make you happy!"

The only thing reflected in the mirror was Yoo's massive head, cocked to one side with the puzzled expression dogs sometimes have. "Come on up here, boy," she said with a sob and patted the seat. Yoo eagerly scrambled over the armrest and settled beside her. He was a living thing that actually wanted to be next to her. With that thought in her head, she slowed the car to forty, scruffed his head, and hugged him a bit closer. Together they began the trek across Route Sixty.

They traveled eastward for almost an hour before Louise noticed the storm coming from the south. In the upper right-hand corner of her windshield she spotted a row of black clouds churning across the sky. It was impossible to tell how far away they were, but they appeared to move rapidly. She pressed down on the gas pedal and took it up to sixty, hoping to outpace the rain. Yoo snuffed at the air and tensed. A big dog, he cowered at the sound of a storm. Already he'd sensed it. Maybe he'd caught the distant sound of thunder or a sudden change in air pressure. Yoo's ears flattened against his head, and he began panting as if in dire need of water.

"Relax, boy," Louise said. "We'll find someplace to stop."

She would have done so gladly, but this was the same route they'd come across on, a narrow single-lane road with blind curves and no shoulder, a road bordered by impenetrable patches of palmetto and barbed wire fences. Before she could find a place to turn off she saw the spiral of black clouds and a heavy curtain of rain coming from her right. *Maybe I can outrun it,* she told herself. She pressed hard on the gas pedal and the speedometer moved past seventy, inching its way up to eighty.

The first splat hit the windshield seconds later, not a raindrop but a bullet of water the size of an egg. It was too late for running and Louise knew it. She slowed and turned the wipers on. If only she hadn't taken time for breakfast she'd be on the interstate by now, a place with overpasses and dozens of rest stops. Why did she always do the wrong thing? She turned left when it should have been right, said yes when it should have been no, stayed when she should have gone, gone when she should have stayed. For the first time since she pulled out of the driveway the thought of turning around crossed Louise's mind, but with the rain now coming in torrents she pushed it aside.

Louise slowed her speed to thirty and reached over to comfort Yoo who was now shaking like the last leaf on a windblown tree.

Suddenly something pinged off of the hood. At first she thought it might be a loose pebble that had flown up, but then there was another on the roof, then another, and another. The sky turned black as night and within the span of a few heartbeats, a cascade of ice balls began battering the car. She clenched the steering wheel and prayed she wouldn't get caught up in a tornado. Yoo whimpered and crouched on the floor.

"It's okay," she said, trying to sound brave, but she doubted he heard her. The noise of the storm roared like an avalanche. She struggled to hold the car on the road but could barely see beyond the front bumper. She finally caught sight of the yellow line and focused her eye on it, which was why she didn't see the tractor trailer coming from the opposite direction.

Before Louise knew what hit her, a thundering sheet of water smacked the windshield and left her with no visibility. In a moment of panic she yanked the wheel to the right, causing the car to slide one way and then another. The tires skidded across the blacktop through the sloshy mud at the edge of a cow field and back onto the blacktop, so she slammed her foot down on the brake. The car veered to the left, then right, and when Louise tried to straighten it, the car spun out of control. When it finally came to a stop it sat crossways on the road, heading neither east nor west.

The engine had stopped, but the windshield wipers continued to swish back and forth. For a moment everything was a blur and Louise envisioned herself dead; then her foot began to quiver. Next her arms and legs trembled, and she jerked forward as the English muffin rumbled up into her throat. In a single instant her entire life had run through her brain. She had died five times and the world had twisted itself sideways, yet through it all the hail continued to beat against the windshield.

She swiped her hand across her face and twisted the ignition key. The motor whined a few times, coughed, and finally chugged to life. With the taste of coffee still pushing up in her throat, Louise inched the car around and headed east. She moved slower than a crawling baby, so slow that the speedometer hardly budged. In time, the hail switched back to rain and a flood of water cascaded down the windshield. Only now tears also flooded her eyes. Somehow she managed to keep moving until a car came up behind her, blasted its horn, and sped by. At that point Louise broke into heart-wrenching sobs.

"I'm doing the best I can," she cried, allowing the car to roll off of the road and into a cow pasture.

She waited there for the rain to pass. Even after the sky brightened and she saw nothing but a few wispy clouds overhead she sat there, her right foot too weary to press down the gas pedal and the muffin still twisting about in her stomach.

Louise

I've never been so afraid in my entire life. As I sit here shaking from head to toe, I ask myself why don't I just turn around and go back home. The answer almost breaks my heart. Clay, the man I've loved for the whole of my life, simply doesn't care whether or not I'm there. I'm invisible to him. He doesn't hear my words and doesn't see the pain on my face. He has a new life, and, sadly enough, I'm not part of it. I'm the winter jacket he's hung in the back of the closet—a thing that's useless but you're reluctant to get rid of.

Being needed is what gives a person a sense of worth. And right now the only person who really needs me is Billie. I know she's in trouble, or she would have called. I figure I'll find Billie and help her explain the truth to Bradley. Once he understands how good she was to his mother, he'll be quick to forgive her. If not, she can come back to Florida with me. God knows I could use a friend to talk to.

Clay's determined to stay here, and I've no desire to divorce him. Yes, I'm going back to New Jersey, but I doubt that I can stay there. It's a heartbreaking thing to find yourself split down the middle like this. There's no good choice, because whatever I decide will tear apart a piece of my heart. After I've helped Billie straighten out her life, I'll take a look at where mine is going. I pray to God I make the right decision.

Raining Truth

Louise remained in the pasture for a long time. The rain stopped, the clouds moved on, and a brown cow nosed the window, but still she sat there imagining herself dead, emotionally if not physically. Finally it came to her that perhaps the mishap was a sign, a sign that the Louise she used to be was dead. It was time to start a new life—a life as Penny Palmer. Becoming Penny gave her the courage to turn the key in the ignition and inch the car forward until it broke free of the rut it had settled into. She eased the car back onto the asphalt and headed eastward.

After a few miles Louise switched on the radio and found some music, but it lasted only a few minutes then turned to static. She snapped the radio off. The narrow road had few distractions. It was mile after mile of orange groves, rows of trees that stretched as far as the eye could see. Trees rooted to theirs spot on this earth. Trees that never wandered, never moved from one row to the next, content to blossom and bloom in the very same spot year after year after year. It was so wonderfully organized, so neat and self-contained. Louise found herself wishing people were like this.

Her thoughts flitted back to her father—a man who grew irritable and started to itch if he stayed put for any length of time. A man who rolled from town to town until it was too late to change his ways. He spread himself out like a seed dropped on rock hard ground, a seed that sprouted buds but grew sideways and never bothered to take root. If he'd rooted himself to one place or another he wouldn't have been traveling through that last town, the one where he was run over by a delivery van in the alley behind Muldoone's Pub. How sad that a man could waste his life, live day after day, and not care a thing about belonging to anybody or anyplace in particular. Even the wife and child he carted along became just so much extra baggage. Louise knew that if a stranger were to ask her father the color of her eyes, he wouldn't have known the answer.

Probably he would have answered "blue eyes." He wouldn't have known they were hazel, with flecks of green and brown. How could he have known that? He seldom took the time to look square into her face. She was little more than a reflection in the rearview mirror. "Sit down," he'd say, "you're blocking my view. Stop whining. One more word and I'll dump you off by the side of the road." Perhaps, Louise thought as she absently swerved onto the shoulder, it would have been better if he had.

She eased back onto the blacktop and kept going. Every so often she saw a break in the line of the uniform rows of an orchard, split open by a misfit tree, its branches gnarled and fruit rotting on the ground. Louise wondered if those were the trees like her father, trees that didn't want roots and resented the fact that they were stuck in a grove. Maybe they stood there day after day, waiting for a gust of wind to shake their limbs and free them of any little hanging-on oranges. Louise knew how it felt to be one of those oranges. She could still remember the rain drizzling down her back the night she was dumped on Aunt Rose's front porch.

Buckling under the weight of her loneliness, she reached across the seat and hugged Yoo closer. The dog was a lot like her, a cast-off taken in by a stranger. Yoo had her to love him, but who did she have? Uncle Elroy's wrinkled face came to mind, then Clay's sorrowful eyes. She thought about dear little Mandy, Philip and Patty Lynn, Billie Butterman and the Material Girls—they were all pieces of the puzzle she'd spent her life assembling. Scattered images began swirling through Louise's mind. She saw bits of faces, a branch of the oak tree, some white siding, a brick chimney, snippets of her life, but none of them a complete picture.

Louise suddenly felt tired beyond belief, so she pulled into a glass-fronted strip mall just off the interstate. At one end stood a Big K-Mart, the "Big" inserted into the sign with a caret like some kind of afterthought. At the opposite end was Rudy's Root Beer— Ice Cold Drinks & Monster Burgers.

She parked on the far edge of the lot, slumped back into the seat, and watched a leftover drizzle of rainwater slide down the windshield. "Well, here we are," she said, trying to sound as brave as a Penny Palmer would. Her fingers still trembling, she fished the leash from her bag and hooked it onto the dog's collar. As the car door swung open Yoo sucked in a whiff of food and moved toward Rudy's.

The dog followed the scent, tugging Louise across the lot, weaving in and out of rows of cars and almost running headlong into an old woman click-clacking along with a walker. Although she tried to cling to the bravado of being Penny Palmer, Louise kept wondering if she'd done the right thing after all.

Rudy's was the type of place where young people congregate, where they sit for hours sipping a single Coke-a-Cola and sharing an order of fries. Long before Louise got to the walkway she could hear the noise rolling through an open take-out window: a song she'd never heard before and the high-pitched laughter of young people.

A teenager with a red-striped cap and a bridge of freckles stood at the counter and gave her a toothy smile. "Welcome to the home of the Monster Burger," he said. "May I take your order?"

"What's a Monster Burger?"

"A hamburger."

"A regular hamburger?"

"Yeah, but with lettuce, tomato, cheese, chili beans, and onions."

"Oh," Louise said. "That's too much."

"You can have it plain."

"Okay," she answered. "Cheese maybe, but no chili beans or onions." She also ordered a root beer and a cup of water.

"One plain with cheese," the boy repeated, then he whistled across the galley and tossed a frozen hamburger onto the grill. In an odd way he reminded Louise of Phillip at that age. Phillip, with his dark hair and olive skin, looked nothing like this boy, but it wasn't looks, it was something else—a certain kind of gawkiness kids suffered before they grew into themselves. Louise wondered what was worse, being young or growing older. Young people were spared the hardships of age, but they were burdened by the insecurity of facing life with no guarantee of what was to come.

Five minutes later the boy returned. "No chili, no onions," he said and pushed a grease-stained sack through the takeout window.

Louise picked up the bag and set off in search of a bench. She wanted to find one beneath a shady tree. She crooked her head to the left and right. Plenty of trees—willows, oaks, even a few flowering magnolias—but no benches. Across the parking lot sat the dividing islands, thick with hard-edged Bermuda grass and clusters of white jasmine. The center island even had a row of sabal palms. That would have been the ideal place to sit and picnic had she not remembered how the lawn at Tall Pines was alive with fire ants, beetles, and lizards. Continuing along the walkway, she spotted a green bench in front of the glass window at K-mart—a worn bench with the sun blistering down on it and one slat missing.

She had hoped to find a picnic table, perhaps one with an umbrella angled to provide shade. But as she'd come to discover, wanting and having were two different things. Louise dropped down on the green bench and adjusted herself across a span of open slats. Half of her right thigh sagged through the empty hole, and although it was far from comfortable it was better than nothing. She set the cup of water on the ground, then crumpled the hamburger inside a piece of tinfoil and gave it to the dog. "Here you go, boy," she said, and Yoo began wolfing it down. After he lapped at some water, he stretched out in the sun. Louise did the same. The twitch in her fingers had stopped, and the sun felt soft against her face. Her eyes fluttered closed as she leaned against the back of the bench. She was on the verge of dozing when she heard a voice.

"Will I be disturbing you if I sit here?"

Louise popped her eyes open and bolted upright. "Oh."

In front of her stood a crooked little woman no bigger than a twelve-year-old girl. She had a topknot of cottony white hair and wrinkled brown skin. "You mind?" she asked again.

"No, no, of course not." Louise scooted to the side and made room on the bench.

"Thanks, dearie." The woman slowly lowered herself onto the bench. "Gotta be rain coming." She bent over and rubbed her right knee. "The tee-vee says we ain't gettin' rain, but my knee's never wrong."

"Actually, I passed through a downpour on my way here," Louise said.

"I knew it!" She lifted the hem of her flowered dress and nodded at the knee. "See that, swollen! Rain's gonna be here, less 'n an hour."

"Oh, dear," Louise said. "I'd hoped it was over."

"No, indeed, we're in for it. Guaranteed."

Thinking about where she might go to avoid another storm, Louise squirreled her face into a frown and asked, "Do they allow dogs in K-Mart?"

"Allow? I don't know as I'd say allow. Clementine sneaks Baby in and puts her in the basket. 'Course Baby's a poufy little thing. "

"Umm..." Louise looked down at the eighty-five-pound Yoo. "I doubt I could even lift him up to the basket."

"Right." The woman nodded. "Best take him home."

"I sort of live in New Jersey."

"Well, then." The woman again eyed the dog.

"Maybe we could wait in Rudy's."

The woman shook her head. "Unh-unh. That's one place dogs for sure ain't allowed." She turned to Louise. "Clementine don't even bring Baby in there."

"Oh, dear."

"I suppose," the woman said as she rubbed her chin thoughtfully, "if he's not one to pee on the floor, I could let you wait out the storm at my place."

"Oh, he'd never pee, but I wouldn't want to impose."

"No bother. With my joints all swelled up, I'd be glad for a ride home."

Louise felt relief at having somewhere to go. If the weather-forecasting knee was right and the storm was close behind, she surely didn't want to get caught in it again. "Thank you so much," she said, gratitude spilling from the words.

They'd already pulled out of the parking lot before she thought to introduce herself. "By the way," she said, "my name is Penny Palmer."

The woman seemed unimpressed by her two-of-a-kind initials and answered, "Most people just call me Tulip."

"Tulip?"

"Unh huh, like the flower. Okay, slow now. That's it, the blue one on the left."

Louise turned into a pebbled drive squeezed between two trailer homes.

Tulip lived in a tin box with four narrow windows. It was less than half the size of Uncle Charlie's house and flatter to the ground. You could have easily imagined it to be a little girl's playhouse, neat and trim, circled with a garden of pink and purple flowers, except that it sat alongside a bunch of other trailers not nearly as nice. Plastic lawn chairs, bicycles, and broken toys freckled the lawns of the other homes.

"Hurry along," Tulip said. "That storm's about on us."

Louise peeked up at the sky. The sun still shone bright as ever, not a cloud in sight. If in fact Tulip's knee was wrong, this was a waste of time. But there was still a possibility the knee was right. With that in mind, Louise tugged Yoo down the walkway and followed the woman into the squat little house. They went through a living room with lace doilies on every chair and a threadbare green carpet on the floor, then crossed over into a kitchen no bigger than a closet. A small closet at that.

Tulip poured two cups of coffee, and they sat at the table.

"Long drive ahead, huh?"

"Yes, I'm going to New Jersey."

"My girl's in New Jersey," Tulip said wistfully. "She's settled down now, got four boys and a real pretty house in Plainfield."

"Plainfield's right next to where I live," Louise said. "My son and his family live there too."

"Well, bless my soul, ain't this a small world."

"My granddaughter's not ten minutes away." Excited at the connection, the fact that the Palmer house now belonged to the Spotswoods had apparently slipped Louise's mind.

Tulip sighed. "A granddaughter living so close, that's a blessing."

Louise nodded. "Mandy," she said. "Her name is Mandy. She looks exactly like me when I was that age."

"Her daddy, he look like you too?"

Louise shook her head. "He's the spitting image of his father."

"My girl, she don't look a thing like me. She got a nose like George's sister, and she got Elmira's sassy mouth too."

"George is your husband?"

"Was," Tulip answered sadly.

Louise understood the meaning of "was." Was meant things you once had, things now gone. She could fill a bushel basket with things that were now *was*. She stumbled through the sadness of the moment, then said, "I have a daughter, too. Patricia Lynn."

"Well, ain't that nice. I bet you spend lots a time with her."

"Not really," Louise said. "Patty's got an important job. She's always busy working."

"Still nice having two young'uns. Me, I just got the one girl. But I got those four grandsons." The black olive eyes crinkled into a smile. "Granny Tulip they call me."

Without further mention of Patty Lynn, Louise continued. "Back in New Jersey I've also got friends who are close as sisters."

"Friends is good, but they ain't the same as family."

"My friends *are* like family," Louise replied. She leaned forward like she was letting the woman in on a secret. "My friends and I," she said, "we all belong to the same quilting club. We get together and sit around the dining room table working on our quilts. There's nothing we wouldn't do for one another. Nothing."

"Them's good friends," Tulip nodded. "I don't have that sort of friends. Most folks here go north when the sun turns hot."

"You ought to go spend the summer with your daughter," Louise suggested.

"Rosalie?" Tulip shook her head. "Unh-unh," she said sadly. "Kids today, they got their own life, and they don't wanna be bothered. Barging in, that's what they call it when you come for a visit."

"Barging in? Not my Phillip, he'd never think—"

"That's cause you've got your own place," Tulip said. "He ain't worried about you coming and staying there."

"But surely your daughter doesn't—"

"Oh, yes, she does. The minute I say I'm coming, Rosalie's first words is 'How long you staying?' I tell her right off, 'These kids ain't got but one grandma.' And don't she come back with,

'Yeah, and we ain't got but one bathroom.' Ain't that the height of impertinence?"

A crack of thunder sounded overhead. It bounced off the tin roof and caused the cups to rattle in their saucers.

"I knew it," Tulip said. "When my knee is swelled up, I got no doubt."

The storm didn't start with a gentle pitter-pat of raindrops, it roared in with huge beads of water slapping against the roof and a blinding cascade swooshing down the windowpane. Within minutes a downpour began hammering the roof, and they had to shout to be heard.

"Oh, dear," Louise yelled. "I hope this lets up soon."

"It will," Tulip yelled back and stirred her coffee.

For a brief while, neither of the women said anything. They slouched back in the plastic chairs, burrowed in their own thoughts, and listened to the rain. Finally Louise spoke. "I'm certain Phillip would never think of me as barging in."

"I done told you, that's 'cause you got a place nearby. Your boy knows he can send you home if you get to testing his nerves."

"Even if I didn't—he'd never—"

"Tell him you're coming to stay, you'll see."

Tears welled in Louise's eyes.

"Sugar, you got no reason for tears," Tulip said. "You got your own place."

"Not anymore. I used to have a beautiful little house—but it's gone now."

"Gone?"

"Sold, to a woman who's little more than half my age."

"Oh, I see," Tulip said. "Money problems?"

Louise shook her head. "Retirement."

"Well, then, that's a good thing. You get another house?"

"Unh-huh," Louise nodded, "but it's in Florida."

"Then why you going back to New Jersey?"

"My best friend needs my help."

"She in Jersey?"

Louise shrugged. "I don't know. She's missing."

"Missing?"

"She just walked out. No one knows where she's gone."

"Oh, my," Tulip said, the words stretched out like an armful of sympathy.

"Her husband blamed Billie for murdering his mother, so she left and never came back. She hasn't even called."

"Billie, she's this friend?"

Louise nodded.

"Maybe she had a need to get away, be off by herself for a while."

"Away from *me*? Her best friend?"

"Could be. Some folks get a hurt that settles inside of them and hunkers down till it's good and ready to leave. My Rosalie run off when she was sixteen. I didn't hear word one from that child for two years. I about worried my heart out. Then one day she shows up on my doorstep with this cute little tyke. 'Mama, meet your grandson,' she says, like it was the most natural thing on earth."

"Two years?"

"Two long years! I near worried myself to death. My poor knees wore down to a nub, praying for God to take care of my girl. She's a wild one, I told Him, but she got a good heart."

"Why'd she run off?"

"It don't hardly matter no more. What does matter is that when she decided to come home I was there, waiting."

"Did you look for her?"

"Every place I could think of. I took her school picture and went around asking people, 'You seen this girl?' But it didn't do a speck of good. People who don't want to be found ain't gonna get found."

Tulip pinched up her narrow little face and shook her head. "For the longest time I blamed myself. I should've saw this coming, that's what I'd tell my George. But God rest his soul, he'd say, 'Tulip, you're a good woman and a good mother. Rosalie's got problems she's got to sort out. She'll come back when she's ready.'"

"Two years," Louise said in wonderment. "How did you do it?"

"A body does what they gotta do. I did a whole lot of praying. That, and George is what got me through. You got to trust in the

Lord and believe in the goodness of people, George would say, 'cause that's what matters most."

Louise leaned into the woman's words. "By now," she said, "the Lord's probably lost track of where I am."

Tulip chuckled. "The Lord always knows where you is, even when you ain't where He's intending you to be."

"If maybe I knew where He intends me to be—"

"You ain't ever gonna find out 'less you get to praying and quit feeling sorry for yourself."

"I'm not feeling sorry for myself."

"Sure you are, just like I was when my Rosalie ran off. Waiting ain't an easy thing, but sooner or later your friend will come back just like my Rosalie. Long about time you're certain she's gone for good, she's gonna come knocking on the door. My George, now if he was still alive, he'd've said..."

Tulip's story rolled on in a drone of words that Louise heard with her ears but not her heart. Happy endings happened to people with double initials, not her.

"Lord, how I miss George," Tulip said wistfully. "He surely was a man filled with the love of life." After a moment she added, "I miss those four grandbabies too."

By time the storm let up and the last few blobs of rainwater splattered down from the roof, Louise was ready to leave.

"When you get to New Jersey, you go see my Rosalie," Tulip said, pulling out a scrabble of paper with an address written in large shaky letters. "Tell her how I'm doing just fine, got myself a whole mess 'a friends down here, and playing bingo most every evening. Say I'm gonna come visit, soon as I get time. Just don't mention my using a walking stick." Tulip used the four-pronged cane for every step she took, and to Louise it seemed likely the daughter would already know this.

As she pulled away from the drive Louise glanced back, wondering if Tulip would be peering out from inside the glass. She wasn't. There was nothing but a warm yellow light shining through the worn lace curtains.

Louise had no trouble forgetting the trailer park, but Tulip's words kept bouncing around in Louise's head. At first it was just the stories of George, Rosalie, and the four grandbabies already in high school. Then she recalled the way Tulip talked about life as if she were a casual observer, somebody standing on the sideline watching, not the person living through tragedies and heartaches. The words "barging in" eventually got stuck in Louise's head and kept picking at her.

Barging in. How foolish. Strangers like Cherry Melinski barged in. Louise was simply coming for a visit. Mandy would be glad to see her. Phillip would be glad to see her. Rachel, well, she might consider it barging in. *Perhaps I'll stay with one of the girls,* Louise told herself. Maybe Claire. No, Claire had Queen Anne furniture people weren't supposed to sit on. Maybe Ida. Ida had a spare room. Of course, Ida gossiped about everybody, and if Louise showed up with no place to stay—no, not Ida. Maggie's son still lived at home, Eloise smoked like a fiend, and Peg was not at all hospitable. Doris hated dogs. Wilma had two cats. Louise ran through the names on her list and crossed them off one by one. When she'd run out of other options, she decided to call Uncle Floyd's apartment and see if maybe Aunt Rose was ready to return home. If worse came to worst, she could always bunk on Aunt Rose's sofa for a few days.

Louise worked her way back to the K-Mart plaza and pulled up alongside the outdoor telephone. "Wait here," she told Yoo. "I'll be right back." By the time she jingled a handful of quarters from her purse, an old man had taken possession of the telephone.

"Right at the first or second light?" he shouted into the receiver. Scribbling what appeared to be directions, he shifted the phone from one ear to the other. "What's that?" he said, then crossed out everything he had written and started again.

Louise paced back and forth alongside the telephone, hoping he would notice her waiting and speed up his conversation. He didn't.

"Why don't you just run that by me again?" he said and started another page. "Okay, it's right at the first light…"

A full fifteen minutes passed before he hung up and Louise could dial Floyd's number. Rose answered. "Elkins' residence," she cooed.

"Aunt Rose?"

"Oh, it's you, Louise. I thought it might be one of my friends."

"Your friends?"

"Yes, I'm expecting Luanne to call. We're going to the beach this afternoon."

"You're going to the beach?"

"Well, of course. That's what people do when they live in Florida."

"But you don't actually *live* in Florida."

"I do now." Rose began giggling like a schoolgirl. "I telephoned the building superintendent and told him I wasn't coming back. I said he could clear out my apartment and give the stuff to Goodwill."

"Goodwill?" Louise gasped. "All your beautiful clothes?"

"Honestly, Louise, you can be such a ninny. Don't you realize people down here dress casually? They don't wear all that fussy paraphernalia."

"But, Aunt Rose, you—"

"Lighten up, dear," Aunt Rose said, using terminology Louise never believed she would hear coming from her aunt's mouth. "Now that we're living in Florida, we've got to go with the flow if we're to have any fun."

"You're really not going back to New Jersey? Ever?"

"Well, ever is an awfully long time, but I doubt that I'd be willing to leave my friends anytime in the foreseeable future. Now, what was it you telephoned about, dear?"

"Nothing much," Louise answered sadly. "I just thought I'd check on how you were doing."

Louise replaced the receiver and stared at the telephone for a full minute wondering if somehow someone had played a prank on her. Were it not for the familiar voice, she would have sworn the woman on the other end of the line was not Aunt Rose.

Still trying to comprehend the change that had come about, she dialed Billie Butterman's number. Hopefully, Billie had come to her senses and returned home. The phone rang seven times. On the eighth ring, Bradley answered.

"I was so sorry to hear about your mother's accident," Louise said.

"Accident? Who said it was an accident?"

"I just assumed —"

"Don't."

"Is there anything I can—"

"Nothing."

"Billie," Louise said, trying to find a way to work around to what she was looking for, "I suppose she's taking this quite hard."

"Are you trying to get smart with me?"

"Oh, no. No indeed."

"Billie's gone," Bradley said. "For good, I suspect."

"Gone where?"

"You don't know?"

"No." Louise wondered why Bradley would think she knew.

"She told Missus Kelly she was going to Florida. I figured it was to see you."

"Um, I haven't heard from her yet."

"I'm sure you will. Tell Billie if she keeps using my American Express card, I'm gonna have her arrested." Bradley hung up the receiver. No goodbye, nothing.

Trust in the Lord. Your friend will come knocking on the door.

Louise got back into the car, pulled out of the parking lot, and headed westward, back toward Tall Pines.

Louise

I wish I could say my heart understands the way things are, but it doesn't. Aunt Rose is no longer the woman I lived with for all those years. Bradley, a man who was devoted to his wife, is now calling Billie a murderer. And Clay—he's the biggest mystery of all.

There's a part of me that knows Clay loves me, that understands he's simply not a man to express his feelings openly. But there's another part that wants more. A part that wants him to take me in his arms and say his heart would break if I ever left. It pains me to say this, but I doubt he's even realized I'm gone.

I ask myself what changed. Did Clay change or did I? I think it was Clay. He let go of the worry he'd been dragging around for years. Not me. I hang onto everything—worry, heartache, bad memories, regrets. I carry them with me everywhere I go.

The truth is I'm afraid of change. Afraid of what it will bring and what it will take. Can you blame me? A few short months ago, I had everything. Now look at me. I'm a thousand miles away from my family, and I've lost my best friend.

I'm going back to Fairwind, and I'll try to make a go of it. I'll do it because I love Clay, but I'm still praying he'll have a change of heart and we can go back home where we belong.

A Long Road Home

Lost in a string of daydreams, Louise drove for any number of miles before she began to wonder about the time. She glanced at the clock. Five-thirty—later than she'd imagined. Thoughts of Clay came to mind. She could almost see him pacing the floor, wondering where she was. Even if he didn't realize she was gone, he'd notice the dog was missing. For several miles Louise watched the side of the road, hoping to spot a pay phone so she could call.

It's almost dinnertime, she thought. *When there's nothing to eat on the table, he'll start looking for me. He'll probably wander across the yard and ask Cherry if she knows where I am. Once she learns I'm gone, the entire community will know, even Ernie.*

The possibility of Ernie broadcasting the news of her disappearance caused Louise to ease back her pressure on the gas pedal. The car slowed to forty. *Billie will know how to handle Ernie,* she thought, *Cherry Melinski, too.* Louise chuckled and began wondering how long she'd have to wait for Billie to arrive in Florida. *I should have asked Bradley,* she mused, but then she remembered the anger with which he'd slammed down the receiver. In all likelihood he wouldn't have answered anyway.

Louise continued westward, all the while imagining what Billie would say about one thing and another. Could she possibly already be at the house? Maybe sitting there, having a glass of lemonade while Cherry downed her beer straight from a can? Just as she moved on to wondering what Billie might have to say about Monroe, the traffic slowed to a near stop. Ahead of her she saw an endless string of cars, trucks, and vans lined up bumper to bumper. Not one moved faster than a snail's pace.

Moments later the line came to a dead stop.

"Drat," Louise said, annoyed. She'd now grown anxious to get back home. She snapped on the radio and twisted the dial. Static,

static, static until she hit on 97.1 and found "Tunes of the Day with Crazy Jay."

"Hey, hey," Crazy Jay said. "Looks like we've got an ugly fender bender out on Route Sixty. Our traffic watcher, Clyde Willis, tells us a big rig plowed into a grove truck, and they're gonna be a long time clearing away the mess.

A long time?

"Yep, a real long time. You folks out there in radio land, listen to Crazy: steer clear of the intersection at Sixty and State Road Thirty-four. If you gotta go that way, save yourself several hours, scoot over to the old Jensen Road cutoff, and swing around behind the Cartwheel farm."

"Several hours?" Louise moaned.

"Y'all keep your radio dial right where it is for more tunes of the day with Crazy Jay. And don't forget, steer clear of Route Sixty."

"Oh, dear," Louise murmured. She was already on Route Sixty and had no idea where the Jensen Road cutoff was, much less how to scoot around behind the Cartwheel farm. She wouldn't know the Cartwheel farm if it stood smack in front of her. Apparently that was insider information, something only people who belonged here knew.

Louise settled back into the seat, wishing she had stopped for something to eat. Ready to jump on even the slightest bit of forward movement, she sat with the engine idling for nearly twenty minutes, then lowered the windows and clicked off the motor. The typical Florida early summer evening felt warm and muggy, the air thick with the threat of more rain and charged with smells of gasoline and cow manure. Hungry and damp with perspiration, Louise felt weary of the trip. It was a foolish idea to begin with, and now she wanted nothing more than to return home. The thought of kicking off her shoes and settling down in front of Uncle Charlie's old television suddenly seemed appealing. Maybe she'd make a meatloaf for supper—if she got there in time to make supper.

The dashboard clock ticked off another fifteen minutes, and still the traffic didn't budge. Yoo whined, snuffed at the air, then climbed over the armrest and repositioned himself in the back seat.

Louise took a grocery list from her purse and fanned her face. She could already feel rivulets of perspiration running down her back. What little breeze there once was had died away, and the air settled around them like a too-heavy comforter. Nothing moved except tiny gnat-like things that swarmed in and out of the open windows, nipping at her ears and neck. Nearly invisible, they darted in front of her eyes, then disappeared so quickly she wondered if she'd simply imagined them.

The longer Louise sat the more thoughts of food took possession of her mind. Meatloaf, mashed potatoes with brown gravy, buttered corn. As time passed it became steak, a whole loaf of French bread, a big slice of apple pie with cheddar cheese melted on top of it. She felt hungrier than she could ever remember, and her stomach rumbled like a volcano about to erupt. She rummaged through the glove compartment looking for a breath mint or stick of gum to ward off what felt like starvation. Nothing. Thinking there might still be some of that Stuckey's fudge she'd hidden in the trunk of the car, she got out—but before she had time to check, the line of traffic began to move.

It was almost eleven o'clock by the time Louise got back to Tall Pines.

Not much ever happened in a place like Tall Pines, so when Louise rounded the corner and saw the line of cars and flashing red lights in front of Uncle Charlie's house she was taken aback. She counted not one but two patrol cars, the second of which blocked the driveway. She passed the house, went all the way to the corner, and parked between an antiquated Buick and a Jeep covered with a thick layer of mud, neither of which looked familiar.

Before anything else she searched the line of cars for Billie's Cadillac. It seemed to be the only car not there. Untangling herself from the seat belt, Louise hooked the leash to Yoo's collar and tugged him from the car. Then she went in search of the nearest blue uniform, which as it turned out was a middle-aged man with a paunch that gave him more the look of a bus driver rather than a law enforcement officer.

"What happened?" she asked, her voice sounding a bit panicky.

"Not sure yet. You'll have to stay back, we're working the crime scene." He was as puffed out as the chief detective on a TV show.

"What crime?" Louise gasped. "Where?"

"Right there," the officer said pointing a finger in the direction of Uncle Charlie's house.

"I knew it!" Louise said angrily before the policeman could go any further. "It was Ernie! Just yesterday I caught him trying to steal our television. Ernie Tobias. I'm telling you, that's who did it!"

Louise started to say she'd suspected Ernie right from the start, but the policeman eyed her with a bewildered expression and asked, "Did what?"

"Robbed the house."

"There's been no robbery!" he replied sharply. "It's a missing person case. The husband thinks the woman's been kidnapped. But me, I'm thinking she's most likely run off with some passing-through Romeo."

"Passing-though Romeo? Good heavens! Who would do—"

"The Palmer woman." He again pointed to Uncle Charlie's house. "She lives there."

"Why, I'm not missing!"

"That's your house?"

"Yes," she answered indignantly. "And I've never even glanced at another man, let alone run off with some so-called Romeo!"

"You're the Palmer woman?"

"Yes!"

He pointed to Yoo. "Is that the kidnapped dog?"

"He wasn't kidnapped. He came along willingly!"

The policeman cupped his hand to his mouth and yelled, "Hey, Mike, I got her!"

"Got me?" Louise echoed. It had the sound of a captured criminal.

Officer Paunchy puffed his chest out a bit further, his jacket now straining at the seams and the brass buttons pulling sideways. "Do you mind telling me where you've been?" he snorted in a tough detective voice.

Before she could answer, Clay came running from the house. Another policeman followed Clay, this one a bit older, late fifties maybe, silver-haired, slender, a Paul Newman sort of face. His nametag read Michael M. Mobley.

Triple initials! Never before in her life had Louise met a person with triple initials. She couldn't help but smile.

"Okay, let's back off," Mike Mobley said. "Let the lady talk." He acknowledged her smile with one of his own. "You want to tell me what happened?"

She should have explained how there'd been an accident—a big rig that ran into an orange grove truck and stranded everyone on the roadway for hours. But instead of saying what was perfectly understandable, Louise zeroed in on Michael M. Mobley's nametag and stammered something about how he ought to be sure to buy a lottery ticket.

"Lottery ticket?!" Clay shouted, the veins in his neck a three-dimensional roadmap.

"Well, yes," she answered, "have you noticed his name? He's got three—"

"I'm in no mood for this foolishness," Clay said, trying to control the anger in his voice. "Where were you? I've been sick with worry!"

Louise noticed the twitch in his right eye. "I got stuck in a traffic jam," she said.

"Traffic jam?" Paunchy echoed. "You think this is some kind of joke?"

"Calm down," Mike said. "Let's go inside, sit down, and listen to what Missus Palmer has to say." He took Louise by the arm and started for the door.

Yoo tagged along of his own accord. No one had him by the collar, so Louise assumed they didn't consider him an accomplice.

The living room was crowded with things that had finally arrived from Westfield—a sofa, chairs, boxes piled upon boxes, tables set one upon the other, silk lampshades squashed inside a laundry basket, a broken step stool, a rolled-up carpet. She gasped—not at the sight of her treasured possessions but at the lineup of neighbors squeezed shoulder-to-shoulder along the sofa. Monroe Schramm, Cassandra Willoughby, the Feingold twins—a row of concerned faces with furrowed brows and rigid mouths. They whispered among themselves, but no one said a word to Louise as Michael M. Mobley marched her across the room and into the kitchen. No one but Clay, that is.

"Give me one good reason for your doing this," he said. "One reason, just one!" He paused for two or three seconds then growled, "No answer, I knew it!"

Mike Mobley glared at Clay, then turned to Louise. "Okay now, why don't you tell us exactly what did happen." He pulled a chair back from the table and nudged her into it. "No need to be nervous; take your time." His eyes crinkled at the corners, kind of like a smile. Not a full smile; just a trace of one.

Louise noticed it whether or not anyone else did—handsome, blue-eyed Mike Mobley had the look of luck wrapped around him like a Superman cloak. "Do you suppose if I gave you twenty dollars you could buy a bunch of lottery tickets for me?" she asked.

Mike laughed. "I don't think—"

"Forget lottery tickets!" Clay shouted. "We've been worrying ourselves crazy—me, the neighbors, your friends out there—and all you can think about is lottery tickets?! If that's what you want, I'll buy you fifty of the blasted things!"

Louise started to tell Clay that his buying the tickets wouldn't work—his initials weren't even double, let alone triple—but with him already acting like he would explode, she figured it probably wasn't a good idea. "Believe me," she said, "I had no idea there'd be all this commotion. I didn't think anyone would even miss me, let alone be so upset."

Clay looked at her, his face somber as a gravedigger. "Well, now, just what did you expect? One minute you're sitting here, then without a word of goodbye you and the dog both disappear! Kidnapped, I thought, for certain!"

"Kidnapped? Why, who in the world would kidnap *me*?"

"Kidnapped. Held for ransom. Or murdered and tossed in a ditch!"

"That's ridiculous."

"Ridiculous?" Clay slammed his hand against the table so hard the salt shaker toppled over. "How can you say there's no cause for concern when you just up and disappear like that? You could have told me where you were going, you could have left a note—"

"Okay," Mike said. "Everybody needs to calm down. Obviously what we've got here is some sort of misunderstanding."

"Misunderstanding?" Clay grumbled. "Stealing a dog? Falsified kidnapping?"

"Why, I never!" Louise squealed.

Mike draped his arm over Clay's shoulder and led him to the side of the room. "Seems to me," he said, "this is simply a case of an angry wife letting off steam. She's back safe and sound, no harm done. Let's leave it be."

Clay glanced over at Louise, and she gave him a little half-smile. "Okay," he answered. "I guess we can leave it at that."

Clay never realized that Louise wasn't smiling at him. She was smiling past him. She was smiling at the man with triple initials.

Suddenly Louise felt the heat of a blush creep into her cheeks. Mike obviously knew what she was thinking. When he walked over, squatted down beside her and laid his arm across the back of her chair, she was certain.

"You've caused quite a ruckus, running off like this," he said. "Can I trust you not to do it again?" His voice, soft and gentle as a butterfly's wing, brushed against her ear. "If there's some sort of domestic situation that needs to be discussed, you can give me a call." He smiled and handed her a card with his telephone number on it. It seemed to Louise that he squatted beside her much longer than actually necessary.

Mike stood and said something to Clay but Louise didn't know for sure exactly what it was, probably because she was listening more to the melody of his voice than the words. He had the slightest hint of an accent—not a Florida twang, just a soft roundness that made the words as pleasant as jasmine in summer. Here he was, a man with triple initials, and she was almost certain he'd been flirting with her. Momentarily lost in the loveliest of daydreams, she heard Mike say, "Y'all take care now," and then he left.

Louise now faced Clay and a house full of neighbors waiting to hear the full story. Cherry Melinski appeared to be running things as she circled the living room in her dizzying whirl of brightly-colored toreador pants and jangling bracelets, passing out goodwill and home fried wisdom like the ringmaster at a circus.

All of it was simply too much. The only thing Louise wanted was to have a sandwich and go to bed, but given the situation that was pretty much impossible. There were a dozen people in the living room. No one rose to leave, and they all seemed to have questions. She took a deep breath and casually strolled into the midst of them.

Everyone spoke at once.

"Thank God, you're okay."

"Clay was so worried."

"We were all worried."

"Where'd you go?"

"Why'd you do it?" five or six people asked at the same time.

Oddly enough, Cherry rushed to Louise's defense. "Enough of this," she said. "It's been a long day. Louise is home and she's okay, that's all we need to know. Now let's head on home so the Palmers can get some rest."

Louise felt so grateful she could almost imagine Cherry Melinski becoming one of the Material Girls. Of course, she'd have to get rid of the bangle bracelets and bright yellow stretch pants first.

When the door closed on the last of them, Louise started down the hallway to the bedroom. Clay came right behind her. "I still can't imagine why you'd leave like that," he said. "Here I was worrying myself to death—"

"Didn't you listen to what the policeman said? I was angry."

"So, make a fuss, or don't talk to me. Go buy something expensive. Don't just walk off and leave me thinking that something terrible has happened to you."

As he spoke Louise noticed how sorrowful he looked, like one of those worn gray rags stored beneath the kitchen sink. It seemed that his entire being had suddenly began to slope downward—his brows, eyes, the corners of his mouth, his shoulders, even the fingers that dangled lifelessly alongside his body. She thought back on all the years of love they'd shared, and a feeling of caring she hadn't felt in months came over her. "Well," she finally said, "I came back, didn't I?"

He didn't answer but focused on folding back the comforter and arranging his pillow just so. He then climbed into bed and clicked off the light.

With only a sliver of moon glinting through the tear in the window shade, Louise could no longer see his expression or the posture of his body. She knew he had not yet fallen asleep, because she heard the ragged meter of his breath—whoosh, pause, whoosh-whoosh, pause-pause-pause, whoosh. Each pause it seemed grew longer, forcing her to wonder if his heart might actually stop beating.

After several minutes he asked, "Why?"

"Why what?"

"Why did you come back?"

"Billie Butterman's on her way down here."

He bolted up, snapped on the lamp, and turned to her with a wounded expression. "You came back because of—Billie?" His words sounded splintered, raw with emotion, nothing like the way Clay usually spoke.

"Not just Billie."

"What then?"

Louise understood the question hidden behind the words—was he less important than her friend? Was their thirty years of marriage meaningless? She thought about it for a long moment and realized that underneath her hurt and anger, there was still love. She knew when the harsh light of reality dawned she wasn't ready to live a life without Clay. Yes, she'd lost a piece of her heart, but for the most part she'd held onto what was most important.

"I would have come back anyway," she said. "I came back because of you, because I love you and you're my husband."

He sighed. "Well, I should hope so," he said and flicked off the light. Once he was enveloped by darkness, he spoke again. "I may not always show it, but I do love you, Louise. It looks like that's something you'd know by now." He rustled around for a moment then drifted off to sleep, his breathing pattern smooth, even, measured.

Louise had given Clay all she had to give, but was it enough? His declaration of love had sounded a bit of an afterthought, like a P.S. stuck at the end of a letter. She wondered if he truly felt that way. Or did he now harbor the type of resentment she'd known as a child?

Being left behind is something a person never forgets. Louise could still remember the taillights of her mama's car getting smaller and smaller until they eventually disappeared. She tried to call the image to mind, pull it out of her head, and study it as she had zillions of times before. But this time the picture was different. The disappearing taillights belonged to her car. Louise was the woman behind the wheel.

A million, two million, maybe even ten million times she'd wondered how her mother could leave behind a daughter who loved her. Now here she was on the verge of doing the very same thing to Clay. *Like mother, like daughter.* The thought didn't rest easy in Louise's head. At one time or another she had imagined herself to be any number of people—Miss America, Billie Butterman, a history teacher, even Sweetie Spotswood—but never her mother.

A queasy sensation pushed against her ribcage and slowly worked its way up into her throat. Louise tried telling herself it was because she had skipped dinner. She swung her legs over the side of the bed and fumbled into her slippers. *A sandwich, or maybe a few cookies.* Rather than put on a light, she felt her way through the darkness, down the hallway, through the living room, and into the kitchen. A plug-in nightlight glowed somewhere behind one of the cardboard cartons she passed—not bright enough for her to avoid stubbing her toe, but bright enough to cause a disconcerting glimmer in the catfish's eye.

With the refrigerator door hanging open, Louise slapped together a cheddar cheese sandwich and poured a glass of milk. Two-thirds of the way through the sandwich, she started to picture herself growing to look and sound exactly like her mother. That's when she gagged, bent over the sink, and threw up what she had eaten. Suddenly the overhead light popped on.

"What's the matter?" Clay asked.

"I'm sick," she mumbled, not lifting her head.

Still rubbing the sleep from his eyes, he took a dishtowel, wet it with cold water, and pressed it to her forehead. "Better?"

"Some," she answered and allowed him to lead her back to the bedroom.

Louise mentioned nothing about the fear of being like her mother churning in her stomach. Instead she dutifully climbed into bed and closed her eyes. She closed her eyes but didn't sleep. For several hours she lay there thinking—thinking about the yellow house, the house in Westfield, the endless roads that had carried her family from one place to another. The people she missed, the people gone from her life forever, the man sleeping beside her. Clay was a good man, a man she loved dearly, but somehow time had taken the luster from their love and turned her glass slipper into a comfortable moccasin. A woman could wear a moccasin every day, whereas a glass slipper would splinter and break if life became a rocky road.

Shortly before dawn she remembered Tulip, a woman all alone and yet happy in her tin box house. "Remember to trust in God and the goodness of people." Those words took root in Louise's head, and before the sun had cleared the horizon she promised herself that she would follow through on her decision to settle in at Tall Pines.

Clay

I still find it hard to believe that Louise would walk out the way she did. No note, no goodbye, no explanation whatsoever. Yes, I know she's not crazy about living here, but she hasn't given it a chance.

Maybe I pushed too hard. Maybe that bit about the heart attack was over the top. I knew it would get to her, and I guess I thought once we were here she'd like it as much as I do. With Louise, you never know. The truth is that once Uncle Charlie left us the house I got to thinking about the great life he had down here, and I wanted that same life. Yeah, it's selfish, but I honestly did think Louise would eventually find the same comfort level I have.

It floored me when she said the reason she came back was Billie. They're friends, that's it. Friends. For God's sake, I'm her husband. I'm the one she should be concerned about, not some lady friend who's back in New Jersey.

I know Louise probably wants more than I'm giving her, but that's unrealistic. We're not teenagers. We've been married for thirty years, and not once have I strayed. If by now she doesn't know I love her, then I might as well give up. I think she does know.

How can she not?

Pots, Pans, & Possibilities

"Gone fishing" was scribbled on the back of a cash register receipt from Bigwig. There was no mention of what time Clay would be home. Louise looked at the scrap of paper for a second time, then frowned and tossed it into the garbage can. Given the events of yesterday, she thought he'd want to spend the morning together, have a cup of coffee and talk things through. But no, Clay had headed off in some other direction.

It seemed he had no interest in a discussion of what troubled her. He would do what he always did: wait for the unpleasantness to pass. That wasn't something new. Louise thought back through the years and remembered times when she'd been furious about one thing or another, and instead of facing up to the problem Clay had wandered off to someplace else. Several times he'd gone to work on a Saturday. Once he went in search of a new garbage can, and another time he went down to the blood bank and donated blood rather than deal with the problem.

Louise poured a single cup of coffee and sat at the kitchen table. Tulip's coffee seemed to have a better taste. It was less bitter and had something added to it—chicory, maybe, or hazelnut. She remembered how Tulip said Rosalie had been gone for two years before she came home, and just as Louise was starting to wonder if it would take Billie that long the front door banged open and Cherry came yoo-hooing through the house.

"Whew, this is some big mess," Cherry said, frowning at the pile of boxes stacked along the dining room wall and spilling over into the kitchen. "You outta have help unpacking this stuff."

"I suppose Clay will—"

Cherry laughed that deep throated guffaw of hers, the laugh that rubbed up against Louise's nerves like a piece of sandpaper. "He's a man," she said. "Men, they don't know a thing about unpacking. Let a man help, and you'll find your underwear stuffed in the potato bin." Cherry tugged loose the top that was hanging half-in and half-out of her shorts and flashed a wide-open grin. "Now, when it comes to unpacking," she said, "*I'm* an expert." She elbowed her way into the pile of cartons and heaved a mid-size box to the top of the heap. "Got something to open this with?"

"Really, you needn't bother," Louise replied, but by then Cherry was already rummaging through the utensil drawer.

"A knife, just what we need!" The redhead slashed open the first box, then leaned the roundness of her body against a chest of drawers and nudged it over toward the wall.

Cherry Melinski's face was painted with blue eye shadow and fuchsia lipstick, the same as always, but on this particular day she was not wearing her bracelets so she didn't jangle and she wasn't wearing her yellow wedges so she didn't clunk. Louise felt grateful for that.

The first carton Cherry opened was filled with books. "You got a shelf for these?" she asked, already hefting a second box to the top of the heap.

"No actual bookcase. We never needed one in Westfield. We had a whole wall of shelves built in alongside the fireplace. Those shelves," Louise added sadly, "were big enough to hold everything—knick-knacks, pictures, books, everything."

"Okay, we'll pile them on the floor of the closet." Cherry went tromping down the hall with an armload of books. "You're lucky," she called back.

"Lucky?"

"Yeah. Me, I never had such a place." Cherry walked back down the hall mopping a river of sweat from the crevice in her bosom. "My last ex was career army. He dragged me from one base to another. This here's the first real house I ever had."

"Last ex?"

"I had two. The first, he was a guitar player, a real no-good."

"You've been married two times?"

"Three, including Wilfred."

"What happened?" Louise dropped the colander back into the box she'd been unpacking and sat down to listen.

"I left Larry when he took to beating up on me. He'd come home drunk and say, 'Mabel, how come there's no beer in this refrigerator?' He called me Mabel on account of that's my real name. Anyway, I'd tell him that it was 'cause he didn't give me no money to buy food, let alone beer. That's when he'd haul off and take a swing at me. That last time he whacked me in the head while I was peeling potatoes, so I turned on him with the paring knife and took a slice out his cheek. Then I took off running and didn't slow down to look back."

"Oh, how terrible!"

"It was for the best." Cherry shrugged and continued to unwrap a turkey platter. "I was only with Larry for seven months, so he was easy enough to get over. But the situation with Ed, that nearly broke my heart."

"He was worse than Larry?"

"Much. I *really* loved Ed. We were married twenty years and four months."

Louise leaned forward.

"Far as I knew, we were happy. I never dreamed he'd do what he did."

"What did he do?" Louise moved over and sat on a carton right next to Cherry.

"The day after he's discharged from the army, Ed looks me square in the eye and says, 'Mabel, I had enough of you. It's time for me to get on with my life.' I asked him what he was talking about, but he just shook his head and went on about how I could be so stupid. 'Ain't you ever noticed I don't care much for *women*?' he finally says, then heads off north and tells me to go the other way."

Louise shook her head, focusing on the thought. Somehow surviving such a cruel life made Cherry seem more acceptable; it explained the sharp snap of her words, the garish mix of clothes. Of course, Cherry would never be a Billie Butterman, but then neither was Louise herself.

Cherry unloaded another carton. "These pots go in the kitchen?" she asked.

"Bottom cupboard," Louise answered.

All afternoon they worked side by side, resting only once when Reverend Horchum stopped by. He squeezed through the aisle of boxes and flopped down at the kitchen table. Louise, remembering how Tulip said to trust in the Lord, brewed a fresh pot of coffee and set out the last of a leftover apple crumb cake.

"Lord, bless this food," the Reverend mumbled and reached beyond his stomach to carve off a piece of cake. With the first bite still in his mouth, he added, "A chunk of cheese would go right well with this."

After Reverend Horchum polished off all there was of the cheese, the final crumb of cake, and two salami sandwiches, Louise ushered him to the door. If trusting in the Lord meant feeding Reverend Horchum, she would have to stock up on groceries. When she turned back inside, Cherry had already begun unpacking another box.

"What in the world are you going to do with this?" Cherry held up the red reindeer sweater.

"I wear it every Christmas."

"It's too hot down here!" Cherry set the sweater to one side. "You ought to send it back home to your daughter, or a friend maybe. They could make use of it."

"We might get some frost in December." Louise carefully refolded the sweater and tucked it into the dresser drawer. "You never know."

"It ain't ever gonna get cold enough for that sweater." Cherry swiped her arm across her face. "It's hot down here. On the coldest day of the year, it's still hot." She'd sweated and smudged her mascara so her eyes had the look of a raccoon. "Oven hot," she said, then stomped down on the empty carton and flattened it like a pancake.

Louise didn't want to think about it, so she trotted off to hang her sequined dress in the closet. They unpacked several more cartons, and when she ran out of room on her side of the dresser Louise used two of the drawers on Clay's side. Luckily with all the things that had gone off to the Salvation Army, they had plenty of room.

After the dresser was stuffed with ski sweaters and the bedroom closets crammed so full one of the doors wouldn't close, they stacked sheets and towels in the hall closet, finding a nook or cranny for almost everything, except Louise's quilt-making supplies. By the time they got to those, every shelf was taken. "I probably won't be using these anyway," Louise said wistfully as she packed the colored bits of fabric into two empty suitcases and slid them under the bed. Without the Material Girls, she would find no joy in quilting.

Once they'd stored everything away and had carted the last of the flattened boxes to the garage, Louise studied the living room. With everything in place she expected the room to look as it did in Westfield. It didn't. She rearranged the throw pillows and placed a lace doily in the center of the coffee table. It still looked like Uncle Charlie's house.

"Maybe it's the dented lampshade."

Cherry twisted the shade, moving the dent back to the wall.

"That's not it. Maybe if the sofa was over by the window…"

"Okay." Cherry leapt to the task and single-handedly started shoving the sofa to the other side of the room. She got up momentum, knocked over the three-legged table, and put another hollow in the already-dented lampshade.

"Hmm. That helps, only…"

The sofa overlapped the front door by about ten inches, leaving less than an inch of space on the far side.

"Maybe if we turn it kitty-corner?"

After a few minutes of considering whether or not there was a way to make it fit, they wrestled the sofa back to where it had been underneath the glass-eyed catfish.

Next they moved the chairs first one way and then the other. They twisted the coffee table to the side and tried the three-legged table at a right angle, but neither of those things worked. It was almost four o'clock when they returned all the furniture to where it had been to start with.

Cherry dropped onto the sofa with a grunt. "Whew," she whooshed. "I'm glad that's done." She pulled a plastic pick from the pocket of her shorts and began fluffing her hair. "I must be a sight," she said.

"Unh-unh, you look just fine," Louise replied, and oddly enough she meant it. With the blue eye shadow worn away and her hair flattened to her head, Cherry looked a bit like Ida. In fact, if Louise squinted, Cherry looked exactly like Ida. Louise could almost imagine Cherry sitting in Ida's seat at the next Material Girls meeting; then she remembered she herself wouldn't be there for that meeting or any other meeting.

"Land sakes, it's hot," Cherry said. She opened the top button of her shirt and blew a puff of air down into her bosom. "You got something cold to drink?"

"Soda? Iced tea?"

"Beer's more to my liking." When Louise started for the kitchen, Cherry called after her, "Don't dirty a glass."

Louise revised her thinking. Obviously, Cherry *wasn't* Ida. Ida would never drink from a can, but then Ida was also not one to lend a helping hand. Louise plucked a Budweiser from the refrigerator and headed back to the living room. In fact, if she remembered right, Ida was lazy as sin. Two years ago Louise asked for some help carting a stack of quilts to the church bazaar, and Ida said she couldn't possibly do heavy work like that. Louise set the can of beer on the table in front of Cherry. "Thanks for all the help," she said.

"That's what friends are for," Cherry replied and chugged down a hefty swig.

Friends? Louise stumbled over the thought. Billie Butterman was a friend. Ida and Claire were friends. Maggie, Eloise, Doris, they were all friends. Maybe not the kind of friends who'd pitch in and move furniture about, but friends all the same. It wasn't that Louise didn't appreciate Cherry's help, but becoming friends— well, something like that took years and years.

Cherry gulped down the rest of her beer, then stood. "I got to get going," she said. "Wilfred will be wanting his supper, and I don't have a thing defrosted."

"I do," Louise said like a woman on top of the situation. "I'm planning on making a meatloaf. You and Wilfred want to come to dinner?"

"Yeah, thanks." Cherry gave a wide grin. "Six? Six-thirty?"

Louise nodded. "Six sounds good."

Clay came home alone and without fish.

"Hurry and change," Louise told him. "Cherry and Wilfred are coming over."

"Nice," he answered, a smug turn to his mouth. "Nice you're making friends."

"I don't know that I'd call her a friend." Louise patted the meatloaf into a log and slid it into the oven. "More an acquaintance, I'd say." For a moment or so she wondered if moving furniture shouldn't automatically slide Cherry up to status of friend. *Possibly so,* she thought, but then she remembered the bangle bracelets and Cherry dropped back to acquaintance.

At quarter of six Cherry burst through the back door. Louise had bent over to check on the meatloaf and when the door flew open with a wham, she jerked back and hit her arm on the oven rack. "Yoooowwww!" she screamed and grabbed the stick of butter sitting on the countertop.

"Not that!" Cherry shouted. "Cold water!" She took hold of Louise's shoulders, eased her over to the sink, and turned the faucet to cold. "Using butter on a burn," she said, "that's an old wives' tale. Butter makes it burn more."

Louise dutifully held her arm under the running water, and as the pain subsided she began to wonder how Cherry knew about handling burns.

After almost five minutes, Cherry turned the tap off and said, "Now, let's take a look at that." A large welt had appeared on Louise's forearm. "I'm sorry," Cherry stammered, "I should've used the front door."

"It's not your fault," Louise told her. "I was thinking about this friend of mine who's got a far worse problem, and you just startled me."

"I've a way of doing that," Cherry went on. "Ed used to claim sooner or later I'd give somebody a heart attack. 'Mabel,' he'd say, 'do you have to come through *every* door like a rampaging bull?' I suppose he thought I ought to walk around on tippy toes." She laughed, a small polite noise, not her usual guffaw, then scurried off toward the medicine cabinet. She came back with Unguentine and gauze.

"I believe that's got it," Louise said after Cherry had salved the burnt arm from elbow to wrist and wrapped it in two rolls of gauze.

"We'd better make sure." Cherry wound another roll of gauze around Louise's arm, then stopped. "How's it feel now?" she asked.

"Over-bandaged." Louise held up an arm swaddled to the size of a tree trunk and laughed.

Cherry stayed to finish preparing the meal. She sliced tomatoes, shredded lettuce, cleaned corn, and before Louise could tell her not to she also dumped half a can of spaghetti sauce on top of the almost-cooked meatloaf. "Clay prefers brown gravy with his meatloaf," Louise said, but by then it was too late.

When they sat down to dinner, Clay commented that this was the tastiest meatloaf Louise had ever made.

The zap-zap-zap of Clay's hedge trimmer woke Louise the next morning, and although the sun had barely crossed the horizon it was already blistering hot.

"Will you quiet that thing down?" she called from the window.

"Sorry," he said, fumbling with the switch. "Didn't know it would wake you."

By then she had already turned away.

She showered, fluffed on some talcum, and reached for a pair of khaki trousers. Halfway up her leg she stopped, pulled them off, and switched to the mid-thigh shorts she had bought at the Bluebird Shoppe, the shorts she'd stashed in the bottom drawer. *Today could be the day Billie arrives,* Louise thought as she added an extra stroke of blush to her cheeks. Living in a squat-roofed house was unseemly enough; she didn't also want to look like a frump.

She added pearl gray eyeliner and carefully coated her lashes with mascara. Close up she could see a grandmother, a woman with uncontrollable gray hairs and spidery crow's feet. But if she took a few steps back and narrowed her eyes, she could almost imagine a more youthful woman, a Priscilla, someone with the self-assured look of a Billie Butterman.

Louise had breakfast on the table when Clay tromped into the kitchen. He plopped down in the chair, broke off a sizeable piece of toast, and dunked it into the yolk of his egg without even saying good morning. He was halfway through the bacon when he finally looked up. "Is today something special?" he asked. "You look nice."

She started to explain that quite possibly Billie would be arriving today, but the telephone interrupted her. Louise quickly grabbed the receiver. "Hi," she said as if she were waiting for the call.

"Morning," the caller replied. "This is Bill Farrity. Farrity Painting. We've got a summertime special guaranteed to knock your socks off—"

"Oh." Her voice flattened out. "I don't think—"

"We paint your house at our low discounted price, and you get a free mailbox."

"I'm afraid not."

"Completely installed."

"No, I don't—"

"A *rustproof* mailbox."

"Really, I don't want the house painted," Louise repeated. "But, if I change my mind..." Had there been a pencil handy she would have made note of his number, so she simply pretended.

Louise had hoped the caller was Billie. In fact, she'd expected it to be. When she hung up the phone, a feeling of disappointment settled into her chest. "I thought that might be Billie."

"Why would you think that?" Clay replied absently, then he began searching for the work gloves he needed to trim the palmetto. Without waiting for her answer, he walked off.

Louise dumped the remainder of her coffee down the drain and began waiting. Every few minutes she stuck her head out the door, looking up and down the street. Nothing. Not even a FedEx delivery man. She checked the spare bedroom and plumped the pillows. She tried to read a book but never got past the author's acknowledgments. When she read how he thanked his dear friend it made her miss Billie all the more, so she closed the book and placed it on the coffee table.

About four o'clock, Cherry Melinski rapped on the screen door. "I didn't want to startle you by walking right in," she said.

"Don't be foolish," Louise told her. "I expect you to just walk in."

"Oh. Okay." Cherry got this wide grin on her face. "There's a sale I've got to get to and Wilfred's taken the car to go fishing," she said. "Could you could run me over to Worthmore?"

Louise could hardly say no after all the help Cherry had given her, so she called out to the backyard. "Clay, I'm going shopping."

"Fine," he answered and kept chopping away at the palmetto.

Palm Trees and Polka Dots

Shortly after Louise turned onto the stretch of road west of Moore's Dairy Farm, Cherry pulled a snippet of paper from her pocket and waggled it in the air.

"Guess what," she said. "I've got a coupon!"

"Coupon? Coupon for what?"

"The Bluebird Shoppe!"

"The Bluebird?" Louise repeated. "How'd you get a coupon to The Bluebird?"

"It came in the mail."

Of course, it made sense. People with real double initials have good luck even if they use some ridiculous nickname. Calling herself Penny wouldn't change a thing; she'd more than likely still end up with coupons for corn plasters and dog food.

"Twenty-five percent off everything I buy," Cherry said. "And," she gave a toothy grin, "you too."

"Me too, what?"

"You get twenty-five percent off everything too."

"Me?"

"Yeah, it says right here—coupon good for you and a friend."

Friend? In a situation like this Louise thought they could conceivably be considered friends, if you sort of stretched the definition. "Well, I did see this yellow outfit—"

"Yellow, now that's a color you ought to be wearing," Cherry said. "It would look a lot better than that awful khaki."

Louise took a sideways glance at the orange polka-dot blouse Cherry was wearing. "There's a certain quality of dignity in khaki," she said.

"Dignity? Dead people need dignity! What you need is something to brighten up that pale coloring of yours, put a little life in your face."

Louise glanced at Cherry again. The green stretch pants made the polka-dot blouse even more objectionable. Drab or not, she certainly didn't want to end up looking like *that!*

By the time she parked in front of the Bluebird Ladies Shoppe, Louise had decided against the canary yellow outfit she'd seen last time. She remembered liking it, but she'd walked out of the store and left it hanging on the rack. After careful consideration, she'd deemed it too flamboyant for a grandmother.

They had barely walked inside the store when Cherry latched onto a red tee-shirt with a sequined palm tree on the front of it. "Look at this!" she squealed and held it up for Louise to see. "It's a size ten. You think it'll fit?"

Louise looked at the shirt in Cherry's hand. The narrow little thing didn't look big enough for Mandy. She eyed the size of Cherry's bosom and said, "You probably ought to try a twelve or fourteen."

"It does look like it runs small," Cherry replied and hung the shirt back on the rack. Then she grabbed three other size tens and kept moving through the store.

"What about you, honey?" a chubby-faced clerk asked Louise. "You looking for something special?"

"Not really," Louise answered. "I'll just browse awhile."

From clear across the store, Cherry yelled, "Yellow!"

"You want yellow?" the clerk said. "We've got an outfit that would look *darling* on you. You could use a brighter color around your face."

"I told her that!" Cherry echoed.

"I suppose it wouldn't hurt to try."

The clerk handed Louise a yellow outfit—the same outfit she'd looked at last time. "Bright colors should look stunning on you," the clerk said. "Give you a whole new image. You also ought to try this one and this one and..."

Before Louise knew what had happened she found herself herded into the dressing room with six different outfits, not one of them khaki. The first thing she wriggled into was the yellow skort.

"How's the fit?" the clerk asked, poking her head through the curtain.

Louise suddenly felt foolish. The yellow outfit seemed even more outlandish than it did on the hanger. "I don't think this is for me," she said, eyeing the skimpy skort in a three-way mirror.

"Nonsense, you look terrific. Fit's good, color's perfect."

"Isn't it rather short?" Louise tugged at the leg. "For a woman my age?"

"That's who wears skorts. You look better than most."

"Really?"

"I wouldn't say it if it wasn't so. Not two days ago another lady tried that very same outfit. Now she looked like a butterball."

"It's not too short?"

"Short? That's not short, Sugar. You're in Florida!"

Louise stepped back as far as she could and squinted at the three-way reflection. Sure enough, in the mirror she saw a younger woman—a Priscilla or Penelope.

One after the other Louise slipped in and out of the outfits, the clerk clucking her approval each and every time. "You've a nice little shape," the clerk said, "round where a body ought to be round."

As a friend Louise could take advantage of Cherry's twenty-five percent off coupon, so she bought the yellow outfit, a turquoise short, and two matching tops. She felt tempted to buy all of the outfits she'd tried on, but she needed to ease her way into a new image. Cherry eventually squeezed into the size ten palm tree shirt and found a pair of Lycra toreador pants that emphasized the ampleness of her figure. Those she bought in a size eight. Both women left the store with good-sized bags under their arms and smiles on their faces.

At first Louise didn't notice him squatted down beside the wheel of her car, but once she caught sight of the silver hair and the dark blue uniform her face brightened. "Hi, there," she said, and Michael M. Mobley looked up.

"Looks like you've got a flat." He stood and rose to his full height.

"So I see," she said without looking at the tire.

"If you've got a spare, I can change it for you." He flashed the smile she remembered.

Instead of answering, Louise stood there with her gaze locked on Mister Triple Initials' face.

"A spare?" he repeated.

Cherry elbowed Louise in the ribs. "Oh, it's in the trunk." Louise pulled the key from her bag and handed it to Mike.

Mister Triple Initials opened the trunk and tugged the jack loose from beneath a carton. When he turned back, he stood nose to nose with Louise who had leaned in beside him. Cherry grimaced and rolled her eyes.

"Did you find it okay?" she asked but made no effort to move away.

As she watched him work, Louise found herself wishing he'd slow down a bit. Clay would have taken all afternoon to change that tire, but without mustering up a bead of sweat Mister Triple Initials hauled out the spare and bolted it onto the wheel. The jack was back in the trunk before she had time to get going on a meaningful conversation.

"Well, now," he said, wiping his hands with his handkerchief. "This'll hold you for a while, but have Ernie fix that tire soon as you can."

"Absolutely," Louise nodded. "I'll see to it this afternoon."

Once they'd gotten back in the car and headed back down Center Street, Cherry asked, "What was that all about?"

Louise smiled. "You don't know?"

"Know what?"

"His name is Michael M. Mobley! Do you know what that means?"

"What what means?"

Louise rolled her eyes. "Triple initials! If double initials are lucky, then just imagine—"

Cherry gave a loud guffaw. "Mike ain't one bit lucky!"

"So you say. But if I could get him to buy twenty lottery tickets for me—"

"He ain't never won so much as a fruit basket."

"Maybe he doesn't realize—"

"There ain't no such thing as lucky double initials."

"It so happens I've known any number of people who—"

"Only luck Mike has is marrying Marion."

"His wife's name is Marion?"

"Yeah."

Louise knew that was the way it happened. Only a double initial woman could be lucky enough to win the heart of a triple initial man. "I'll bet the problem is that she's never once suggested he buy lottery tickets."

"There ain't no problem." Cherry laughed. "Him and Marion is the happiest couple in town, outside of me and Wilfred."

Louise left it at that, although she knew if she ever met Marion Mobley she'd most certainly suggest buying lottery tickets. "Goodness," she said, "look at the time. Clay's probably wondering about supper."

"Come on over, eat with us," Cherry suggested. "Wilfred caught three big bass yesterday. They're cleaned and ready to pop in the oven."

"I'm sort of expecting company," Louise said hesitantly.

Cherry gave a wide-eyed look of surprise. "Who?" she asked.

"My friend, Billie. She's coming from New Jersey. Driving, I think." Louise gave a sorrowful head shake. "Poor Billie," she continued. "She's got problems way worse than ours."

"Yours," Cherry corrected. "Me, I'm the happiest I ever been."

"Consider yourself lucky."

"What time's your friend coming?"

Louise shrugged her shoulders.

"Bring her along. Three of them bass is plenty enough for five people, even if one eats as much as Wilfred." Cherry laughed at her own joke.

"Billie may not be here until tomorrow or the next day."

"Well, shoot, there's no sense in just waiting. Come on over, we'll keep an ear out for her."

Louise had to admit the thought of not cooking appealed to her, and odd as it might seem she'd actually enjoyed the afternoon with Cherry. After a certain amount of time, you apparently deafened your ears to the sound of jingling bracelets. Besides Wilfred had caught bass, which tasted nowhere near as disgusting as catfish. "Okay," she said, reasoning that an afternoon of shopping and dinner two nights in a row still didn't make people best friends. True friendships took years and years to develop.

The evening turned out better than expected. Wilfred popped open a bottle of wine to celebrate the fact that he'd caught three bass, a first. And Louise, after two glasses of wine, said the bass weren't the least bit fishy-tasting.

"That's cause I caught them back by the marsh," Wilfred replied.

"The marsh?" Clay's eyes practically lit up. "So that's the place, huh? And all this while I've been fishing alongside the landing."

"That's why you ain't caught fish like these!" Wilfred said. "You and Monroe come fishing with me. I'll show you the spot."

Much preferring the bass to a platter of greasy catfish, Louise said, "Yes, Clay, that's exactly what you should do."

Once the men got to talking about fishing the women moved from the kitchen table to the backyard, and even with a dozen or more mosquitoes buzzing around them they sat and talked. Louise told Cherry what had happened to Billie Butterman. "It's hard to believe," Louise said, "because Billie's had double initials all her life."

"Double initials? Oh, we're back to that good luck thing you believe in?" Cherry chuckled. "Me, I can tell you for certain there ain't no good luck comes from double initials. When I was married to Ed my name was Mabel Malcovitch, and he left me all the same. No, ma'am, I didn't get one speck of good luck till I married Wilfred and turned myself into a Cherry."

"Well, I suppose there are *some* instances…"

When Louise finally got ready to go home, Cherry reminded her about the Hands Down Card Club meeting the next day.

"Oh, I really don't think—" Louise stammered.

"You've *got* to come," Cherry said. "I've already signed you up!"

"Well, I suppose—"

"Eleven o'clock at the clubhouse, and don't forget a sharing dish."

"Sharing dish?"

"Yeah, everybody brings one. You know, some nuts, a salad, anything."

"Okay." Louise already thought that she would put together a platter of little red tomatoes, green olives, and chunks of yellow cheese. It was such a colorful presentation, people felt good just looking at it. She imagined the Hands Down Card Club would be a lot like the Material Girls. They'd serve chilled wine and deviled eggs, use fancy glasses and silver forks. The only difference was this group shared tidbits of gossip over hearts and spades instead of patches of calico.

The next morning Louise got up before seven-thirty and bustled about the kitchen. She pulled out her silver serving platter and polished it until every last shadow of tarnish had disappeared. Then she arranged circles of cheddar skewered with cherry tomatoes and black olives. She had planned on using green olives, the fancy kind with bits of pimento in the center, but she had neglected to buy them at Bigwig. Tomorrow she would make a special trip over to Worthmore so she'd be sure to have the right olives on hand next time. She backed up and eyed the platter, then added a few sprigs of parsley and four carrot curls. *Presentation,* she thought, *that's the difference.*

By nine, she'd gotten in the shower; her dress—pink linen, the exact color of her lipstick—hung on the bedroom door already pressed. Getting ready took longer than usual. She applied an extra dab of foundation, and, with the artful hand of a Michelangelo, ruled liner both above and below her lashes. When her makeup was perfect she slipped the dress over her head, stepped back, and squinted at the mirror. *Ah, yes, Priscilla!*

At ten-thirty Louise started toward the clubhouse. "Nice to get dressed up for something special," she mumbled to herself, marching across the walkway. Possibly Tall Pines was more like Westfield than she had originally thought.

Carefully balancing her tray so it wouldn't tip—she wanted none of the tomatoes or olives askew—she backed through the door. When she turned to face the other women, a flush of embarrassment ran from her hairline down to the small toe on her right foot.

She should have stayed home.

There were fifteen other women in the room, and not one of them was dressed as she was. A blonde as wide as a Buick wore purple stretch pants and a tee shirt that read "If all else fails, ask Grandma!" A beanpole redhead had on the same outfit, except her shirt had "Grandma" spelled out in rhinestones. Almost everyone had on plastic flip-flops and comfy elastic-waist shorts, outfits that made her old khaki pants seem like eveningwear. Not one of them wore a dress, but there she stood in full regalia—stockings, high heels, even eyeliner. Her fussy tray of cheese cubes looked ridiculous alongside the paper plates piled high with potato chips and sliced liverwurst.

"Oh, my," Louise said, wishing the floor would suddenly develop a sink-hole and swallow her up. "I didn't realize it was *this* casual."

"Come on in," Cherry bellowed. "Take a load off."

"I really shouldn't stay," Louise answered. "I have some errands..."

"Why, that's sheer nonsense!" Beulah Mason, a woman with a tidy twisted-up bun atop her head, marched across the room and took Louise by the hand. "You're supposed to sit over here, with me. We're partners today."

"Partners?"

"Rummy. Five hundred points."

"Oh."

"You do play, don't you?"

"Canasta and Bridge."

"Rummy?"

"Not really. I honestly do think I'd better be going."

Beulah Mason had a number of chins that rippled when she spoke then cascaded down her neck into the folds of a full bosom. A big-boned woman, you could view her as overbearing or bossy, certainly not someone you'd expect to be tolerant of a newcomer.

Much to Louise's surprise, Beulah said, "That's okay, Rummy's easy enough to learn." Then she launched right into an explanation of the game. "Now, what you don't want to do is get caught holding a slew of points in your hand. That goes against you."

"Umm..."

"It's like poker. You match up the cards. Except when you know I need a certain card, then discard it, and I'll pick it up the next time around."

"But—how do I know what you need?"

"Well," Beulah raised an eyebrow and winked her right eye. "You don't *know* exactly, it's something you sort of catch on to." Again she winked, this time considerably more pronounced.

Whatever the message, Louise knew she didn't get it.

Within the first five minutes Clara Mae Abernathy shouted "Rummy!" and caught Louise with a full hand. When she spread her cards to count the points, Beulah looked over and sighed. "I needed that king of clubs."

"I'm sorry," Louise said. "I didn't know."

"Watch my face, honey." Beulah winked again, this time so deliberately it seemed her right eye remained closed for a full minute. "Watch carefully!"

Louise still didn't understand how she was supposed to know what card was needed. The second time around she was caught with eighty-five points, and Beulah's eyelid bobbed up and down like a yo-yo.

When they broke for lunch, Beulah asked, "Didn't you see me blinking?"

"Yes, but I didn't—"

"Well, it's surely easy enough. One blink for each number."

"Really? Each number?"

"Exactly. A king or queen, I wrinkle my nose. I lean forward it's spades, backward it's clubs, to the right hearts, and to the left diamonds."

"Isn't that cheating?"

"Of course not. We all do it."

"Why doesn't everyone just say what card they want?"

"Because," Beulah folded her arms across her bosom and crumpled her face, "that's not how the game is played." With that

Beulah headed for the buffet, and like the others she loaded her plate with bologna, potato salad, and pickles.

When they sat down to play again, Beulah looked over and winked. In fact, she closed her eye for so long that if the other eye weren't still open, anyone would have thought she had fallen asleep. "Now, don't forget," she said.

Louise nodded and tried to stay with Beulah's face as the game got going. The problem was she'd glance down at her cards, and when she looked up Beulah's eyelid would be bobbing up and down so rapidly she'd lose count. Beulah would want a nine and Louise would lay down a seven, or she'd wrinkle her nose for a sneeze and Louise would throw down a king—a king she could have otherwise used for her own hand. Once, when Beulah leaned over to scratch an itch on her left thigh, Louise threw down an ace of diamonds and it turned out to be the very card their opponents needed to rummy. That time Beulah gave Louise a swift kick in the shin.

After that Wanda Tattinger suggested they play without signals and Beulah won two hands, which put her in a much better frame of mind. All in all, Louise considered it a reasonably pleasant afternoon. Once you got to know them, the ladies were a nice enough group. Nothing like the Material Girls, but nice enough. Despite the fact that she caused Beulah to lose four dollars and thirty-five cents, they invited her to come back. Louise happily tucked her silver tray beneath her arm and started home, content to see that not a single olive or cube of cheese remained. Someone had even gobbled up the sprigs of parsley.

Louise

Next week I'm making franks-in-a-blanket or meatballs to bring to the Hands Down meeting. Those women are definitely NOT a cheese-and-olive group. Why, most of them showed up dressed like they were ready for a day of housecleaning. I'm thinking I could even wear that yellow skort and be perfectly acceptable.

I'm glad Cherry pushed me into going today. They're a strange group, but once you get used to their ways they're not bad people. Beulah was particularly nice. When I offered to pay back the four dollars she lost, she wouldn't hear of it. She said she'd won seven dollars the week before, so she was still ahead of the game.

Getting to know Cherry at least gives me someone to talk to. It's funny, but hearing about the hard life she had makes me more forgiving of her faults. Today I don't think I heard her bracelets jangle one time. It used to be that sound went through me like a person scratching their nails against a blackboard. If I was a true friend I'd take her aside and explain that those spandex pants don't do a thing for her figure, but being we're just neighbors I feel it's not my place to mention it. When Billie gets here and Cherry sees the way she dresses, Cherry might get the point on her own. I hope so.

Now that Ernie's fixed up the house it's not half-bad. Some days I find myself even thinking of it as home. Not a real home, but a place that's comfortable enough to live in. I guess it wasn't the house I was so attached to but the people. I miss Billie and the Material Girls something awful. And little Mandy—I'll bet she's crying her eyes out because I'm not there.

Clay goes fishing most every day and never mentions New Jersey or all the things we left behind. I hate to face up to it, but I think the reality is that we're never going back. Never.

Postcards & Visitors

Two months passed without a word from Billie. The first few weeks Louise sat by the window from dawn till dark watching for the big white Cadillac but eventually her watchfulness waned, and although she occasionally found herself standing by the window she could no longer picture Billie coming up the walkway. In time Louise began to believe her lifelong friend had deserted her just as she'd deserted Bradley.

When the warm spring turned to a blistering hot summer and Louise had all but lost hope of ever seeing Billie again, a postcard arrived from Philadelphia. On the front was a picture of the Liberty Bell and on the back was written, "I haven't forgotten you, but right now I've got to sort out the mess I've made of my own life. Feeling as I do, I'm not the person you want for a friend. Hope all is well with you. Love, Billie."

Louise read the card over three times; then she sat down and cried. It started out as a bit of sniffling but escalated into a wail that someone could hear a block away. As soon as Cherry caught wind of the noise, she came running.

"What's wrong?" she asked, her eyes big and round as Moon Pies.

"My best friend is gone." Louise handed Cherry the postcard.

Cherry read the card over. "I don't get it," she said with a puzzled expression.

"What's not to get? Billie is gone from my life. I'll never see her again. She's been my best friend for thirty years and now—" Louise started sobbing louder than ever.

"This card don't say that." Cherry turned the postcard over and studied the picture of the Liberty Bell as if she might find a continuation of the message there.

"That's what it means," Louise sniffled. "It's obvious. The other Material Girls have turned their backs on Billie, and she's assuming I'd do the same."

"This says that?" Cherry read the card again.

"It does if you read between the lines."

Cherry read the card again. "I still don't get it. What's she mean about not being the kind of person you want for a friend?"

"It's not true. Do you think I'd turn my back on my best friend just because people think she murdered Missus Butterman?"

"She murdered somebody?"

"I'm not saying she did, but if she did she'd have been justified. I don't care what Bradley says, I know Billie. Even if she hated that miserable old lady, she'd never push her down the stairs."

"You lost me," Cherry said. She pulled up a chair, sat next to Louise, and leaned in so close their noses practically touched. "Okay, now start at the beginning."

Louise did. Even though she'd been twelve hundred miles away at the time of Missus Butterman's funeral and Billie's disappearance, her story rambled on for almost two hours. Louise covered everything from the fact that Billie was born with double initials right through her last conversation with Bradley.

"Whew," Cherry said. "You're right, she does have worse problems."

"Remember the night Clay claimed I was kidnapped?"

Cherry nodded.

"Well, I wasn't. I'd started back to New Jersey thinking I might help Billie out, but when I tried to call her I found out she'd disappeared."

"That's why you came home?"

"It's one of the reasons. You see, I met this woman, Tulip. She told me about her daughter, Rosalie, who was gone for two years, then came home with a baby."

"So, you thought Billie was pregnant?"

"Pregnant? At her age?"

"Oh. Right."

"I figured if Rosalie came home after two years, then Billie would probably come here looking for me. After all, we were almost like sisters—" Louise started to sob again.

Cherry circled her arm around Louise's shoulder. "Go ahead," she said, "cry all you want to. When a person loses a friend, they got a right to be sad."

Cry is precisely what Louise did. For nearly a half-hour, she leaned into Cherry's ample bosom and gave way to tears.

Afterward Cherry fixed both of them a cup of tea. "This don't solve anything, but it makes you feel better." She stirred two heaping spoons of sugar into the cup and set it down in front of Louise. "I got sympathy for how you're feeling," Cherry said. "One time I had a best friend."

"What happened?"

"When Ed run me off, I didn't get to see her anymore. We swore we was gonna write and keep in touch with each other, but it didn't work out that way."

Louise stopped sniffling and listened.

"I wrote her four letters and never did get an answer. The fourth letter came back marked 'no longer at this address,' but it didn't say where she'd moved to."

"How terrible," Louise said with a sigh.

"Yeah." Cherry's eyes started getting watery. "They got a big sale at Bluebird," she said. "Let's go. It'll make us both feel better."

"Okay," Louise answered. Ten minutes later they were on their way to Worthmore.

During the next few months three more postcards from Billie arrived, every one of them mailed from a different city and not one giving any indication of when she'd arrive in Florida or if she was headed in that direction. They simply said she was managing to get by and hoped all was well with Louise. Every time a postcard arrived, Louise slipped into a malaise of memories that lasted for days. When there were no more postcards, she began to believe

Billie was forever gone from her life and for nearly a month she carried the thought around like a sack of stones.

Four times she called Rose Elkins to see if perhaps she'd heard something of Billie, but Rose claimed she was busy living her own life and didn't bother to keep in touch with anyone from New Jersey. "But Aunt Rose," Louise said, "what about all your friends? What about Missus Henkley?"

"Missus Henkley?"

"The woman next door. Brown hair, very nicely dressed?"

"Oh, that Missus Henkley," Rose answered. "I suppose she's okay."

"She was your best friend. Don't you think you should call and—"

"Louise, dear, the woman was an old fuddy-duddy. Why, she wouldn't even fetch the newspaper from outside her door unless she was fully dressed." After that Rose said she hated to cut Louise short, but she was on her way to a pizza party and didn't want to be late.

"Well, if you do talk to someone, would you ask if they've heard anything about Billie?" Louise asked, but by then Rose had hung up the telephone.

In June Rose and Floyd came for a visit, and Louise did a double-take when she opened the door. Aunt Rose wore cut-off pants and neon green flip flops. "Good grief," Louise gasped. "I almost didn't recognize you!"

"That's because I've had my hair cut," Aunt Rose answered.

"And you've colored it platinum blonde!"

Rose nodded. "Becoming, don't you think?"

"Well, I sort of liked the silver you had—"

"Louise, dear, you tend to see things as you want them to be. My hair wasn't silver it was grey, and everyone knows grey hair can make a person appear old."

Floyd and Aunt Rose stayed just long enough to have lunch and then they drove off, headed for what she called three days of "bumming around" the Florida Keys.

"You might want to visit Ernest Hemmingway's house while you're down there," Louise suggested but Rose said it was not likely, because they planned to do a fair bit of fishing. After they waved goodbye and drove off, the memory of Aunt Rose dressed in a shirt covered with palm trees brought on a headache that lasted for three days.

In August Phillip called, saying he'd booked a trip to Disney and figured they'd swing by for a visit. "When exactly would that be?" Louise asked, hoping he wouldn't say the same week as Dora's Tupperware party.

"We'll be arriving Tuesday after next, and we'll start for home the following Monday."

"Oh, dear," Louise said. "I'm going to miss the Hands Down meeting and—"

"Well, would you rather we didn't come?" Phillip asked sarcastically.

"Of course not!" Louise replied. Given his attitude, it's a good thing she hadn't told Phillip she'd also miss out on Dora's Tupperware party where there would be a buffet *and* valuable door prizes. Although she would have preferred they come another week, one not so crammed with social events, she would be truly glad to see sweet little Mandy. Of course, she'd be glad to see Phillip and Rachel also, although Rachel could be a bit tedious at times. But it was Mandy she'd missed the most. Louise thought back on the way her granddaughter made her feel special. Actually more than special. Downright godly.

On the Tuesday they were to arrive, Louise woke up before the sun cleared the horizon. "I thought they'd be here by now," she told Clay.

"At six o'clock in the morning?"

"I hope they haven't had some kind of trouble, a flat tire or an accident." She absentmindedly turned back to fixing breakfast and cracked an eighth egg into the bowl.

"I'm not *that* hungry," Clay said as he stood there watching.

"Oh. Okay then, I'll scramble them."

"Eight eggs are eight eggs, whether they're fried or scrambled."

"Stop making such a fuss," Louise said and poured the half-scrambled eggs into the frying pan. "You want sausage or bacon?" she asked.

Although Clay told her he'd prefer the sausage, she took out a pound of bacon and fried up the entire thing. Every few seconds she turned to look at the clock. "Is this clock broken?" she finally asked, and right after that she pushed the toaster lever down again even though black smoke had started to curl through the kitchen.

"I think that toast is done," Clay said.

"Okay." She took the toast, black and crusty as a piece of coal, slathered butter on it, and sat the plate in front of Clay.

"This toast is burnt," he said. "I don't want burnt toast."

"I'm tired of all this complaining," Louise said and trotted off toward the living room window. She looked to the left and craned her neck until she could see all the way to the bend in the road—nothing. She looked off to the right, which was a dead end. The only thing she saw was a rusted truck with a flat tire. "I hope they haven't run into a storm," she murmured, thinking back on her own experience. "A sudden downpour is sure to cause an accident, especially since Phillip is not used to driving in that kind of rain. Clay," she called with a sudden sense of urgency, "we'd better go look for them."

He still sat in the kitchen eating eight eggs and a pound of bacon. "Look for them where?" He scraped a large helping of bacon and eggs into Yoo's bowl and went into the living room. "You don't even know which way they're coming."

"Of course I do," she answered. "From Orlando."

"And where exactly did you want to look?"

"We could cross over Route Sixty and back track to Disney."

"And what if they show up here while we're driving around the countryside?"

Louise gave an agitated huff. "You have all the answers, don't you?" With that she tromped back to the kitchen and looked at the clock again. "This thing is broken," she called out. "I'm positive it's broken!"

"It's not. It read nine-twenty-five before, and now it reads nine-twenty-eight."

"They're probably stranded alongside the road."

"They'd call if that was the case."

"If they weren't in trouble, they'd be here by now."

"They said early afternoon."

"Well, it's already," Louise checked the clock again, "nine-twenty-nine!"

"They'll get here in their own good time," Clay said. He picked up the small axe he'd left alongside the door and walked out. Chopping away at the palmetto had become a daily thing.

"Hopefully they'll get here soon," Louise mumbled nervously. "I wouldn't want to start a project and be wrapped up in it when they arrive." She conveniently forgot her last project was the half-finished quilt she'd brought from New Jersey.

Close to three o'clock Phillip's car pulled into the driveway. Mandy jumped from the car shouting, "Grandma! Grandma!"

Louise scooped her up and hugged hard. "Oh, sweetheart, I've missed you so very much," she whispered.

"I missed you too," Mandy answered and wriggled free. "Grandma, guess who came with us—Victoria!"

"Victoria?"

"Unh-huh. She's my new best friend."

Mandy turned back to the car and urged a little girl with cascades of curls and huge brown eyes from the back seat. "Come on," she said. "It's only Grandma!"

Only *Grandma?* Louise considered herself so much more than that. She had morphed into someone with a colorful wardrobe of shorts, a person invited to parties, a player who could catch the signals for Rummy. She looked down at the bright red toenails poking out of her yellow sandals. The change seemed so obvious; how could they not notice?

That was the start of a very trying week.

Apparently, Phillip had caught a cold the day after they'd left New Jersey and hadn't felt up to stopping for a round of golf in Hilton Head, which put him in a particularly sour frame of mind. Then halfway through Georgia Rachel's allergies started acting up, so that by the time they got to Disney her nose was as red as a ripe tomato. Minutes after they pulled into the driveway Rachel gulped down a double dose of Benadryl and went off to bed, leaving

Louise to cope with two little girls who wouldn't listen to a word she said.

"Don't jump on the sofa," she told them, but they did anyway. "Don't sit on the dog. Don't spill the soda. Don't wake your mother. Lower the sound." It was all Louise could do to hold back from disconnecting the television, because they blasted it from morning till night, one silly cartoon after another.

Rachel came out of the room just long enough to eat. She'd plop herself down and make quick work of a good-sized stack of pancakes or three sunny-side-up eggs, then honk her nose a few times and head back to the bedroom. For three afternoons in a row, Louise took Mandy and Victoria to the swimming pool while Phillip headed off to go fishing with Clay and Monroe Schramm. The girls, so even in size you could lay a board across their heads, pranced along hand-in-hand, giggling in each other's ears and whispering secrets, paying little or no attention to the tag-along grandma. The visit wasn't going at all the way Louise had thought it would.

The only good thing about the entire week was that Mandy leapfrogged onto the sofa and sent Uncle Charlie's catfish flying off the wall—smashed it into nine pieces, not including the glass eye, which rolled off under the sofa never to be found. Louise was sorely tempted to scold the girls. After all, she'd told them to stop jumping on the furniture any number of times. Luckily they hadn't listened. When the catfish went sailing through the air, Victoria leapt up and shouted, "Not me, it wasn't me!" But Mandy, she just sat there with those blue eyes wide open.

"Well! Maybe you'll stop jumping now!" With a piece of green fin stuck to her shoe, Louise walked away so they wouldn't see her laughing.

She might have enjoyed the whole thing more, but by that time she was worn thin with bumping into Rachel or Phillip every time she turned around, cooking meals, cleaning up, and babysitting two girls determined to be downright troublesome. On Friday, a half-hour after the dinner dishes were cleared from the table, Cherry came yoo-hooing through the door. Not bothering to ask Louise "How was your day?" Cherry flopped herself into the recliner and said, "You missed a great game last Tuesday."

In a snit, Louise replied, "In case you haven't noticed, I've got company."

"Tough luck. You were supposed to be play with Esther."

"Esther Plugett?"

Cherry nodded, grinning in the way that made her cheeks puff out.

"So, what'd she do?"

"Got another partner."

"Another partner?"

"Yeah. Minnie Hawkins."

"Minnie? She doesn't even know all the signals!"

"Maybe not, but they won."

"Minnie won?"

"Yeah, eight dollars. Esther got four Kings and rummied on the third hand."

Louise moaned. This could be added to the list of things that didn't go her way. For almost two months, she'd waited for this chance—Esther was the best Rummy player in the group and won something almost every week. Now it would probably be three, maybe four months before they were paired again.

When the days started to feel as if they were thirty or forty hours long, Louise found herself itching to break free. She'd already missed the Hands Down Meeting and Dora's Tupperware party, and she was on the verge of missing The Bluebird Shoppe's summer clearance. "Think I'll take a run over to Bigwig," she told Clay. "We're almost out of peanut butter."

"Peanut butter? No, there's several jars in the cupboard."

"That's the crunchy kind."

"Oh."

"Not good for your digestion. Besides, the little chunks of nut stick in your teeth."

"But isn't that the kind we always have?"

"It's time we changed."

"After all these years?"

"And milk. We need milk."

"We've got two gallons."

"Growing children need a lot of milk."

"Okay," Clay shrugged. "I'm going over to Giant Hardware anyway, so I'll pick those things up. At least it'll save you the trip."

To push the issue would have been awkward, especially with Phillip and Rachel sitting right there. "Okay," Louise answered, consoling herself with the thought that Phillip and his family would be leaving day after tomorrow. Somehow in just six days she had grown as anxious for them to be gone as she had been for them to arrive.

Phillip had planned to leave Monday morning, but Sunday night the weatherman announced a storm front coming through.

"I wouldn't worry," Louise assured him. "These things blow over quickly, ten maybe fifteen minutes."

"Hmm." The corners of Phillip's mouth had a natural droop that made him appear constantly worried, a feature inherited from his father. "I don't know," he mumbled. "They did say heavy rain."

"Comes and goes," she said again. "Nothing to worry about. I've been caught in it any number of times."

"Hmm."

"You'll see. Tomorrow morning it'll be sunny."

During the night the storm front rolled in, came from the west, and stalled overhead, just as the weatherman had predicted. When they woke on Monday, a blanket of dark gray clouds hung so low it felt as if you could stick a finger in the air and poke rain from them.

"I don't think I want to drive in this," Phillip said, his eyes now sloped at the same angle as his drooped mouth. "We probably should wait a day or so and let it pass."

Mandy and Victoria flopped down in front of the television and settled on a cartoon. Phillip and Rachel went back to the kitchen for another cup of coffee. The rain started moments later. Not a typical Florida storm with booming thunder and lightning zigzagging across the sky but a steady downpour, a heavy sweep of water pushed sideways by the wind. "Strange," Louise said as she refilled everyone's cup. "I thought it would have blown over by now."

It was close to eleven when Phillip said, "We'd better wait and leave tomorrow."

"I'm inclined to agree," Clay said as they stood watching the rain—father and son, two faces with the same rubber-stamp expression.

After supper the storm moved on and a clear white moon appeared, and Louise breathed a sigh of relief. Tomorrow would be a beautiful day.

Tuesday morning dawned with a sun-filled sky, just as Louise had predicted. After breakfast Phillip and his family climbed back into the car and started home. At ten o'clock Louise called Cherry. Twenty minutes later they were on their way to Worthmore.

"So," Louise asked, "how was the Tupperware party?"

"You didn't miss much. The buffet was pickles and sliced bologna. Dora was gonna make sandwiches, but she forgot to buy bread. Beulah, you know how she likes to eat, well, she told Dora since she had all that Tupperware she could've bought the bread a week early. Of course Dora got real up in the air and said Beulah ought to know the Tupperware was for demonstrating, not using."

Louise laughed. "What about the door prize?"

"Door prize?" Cherry said mockingly. "A plastic lettuce keeper. Round, the kind you can only use for iceberg. Nobody buys iceberg anymore."

"Well, then, I don't feel so bad about missing the party."

"I could have easy enough done without going," Cherry said. "How was your visit with the kids?"

"Okay," Louise said. "Kind of disappointing, but okay."

"Disappointing?"

"Unh-huh." She paused a long time and made it seem as though she was looking for some sort of a road sign, even though she could have driven to Worthmore blindfolded. "I guess I expected it to be the way it used to be, but it wasn't."

"It wasn't?"

"No. Mandy used to say I was her best friend, but now..." Louise sighed and shook her head. "And then Phillip...well, he flat out said my outfit was too short for a woman my age."

"What was you wearing?" Cherry asked.

"My yellow skort."

"Pffft," Cherry puffed. "That ain't even close to being short. He was probably just in an out-of-sorts mood."

"Maybe," Louise answered. "But it does seem like they've changed."

"Me, I'm used to that. Every time I get something settled in my mind and think, okay now this is how things are, whammo! Everything changes again."

"Don't you just hate that?" Louise replied and then wondered whether Bluebird would have a pair of purple plaid shorts in her size.

The Accident

The Thursday it happened, Cherry was at the Palmer house watching as Louise demonstrated how to make deviled ham canapés. They were in the middle of rolling out the crust when they heard a knock. The knock itself surprised them since most of the people at Tall Pines simply came yoo-hooing through the door. "You finish up," Louise told Cherry as she turned toward the front door.

Michael M. Mobley stood there. "Missus Palmer," he said. "I'm sorry to have to tell you this, but there's been an accident."

"Not our car," Louise replied with a fair amount of confidence. "It's in the driveway. Hasn't been driven all day."

"I'm afraid the accident—"

Cherry came scurrying into the room. "Accident?" she said.

"Yes." Mobley's face looked as somber as that of a gravedigger. "Were Wilfred and Clay together today?" he asked.

Both women nodded. "But I doubt they'd be driving around," Louise said nervously. "They went fishing."

"This was a boating accident," Mobley said. "Out at Snake Lake."

Cherry teetered a bit, and Mobley grabbed hold of her arm. "It appears a tourist who'd been drinking lost control of his speedboat and ran into Monroe Schramm's boat. We've had reports that three men were on Schramm's boat. The rescue team is pretty certain one of them was Monroe. They think the other two might have been Clay and Wilfred."

"Might have been—" Louise felt her heart drop. It hurdled past her stomach and down through the soles of her feet. "Might have been? Clay? Wilfred?"

"Not Wilfred," Cherry said. "Not Wilfred, why he's—"

"We're not sure yet," Mobley said, making it sound as if there was hope. "The rescue team has already pulled somebody from the water. They think it's Monroe Schramm but they don't know for certain, because he's still unconscious."

"Where's Clay?" Louise asked, her voice high-pitched and threaded with panic. "Have they gotten Clay out of the water?"

"As far as I know they've only taken one person from the—"

"Clay can't swim!" she gasped. "He can't swim a stroke!"

"Wilfred can," Cherry said, reaching for Louise's arm. "He's a good swimmer. He can tread water and—"

"Clay can't!" Louise screamed. "He can't swim. Not at all!"

"Try to calm down," Mobley said. "It's too soon to jump to conclusions." He reached for Louise's shoulder, but she yanked herself back.

"Didn't you hear me?" she screeched. "Clay can't swim! Do you know what happens to a man who can't swim?"

They drown, her mind said, but she couldn't speak the words. Her eyes overflowed as she turned to Cherry. "We've got to go look for them," she said tearfully.

"Come on." Mike led them to the squad car. "By the time we get there the rescue team will probably have all of three of them."

"Clay can't swim," Louise repeated, but this time it came out in little more than a tearful whisper.

Mike turned the siren on and stopped for nothing. Although he made it to Snake Lake faster than anyone might have thought possible, to Louise it seemed the patrol car moved at a crawl. Cherry nervously babbled on about how Wilfred was such a good swimmer. "In high school he won a medal," she said. "A medal! Being such a good swimmer, he'd surely be able to—" The words crackled and broke apart as she spoke.

Louise simply stared out the window mumbling a prayer about how she didn't wish Wilfred or Monroe any harm, but would God please make it *her* husband who was hauled up from the water. A long stretch of tangled-up pines swished by and then a clump of palmettos, and the sight of them made her ache to hear the sound of Clay's axe whacking away at a palmetto little more than stump.

"We're here," Mike finally said and turned into the boatyard.

With all the stories she'd heard of Snake Lake, Louise felt as if she'd been there before. She had a picture of the place fixed in her mind—shiny, bright pleasure boats drifting across soft waves of blue satin, open-air restaurants, umbrella tables. But as soon as they swung into the boatyard, she saw the truth of what it was— ugly and forlorn, a place unlikeable from the moment you set eyes upon it.

Patches of sawgrass taller than a man dotted the lake, a good part swamp. She saw no sand, no beach, just a narrow strip of muddy shoreline with moss-covered trees, clutters of cattails, and a chained-down garbage can. Louise had always imagined the water to be blue and so clear a person could watch fish swimming, but it was scummy and black. The blackest black imaginable. A black so thick and dense that everything beneath the surface disappeared from sight. In place of the lakeside breeze she'd expected, the heavy stench of rotted plants and algae came to her.

Gawkers salted the shoreline, people who wandered in from nowhere to stand around and stare, expressionless eyes fixed on the gray dinghies bobbing in the distance. A few fishermen who had joined the gawkers clustered together and thanked God such a thing had not happened to them.

Was it possible Clay knew these people? Raggedy little groups of men whispering about what might have happened? A bleak-faced woman fingering a string of rosary beads, another toting a baby on her hip? The gathering had the look of a wake mixed with the tawdriness of a two-dollar carnival. Two boys flopped around in the mud. "Look at me, I'm a drowned man!" the bigger one shouted. He clutched his throat and let his tongue hang loose from his mouth. A menacing look from the woman with the baby silenced him.

Mike steered Louise and Cherry through the crowd, beyond the bait shack plastered with signs for beer and hot dogs, past the "No swimming" sign, and toward a giant heft of a man drinking coffee from a paper cup. "Captain Ritter," he said edging the two women forward, "This here is Louise Palmer and Cherry Melinski."

A mountain of a man, the captain had a sizable stomach hanging over his belt and a wiry red beard covering most of his face. He shook his head sorrowfully. "Nothing yet. We've got Schramm and the tourist who was in the speedboat. The searchers are still out there looking." He had a gentle voice for a man of his size, not something one expected.

"My Wilfred's a good swimmer," Cherry said. "Surely the searchers can see him."

Captain Ritter shook his head again. "We've got reports that Schramm was the only one wearing a life vest—"

Louise's face turned ashen. "Not wearing a life vest? But Clay can't swim—"

"Nothing's for sure. We've just got to wait and see."

"Wait?" Louise repeated after him. "A man who can't swim can't possibly—" She grabbed at the air as if it were something to hold on to.

"Mobley, find these ladies a place to sit," Captain Ritter directed and patted Louise on the shoulder. "I'll come and get you the minute we have something."

She didn't answer. She couldn't. Her throat had filled with the words she should have said to Clay, all the things he needed to know so that he'd fight to stay alive. Just three days earlier she'd threatened to return to New Jersey with or without him, but she'd said it in the heat of anger. She'd never leave. She loved Clay; surely he knew that. After all these years how could she not love him? He was the father of her children, he was... Suddenly the old heartaches flooded her thoughts, the bitter memories, and the pain of losing what she loved. Despite a relentless sun, a sun so hot that it caused steam to rise from puddled water, Louise shivered. Her hands and feet felt cold as a box of frozen spinach.

Cherry wrapped her arm around Louise and they stood there, huddled together like women awaiting execution. "Don't worry," Cherry whispered. "Wilfred's a good swimmer. He'll save Clay." Louise wanted to believe that, but her heart knew better.

On the far end of the beach, Cherry noticed a crowd of people gesturing and moving about. "Maybe they see something," she told

Louise. The two women linked arms and set off in that direction, making their way through the crowd of people. Inch by inch they moved toward the shoreline, their eyes fixed on the far horizon. Although Cherry believed Wilfred a strong enough swimmer to save himself and his friend, Louise imagined Clay could at any moment be taking his last breath. Even worse, he could already be dead, lying motionless beneath the black murkiness of that God-forsaken lake. When they finally reached the area where they'd seen the flurry of activity, they discovered the commotion was caused by a few sand fleas nipping at people's feet.

As Louise and Cherry stood there side by side searching the stretch of black water for any moving thing that could perchance be their husbands, the sun blistered the beach and the buzz of mosquitoes grew louder. Every now and again a long-legged bird skittered in or out of the marsh, but little else moved. Louise dug her heels into the ground and craned her neck toward the spot where the rescue boats circled round and round. Occasionally the flutter of a bird's wing would ruffle the sawgrass or the sun would cause a glimmer of light to dance through the water, and she would shift her eyes to that spot. Soon she began seeing things the others didn't.

She saw Clay's shriveled arm rise from the water and take hold of all the things she loved. A young Louise dressed in a white satin gown appeared and then disappeared. Odd pieces of furniture, babies, houses, even the storage shed in Westfield—all of them followed Clay down into blackness. Even Yoo. She saw the dog's head bobbing back and forth for a moment; then it too disappeared. Everything that mattered in her life was gone.

Neither woman could say how long they remained there—a minute, two minutes, five minutes? It felt like hours, because as the heartbeats landed heavily one upon another, Louise began to believe she would never see Clay again. Suddenly Cherry spotted a black speck bobbing up and down in the water. "Look!" she screamed, stretching her arm toward the horizon. With babies whining, dogs barking, and people talking, her shout disappeared in the noise. She began jumping up and down and waving her arms about. "I see Wilfred swimming!" she screamed. "Over there!"

In three long strides Captain Ritter came to their side. "You see something?"

"A splash! It's Wilfred, I know it's Wilfred!" She pointed again. "There he is!"

The Captain tilted his head left, then right. "Where?"

Louise stretched her neck and leaned toward the water, hopeful but somehow realizing that Cherry now saw what she had seen—the lake swallowing up everything that mattered.

"It's gone now," Cherry said, lowering her arm.

Ritter shielded his eyes and squinted at the lake, not momentarily but for a decent while. Finally he turned away. "Holler if you see anything else."

Louise remained where she was, her eyes fixed on the spot Cherry had pointed to. Maybe Wilfred was strong enough to save Clay... Maybe Cherry *had* seen something...maybe...but then again...maybe not.

Suddenly the shadow became visible again, a black head, a shade darker than the lake, making its way through the water, a small but steady ripple. "That's Yoo!" Louise screamed.

Just as Ritter turned back, a voice squawked across his radio.

"Captain, you ain't gonna believe this. There's a dog out here."

"Get over there and pick it up." Ritter watched as the little motor boat cut westward. "Good work, Pete," he mumbled. "Good work."

For a while Louise felt certain she could see Yoo. She even thought she might have heard him bark. But then the black speck disappeared behind a stand of sawgrass, and she began to wonder if it had been nothing more than a mirage—something wished for and imagined as real. As the rescue boat slowed and edged its way into the marsh, she prayed to hear someone call out that they had found Yoo and Clay, Wilfred too, of course. All she heard was the jumble of unfamiliar voices, the crackle of static, and the sound of birds.

Someone on the other end of the radio shouted, "Looks like—!" but after that the sound of birds squawking covered anything else he had to say.

"What?" Cherry screamed. "What?" She held tight to Louise's arm.

"Is it Clay?" Louise's voice sounded thin and so pitifully small a gust of wind that suddenly came up carried it off.

"It's Wilfred! It's got to be Wilfred!"

Captain Ritter did not turn to either of the women but kept his eyes glued to the water. "Got anything?" he asked the radio. No response. Ritter waited a moment then repeated the question.

"Debris... green boat..." the radio finally crackled, but the screeches from a flock of sandhill cranes made it impossible to catch all the words.

"What about survivors? Have you found either of the men?"

"Erk...swimming away . . ."

"Is someone out there?"

"Dog..."

"Can you pick him up?"

"He's going... opposite direction... mangrove thicket...."

"Call him!" Louise cried out. "His name's Yoo. Call him, he'll come." On the horizon she saw other boats suddenly turn toward the marsh and she held her breath, afraid to trust that for once something would turn out as she wanted it to. Moments later she heard the sound of barking, Yoo's barking, a sound as familiar as her own child's cry. "Clay? Is Clay with him?"

"Pete, what's going on?" Captain Ritter asked.

They only heard the far off scrabbling around of things, splashing, and a muffled echo of voices calling back and forth.

"Pete?"

"Cap, we got one of them."

"There's more dogs?"

"No, it's one of the guys from the fishing boat."

"Clay? Is it Clay?"

"Wilfred?" Cherry dug her fingernails into Louise's arm so furiously that a trickle of blood oozed from where she had locked on.

Ritter still didn't turn to either of the women, just focused on the water as though he could see into the thicket with some kind of X-ray vision. "Is he okay?"

"Bad shape... on my way... Charlie's...staying..."

"Lassiter! Shipley!" Captain Ritter motioned for the two officers to follow him as he headed toward the parking area shouting a barrage of orders. "They've got a survivor! Get that ambulance over here! Move!"

It took everything Louise had not to grab hold of Captain Ritter and tug him back. Who? she wanted to know. Who was the survivor? She and Cherry both wanted to ask, and neither wanted to hear an answer. One survivor. One. That meant someone lived and someone died. Each woman understood if her husband lived, her friend's husband died. Whatever the answer, heartbreak would follow.

A flat gray boat chugged out from behind the sawgrass and turned to shore, Yoo's black head poking up just beyond the bow. Still linked arm-in-arm, the two women waded into the black water where they watched and waited.

Louise thought back to the day of old Mister Palmer's funeral and remembered the gloom of it. She could still recall holding Baby Phillip in her arms as she stared down into the casket, into the face of a man with the same somber expression and downturned mouth as Clay. Missus Palmer simply did not believe her husband could be taken from her in the blink of an eye, so she sat on the sofa in the far back of the room pretending someone had made a huge mistake.

For three whole days she sat there, looking at the door as if she expected Clay's daddy to arrive at any minute. She refused to look at her dead husband until the very last minute. Then just as they began to close the casket, Missus Palmer ran up and threw herself across the coffin and began kissing his face. "You didn't have to shovel the walkway!" she cried. But it didn't make any difference at that point.

Once the rescue craft moved into shallow water, Yoo leaped over the side and splashed his way toward Louise. Moments later the two women saw the lifeless body of the man lying at the bottom of the boat.

"Clay!" Louise screamed and reached for her husband.

"Stay back," Shipley commanded as the boat maneuvered into position.

"Clay!" Louise cried out a second time, tears now streaming down her face. She wanted to know if he was alive, she wanted to touch his face and listen to the sound of his breath, she wanted to see him smile, but she could ask for none of these things because his name was the only word that came from her mouth.

Neither of the officers said anything more as they lifted the body from the boat and placed it on the mud of the beach. The ambulance attendant rolled Clay onto his side and brought forth a trickle of water from his mouth, but it looked hardly more than the drip of a broken faucet.

Louise watched for what seemed an eternity as they pressed against her husband's lifeless chest and breathed into his mouth. This, she realized, was the horrible place between heaven and hell, a place where you experienced the worst of everything and the best of nothing. A dumbfounded Cherry stood beside Louise for a few moments; then she wandered off, looking to the horizon and calling out, "Wilfred? Wilfred?"

Eventually a surge of black water gushed from Clay's mouth, and he began to retch violently. His head jerked to the side and another rush of water poured from his mouth, filthy water thick with the scum of the lake. Louise wanted to reach across, clean his face, wipe away the rotted seaweed, but the rescuers hovered over him in such a way that the best she could do was take hold of his hand. After a while Clay ceased gagging and slowly opened his eyes, not totally, but rather like someone waking from a deep sleep. He looked at Louise as if she were someone he didn't recognize. "M…on…roe?" he said, and then closed his eyes again.

"Stay with me!" Shipley shouted as Clay fell back. "Do you know where you are? Do you know what's happened?"

"M…on…roe?" Clay mumbled again."

"He's on his way to the hospital," Shipley answered. "A bit banged up, but he'll be okay. We've also got your dog."

"Wha…about…" Clay fell back a second time and waited until he regained enough strength to finish his question. "…Wilfred?"

"They're still looking."

Clay groaned and twisted his face into a grimace.

Louise clamped his hand tighter. "They'll find him," she said. "They found you, and they'll find Wilfred. Cherry said he's a real good swimmer."

Captain Ritter knelt beside Clay. "What happened?" he asked.

Clay groaned again. "Louise?"

"Can you tell us what happened?" the captain repeated.

Clay didn't answer, just shifted his eyeballs off to the side.

"I can!" an old man in the front row of the crowd shouted. "I seen it all!"

"You saw what happened?"

"I sure enough did. I was fixing to do a bit of fishing myself, but once I spotted that young fella zip-zapping across the water I decided to wait a spell."

"What's your name?" Ritter asked.

"Tom Trumbull."

Louise watched the man speak. Old and stooped, he had a ragged bristle of beard and a floppy hat faded to almost the same shade of gray. Not the type of person you'd figure for such sensibility.

Ritter pulled a pad from his belt and began to write. "Did you actually see the collision?" he asked.

"It weren't no collision," the old man answered. "That young fella ran smack into the side of Monroe's boat. He come across the water whooping and hollering like a man full of loco weed."

"The young man in the green speedboat?"

"Green, yeah, but I ain't never seen no speedboat go fast as that one. That thing was nose up and moving like a bullet when it hit Monroe."

"So you're saying the speedboat ran into the boat the fishermen were in?"

"Worse 'n ran into it. He splintered Monroe's boat sideways to Sunday."

"What happened then?"

"Well..." Tom Trumbull paused for a moment like he was thinking the thing through. "It *seems* I saw somebody jump out of the boat a second or so before the explosion, but that's something I'm not certain on. It happened real fast. Once that green boat exploded, stuff was sailing through the air like spray from a pop bottle."

"Anything else you can tell me?"

"Yeah. You ought not allow them kind of boats out here. This is a fishing lake! A fishing lake for law-abiding citizens."

"Anything more about the accident?"

"Ain't nothing else to tell." The old man shook his head. "A few more minutes and I'd've been out there myself, likely as not dead now."

The captain turned back to Clay who had his eyes open and was listening to Trumbull's story as if it was something he'd never heard. "You able to get up?" Ritter asked, sliding his hand beneath Clay's back and easing him to a sitting position.

"Um," Clay answered, but his head bobbled.

Ritter gave the ambulance driver a nod. "Take him in and have them check him out." He stood and looked back at Clay. "How'd you get in the marsh?" he asked.

"Marsh?"

While the others lifted the stretcher into the ambulance, Mike Mobley walked over and put his arm around Louise's shoulder. "Clay is gonna be okay," he said. "Don't worry." Then he took her arm and helped her into the back of the ambulance.

As the door closed Louise caught one last glance of Cherry Melinski, standing ankle deep in the black water, calling out for Wilfred. The sorrowfulness of such a sight tore a piece from Louise's heart and started a flow of tears from her eyes.

Throughout the months she had grown fond of Cherry, and now she'd come to the point where she'd do anything to spare her friend such pain. Anything, Louise told herself. Except trade places.

Clay

I was in the hospital for three days, puffing on an inhaler that was supposed to clear my lungs and trying to get food to settle in my stomach. That whole while I was thinking about Louise and wondering if maybe she'd been right all along.

I had always looked at Uncle Charlie as the man I wanted to be—somebody without a care in the world, a man with no responsibilities, a man who had caught hold of the brass ring and was taking the ride of a lifetime. Now, I'm not so sure that's true.

Charlie's wife left him seventeen years back. His kids hadn't spoken to him in God-knows-how-long. Once I got to thinking about it, I came to realize he lived a pretty lonely life. Whenever I'd call on Christmas or his birthday, he was always alone. I'd ask what he was doing and he'd inevitably answer watching TV. The only joy Charlie had was going fishing. When he died there wasn't a speck of food in the house, just that rotted fish and a bunch of McDonald's wrappers stuffed in the trash.

Without realizing it, I've been following in Uncle Charlie's footsteps. For the past three months I've gone out on that lake with Monroe and Wilfred almost every day. It might sound like fun, but after a while it gets boring. We sit there hour after hour and retell the same old tired stories. Then we pretend to laugh, even though we've heard it nineteen times before.

Where did all that nonsense get us?

Well, Wilfred is dead and I came precariously close to it. If it wasn't for Yoo, I'd be just as dead as Wilfred. Working at the bank wasn't really all that bad. Every day I had a chance to meet people, interesting people with new stories to tell. They'd come into the bank to make a deposit and stop by my desk just to say hello. I'm starting to miss those days.

If Louise brings up the subject of moving back to New Jersey again, I just might say yes. It's certainly something to consider

The Worry Quilt

Clay came home from the hospital but still felt shaky on the day of Wilfred's funeral, so Louise went without him. She walked beside Cherry, held fast to her arm, and steadied her steps. Bess Claremop skipped the services and stayed back to set up a buffet lunch in Cherry's dining room.

Everyone came. They carted in bowls of salad, casseroles, platters of meat, bushel baskets of fruit, and seven different pies, but no one ate. No one ever eats funeral food. Louise knew that outright. Not imagined. Knew. Oh, to be polite people might take a crumb of this and a morsel of that, but eventually they'd set the plate down, wander off, and help themselves to another drink. When it came to funerals, even the teetotalers who passed up a thimbleful of wine at card games would say, "I suppose I could have a glass of that gin. Make it a double, will you, honey?"

Wilfred's funeral was no doubt the saddest Louise had ever seen. Other than Cherry herself, every single person in the room sipped a hefty drink. Most were on their third or fourth. But Cherry wouldn't touch a thing. She just sat there on the sofa like a fizzed-out firecracker, not a stitch of make-up on her face, and her eyes redder than her hair. At one time Louise would have sworn Cherry married Wilfred Melinski just so that she'd have a permanent place to live, but the misery on her face told a different story.

"Have a drink," Margaret Klumpmeyer urged. "It'll help you to forget."

Cherry answered, "I don't want to forget."

After everyone else had gone home, Louise packed away the leftover food and cleaned the kitchen until the counters glistened. Then she pushed her way through the hibiscus bush, searched her medicine cabinet, and came back with two sleeping tablets.

"Take these," she told Cherry. "Not to forget, but just so you can rest."

Cherry didn't argue. She simply stuck out her hand to accept the pills and swallowed them down like a little kid. As her eyelids were fluttering closed, she whispered, "Please don't leave me alone."

Louise didn't. She stayed the night, dozing in the recliner and keeping watch as Cherry tossed and turned on the sofa.

For two months after the funeral, Cherry never left the house. It was as if she died right along with Wilfred. Every morning Louise came bringing coffee and some sort of pastry. But Cherry, once capable of eating a dozen doughnuts in one sitting, would break off the teeniest little corner and leave the rest on the plate. "You've got to eat," Louise told her, but every time Cherry shook her head and pushed the plate further away.

When the grass in the yard grew ten inches tall, Walt Wisnowski came over and mowed it for Cherry. Then Ernie came by and tightened the spring on her screen door, tightened it so much that it snapped shut before people were halfway through. Reverend Horchum planted a pink hibiscus alongside the walkway. Clay washed her windows. While all this attention did in some way please Cherry, at least enough to generate an occasional smile, the big goofy-faced grin she used to wear had disappeared.

As the weeks and months passed, life started to slip into a daily routine. Cherry got up in the morning, got dressed, dusted the furniture, and vacuumed the carpet. Then she sat down and waited for the day to end.

With Cherry making no effort to leave the house, Louise began to pop in and out frequently. Without warning, she'd come barging through the door and ask, "You need milk?" But Cherry would shake her head and indicate there was already a container in the refrigerator. "Why, that's soured!" Louise would say. Then she'd empty the curdled milk down the drain and go fetch another quart. She brought bread, canned pork and beans, microwave dinners—mostly things she could buy at the Super Gas convenience store. She seldom went to Worthmore, and when she did it was only because Cherry had specifically requested something like a fresh cantaloupe or tin of sardines. On those few occasions, not once did she visit the Bluebird Ladies Shoppe.

Day after day Louise would plop herself down on Cherry's sofa and try to start up a conversation. She hauled out every bit of gossip she knew and then began to manufacture a bit more. "Rumor is..." she'd say, but it was obvious Cherry wasn't even listening. When she finally became worried to the point of frustration, Louise took hold of Cherry's shoulders and gave her a gentle shake. "Look at you," she said. "Why, you're falling to pieces!"

Cherry glanced down at her arms and legs as if she expected them to be disconnected from her body, but once she saw they were still there she replied, "No, I'm not." Then she slid right back into that solitary world of hers.

Without Cherry slamming the screen door open and hollering her way in, the Palmer house grew quieter. Too quiet for Louise's liking. One morning at breakfast she told Clay, "I really miss Cherry coming over."

"You do?" He started fingering his chin the way he always did when something puzzled him. "But didn't you say she was rather—"

"Forget it!" Louise snapped and handed him a piece of burnt toast. "I just knew you wouldn't understand!" By then she had reached the point where she would have paid money to hear Cherry's bracelets cling-clanging through the door.

Louise didn't give up. "Beulah's been asking for you," she told Cherry. "So have Bess and Martha. Now that the club's short a person, Nora Newman has to play two different hands."

"Nora Newman?"

After several stories that had no truth whatsoever, Louise finally convinced Cherry to come to the next Hands Down meeting. Even then, it didn't turn out quite the way she had expected. Cherry just sat there with a spread of cards in her hand

and stared like she'd never before seen a jack of spades or king of diamonds. Louise blinked like a firefly when she needed the seven, even nudged Cherry beneath the table.

"Is anything wrong?" Cherry asked.

"Wrong?" Louise blinked seven times as deliberately as she knew how to. "What could possibly be wrong?"

"Oh." Cherry laid down an ace. Then Martha rummied and caught Louise holding one hundred and eighty points in her hand.

After that Louise went to the meetings alone. "Cherry's still not feeling up to it," she told the girls. By then Nora Newman had started grumbling about why she was always the one who had to play two hands.

"When is Cherry coming back?" they asked.

Louise just shrugged her shoulders.

Clay had not gone back to Snake Lake since the day of the accident. Twice, he and Monroe Schramm went down to the canal and fished off the riverbank, but they never so much as stuck a toe in the water. Instead Clay busied himself with doing this and that around the house, mostly things that didn't really need to be done. Every morning he would fire up the weed-whacker and set to work. He chopped at the palmetto until it was whittled down to a nub—a thick stalk with five leafless stems on one side.

"You're killing that plant," Louise said, but then he took off another two stems.

After that he started building a doghouse. Not a simple little doghouse, but an elaborate two-story thing big enough for grown people. It had glass windows, carpet, even a shingled roof. "I owe you, boy," he'd say, scruff Yoo on the head, then turn back and hammer another nail in place.

One morning as Louise made breakfast, she noticed Cherry's car back out of the driveway and speed off. "Now where in the world would she be going this early?" Louise absently shoved the already-toasted muffin back into the toaster.

"I don't want that too well-done," Clay said. "Not black on the edges."

"Didn't you hear me? Cherry left here like it was some sort of emergency."

"Maybe she was in a hurry to go shopping."

"Shopping? Cherry? Since Wilfred died, she hasn't stepped foot inside Bigwig."

"Well, then, she's probably out of everything by now." Clay dipped a chunk of bread into the yolk of his egg and handed it to Yoo.

"Stop feeding him so much," Louise said.

"He saved my life!"

"If he ever has to do it again, he'll be too fat to swim."

"He won't ever have to do it again," Clay answered.

"You'd think she'd say something. Maybe ask if I want to go along."

"Where?"

"Shopping."

"Could be that wasn't where she went." Clay handed the dog another chunk.

"Don't keep feeding him."

"Okay, okay," he answered and tossed a strip of bacon to the dog. "Think I'll hose off Cherry's back porch while she's gone."

Louise grabbed the plate away. "Keep feeding him all that fatty food and he'll explode," she said angrily. She would have said more, but Clay was already out the door. Leaving the breakfast dishes in the sink, she walked into the living room and peered out the window, stretching her neck to one side and then the other as if she might see Cherry's car parked somewhere down the street. *Where in the world has she gone?*

The Hands Down luncheon was at one o'clock, but Cherry still hadn't returned so Louise decided not to go. The platter of deviled eggs remained in the refrigerator, and she hung around the front window watching the empty street. As she watched and waited, a prickling of unease began to poke at her brain. It was not exactly a pain; more like a warning bell that kept her on edge. She got the same feeling when there was some kind of change in the wind. And the thing Louise hated most was change.

Long about two-thirty she strolled out to the back yard and asked, "Clay, you sure Cherry didn't say where she was going?"

"Not to me." He didn't look up, just continued mixing up some fertilizer for the palmetto, which he now thought wasn't doing so well. "By the way, what's for dinner?"

"Meatloaf."

"Yum, meatloaf. Yoo likes meatloaf too, don't you boy?"

"He's not getting any." Louise let the screen door slam behind her.

At four, she called Beulah Mason. "Have you seen or heard from Cherry today?" Beulah said she hadn't. Next she dialed Cassandra Willoughby. Then the Feingold twins, and after them Susan Jean Barrow. When the doorbell rang at four-thirty Louise had just hung up from Reverend Horchum.

"Hi," Cherry said.

"Your hair's brown!"

"Yeah, pretty close to my natural color. Of course, this here's dyed."

"Good grief, Cherry! You don't look a thing like—"

"Mabel. My name's Mabel. Don't I look like a Mabel?"

The truth was with Cherry winnowed down to one hundred-twelve pounds and her hair colored a chestnut brown, Louise thought she looked exactly like Billie Butterman. And with changing her name, she now had matching initials. "Well…"

"Of course I do. I'm every bit a Mabel."

Louise didn't know what to say, especially given the sensitive nature of Cherry's state. It was one thing to be named Mabel, quite another to look like one.

"Just be flat out honest. I was never really a Cherry."

"Well, I wouldn't say—"

"This morning, I was sitting on the sofa crying my eyes out when whammo—it comes back to me how I used to be this scrappy little kid who could deal with whatever life dished out. That's when I decided to go back to being Mabel."

"Mabel?" Louise repeated.

A brown-haired Cherry wasn't something Louise could swing right into. She'd go charging over with a pitcher of lemonade or a plate of stuffed peppers, and when she came upon Cherry she'd find herself startled all over again. "Ch-er-Mabel," she'd sputter.

It was close to three months before saying Cherry's real name came natural. But once it did, Louise settled into a newfound friendship. Mabel was a likeable woman who didn't wear seventeen gold bracelets that jingled and jangled whenever she moved, nor did she wear spandex pants and stretched-out polka-dot tops. In some ways Louise missed the hearty guffaw of Cherry's laugh, but Mabel's friendship made up for it.

Well, made up for it as far as Louise was concerned.

Mabel was another story. On warm nights when the windows were open, Louise heard the muffled sound of Mabel sobbing. It was as sad and lonely as the cry of the night bird. On those evenings Louise would grab a chunk of cake or some cheese and crackers and hurry next door. "Thought you might like a piece of this," she'd say, never mentioning what she heard.

"Thanks," Mabel would answer and pretend nothing was wrong even though her face was puffy and red-eyed.

Louise invariably pushed her way into the room and settled down on the sofa, steering Mabel into some unrelated conversation or a television show they simply had to watch. One night Louise brought over a shopping bag filled to the brim with pieces of calico. "You're gonna make a worry quilt," she said.

"Worry quilt? Me?"

"Something simple." Louise thumbed through the pages of her pattern book. "Here's a good one, Fair n' Square."

"But quilting? That's not something—"

"Trust me," Louise said and laid out snippets of calico end-to-end across the table. "Now, take six patches and trim them to five-inch squares."

"I don't think you understand—"

"Use a ruler to make sure they're straight." Louise pulled another handful of material from her bag. "You prefer mostly blue or mixed colors?"

Mabel lowered herself into the chair and sighed. "Whichever."

"My very first project was a worry quilt. Aunt Rose taught me how to do it the year my mother ran off and left me." Louise measured five inches of a cornflower blue check and marked it with chalk. "I'll mark, you cut," she said and chalked another square, this time a yellow daisy print. "That's when I learned, if you want to get the sadness out of your heart you've got to have someplace else to put it."

"That's nonsense."

"It is not." Louise looked over at Mabel and nodded knowingly. "See, the way it works is you sew your troubles into the quilt. Hurt feelings and loneliness, they get threaded right into the pattern, and once it's stitched together they've got no way of getting back to you."

"How can you believe such a thing?" Mabel scoffed, yet she didn't lift her eyes from the square of fabric she was busy trimming.

"From my own personal experience," Louise answered, "that's how. After Daddy got killed, Mama drove to New Jersey and put me out in front of the Elkins' house. 'Ring the doorbell, honey,' she said, 'Aunt Rose is just *dying* to see you,' and then off she went. I sat on those front steps every day for almost a month, watching for her, thinking surely she'd be back. After all, I was her daughter! Finally Aunt Rose, who as it turned out wasn't really my aunt but some sort of third or fourth cousin, said she didn't suppose Mama intended to come back anytime in the foreseeable future so I'd better start doing certain chores, otherwise I could just march myself right down the same road."

"Chores? What did she expect a little kid to do?"

"Make my own bed, dry the dinner dishes, and spend an hour a day working on a quilt for the church auction." Louise grinned sheepishly. "At first I thought she was the meanest woman God ever made, but then I started to enjoy quilting. It got to be so much fun I'd skip going out to play, even forgot about sitting on the steps watching for Mama's big old black Packard to come roaring around the corner."

"Pass me over that purple polka dot, will you?" Mabel waggled her finger at the patch on the far edge of the table.

"When the Ladies League sold my quilt for eighty-seven dollars, Aunt Rose claimed it was the end of my troubles. 'You stitched them into the quilt and somebody else has them now,' she said. For a while that worried me, the idea of passing my troubles on to some unsuspecting person who'd paid their hard-earned money for a quilt. But Aunt Rose said not to fret. 'Your troubles don't worry other folks,' she told me, 'they got their own set of troubles.'" Louise riffled through the stack of patches looking for a matching cornflower blue piece. After she found it, she looked over at Mabel. "You know, when you think it through, it does make perfect sense."

"Got any yellow there?" Mabel asked. "Bright yellow maybe?"

When Louise headed home that night, the eleven o'clock news had already come and gone. There had been a meat market robbery over in Ocala, the county appointed a new school board commissioner, and the weatherman assured viewers that a wide band of thunderstorms would come through day after tomorrow. But none of that made any difference to Mabel Melinski, who still hunched over the table deciding precisely where to place the apple green plaid and robin's egg blue patches.

It wasn't until she reached her own front door that Louise allowed a wide smirk to creep across her face. Had Mabel not jumped right into the project, Louise might have felt a tad guiltier about telling such a whopper. Why, she hadn't even started quilting until after she was a married lady with two toddling babies, and it was Billie Butterman who'd taught her. But this, she reasoned, was a much better version of the story.

The Reunion

Almost eleven months after the accident Louise stood at the kitchen sink and heard the chime of the doorbell. Ever since the incident at Snake Lake, she'd developed a dread of knocks and doorbells. Neighbor's yoo-hooed their way in. Bad news knocked or rang the doorbell. She dried her hands and called to Clay who was out back fertilizing the palmetto. "There's someone ringing the doorbell!" she exclaimed with a sense of urgency.

"You answer it," he said. "I'm busy."

"Oh, dear," Louise said apprehensively and started through the house feeling the weight of dread pushing down on her. With the glare of sunlight behind the visitor, Louise couldn't make out who it was until she was practically on top of the person. But once she saw the bright red lips and wide smile, she flung open the door and shouted, "Billie!"

They wrapped their arms around each other and for a few moments embraced like lovers. "I thought—" Louise had waited for this moment for such a terribly long time, she had stored up so many things to say, and yet all she could manage was, "Good Lord, how I've missed you!"

"Me too," Billie replied, her eyes filled with tears.

"I thought you'd forgotten, found yourself a new friend."

"Never," Billie said. "Never."

"I worried myself sick—"

"I'm sorry... so sorry," Billie said sadly. "I would've come sooner, but..." Her words were slow and measured, almost painful in coming. "The night Bradley's mother died, he turned on me in a way you'd never have dreamed possible. He was like a crazy man, screaming, ranting and raving, blaming me for her death. He told me to get out of the house or else he'd do to me what I did to her. I tried to explain that I wasn't even at home when she fell, but he wouldn't listen to a word I said. It was after midnight and I didn't have any place to go, but I was afraid to stay there so I left."

"Why didn't you call me?"

"That was my first thought—"

"Then why didn't you?"

"I knew what a difficult time you were going through," Billie said sadly, "and I told myself that if you were strong enough to handle your problems, I had to be strong enough to handle mine."

"My problems?"

"Moving down here."

"Oh, that," Louise said, waving a hand as if it were something hardly worth discussion. She tugged Billie through the house and settled her at the kitchen table. "Clay," she called out to the yard, "you won't believe who's here!" She set out a platter of cookies and glasses of iced tea and then began reminiscing about their old friends. "How's Ida?" she asked, "and Claire? Is Maggie's Joe still drinking?"

Billie shrugged. "Wilma Klinefeld is the only one I've seen in almost a year. I ran into her in Seattle."

"Seattle?"

"Yeah. She moved into her sister's place after she and George got divorced."

"How sad," Louise said. "I'll bet she misses the Material Girls."

"She told me there is no more Material Girls."

"No quilting club?"

Billie shook her head. "They drifted apart. Barbara moved to Connecticut, Eloise's arthritis is acting up, and Margo, believe it or not, got a job. Part time of course. She works at that eyeglass place at the mall."

"No Material Girls?"

"Nope. Nancy Spotswood came to two meetings. Then she started making excuses like needing to be there when the kids got home from school. 'What about our coming to your house so we can meet Virginia Gluck?' Ida asked. Nancy just rolled right past the part about meeting Virginia Gluck and said, 'Oh, my house is such a mess, toys all over the place.'"

"I knew it!" Louise snapped. "From the very first I sensed she was the kind of person to clutter up the place."

Moments later the sound of the weed-whacker died, and Clay stomped through the back door shaking loose the bits and pieces of palmetto stuck to his shirt. At first he pulled up short, staring at Billie blank-faced without a flicker of recognition. After a long moment his face lit up, and he said, "Why, Billie Butterman, just look at you! Your hair is *red*!" He made no mention of the thirty or forty pounds of padding she'd stuffed into a pair of too-small spandex pants. "I swear I almost didn't recognize you. With that red hair you look like this other friend of Louise's—Cherry Melinski. Well, she used to be Cherry. Now she's gone back to using Mabel."

"I'm not a Butterman anymore," Billie said.

"Ah, yes," Clay mused. "Louise told me about that."

Louise pulled up a chair and leaned across the table toward Billie. "It's been more than a year since you left," she said. "So what have you been doing?"

"Mostly moving from place to place, trying to keep my head above water."

"Have you tried talking sense to Bradley?"

"Of course. The first time I called, he went off on another tirade about how I was to blame for his mama's death, and when he finished he slammed the receiver down so hard it almost broke my eardrum. The next time, he told me I'd better stop using his American Express card or he was gonna have me arrested. I asked if he'd ever heard of community property laws. Then he slammed the phone down again."

"Did you?" Louise asked.

"Ever hear of community property law?"

"No, stop using his American Express card?"

"Absolutely not. I figured he owed me that much."

Louise grinned.

"But you know Bradley. When he says he's gonna do something, you can just bet he will. Two nights later I go out to dinner in Wilmington and try using the card. The waiter was gone for nearly fifteen minutes, and then when he comes back he leans down and whispers, 'I'm sorry ma'am, but you'll have to pay cash.

I've been instructed to confiscate your card.' I was mortified! The poor waiter, he was just a kid and probably as embarrassed as me. Anyway, I told him that I didn't have any cash on me, but I'd send it to him. As the kid's escorting me to the door, he whispers, 'Don't bother about sending any tip.'"

"How absolutely horrible," Louise said and pushed the plate of cookies aside as if she'd suddenly lost her appetite.

"The third time I called, Bradley hung up before I finished saying it was me."

"That's the meanest thing I've ever heard."

"I should've expected it. His mama was exactly the same—self-centered."

"What did you do then?"

"Found a job. What else could I do?"

Louise leaned into Billie's every word, listening, but all the while thinking, *How could something like this happen to a person who's always had double initials?*

"I had twenty or more different jobs in the past year. Waitress, car hop, check-out clerk. In Pittsburgh, I even took a job as a nanny. That, I quit after four days."

"But couldn't you make Bradley—"

"Pay?" Billie laughed. "Yeah, if I'd had money for a lawyer."

Louise furrowed her brows. "If all you need is money, we'll get it."

"Believe me, it sounds easier than it is."

"There are ways to do it," Louise said with an air of determination. "I'm not sure how yet, but we'll come up with something." She grabbed hold of Billie's hand and tugged her through to the tiny little guest room—a room with lace curtains and a flowered bedspread, a room that for well over a year had remained empty. "This is your room. I knew you'd get here someday." Louise beamed.

After Billie carried in her belongings and squeezed everything into the tiny little closet, Louise began telling her how pleasant it was to live at Tall Pines. "There's no quilting group," she said. "Cherry—or, rather, Mabel Melinski—the woman next door, she's the only person interested in quilting. There's a card club. They cheat and blink signals to each other, but once you get to know them they're a pretty nice group. Real casual. You'll feel like a fool wearing anything fancier than shorts and a tee shirt," Louise said, remembering her first encounter. "Tall Pines takes a bit of getting used to," she added with a laugh, "but once you settle in—"

"Oh," Billie said, "I don't intend to stay."

"Not stay? Don't even think it!"

"Well…I suppose there's really no other place I need to be."

"Good. What we'll do is raise some money and sue Bradley's butt off. I've got a friend who will help us," Louise went on. "Mabel, she's quick to lend a hand when you need one. When we moved down here it was Cherry who…" Louise explained how she came to know Cherry and the subsequent tragedies that led to her becoming a Mabel.

"After her Wilfred died, she colored her hair brown and went back to using her real name." Louise hesitated a moment, then added, "I expect she'll go back to being Cherry once she gets to feeling a bit better about herself."

"If it helps, maybe I ought to go back to using my real name too."

"Billie Balsas?"

"Willamina Balsas."

"Willamina?" Louise gasped, her mouth hanging open.

Billie wrinkled her nose. "I know, it's terrible. I was named after Uncle William and like him called Billie. Being a man, he of course spells his name with a y."

"That explains it," Louise said. "The reason you've had this run of bad luck is that you're an ordinary person just like me. You don't really have double initials."

"I never said I did."

"I just assumed." Louise laughed again. "For more years than I can count, I've been telling myself, 'Billie Butterman's got double initials, which is why she doesn't have to stretch her budget by making meatloaf.' Now you tell me you're a Willamina!"

"I like meatloaf."

"This isn't about meatloaf," Louise said. "It's about all the things, the good-luck things that come from having double initials."

"You can't honestly believe that crap."

"Crap? It's a proven fact—"

"Okay," Billie argued. "Then explain this: if you think my bad luck is because my name doesn't actually consist of double initials, to what do you attribute Mabel Melinski's? She's had it worse, and her real name is made up of double initials."

"Well," Louise stammered, "sometimes one thing or another can cause—" But by that time Billie Butterman had doubled over laughing.

After supper Louise took Billie over to meet Mabel. "Now be sure to call her Mabel, not Cherry," she said. "She's still sort of settling into this new name. And remember, if she's not real friendly don't think badly of her. She's still pretty sorrowful."

Louise had made a strawberry shortcake to bring, so with that tucked under one arm and Billie Butterman latched onto the other she trotted up Mabel's walkway. Ordinarily she would have yoo-hooed her way in, just as the old Cherry used to, but with Billie beside her Louise decided to knock.

"Is that door stuck again?" Mabel called out then she came over and gave the knob a yank. "This wasn't stuck," she said. "Why didn't you—"

Louise cut in. "I've got somebody I want you to meet."

"Well, bless my soul!" Mabel shouted and flung the screen door open with such force that it snapped the new spring Ernie had installed. "This is your Billie Butterman! I'd know her anywhere." Mabel wrapped her arms around both Billie and Louise and squashed them up against her chest. The strawberry shortcake was pretty well squashed too. "I can't imagine a more welcome sight!" she squealed and tugged them inside.

"And you," Billie cooed. "You're exactly as I pictured!"

Louise wondered how they'd gotten such an accurate image of each other when both of them had changed so much she could just barely recognize them.

"What you've been through," Mabel said with a sympathetic moan.

"You too," Billie said with a sigh of her own.

"I think the cake is ruined," Louise said, feeling a bit left out because she herself had no tragedy to contribute to the conversation.

"Why, it's not ruined at all," Mabel said. She took the squashed cake and ladled it into bowls. Like lifelong friends, they settled around the kitchen table and began their stories. When Billie told how Bradley had thrown her out without a cent and then cancelled her American Express card, Mabel slammed her hand down on the table and sent a full bowl of strawberry shortcake flying across the kitchen. "That louse!" she said angrily. "He ought to pay for doing a thing like that!"

Both Billie and Louise agreed.

"The problem," Billie said, "is that I don't have the money for a lawyer."

"We can fix that," Mabel replied with her chin set in the feisty tilt that had all but disappeared after Wilfred drowned in Snake Lake.

"See?" Louise gave Billie a wink. "I told you she'd help."

They set about discussing ways to raise money. They ruled out babysitting since not a single soul in Tall Pines had children, let alone babies. Lawn mowing was considered too laborious, in addition to which they doubted that anyone would pay to have their lawn mowed when their husbands would do it for free. A cake sale wouldn't bring near enough money, and without basements no one had enough stuff for a good-sized yard sale. "If only Clay hadn't gotten rid of all that stuff we had in Westfield," Louise said, but by then Mabel and Billie had moved on to considering the possibility of opening up a restaurant.

"We could do it right here, in my living room," Mabel said. "Move out that saggy old sofa and chair and put in some cute little bistro tables with candles, checked tablecloths, you know, a cozy sort of place."

"That's not gonna work," Louise cut in, "because none of us are very good cooks."

"I can make fried fish," Mabel said.

"Yes, but that's the only thing."

"I used to make apple pies for the Material Girls luncheons."

Louise glanced at Billie with a raised eyebrow. "Yes, but didn't you notice no one ever ate them?"

They all agreed the restaurant idea wouldn't work. Then they ruled out starting a dry cleaning establishment and an exercise center because of the cost of the equipment. Besides, Mabel said, "No one but Cassandra Willoughby ever exercises."

Long about eleven-thirty they all agreed their ideas had gotten stale. "Let's get a good night's sleep and start again tomorrow morning," Louise suggested, and that's what they did.

The following morning Louise handed Clay a bowl of instant oatmeal. Then she and Billie headed for the door. "What about my eggs?" he said. "And the bacon?" But by that time they had left.

When they walked in they saw Mabel already at work finishing up her latest quilt. "I think better when I'm quilting," she said, then handed Louise a pair of pinking shears and Billie a sack of calico pieces. "Here, sort these out, and trim them to size while we're thinking."

Billie came up with the idea of dressmaking, but Mabel and Louise both shook their heads. "Folks around here don't go much for fashion," Louise said.

"And," Mabel added, "it'd be hard to beat Bluebird's sale prices."

About ten-thirty Beulah came by with her sister, Francine, who had just recently moved to Tall Pines. "My, but that quilt's beautiful," Francine said.

Mabel nodded. "Thanks." Then she turned back to Billie and said, "What about a lingerie shop?"

"For the ladies at Tall Pines?" Louise raised her eyebrow again.

"Oh, right." Mabel turned back to stitching the yellow print square.

"I'd love to learn to quilt like that," Francine said, and she started fingering the edge of the quilt Mabel was working on. "Do you sell these?"

"Unh-unh," Mabel shook her head. "Besides, we're kind of busy right now. You suppose you could come and visit some other time?"

"Oh, sorry." Francine picked up a patch of blue calico that Louise had just trimmed to size. "This reminds me of a coverlet my mama once had. How I'd love to learn to quilt like this. Old as I am, I'd pay money to learn to quilt."

"Well, we're too busy to teach you right now." Louise wanted to tell Francine that at some time in the future she'd gladly show her how, but before she could Billie bolted upright in her seat.

"That's it!" she shouted. "A quilt shop!"

"A quilt shop?" Mabel and Louise replied in unison.

"You heard her." Billie pointed an accusing finger at Francine, who by now had let go of the quilt she'd been admiring. "She said she'd pay money to learn to quilt!"

"I wasn't trying to insult anyone," Francine mumbled apologetically.

Louise eyed Billie as if she was a woman gone mad. "She's one person!"

"I would too," Beulah said. "I mean, not that I'd want to impose or anything, but if you was to offer paid lessons, I'd surely sign up."

"See?" Billie shouted. "Why, I'll bet there are any number of people—"

"Claudia," Beulah chimed in. "She told me she'd love to have a quilt to cover her feet at night. Last week when we brought those blueberry muffins over here, she even asked Cherry if she'd be willing to sell that quilt. The mostly-blue one."

"Mabel," Mabel said.

"Oh, right. Mabel."

Five minutes later they told Francine they were pleased to have made her acquaintance. Then they shooed both Beulah and her sister out the door.

That very day they started making plans for a quilt shop.

Louise

Life is funny. Just when you think you've got it figured out, everything changes. I've lived my life afraid of change, but I'm beginning to question whether it's always bad.

Last night I got to thinking about how life would have been if we'd stayed in New Jersey. There'd be no more Material Girls, Billie would be gone, and my sweet little Mandy has grown up and wants to be with friends of her own age. All the reasons I thought I had to stay are gone.

And Clay...he's a changed man, a person who takes time to see things he never saw before. I've come to realize just how much he loves me. It's not the wild kind of professed love I had wished for, but the forever kind. The kind that almost doesn't need saying. Without words I know it's there. It's like the sun. You know it's back there even when the day is cold and so clouded over you can't see a speck of brightness.

I've wasted a lot of years looking back, remembering things that should have been forgotten and wishing for things that were nothing more than silly superstitions. I always imagined my life would be different if I was somebody else. Now I know: there isn't anybody else I'd rather be. I'm happy with who and where I am.

The Lucky Ladies Quilt Shoppe

As soon as Beulah and Francine had left Mabel closed the door and flipped over the deadbolt, claiming it would be better if they weren't disturbed. Then she took the telephone off the hook. "Okay now," she said. "Let's get down to business."

The first obstacle they came up against was the supply of material. "If we want to give quilting lessons, we've got to have something for people to quilt with," Louise said. She suggested that Clay's cotton undershorts would provide some excellent patches to start. "And there's that lovely bathrobe he hardly ever wears. Oh, and there's also a blue chamois shirt."

"Well, then," Mabel exclaimed, "I've got a closet full of things I don't wear anymore." She dashed into the bedroom and came back with an armful of brightly-colored blouses and stretch pants still dangling from the hangers.

Billie latched onto a pink polka dot tee-shirt. "Don't tell me you're going to cut this up," she said, holding it up in front of her. "It would look great on me."

"Take it," Mabel said. "There's also pants to match."

"I just love spandex!" Billie twisted herself around to catch a look in the mirror. "It's so slimming, don't you think?"

Mabel nodded, but Louise just sat there wondering how her two best friends had become so switched around.

Billie eyed several other outfits, all of which Mabel insisted she take.

"You might as well," Louise said. "Spandex is no good for quilt making."

Long about one-thirty, Clay came walking over to Mabel's house. When he found the door locked, he started yoo-hooing through the back window. "Louise?" he called. "I'm hungry. Are you coming home to make lunch?"

"No," she hollered back. "Fix yourself a sandwich. There's bologna in the fridge."

Louise heard him grumble something about how feeding a man lunch was the least a wife could do, but she stayed put and listened to Billie's newest suggestion.

"Some people might not have time for sewing," Billie said. "So what we ought to do is also sell finished quilts."

Louise and Mabel both thought that was a fine idea. "The problem is we don't have very many quilts to sell." Louise twitched her brow into a troubled look. "I've got three and one that's mostly finished."

"I've got two," Mabel offered.

"I've got six stored away in the basement of Bradley's house," Billie said. "If only there was a way to get hold of them."

"They belong to you, don't they?" Mabel said defiantly. "The law says he's got to give back anything that belongs to you!"

Billie explained how under the present circumstances Bradley wouldn't give her a booger that had fallen loose from his nose, let alone anything she actually wanted. "I could start working on some new ones," she suggested.

"And let that louse get away with keeping your stuff?" Mabel's nose twitched like a prize fighter waiting to climb into the ring. "No, indeed!"

Billie shook her head again. "Believe me, he won't do it."

"Oh, no? Listen to this." Mabel curled her fingers into a pretend telephone, held it to her ear, and started speaking. "Mister Butterman," she said in a very British accent. "This is Mable Melinski, Attorney at Law. I've been retained to represent your ex-wife, Billie..." She hesitated a minute, then asked what Billie's maiden name was. By that time Louise's mouth had dropped open.

"You're good," Billie said. "Real good. It just might work."

After that they started working out exactly what Mabel would say once she got Bradley on the telephone. For a while they tried having Louise announce the call, but, worried that Bradley might recognize her voice, they abandoned that idea. After three mistake-free run-throughs, they felt ready to place the call.

"Who'd you say this was?" Bradley asked after Mabel finished the part where she claimed to represent Willamina Balsas. Mabel repeated herself and then informed him that they were offering him the opportunity to return his ex-wife's possessions prior to the implementation of legal proceedings.

"I hope you understand," Mabel cooed in the most condescending tone of voice, "that Miss Balsas will get the things she's requesting, either way." By the time she finished, Bradley Butterman had reluctantly agreed to ship the box of quilts and all of Billie's other personal belongings, including jewelry—which for a while was a sticky point—to the Law Offices of Melinski and Melinski. She hung up the telephone, and then all three women danced around the living room whooping and hollering like teenagers drinking whiskey. As soon as they settled down, Mabel scurried out to her mailbox and right below Wilfred's name she pasted a large white label that read "Law Offices of Melinski & Melinski."

"That makes it eleven quilts," Louise said. "Now we're ready to start up a real business—maybe rent one of those little shops over in Worthmore."

"Eleven?" Billie repeated. "We'll need more than eleven quilts to open up a store. We'll need twenty, twenty-five maybe. Bins of fabric, batting, hoops, needles, pattern books—all of that." She reminded Louise of The Stitchery in Westfield. "Remember? Yellow walls? Really nice quilts hung all down one side? Bins of fabric sorted by color?"

"Well, maybe if we get busy sewing—"

"Nice idea, Mabel," Billie said, "but it would take us years to get enough. "

"I know!" Louise jumped up from the table, dashed across the lawn to her own house, and pulled out the suitcases she'd stored under the bed. "It's in here, it's gotta be in here," she kept mumbling as she scrabbled through swatches of calico and brocade. Finally she came upon the tattered leather telephone book, something she hadn't seen since the night she'd decided to come back to Tall Pines. The book held all the addresses and telephone numbers of the old Material Girls, or at least what might be left of them. Without bothering to reorganize the scraps of material, she flopped down on the side of the bed and started dialing.

"Ida, this is Louise Palmer," she said. "Our dear friend, Billie Butterman, is in trouble and needs our help. She needs money for a lawyer—"

Ida cut her off mid-sentence. "Lawyer? Is she in jail? Is this about her killing Bradley's mother?"

"No, she's not in jail, and, Ida, you know very well Billie wouldn't kill anyone. Not even horrible old Missus Butterman." Once Louise got that clarified, she continued to tell of all that had happened to Billie, elaborating at great length on the American Express card incident. She finished with an explanation of how they needed a good number of quilts to get the business going.

"Poor Billie," Ida said with a sympathetic moan. "I can't even imagine..." She promised to send the three finished quilts stored in her attic, along with a used sewing machine she no longer needed, a pattern book, and a carton of fabric squares already trimmed to size.

After that Louise called Claire, then Marie, then Eloise. In each instance she told the story of how Bradley had thrown Billie out without a dime and then taken away her American Express card. "We're setting up a quilt shop to earn enough for her to hire a lawyer," Louise told them. "Do you have any finished quilts you'd be willing to contribute?"

After she'd spoken to Lucy Zuiderman, the last person listed in her book, Louise tallied the commitments. She had thirty-seven quilts, twenty-one stretchers, four pairs of pinking shears, and enough fabric swatches to stitch a runner from Tall Pines to Westfield. In addition to all that Barbara Watkins, who'd already donated all of her quilts to the Church Fair, said she'd send a check for fifty dollars to help out with buying tables and chairs. Louise had been wrong. The Material Girls hadn't forgotten about her or Billie Butterman.

She went trotting back over to Mabel's house with a mile-wide grin. "Thirty-seven more!" she called out as she came through the door. That made a total of forty-eight quilts they had to sell, and according to Louise's calculations, more than enough supplies. Well, other than the thread. They would definitely need thread.

With things falling into place, Mabel began working feverishly on finishing up the quilt she'd started a few weeks earlier. Louise and Billie spent their days scouting out places for the shop. On the first day of searching they walked back and forth along Center Street until their feet puffed up like dumplings, but they couldn't find a single available storefront. The next day they meandered in and out of the side streets until it came up a hard rain, but still nothing. Kara, the manager at the Five-and-Dime, suggested they speak with Reverend Horchum, which they did. He set aside a jelly doughnut he'd been snacking on and told the ladies that they could use the church community room as a place to get their business started. But Louise figured that feeding the reverend would cost a lot more than rent, so she turned down the offer.

On the third day of looking, when it appeared they might run out of options, Louise spotted a sign in the thrift shop window that declared "Clearance Sale!"

"Come on," she said to Billie. "We might find some thread." As it turned out, the shop was almost bare to the walls. A bin held a few pairs of baby sneakers, a stack of foreign-language cookbooks, and a basket chuck full of handmade potholders left there on consignment.

"Looks like you could use some fresh merchandise," Louise told Christine, the girl who operated the shop.

Christine, busy filing her nails down to the quick, answered, "Are you kidding? I been three months trying to get rid of this stuff! Soon as this last bit's gone, I'm outta here!"

"You mean you're closing the store permanently?" Louise stammered.

Christine laughed. "Yeah, permanently. I'm having a baby in case you ain't noticed." She patted the basketball-shaped bulge beneath her blouse.

"Ah, yes, a baby," Louise repeated, looking around the room. "Well, then, I don't suppose you'll want to keep this shop."

"Not on your life. I done told Hank, 'I'm having a baby, so don't expect I'll be working anymore.'"

"Then it's for rent?"

"Not 'till I get rid of this stuff."

It cost Louise seventeen dollars and sixty-eight cents, but she planned to hold on to the merchandise and set up a thrift shop in a corner of the quilt store.

Five days later the three women signed their names leasing the narrow little shop located at the far end of Center Street—a place with chunks of plaster missing from the wall and not a single counter in sight.

"Good gracious," Louise said. "This place certainly needs a lot of fixing up." Billie and Mabel both nodded.

"For sure some plaster," Mabel said, sticking her hand into a hole the size of a pancake. "And paint."

The three women marched down Center Street and turned into Giant Hardware. "Morning, Howard," Louise chirped. Then, moving along like she had experience with this sort of thing, she led the trio toward the back of the store.

"What you looking for?" Howard asked.

"Paint," Louise answered. "We're fixing to open a quilt shop down the block."

"Open up a store? Three ladies? Why, that's never gonna—" When Howard saw six angry eyes looking at him, he stopped dead in the middle of his sentence. "Over here," he said.

Louise turned to the others. "Green, yellow, or white?"

"How about a soft mauve?" Billie said. "Or maybe a robin's egg blue?"

Louise shook her head. "All he's got is green, yellow, or white."

"No," Howard cut in. "You can have whatever color you want."

"When we bought our paint," Louise stammered, "you said—"

"It used to be that way. Now we've got a paint mixing machine. One hundred and thirty-seven colors. You choose."

Howard handed Louise a color chart that stretched out longer than she was tall.

Louise liked the sky blue, but Mabel preferred primrose pink. Then Billie, who had at first waffled between the canary yellow and rose garden, finally suggested they use white so the colors of the quilts hanging on the wall would show up better. Louise and Mabel agreed. They bought six gallons of paint, three brushes, some turpentine, and a can of already-mixed plaster. Howard, in an effort to make up for his comment about three ladies owning a business, offered to lend them a step ladder and deliver it himself.

By mid-afternoon they were busy at work—Mabel plastering the holes, Louise and Billie painting. Since Howard hadn't yet delivered the ladder, they started down at the baseboard and painted up. Once the ladder arrived, Louise started on the upper portion of the room while Billie continued working her way along the bottom.

They weren't even halfway through with the painting when Ernie Tobias popped in. "Whatcha doing?" he asked, and Louise's mouth curled into a smile.

"Well, come on in," she said. "Don't stand there like a stranger." She climbed down from the ladder, pulled a soda from the cooler, and held it out to Ernie. "Have a Coke," she offered. "Chips, maybe?"

Ernie popped open the can, then eyed the spot where Louise had been painting. "How you gonna do that top part?" he asked. "And the ceiling?"

"It's a problem." Louise shrugged. "I can't reach that high."

"Nobody can. You gotta have an extender."

"Extender?"

"A pole that hooks onto your paint brush. I got one."

"Do you think—" Louise cooed, but before she could ask if he'd do it Ernie said he had bowling that night.

"Gimme a key," he said. "I'll see to it first thing tomorrow."

Louise twisted the shop key from her key ring and handed it to Ernie.

The next morning when the ladies arrived, Ernie had already come and gone. Not a single hole remained in sight, the walls were painted right to the top, and the ceiling looked as white as an overhead cloud. Not only that, but the brown linoleum had been waxed and scraped clean of paint spatters. "Wow!" Billie exclaimed. "That Ernie is really something."

"He sure is," Louise replied.

With the painting finished, they began looking for furniture. "We'll need a counter," Louise told the others, "a table and some chairs. Fabric bins, a rack for hanging stuff, scissors, and the like."

Louise started asking at the nearby shops, then worked her way along Center Street until she reached Bigwig, located at the far end of town.

"As it so happens," Mister Doppler, the manager, said, "we've remodeled our produce department, and I've got some vegetable bins you'd be welcome to. They need a good scrubbing, maybe even a coat of paint, but other than that..."

Reverend Horchum gave Mabel a pew with a broken arm on one end, but she smiled and said they could cover it with a plumped-up throw pillow. Billie got a card table and eight folding chairs from Rose Marie Chester in exchange for letting her sit in on the first quilting class. No one found a hanging rack but Ernie tacked up a pegboard, which served the purpose.

The following week quilts and supplies started arriving. Most of the cartons had letters tucked inside wishing Louise and Billie well in their new business and saying how much everyone missed them. Some had checks. Margot sent her lucky frog statue along with a note saying how the frog would surely bring success.

Louise and Mabel unpacked quilts, sorted fabric swatches by color, and arranged the collection of pattern books into an eye-catching display. Ernie hung the quilts, and as it turned out there were so many that they covered one whole wall and half of another. Billie spent the entire week painting a sign that read "Lucky Ladies Quilt Shoppe."

On the first Saturday of October, the store opened for business. That day seventeen women, not including Rose Marie Chester, signed up for quilting lessons. And Billie sold Mabel's mostly-blue quilt for two-hundred and sixty-nine dollars. The sign on the door read "10AM – 5PM," but the shop still bustled at seven-thirty. Louise called home and told Clay that she'd be at least another hour.

"What about supper?" he asked.

"Peel some potatoes and put them on to boil," she told him. "I'll bring home one of those rotisserie chickens from Bigwig."

"Rotisserie chicken," he grumbled. "I was in the mood for fried fish."

"I don't think Bigwig sells fried fish," Louise answered, then clicked down the receiver and went over to wait on Ruthie Merrigan who wanted to register for the advanced class.

The following Tuesday Louise again called Clay from the shop. This time she instructed him to bread the pork chops and chop up some greens for a salad. "Make sure to put in enough lettuce," she added, "because Billie and Mabel are having dinner with us." When he started to fuss about how such things shouldn't be a husband's duty, she claimed he was making a mountain over a molehill. "After all," she said, "it's not like you're working."

On Friday Louise left a pound of hamburger defrosting on the kitchen counter and scribbled down the directions for making a meatloaf. "Sorry," she wrote at the bottom of her note. "I'm teaching a class and won't be home until about eight-thirty."

A Year Later

On the first anniversary of the quilt shop's grand opening, Louise, Billie, and Mabel, who by then had gone back to being Cherry, popped open a bottle of champagne. "Here's to the Lucky Ladies Shoppe," they said in unison. They clinked the crystal flutes and each downed a full glass of champagne.

Just two days earlier Mark Silver, Billie's real lawyer, had informed her that Bradley would agree to a fifty-fifty property settlement if she would be willing to drop the defamation of character suit. By that time she'd already gotten her own American Express card and moved out of the Palmer house into a cute little apartment less than one block from the shop. Once the settlement went through Billie would be able to buy any house she wanted, but she'd had her fill of moving so the only thing she wanted was to remain right there in her own tiny apartment.

Although Cherry still had a picture of Wilfred sitting on her dresser she'd started dating Roger Bushmeyer, the man slated to become the next mayor of Worthmore. With her campaigning alongside of him for almost three months straight, Roger was practically a shoo-in. He'd been seen in Jay's Jewelry three different times, and rumor had it that he'd ordered a good-sized diamond ring to fit Cherry's finger.

With Billie wrapped up in the lawsuit and Cherry busy campaigning, Louise managed the Lucky Ladies Quilt Shoppe. She worked at the store most every day, and now had women friends as far north as Orlando and as far south as Hialeah Park. All day long the telephone kept jingling, ladies wanting to know about this or that. "Ask Louise," they told each other, for they considered her a guru on not just quilting but area folklore. "Fort Pierce?" Louise would say. "Why, there's an excellent quilting club in Fort Pierce. And did you know that it actually is a deep water port?" It seemed that no matter what obscure little place a person might mention, she knew something of it.

Clay, on the other hand, had given up on fishing. He'd decided that it was not at all what he'd expected it to be. He'd also grown tired of making meatloaves and fixing salads. He began complaining about not having a hammock like he'd had in Westfield, so Louise suggested he get a new one. "Set it up in the back yard," she told him, but he was none too enthusiastic about the idea and said Florida was too hot for napping outdoors.

That June Clay asked Louise if she'd like to take a trip back to New Jersey. "Maybe we could get a little efficiency apartment," he said. "Spend the summer there and the winter down here."

Louise said with the quilt shop as busy as it was, she couldn't even consider such an idea.

"What about Patty Lynn? Phillip? Little Mandy?" he argued. "Don't you want to see them?"

"They'll come and visit when they're ready," she replied. Then she asked Clay if he knew St. Augustine was the oldest city in America.

In early November a slender blond walked into the quilt shop and began browsing. She stopped in front of a quilt Ernie had hung just a week ago—an original design Louise created. A stretch of flowering plants covered the width of the quilt, and above it Louise had placed a field of pink stars scattered over a patchwork meadow.

"That yellow's the moon, isn't it?" the woman asked, pointing to a circular-shaped patch at the far right.

"Yes, it is," Louise answered. "It represents the fullness of life."

"And the plants?"

"The rooted parts of a person."

"Rooted?"

"People and places that stay in your heart, no matter where you are."

The woman smiled. "What about the stars?" she asked.

"Friends," Louise answered. "The ones who somehow find a way to shine through the patches of darkness to light the way for you."

"Oh, my," the woman said somewhat wistfully. "What a wonderful vision of life."

"Yes," Louise replied with a smile, "but unfortunately, it sometimes takes the better part of a lifetime to come to the realization of it."

When the woman asked if the quilt was for sale, Louise shook her head. "No," she said. "That quilt reminds me of the things I'd almost forgotten."

Five days before Christmas, Louise had Ernie take the Fullness of Life quilt down from the wall. She folded it carefully and packed it in a sturdy brown cardboard box. Then she took out a piece of paper with an address on it—a piece of paper that she'd tucked into her purse when she stood in a mobile home what felt like a lifetime ago—and copied the address on the box. Beaming, she carried the box off to the post office.

The box arrived at Tulip's trailer late Christmas Eve. When the old woman opened the box, she found Louise's quilt along with a note that read, "Thank you for helping me to remember what matters most." Although the note was unsigned, Tulip knew who had sent it. She pulled the quilt from the box, ran her fingers across the evenly-measured stitches, and smiled.

If you enjoyed reading this book, please recommend it to a friend or fellow reader and share your thoughts in a review on the website for Goodreads, Amazon, or Barnes & Noble.

For book news, reviews and fun,
join Bette Lee Crosby on her blog at

www.betteleecrosby.com

Acknowledgements

A novel does not come together without the help of many people—readers, editors, designers and the technical geniuses who translate an author's words into readable electronic formats. I am fortunate to be working with some of those that I consider the best in the business, and I am eternally grateful to the following people for their contribution in making What Matters Most a reality:

Michael G. Visconte…Creative Director of FC Edge in Stuart, Florida… a design genius who finds the heart and soul of every story and transforms it into a breathtakingly beautiful cover. Thank you Michael.

Ekta Garg…Editor extraordinaire and a woman who catches all my mistakes without ever losing sight of my voice. No easy task, but she does it with grace and charm. I count Ekta among my many blessings.

Danielle Benson…The absolutely best formatter in the universe. Thank you for having the ability to find even the oddities that seem to sneak in and out like thieves in the night.

Naomi Blackburn… Thank you for being an early reader and helping me to see beyond myself. Your suggestions are both wise and wonderful.

Geri Conway…I am blessed to have you as my sister and thankful for all the other roles you play—those of a listener, sounding board, advisor, early reader, and constant supporter.

Lastly, I am thankful beyond words for my husband, who puts up with my crazy hours, irrational thinking, and late or non-existent dinners. I could not be who I am without you, Dick, and I pray that neither of us ever lose sight of this awesome blessing God has given us.

CPSIA information can be obtained
at www.ICGtesting.com
Printed in the USA
LVHW051835251119
638450LV00005B/890/P